Head Over Heels

Mama's Boys

Crystal B. Bright

LYRICAL PRESS
Kensington Publishing Corp.
www.kensingtonbooks.com

Lyrical Press books are published by
Kensington Publishing Corp. 119 West 40th Street New York, NY 10018

All Kensington titles, imprints, and distributed lines are available at special quantity discounts for bulk purchases for sales promotion, premiums, fund-raising, and educational or institutional use.

Special book excerpts or customized printings can also be created to fit specific needs. For details, write or phone the office of the Kensington Special Sales Manager:
Kensington Publishing Corp.
119 West 40th Street
New York, NY 10018
Attn. Special Sales Department. Phone: 1-800-221-2647.

Kensington and the K logo Reg. U.S. Pat. & TM Off.
LYRICAL PRESS Reg. U.S. Pat. & TM Off.
Lyrical Press and the L logo are trademarks of Kensington Publishing Corp.

First Electronic Edition: August 2016
eISBN-13: 978-1-61650-715-2
eISBN-10: 1-61650-715-2

First Print Edition: August 2016
ISBN-13: 978-1-61650-716-9
ISBN-10: 1-61650-716-0

Printed in the United States of America

Sometimes it takes hurt to open your heart...

At twenty-two, Thane Wells is the highest-paid pitcher in Major League Baseball—and he owes it all to his adoptive Mama, "Queen" Elizabeth Sommerville, a wise, beautiful, entrepreneurial African-American woman who always encouraged him and his two white brothers to reach for the stars...the woman Thane still talks to daily. He never dreamed their most recent conversation would be their last. With his beloved supporter suddenly gone, Thane is grief-stricken, shaken, and vulnerable—especially to a woman like Kari Meyers.

Kari's had her eye on Thane for a while, but strictly for business. As a junior sports agent, she's hungry to sign him, especially when she hears his current agent will be retiring soon. When she finally locates Thane, she's shocked to discover he's attending his mother's funeral—and he's shocked to find Kari in his hotel room. Assuming she's an escort is just the beginning of their misunderstandings. But one thing that's clear is their mutual attraction. As a single mom with an NBA ex, Kari has a rule against dating athletes. Yet as circumstances bring the two closer together, they just might find they're on the same team, heart and soul...

Books by Crystal B. Bright

Mama's Boys
The Look Of Love
Forget Me Not
Head Over Heels

Published by Kensington Publishing Corporation

This book and this entire series are dedicated to everyone that contributed to my writing journey. Every book I read, every class I took, every conversation I had about the writing process all got me to where I am right now. I'm so grateful and thankful for every arduous step in my journey. It was all worth it.

To all the mothers out there, whether your children are biologically yours or chosen for you to raise or the four-legged kind, thank you for building the foundation of happy and healthy adults. For Ireleen S. Bright – you will always be my hero.

Author's Foreword

I'm almost sad to end this series. I have thoroughly enjoyed writing about the Wells boys and their journey to find love. Although I love Gunnar and Gideon, Thane's character pulls at my heart, mainly because he's the baby of the family just like me.

No matter how big the family, there is always some sort of misunderstanding that pulls the family apart. I wanted to explore that dynamic with this family. Sometimes the "rock" that holds the family together may not always be the parent.

The main message I wanted to express in this series is that forgiveness is powerful and love is everywhere if you open yourself up to receive it.

I hope you all enjoy my series. I certainly had fun writing it.

Keep reading,
Crystal***

Acknowledgements

Thank you Alicia Condon, Renee Rocco and the entire Kensington and Lyrical Press family who took a chance on my series. This series wouldn't be half of what it is without the hard work of my editor, Heidi Moore. She kept me on track and challenged me. I'm a much better author because of her.

Thank you to the love of my life, Jim Stark, who supported me in so many ways. I love you.

Chapter 1

Five years ago

Kari Meyers stared at her reflection in the ladies' room mirror at the Hilton Hotel in New York, trying to will herself to appear more important than she felt. She hadn't waited for the ink to dry on her diploma from Old Dominion University when she made the trek to this hotel on the heels of a man. No, a boy. Hell, who was she kidding? Even at seventeen, Thane Wells looked like a grown man with a lot of stories.

She could have kicked herself for her salacious thoughts. No other sports agent, especially one starting out, would think of a potential client like a sexual being—even if the client had thick, dark brown hair that begged to have fingers raked through it, and aquatic-blue eyes that made her want to dive in deep and get lost in them for years without coming up for air. She couldn't forget his strong jaw, sleek nose, and his set of full, kissable lips.

For a white boy, he had swagger. For a college freshman, he had an impressive pitch. Kari had to remember that and stop contemplating whether he would find an African-American woman a few years his senior attractive.

Her phone rang in her purse at the same time the door to the bathroom opened. Kari ignored the woman that had come into the restroom when she saw the name on her caller ID.

"Hey, Grandpa." Kari smiled.

"My baby. How are you doing up there? Did you get Thane to sign on as your client?" His strong voice powered through the few cracks that riddled his speech.

"I haven't met him yet. Psyching myself up first." The wild, flapping vultures in her stomach hadn't settled since she'd arrived by Amtrak that afternoon to crash this baseball-recruiting event.

Llewellyn Meyers didn't mince words. Never had. "You know sports. You're the one who found this cat's information when he was in high school. And you just got that degree."

Kari heard a giggling sound through the phone that made her smile and almost tear up.

"And you have this little guy here depending on you."

Kari could almost see her grandfather smiling.

"Say hi to your mother."

"Hi, Mama!" Michael screamed.

Little kids her son's age had no volume control. Kari loved it.

"I shouldn't have taken this trip right now. I just graduated last week." Kari peered over at the stately looking African-American woman who busied herself by slathering a coat of red lipstick over her lips.

She looked flawless. Her eyebrows sat perfectly arched over her full brown eyes. Her eyelashes looked good enough to be fake—full, long, and curly. She wore a sensible skirt and matching jacket, but with the cream-colored silk shirt underneath, she pulled off a feminine yet strong look.

Kari scanned her own outfit. She wore a simple red wrap dress and had her shoulder-length brown hair in simple waves around her face. She'd thought she looked appropriate...until she saw this woman.

"Don't be silly," Llewellyn said. "I don't mind watching this little guy. You've worked hard. You've put yourself through college. You recognized that young man's talent before all the other big agents, including Alec Fogel. Sign him and come home and tell us all about it."

Kari smiled. "You always believe in me, even when I screw up."

"Hey," Llewellyn said quickly. "You haven't made a mistake in your life. People have disappointed you. But things happen for a reason. That boy that left you years ago gave you a great little son."

She smiled. "Michael is a blessing." She took a deep breath. "I'll do my best, Grandpa. As soon as I meet Thane, I'm coming right back home."

"Do what you need to do. Love you."

"Love you. Give Michael a hug and kiss from me." Kari made a kissing sound on the phone before disconnecting the call.

She surveyed her appearance again. Feeling a tad casual next to the Queen of England standing next to her, Kari pulled out a tube of lipstick and painted her lips a rose color.

"First time leaving your child at home for an extended period?" the woman asked out of the blue.

Kari turned to her. Her bathroom companion's simple and genuine smile made Kari relax a little.

"Was it that obvious?" She tossed the lipstick in her purse and exhaled. "I felt mommy-guilt when I went back to college. Now that I've graduated, I'm trying so hard to make a good life for the two of us. I feel bad leaving him, even if it's only for a day."

"I understand. I had three young boys myself at one time and was running my own businesses."

Kari blinked. "You did all that on your own?"

She nodded. "At one point, I had a husband. But he was more of a nuisance than anything else. Got rid of him but kept my boys." She smoothed her hand over her hair. "So you're here on business?"

Kari nodded. "Trying to become a sports agent. I want to start my own business and not work for someone else. I know it'll be difficult. But I'm not going to give up."

Kari's new confidante nodded and carried the biggest grin.

Kari continued. "I thought if I could get this player I've been watching since his high school days, it would get me noticed."

The woman raised her eyebrows. "Wow. So you came here on your own to sign an athlete as a client, and you haven't even started working yet? That takes a lot of nerve and guts. I admire that. You're not looking for anyone to hand you anything. You're willing to do it all on your own. Reminds me a lot of myself several years ago." She held out her hand. "Elizabeth."

Kari shook it. "Kari. Nice to meet you." She should have guessed the woman's skin would be soft to the touch. "Do you live in New York or just visiting?"

"Here on business. So you're meeting an athlete here?" Elizabeth tucked her clutch under her arm.

Kari nodded. "I don't have a meeting set up with him or anything. I was hoping to see him and talk to him." Her body felt warm all over as she thought about Thane Wells. "He's going to be amazing on a major league team someday."

"Who is that? Someone named Thane?"

"Yes, Thane Wells. He's a great pitcher. I know all his stats now that he's in college. I understand he got invited up here by the Yankees. I don't know if he has an agent yet, but I would love to get in on the ground floor." She lowered her voice and leaned closer to Elizabeth. "It doesn't hurt that he's extremely good looking."

"He just started college. Don't you think he should finish?"

Kari blinked. "You *are* a mom. Yes, he should finish if he can. But his best earning years are now."

"And you sound like an agent." Elizabeth moved in closer to Kari. "Let me give you a bit of business advice. It appears that you've done your homework. For that reason, you should come at him in a more businesslike way and not, um, with putting all your assets out there."

Kari peered down at her attire again, this time catching a glimpse at her exposed cleavage. "I thought I looked professional." She pulled the top of her dress together.

"If you truly did, you wouldn't have adjusted your dress." Elizabeth lowered her voice. "You might be seeing a male client, but you need to look like a professional woman. Don't think you can snare him with your looks. You're smart. I can tell that from our short conversation. Show him you care about propelling his career and he'll be happy to sign. Don't expect him to do it because he's attracted to you or because you're attracted to him."

Kari shook her head. "I was planning on winning this guy over by spouting his stats. Nothing else."

"Do you have any contacts yet?"

Kari remained quiet. She'd made some connections with minor league teams, but nothing on the level of a major league team. Her silence must have answered Elizabeth's question.

"The meet-and-greet may happen, but you may not get him to take you seriously now. Maybe in a few years." Elizabeth put her hand on Kari's shoulder. "But I do like you. I wish you all the best. I'm sure you're going to do great things in the future."

Too stunned to talk, Kari remained quiet as Elizabeth walked out of the bathroom. Great. Now she felt self-conscious about everything—her look, her approach, her pitch. She grabbed a paper towel and scrubbed the abrasive gray material over her lips to remove some of the lipstick.

Although Elizabeth had talked to Kari like a mother, Kari appreciated the words of wisdom. Kari hadn't realized she had dressed more like a bar hopper than an agent. Since she didn't plan on staying overnight, she hadn't brought extra clothes. She pulled her dress together even more to cut down on the view of her cleavage, and she cinched the belt tighter. Then she stopped.

She'd come to New York on a head full of steam and her nerve. Her grandfather believed in her. She had done all of this for her and Michael's future. She couldn't let the words of a stranger make her doubt herself.

Kari reapplied her lipstick, fluffed up her hair, and marched out of the bathroom. Confidence would get her through this moment. So far, her nerve had gotten her to a city she'd never been, to meet a man she'd never met and make a proposition to catapult her career.

The silence of the bathroom had shielded her from the noise and activity in the hotel lobby. Guests and employees strolled by her. Working on instincts, she walked down a hallway that led to several conference rooms. She stopped when she spotted Thane standing at the end of a hallway.

Even in jeans, a collared shirt, and sneakers, he didn't come off as a kid. Maybe it had something to do with his height or his slightly muscular frame. He had his back to her for a moment in the empty corridor. When he turned around and spotted her, he froze. He stared at her before a smile rose.

Kari's heart pounded. The words of a stranger echoed in her head. She had to go into this with business on her mind and forget that even from several feet away, his incredible eyes pierced right through to her soul.

Thane took a step toward her, but a couple of men, coming from a nearby conference room halted his movements. They spoke to him simultaneously as they guided him into the room and closed the door.

"Damn." Kari marched back and forth in a tight three-foot area. She couldn't just barge in and interrupt the meeting. She wanted a chance to talk to Thane first.

"Ma'am, are you a guest of the hotel?"

Kari felt the hand on her shoulder before she heard the question. She turned to see a hotel security guard standing behind her.

"No, I'm not a guest," Kari answered honestly. When she saw the guard gearing up to boot her out, she continued. "I'm with the Yankees talking to a recruit. They have Thane Wells in the room down there." Part of her statement held some truth.

The guard held up his hand. "I apologize. Let me know if there's anything I can get you."

"Bottle of water would be great." She might as well play this up for all she could.

"Of course." He walked away.

As she waited for Thane to reemerge, she thought of all the arguments she would make to get him to take a chance on her as a new, untried, untested agent. She paced around and caught sight of a couple of businessmen sitting in the lobby. As she stared at them, she recognized one. Legendary sports agent Alec Fogel had made a trip all the way to New York for Thane. She knew it.

She didn't recognize the man beside him. It didn't matter. The fact that she'd spotted talent that had attracted a monumental agent like Alec Fogel made her want to pat herself on the back. She heard the conference room door open and laughter coming from down the hallway.

Kari brought her attention back to that area. She saw Thane emerging with one of the Yankees' coaches. She started to approach them when she stopped in her tracks again. This time, Thane's great looks had nothing to do with her hesitation. Someone else strolled out of the room that she'd never expected she would see. The woman Kari had had a conversation with in the bathroom followed the duo and stood next to Thane. Was she another agent?

No, she'd given Kari advice and wished her luck. Or maybe she'd done that to get into Kari's head. Only one way to find out. Kari started down the hallway when she felt a vise-like grip around her upper arm. She turned to see the security guard again and another employee.

"All the Yankees' employees have been checked in already. Nice try, lady," the employee said. "Please escort her out of the hotel."

"Wait. No. You don't understand." Kari attempted to dig her heels into the sandy-colored ceramic tile floor. "I need to talk to Thane Wells. If I can do that, I'll leave."

"Honey, I'm sure someone in your business would love to talk to some clients. You're not doing that in here." The security guard pulled her roughly toward the door.

"Stop. I'm not who you think I am. I'm a sports agent." She managed to crane her head around the guard to see Thane, Elizabeth, and the real Yankees staff members walking out into the lobby. This would be her only chance to make an impression. "Thane! Thane!" She waited for him to look at her before she could be thrown out into the street. "Finish college and then sign with a team. Get with a good farm team. With your pitching stats, you can get top dollar."

"Be quiet and leave the premises," the guard spoke between gritted teeth.

Kari ignored him and made one final plea. "You would be worth every penny. Sign with me, and I can take you far."

Before she could see if she made an impact, she got pushed outside the door, nearly toppling to the ground. Kari managed to keep her balance. She wouldn't be caught flailing even though she had failed.

"And stay out." The guard pointed at her and turned back into the hotel.

Kari stood on the sidewalk and tried peering into the glass doors to see if her words had gotten through to Thane. Had he heard her and, more importantly, did he believe her?

After waiting an hour in front of the hotel, Kari chalked up her stunt as a disaster. Thane had probably heard her pleas, but apparently her words hadn't made any impact. Or maybe they had, and whoever this Elizabeth woman was to him had convinced him that Kari couldn't represent him or his career.

She glanced at her watch. If she hurried, she could make it down to Penn Station and get home to tuck her baby into bed.

Kari started to head down the street when she heard a voice behind her. "Hey!"

She turned, hoping to see Thane calling for her. Instead, she saw the other businessman who had been sitting with Alec Fogel. Out of curiosity, she waited as he walked up to her.

"Do I know you?" Kari asked as she held on to the strap of her purse.

"No. And I don't know you, but I'd like to." The statuesque older man ran his hand over his silver hair. "My name is Frank Milliner. I'm the owner of the Winning Edge Agency. I heard what you said in there to Thane Wells. What agency do you work at now?"

Kari regarded him for a moment before speaking. "I don't. I was hoping to sign him up as my client."

"Wait. You don't work at an agency? How did you even know about him?"

Great. Another man who probably underestimated her passion for sports and her drive for a career. She would have to correct that perception right now.

"I review high school teams and watch players like a scout. Thane came up on my radar when he threw that no-hitter during his senior year of high school. He's only gotten better in college. He's going to be a beast on the field. I'm guessing Elizabeth knew that."

Frank furrowed his eyebrows. "Who's Elizabeth?"

"That woman who was with him." She pointed into the hotel.

He chuckled. "That's Elizabeth Sommerville, Thane Wells's mother. She adopted him and his two brothers."

"I know about Gunnar and Gideon Wells. I had no idea they were adopted. But I've focused on Thane." *With good reason*, she wanted to say.

Gunnar had already become an MMA champion by the time Kari had found out she would be a mother at the age of sixteen. Gideon began his career as an NFL quarterback during her freshman year of college.

Now she understood Elizabeth's motherly advice. She hadn't been trying to steer Kari clear of Thane because she wanted his business. She'd been protecting her son from a potential gold digger or worse. Of course, it would have been nice if Elizabeth had told Kari of her relationship to Thane. Then again, if she had, it would have made Kari even more nervous.

"I could use someone like you in my company. I'm assuming you've finished school." Frank crossed his arms over his chest as he studied her.

"Just graduated."

He laughed and shook his head. "Yes, you are exactly what I need for my business. We should talk." He tried to guide her back into the hotel.

Kari stayed cemented to the cracked walkway. "I'm not exactly welcome back in there. Can we meet somewhere else?"

Frank smiled. "Of course."

Although she'd missed one opportunity, she hoped this one would turn out to be a winner. That didn't mean she would be giving up on Thane Wells. He wouldn't be the one who got away.

Chapter 2

"I shouldn't do this." Thane Wells stared at his reflection in his hotel room's bathroom mirror.

He braced his hands on the granite countertop as he gathered himself. The slight pain in his abdomen still throbbed. Thane took a couple of deep breaths and hoped that it would help ease the gut-wrenching feeling.

He grabbed a bottle of a pink, thick fluid. He downed a couple of gulps and waited for it to make it to his stomach before he followed it with some mouthwash. He spat out the minty, green liquid and took another cleansing breath before he left the bathroom.

The Carolina Wrens spared no expense for his comfort. His shoes clicked against the marble floor with its dark, soothing brown tones. The opulence of this hotel matched the great season the baseball team had had and would have this coming year.

He combed his hair back and added a slight part on the side. Thank God, he'd gotten a trim before his meeting that night. He didn't want to be labeled as a disheveled athlete.

He did leave his face stubbly though. Between keeping himself clean shaven and looking like he'd been partying all night, he found women approached him more when he resembled a bad boy. For this meeting tonight, he needed an ally.

Of course, his mother, dear Queen Elizabeth Sommerville, would hate his appearance despite his crisp white button-down shirt and complementing midnight-blue jacket and pants, courtesy of some designer who wanted Thane to model his clothing.

Thane hadn't given the designer his answer yet. He still had to figure out a polite way to say no. His main opposition to being the label's spokesman had to do with the quality of the clothing. The stitching didn't meet his standards. Each time he'd gotten a shirt from this designer, he had to let it out in the chest area. He couldn't trust a tailor with the work, not when he knew his body better than anyone else, and he could do the work better than most.

He pulled his shirt sleeve down under her jacket and straightened his belt. To finish off his look, he sprayed some cologne over his neck and chest. The musky scent added a nice aroma. For what he hoped would be a brief encounter, he wanted to appear pleasant, approachable.

Thane snickered when he recalled the few times he had been out while wearing the scent. Even in crowded clubs, he managed to get noticed among other men. He would have to work hard for attention down in Florida.

"I guess this will have to do."

When his cell phone rang, he assumed the call came from the reporter he needed to meet. He saw the number, and even without it being saved in his list of contacts as one of his friends or associates, he knew the caller. He could be delayed from his meeting a bit to have this quick conversation.

He tried hard not to smile before he answered it. "Good evening."

"Hello, Mr. Wells. Did I catch you at a bad time?"

Thane took a deep breath and exhaled loud enough for the persistent agent to hear him. "Does that ever matter to you, Ms. Meyers?"

"Of course it matters. I not only care about your representation, I also am concerned about you as a person."

He laughed. "I needed that. That's one thing about you. You can make me laugh."

"Not everything I do or say is funny." Her tone became serious. "I would like to represent you."

For as long as he could remember, Kari Meyers had been after him for his business. Her daily calls during his first year at the Carolina Wren farm had flattered him at first. After he'd signed on with another agent, he assumed the calls would stop. They didn't. She continued to sell herself. Too bad he didn't need to make a switch.

"So why did you stop calling me daily? I think you're down to once or twice a month now." Not that Thane cared.

"Believe it or not, I'm trying not to be a total pest. I feel that I'm the best person to represent you." She lowered her voice but still kept it strong.

Her husky tone had a strange affect on Thane. His gut-wrenching ache went away. He didn't think about baseball or his brothers. He often wondered what this woman looked like.

"Why are you calling me so late? Shouldn't you be out on a date or something?" He had to get his mind to stop imagining more with this tenacious woman.

"When I'm your agent, my personal life goes out the window. I'll put my full time, effort, and focus on you." She spoke sincerely, not like a politician, but like a true businesswoman.

"I could be very demanding." He chewed on his lower lip to keep from laughing. "I could ask you to stock every locker room with green M&Ms. Would you do that for me?"

"No."

Thane blinked. "What happened to you putting your time, effort, and focus on me?"

"No candy while you train."

The slight lilt in her voice had him imagining her smiling at her cheeky statement. He fantasized about her look. How old was she? Was she tall or short? Was she attracted to him beyond being a baseball player?

"If you would like to meet, I can schedule some time," Kari said.

"Why don't you give up?" Thane looked at his reflection in the mirror one last time. "This was cute and funny at first. Now you're just wasting your time. No matter how many times you call, I'm not going to change my mind. Why don't you stop?"

After a slight pause, Kari answered, "Why haven't you blocked my calls already?"

He stared at his reflection for a bit, stunned by the question. Why *hadn't* he blocked her, or even changed his number? In a twisted way, had he come to enjoy these conversations? Did he like hearing from Kari Meyers on a regular basis? He had no idea about this woman's identity or her appearance. He'd never met her.

"Enjoy your evening." He disconnected the call.

A small part of him did want to block her number. Then again, that wouldn't stop her from using other phones to reach him. Damn. Was he so desperate for companionship since his breakup over a year ago that this strange exchange qualified as a relationship?

He glanced down at the pricey timepiece on his wrist. *Shit. Ten minutes late.*

Thane stuffed his wallet into his jacket pocket and started to slide his phone into pants pocket. At that moment, it rang and vibrated in his hand. When he saw the name on the screen, he knew he couldn't ignore it.

"Mom. How are you?" He smiled every time he talked to the only person who stood by his side and believed in him.

Elizabeth let out a long exhale. "My baby. Are you eating right?"

Her words came out slower than her normal Southern drawl. At only ten minutes after eight, it seemed early for her to be in bed. He knew the reason for her exhaustion.

"I'm fine. Eating all of my vegetables and being a good boy." He plucked a piece of lint from his jacket.

His mother didn't need to know that he hadn't eaten that day. No need to worry her, especially with her being all the way in Virginia. She couldn't see him right now in Florida.

"That's my son." She coughed. "Big plans tonight?"

An uncomfortable tickle crept up the back of Thane's neck. "Interview with a writer from some sports magazine. My agent thought it would be a good idea to help soften my image. I think those were his words."

"Don't do that issue where they have all the athletes in there naked. I don't want you showing what God gave you in some magazine."

He laughed. "What? You don't think I have a good enough body for it?"

A pause lingered before he heard a beeping sound through the phone and another one of her long breaths.

"Mom, are you back in the hospital?" Thane sat on the king-sized bed.

As he scanned his room, it didn't escape his attention that here he sat in the lap of luxury while rough hospital sheets surrounded his mother's body. He didn't deserve this, and neither did Queen Elizabeth.

Elizabeth's voice hitched before she spoke again. "Don't worry about me. Darling, I want you to do something."

"Anything. You know that." He pressed his fist against the bed as he listened to her. His hand sank into the plush, tan comforter.

"Work hard. Don't ever give them half of your effort." Her voice trailed down to a whisper by her last words.

"Of course. Always. I give one hundred and ten percent at every practice. I wish you were well enough to come out to spring training. I think you would love it here in Florida."

She coughed again. The wheezing that followed worried him.

"Mom?"

She continued. "You need to find yourself a good woman."

Thane rolled his eyes. "I have. There are really good women all around me."

"I'm not talking about you jumping into bed with every woman you meet. Don't think I don't know what you've been doing. Be...kind."

He stood when she hesitated. "Do you need to call a doctor? You're not sounding—"

"And make up with your brothers." She coughed again. "I apologize for interrupting you."

"No, it's okay." He rubbed his hand across the back of his neck. "I don't have a problem with them. I've just been busy."

"Don't lie to me, son. Gunnar and Gideon love you. The family is growing. You need to reconnect with them." Her breath caught.

"Which hospital are you at?" Thane paced.

He knew he should have gone home, despite his brothers being there. He didn't want to see them, but he always had time for his mother.

"I told you not to worry about me."

Thane could almost see her smiling as she spoke. His stately African-American mother, who never treated him or his brothers differently despite them being white, had managed the impossible. She had started and operated three successful businesses and raised three adopted boys as her own. Damn it. He should have gone back to his childhood home.

"You are my best girl." He smiled. "I can be on a plane and back to Virginia tonight."

"No." The word came out so strong. "You are about to train. Baseball is your career. I'm so proud of you. I would love to see you win a World Series."

"You and me both." He cleared his throat when it became scratchy. "Fine. My next break, I'll come home to visit."

"Sounds. Good."

The spacing of her words heightened his concern. He balled his hand into a fist. "I love you, Mom. I love you so much. You know that, right?"

"Always. Never a doubt. You are my baby." Elizabeth made a kissing sound over the phone. "Love your family. *All* of them. I mean it."

"Sure." For this one request, he would have to tell her what she wanted to hear. Even though he would rather beat himself senseless with a baseball bat than talk to his pigheaded brothers.

"Family. Is. All. You. Have." She coughed again. "I love you."

"Love you, Mom." He covered his mouth, afraid to say more than that.

"Go. Be...strong." Elizabeth disconnected the call.

Thane stared at his phone. He brought up Gunnar's number. His finger hovered over the screen, only a hair away from pressing *send* to contact his oldest brother about their mother. She hadn't sounded like her normal self.

He stopped and canceled the call. Elizabeth told him not to worry. She promised to come see him when she felt better. She never lied to him in the past.

The niggling voice in his head told him not to discount his feelings this time. He called Gideon's number first. After three rings, someone answered.

"Hello?"

Thane blinked when he heard a female voice. He looked at the screen to see if he had dialed the right number.

"I'm looking for Gideon Wells." He didn't say more in case he had called an old girlfriend by mistake.

Girlfriend. More like play thing. His mother would be disappointed if she knew how he'd been treating some women lately. Since none of them had complained afterward, especially when gifted with something from a robin's-egg-blue-colored box, courtesy of Tiffany's, he saw his behavior as a victimless crime of passion.

"This is his brother Thane, right?" she asked in a whisper.

"Who's this?" He wouldn't be confirming her claim until he found out the identity of this woman.

"I'm Janelle Gold. I'm Gideon's girlfriend, I mean, fiancée."

Thane couldn't move, couldn't say anything. Gideon had gotten engaged and hadn't told him? Gideon hadn't even shared with him that he'd been thinking of getting married.

Thane couldn't blame his brother for cutting him out of his major plans. Thane had practically ignored him each time Gideon called. He squeezed his eyes shut and took a deep breath.

"Congratulations on the engagement." Thane meant the sentiment even though he felt his own heart shattering.

Janelle gasped. "I shouldn't have told you that until I found out for sure if you're Gideon's brother. Are you? He'll be so disappointed if this gets leaked to the press."

Thane smiled at her naïveté. Yes, she would be perfect for his middle brother. "I'm Thane. I was hoping to talk to him. Is he around?"

"Sleeping. The surgery took a lot out of him. Since your mom had to go back to the hospital, he's been a wreck."

Thane had almost forgotten about the surgery. Gideon had called him shortly after the Super Bowl and before the procedure on his knee, but Thane hadn't talked to his brother since to see how he'd fared.

He heard a door closing through the phone.

"Is there something I can tell Gideon when he wakes up? Or do you need him right now?" She exhaled. "I would hate to wake him."

"No. Let him sleep. I'll catch up with him later." Thane ran his hand over his head.

Janelle's voice lightened. "Gunnar went to the hospital with Eboni. You can get him."

So Gunnar had gotten back with his old high school sweetheart. Good. Thane remembered Eboni from when the two of them had dated. He recalled that she had been the one with the wild orange hair who would give Thane candy when she visited. Now he realized she used the candy to keep him quiet whenever she and Gunnar went out after Gunnar's curfew. Everyone had secrets.

Thane really didn't want to talk to Gunnar, especially about Elizabeth. To fake his true feelings, Thane smiled. "Thanks. You get some rest yourself. Nice talking to you."

"Same here. I hope I get to meet you soon."

Thane disconnected the call and took a moment to think. Even though he wanted to ditch the idea of calling Gunnar, he remembered his mother's cough and her gasping breath.

He pushed the number to reach Gunnar. After one ring, his oldest brother answered.

"You've got some fucking nerve." Gunnar sounded like he spoke through gritted teeth.

"Hey, bro. What a welcome. You kiss your mother with that mouth?" As usual, sarcasm would help him deal with Gunnar.

If he knew Gunnar, his hulking brother probably looked like a charging bull, complete with red eyes and drool dripping from his mouth. Smoke probably billowed out from his ears.

"Don't you dare bring Mom into this. I'm about to go up to see her now."

Thane heard a ding like in an elevator and a canned voice announcing the floor and direction of the ride.

"Good. I wanted to tell you—"

Gunnar cut him off. "Don't tell me anything. For months, I've been trying to reach you, and you've ignored me and my messages. Mom had a triple fucking bypass. Gid had surgery."

"And you were shot. I know." Thane didn't mean for the statement to sound dismissive, but he didn't call to get a lecture.

"Glad you care." Gunnar released a long, low grumble. "You know all this and you can't bother to bring your ass back home to see any of us. Don't you give a shit about your family?"

"Yeah, I do. That's why I'm calling." Thane clenched his teeth. "But you know what? You know it all. I'm sure you'll handle everything and be the big hero as always and I'll be the screw-up. I've got to go."

Gunnar snickered. "Of course. Fucking a model this time? Or is it a groupie?"

Thane walked out of his room. "Give Mom my best. Tell her I love her."

"Whatever. Do it yourself, you spoiled brat. No matter what you do or how low you stoop, you will always be Mom's baby. It still amazes me that it's her heart that's killing her since she has such a big one. Have a great evening." Gunnar disconnected the call.

Thane slid the thin phone into his jacket pocket. He hated going down to his interview with everything weighing on his mind. Even as he entered the elevator, a nagging voice in his head begged him to follow up with someone about his mother. Gunnar had been heading up to see her. He told himself that as usual, his brother would make sure Elizabeth had everything she needed. He would keep her safe.

Thane didn't want to do this interview. He'd been pushed to do it by his overbearing agent, who'd managed to get him the most lucrative deal in Major League Baseball history.

When the elevator doors opened to the lobby level, he saw a very frustrated woman glancing at her watch and pacing. Thane at least owed the journalist an explanation. The closer he got to her, the more he noticed something odd. Her marching step had an irregular pattern. She kept looking down at her feet as though unsure of her footing. At peculiar moments, she would giggle and cover half her face and mouth with her hand.

As soon as she headed for the door, he went after her. She stumbled back and nearly fell to the floor before she caught herself.

"I'm late. I know." He stood in her path to stop her.

"Yes, you are, Mr. Wells." The feisty blonde glared at him as she crossed her arms over her chest. "I've heard stories about you. I hoped you wouldn't dismiss me like other women in your past."

Damn. He had that kind of reputation? He couldn't catch a break today. He took a deep breath and caught the scent of alcohol in the air. Not unusual for a journalist to imbibe once in a while, sometimes during the interview. This one looked like she couldn't hold her liquor.

He held up his hands in surrender. "I'm not that man, Ms. Toplee." He shook his head. "However, I do have to apologize. I need to catch a plane and go home for a family emergency. My mother isn't doing well."

The journalist's face softened. "Your mother? I heard about Gunnar and Gideon. Are they going to be okay?"

"I could explain more, but I really do have to go. I apologize for making you wait and skipping out on you." He shook her hand and bowed his head. "Please call my manager to reschedule." He started toward the elevator.

"I can do that or I can make something up."

Thane stopped at her threat. He wished he could be more like his brothers. They didn't care about doing interviews or how the media portrayed them. Not Thane. Call it his overwhelming need to please, but he hated the idea that he could craft his image but didn't.

He turned to her. "Whether I stay here or not, you were going to do that anyway, right?"

She smirked and shrugged. "I'm a good writer. I'm an honest journalist. I would rather tell the story of a hot, young major league pitcher than one about the irresponsible player who arrived late for the interview to only bail with a flimsy excuse."

"I've been called worse." Flames encircled Thane's head. "And it's not an ex—"

"Let's talk." She headed toward the elevator. "We can do the interview in your room while you pack. You can tell me about this mysterious illness that you may or may not have that the keeps popping up in the rumor mill."

Thane wouldn't be talking about that. He'd worn the right outfit and splashed on some expensive cologne in order to make himself more appealing to this writer so that he could avoid talking about the personal problems plaguing him. Before he could respond, she gave him another option.

She put her hand on his arm. "Or you can come to my room."

Thane recognized where she wanted this to go. Ordinarily, an invitation like that would get his lower half tingling. Right now, he only felt numb. He didn't know his mother's status, and he couldn't rely on Gunnar to share any information.

He pointed to the hotel's dimly lit bar. "We can go in there to talk. We can get right to the interview so that you can get home to your husband."

That got the brown-eyed beauty to smile. "I'm not married."

Thane feigned surprise. "No man has captured you yet, huh? Boyfriend, right?" He put his hand to the small of her back to help guide her. The less complications he had in his life the better.

"Nope. No boyfriend either." She walked next to him as they stepped into the bar.

Couples and groups littered tables, keeping their heads hung low to hold intimate conversations with each other. Popular music thumped through the place to keep the gyrating bodies on the tiled, square space in the front of the room moving, twisting, and waving back and forth. Thane saw them simulating sex on the dance floor. He kept his attention directed to an empty table in the back of the room.

During his trek, he leaned down and whispered, "Girlfriend?"

That got her to laugh out loud, an almost donkey-sounding guffaw that drew the attention of several patrons in the bar. Thane had to remember not to make the mistake of amusing her again.

"Mr. Wells." She shook her head as he held out a chair for her at a back booth.

"Call me Thane." He made sure to get her comfortable before he occupied a seat across from her.

"Ah, if we're on a first-name basis, call me Lora Ann." She held out her hand to him.

"Good." He shook her hand, careful not to get too intimate too quickly. "Let's get this started so I can get going."

Putting his hand on her back had been pushing the familiarity level, but he knew the touch would make her comfortable with him. He could tell under her conservative pantsuit she hid the body of a tall, lithe cheerleader. If he had more time, he could think about having her long legs wrapped around his body. He didn't want to hear her talking though.

"Shall we get started?" She took out a small digital recorder.

"Is this the way you always do business? By blackmail?" *And drunk*, he wanted to add. He punctuated his query with a smile.

She crossed her legs and leaned back. "No. I have other methods of persuasion in my arsenal."

Sex, of course. Thane kept his face stoic as he regarded her. He didn't need to tip her off to what he thought of her interview tactics. Plus, he needed to do this interview quickly.

Lora Ann ordered herself a drink before she dove into questioning. "First things first. How is your family?"

Lora Ann's question shouldn't have disarmed Thane, but he felt his gut tighten at her inquiry. He shook off his nerves to bring out his business side.

"Gunnar is his normal fighting self." He didn't have to reveal the nasty blowout he had with his stubborn, judgmental brother.

"The ultimate fighting world will be glad to hear that, although I'm still shocked he's not coming back to the sport. Rumor has it his own manager arranged the hit against him. Is that true?" She nudged the recorder closer to Thane and took a lengthy sip of her Long Island iced tea.

"You'll have to ask Gunnar about that." Thane couldn't answer anything about his combative brother, even if he did want to reveal some of his secrets. "Gideon is resting up so that his body can properly heal. But I'm sure he'll be back next season a stronger and faster athlete."

"It's great that his team is supporting him. I saw Dennis the Menace's press conference yesterday. He said some pretty nice things about your quarterback brother. Did you catch it?" Lora Ann ordered a second drink before Thane even tasted his ginger ale.

"No, I missed that. Traveling at the time, I think." He stared at her empty glass. "Thirsty?"

"Very." She ran her tongue over her lips. "And your mother? You mentioned something about her earlier."

Thane glanced down at the recording device. "Let's keep this interview on me."

A waitress placed a second drink in front of her. This time, Lora Ann went for a white wine.

Lora Ann giggled as she picked up her glass. "Fine. Let's talk about your agent. Word on the street is he's looking to retire soon."

Alec Fogel had been the mastermind behind some of the greatest athletes in professional sports history in all fields. Thane considered himself lucky to have even caught the old man's notice. At the time, Thane had been a senior at Northwestern University. He had always thought Alec had only wanted to sign him because he liked Elizabeth. The old man fawned over her at every meeting.

"Did you hear that from Alec?" Thane twirled his frosty glass between his hands.

"I didn't ask him." She took a healthy gulp of her wine and held on to the glass. "I wanted to hear what you thought."

"I think my skills and talents as a pitcher got me to where I am today. It's those skills that will keep me in this sport for a long time." He watched her finish off her drink and signal for a third. "And I think you might have had enough to drink."

Lora Ann raised her eyebrows. "A caring, compassionate baseball player." She puffed out a sloppy chortle, one complete with a bit of slobber that oozed from the side of her mouth. "Stick with the bad-boy persona. It works better for you."

Thane shook his head. "This interview is over." He threw a hundred-dollar bill on the table before standing. "I would strongly suggest you sleep off your single-girl party." He started to walk by her when he stopped and glared down at her. "Write anything negative about me, and I'll have my attorney all over you and your magazine faster than you've been pounding back drinks."

Thane walked out of the bar and went to the elevator.

"Wait!"

He pressed the *up* button as soon as he heard the shrieking cry behind him, but he didn't bother turning around. His efforts to present a pleasant demeanor didn't make a bit of difference.

"Please, Mr. Wells." Lora Ann gripped his arm.

He turned to her for a brief moment. The desperation that filled her eyes covered their previously blood-shot appearance. "I'm sorry for the way I acted. I was nervous to meet you so I drank to take the edge off."

"Are you feeling smooth now?" Thane kept his disapproving stare on her even when the elevator doors opened.

"Not really." She wobbled back and forth on her feet before she nearly hit the floor.

With his gentlemanly nature kicking in in full force, he darted to her in enough time to scoop her up in his arms. "Let's get you back to your room and into bed."

"Oh, God. I'm so sorry." She covered her face with her hand and cried.

Thankfully, no one else occupied the elevator. Her cry sounded as loud and annoying as her laugh. Like a baby, he continued to cradle her.

"What's your floor?" he asked.

"Nineteen."

Great. Same as his. He waited until the elevator stopped before he set her on her feet and draped her arm around his shoulders.

"What room?" He peered down the hallway, hoping that her room wouldn't be far.

Lora Ann dove into her purse and pulled out her room key card. "What's it say?"

Damn, she couldn't even remember her room number? Thane could only imagine what would have happened had she been with the wrong athlete tonight or the wrong type of man, one who would take advantage of her weakened state.

He glanced at the card. Thane rolled his eyes. Her room sat only two doors down from his. "This way."

Thane passed his room as he headed to hers. Once there, he slid her card into the reader and waited for it to flash green before he opened the door. He helped her inside, keeping her propped up while she stumbled. He got her to bed. She sat, the top half of her body swaying back and forth.

"You were supposed to be my first really big interview with a baseball player, and I screwed it up." She placed her hand on her forehead. "They'll never trust me to go out of town again to get a story like this." She peered up at him. "I am so sorry."

Thane thought about correcting her use of the term. His mother always told him and his brothers that you should always say that you apologize. Being sorry meant that your personal state lacked character and had nothing to do with your feelings. As he stared at her, he figured in this case, the statement rang true.

Lora Ann's blond hair looked messy, like she'd already been to bed. He now noticed the pantsuit he'd thought made her look professional had been buttoned incorrectly. Had he been really observant down in the bar, he would have noticed she had her pants zipper halfway down.

Thane lifted her feet so she could lie down. "Get some sleep." He ran his hand over his hair. "Call my manager in the morning and tell him I was a no show. Arrange for another interview. You come there drunk again, and God help you."

Lora Ann's face screwed up into an unpleasant expression like she wanted to cry before her eyes widened and she leapt off the bed. She rushed past Thane to the bathroom where she hung her head over the toilet and purged her guts.

Although not interested in seeing a woman getting sick, Thane couldn't help but stand in the doorway to check on her. "You going to be okay?" He picked up a glass next to the sink and filled it with water. "I hate to leave you like this." He handed it to her.

"Will you stay with me for a little while?" She held the glass with both hands and drank from it.

"I can't. I need to go. My family—"

"I know. I know. I shouldn't have asked." She waved her hand in the air.

Holding the glass with only one hand weakened her grasp. She dropped it to the floor. It shattered into large sharp shards around her knees.

"Shit!" She reached for a piece and quickly drew her hand back like she'd been bitten.

"Don't move." Thane saw the bright red trail of blood sliding down from her palm to her wrist. He held her arm up and grabbed a towel to stop the bleeding. "I'll have them call for an ambulance to take you to the hospital."

Lora Ann could be someone else's burden tonight.

"No! Please! It's bad enough my magazine paid for this room and I'm coming back with no story. If they find out I got drunk, got sick in front of you, and cut myself, I'll be so fired." With her free hand, she wiped her eyes with the back of her hand. "Please, can you help me? I swear I'll do you right on the interview."

Thane had less interest in how he would be portrayed than getting home. He could hear his mother's voice in his head, telling him to help this woman. Be a gentleman.

"Let me clean up this glass first, and then we'll get you back to bed. As soon as I get this cut dressed and you get to sleep, I'm out of here." He crouched down and started dumping the broken glass into a nearby trashcan.

"Understood. Thank you so much." She patted his shoulder.

As soon as he had all the large pieces removed, he wiped the floor with a towel and shoved it next to the commode, making sure to sweep away all of the glass slivers. He helped her to her feet and picked her up in his arms. He didn't need her injuring herself again by stepping on pieces of glass.

He placed her on the bed again. "I'll be back." Thane left the room and went to his own.

As a baseball player, he'd gotten used to having the occasional abrasion. He couldn't run to the hospital with every scrape and cut. He pulled out his travel-size first-aid kit from his suitcase and went back to Lora Ann's room. He placed her room card key on the nightstand next to her. He didn't want to have it on him any longer than he needed.

Thane took off his jacket. He should have removed it in his room but he hadn't thought about his own comfort then. He slipped on a pair of latex gloves.

"Wow, you are very thorough." Lora Ann sobered up to the situation as she watched him.

"I have to be." He removed the towel from her hand. "Baseball is a team sport, but after the game, you're on your own."

"You seem pretty close to your family." She smiled.

Thane didn't answer. He cleaned her wound, which had at least stopped bleeding. With the blood cleared, he saw that she hadn't cut herself too deeply. He placed a sterilized pad over it and taped it down.

"That should hold you, but you may want to see someone about it if it gets irritated." Thane removed his gloves and prepared to leave again.

"Wait." Lora Ann grabbed his arm with her unaffected hand. "Will you wait here with me until I at least fall asleep?"

"I really should—"

She cut him off. "Please? I don't want to vomit in my sleep and choke on it."

Thane had an answer ready for her for that situation. She needed hospital care. He didn't have the time or the inclination to be her babysitter. Again, the voice of his reasonable mother filled his head.

Help her, he imagined Elizabeth telling him. *Be there for her.*

Thane grabbed a chair and put it next to the bed. He plopped down in it. "One hour. That's it." To punctuate his statement, he glanced at his watch.

Lora Ann nodded. "Thank you. I know I have been a—"

He held up his hand. "Please get some sleep." He didn't need to hear any explanations or apologies right now.

She slipped under the covers and closed her eyes. To help her get to dreamland, Thane extinguished the light. In the dark and silence, his mind wandered. He replayed his conversations with Queen Elizabeth and Gunnar. Neither gave him a warm and fuzzy feeling. He leaned his head back and closed his eyes, hoping to forget both situations.

What felt like only a minute passing by must have been longer. Thane felt an ache in the back of his neck that throbbed as soon as he moved his head. He put his hand to his forehead while keeping his eyes closed. He became alert when he put his other hand to his chest and felt his bare skin under his touch. He hadn't undressed.

Thane peered down. With the light in the room now on, he saw that not only had his shirt been unbuttoned and opened, his pants had been undone and unzipped.

"What the hell?" He bolted to his feet in time to see Lora Ann coming out of the bathroom completely naked.

He had been right that she had long legs under her conservative pantsuit. She also hid a myriad of colorful tattoos over her body. Dragons crept over her belly. Tigers ran down her thigh. An eagle's outstretched wings cradled her breasts.

"You looked uncomfortable in your suit." She sauntered to him. "I was making sure you were relaxed."

He glanced at his watch. "Damn!" He'd slept for several hours.

How the hell did that happen? He had a lot on his mind, but nothing plagued him that deeply to cause him to sleep for hours with a complete stranger.

Thane zipped up his pants and headed to the door. "Looks like you're doing fine now, so I'm going to go."

"Wait. Don't you want to—"

"No." He opened the door and stumbled out of her room. He had to get packed and get home.

When Thane turned toward his room, he saw someone else he really didn't want to see right now.

"Christ. You came all the way down to Florida to yell at me?" Thane closed his shirt as he glared at Gunnar.

Gunnar's mouth looked tight as he stood by Thane's door like a guard. He balled his hands into fists. Wearing black boots, dark colored jeans, a dark T-shirt and black jacket, Gunnar looked like a knockoff hit man.

"Were you with a woman last night?" Gunnar's eye twitched.

He blocked Thane's door, preventing Thane from gaining access to his room.

Thane turned back to Lora Ann's room. "Long story." He sighed as he looked at his brother in front of his hotel room door. "Why did you come all the way down to Florida? Want to see me train or something?"

Gunnar's jaw flexed. "Mom—" He stopped.

The one word felt like a stone dropped down into Thane's gut.

Gunnar took a deep breath and stood straight. Thane noticed the redness coloring his eyes. The glossy sheen gave away his reason for being there.

Gunnar took a deep breath and on the exhale said, "Mom died last night."

Thane's heart stopped beating. He took a step back. "Stop lying." He shook his head. "That shit isn't funny."

Gunnar stomped to Thane and grabbed his lapels. "Mom had another stroke last night. She never recovered." He let Thane go. "Pack your shit. I'm taking you home."

Thane stared at his brother, wanting the words he'd spoken to be untrue. No way could Queen Elizabeth be gone. He'd just talked to her. She said she would be fine. Now he felt alone.

Chapter 3

Kari Meyers sat at her cubicle at the Winning Edge Agency with her phone pressed to her ear. She crossed her legs while listening to the worst Musak ever created. She would rather hear fingernails scratching down a blackboard than the light and easy version of a Beyoncé hit.

She heard a knocking sound that grabbed her attention. She glanced up to see her boss's assistant tapping her wrist and shrugging her shoulders.

Having after-work drinks with Chelsi would be the highlight of her week. Kari shook her head as she waited to talk to Jean, her temperamental client, a French professional tennis player who refused to leave the locker room during the first day of a major tennis tournament. As an agent, Kari knew there would be a lot of handholding. She didn't expect to also be a babysitter. Her ten-year-old son acted more mature than some of her clients.

Kari shook her head as she watched Chelsi cleaning up her desk area.

"I'm not going." Jean cut through the music with his thick French accent. "You can't make me."

Kari plastered a smile on her face, determined that if she carried a pleasant countenance here, she could convince this prima donna to do the right thing. "Jean, I understand. I'm not telling you to play. Whatever reason you have for keeping yourself in your locker room is justified."

"*Oui.* They gave me half the time to practice."

Kari rolled her eyes. Her grandfather would have been so disappointed to see her doing that. "That is unacceptable. You are ranked one of the top twenty tennis players in the world." She would leave out the fact that had another player not broken his wrist, causing him to bow out of several tournaments, Jean wouldn't have cracked the top twenty.

"*Oui.* They treat me like the ball boy or something." He snorted.

"Unacceptable. I won't stand for them treating you less than the international star you are. Here's what I'll do. You pack up and come back to the States." She heard some rustling on the other end of the line. "I'll tell them to hold off paying your appearance fee." The movement stopped. "And the sponsors will not be happy not seeing you play and wearing their sneakers and clothing. But, hey, it's only endorsement money. It's not like you're living off that. You're young. You can keep playing for tournament money—that's if you place."

The line became silent for a moment.

Kari filled the void. "I'll have Chelsi get plane tickets for you to come back."

"No. Hold on." Jean cursed in French. "The sponsors will drop me if I don't play?"

"Of course. They're counting on fans seeing their logo all over you." She cleared her throat to keep from laughing. "But you have standards. I'll call and let them know to hold off payment."

"Wait." A pause lingered before he continued. "I'll play. I need more practice time."

She smiled. "That should be easy. Contact your manager and he can call the organizer and make that happen." Good thing she'd done that before even calling her client. "You're going to be amazing."

"I know." He snorted.

"What else can I do for you?" She opened her desk drawer and pulled out her purse.

"There are no good wines here."

His whining rivaled a classroom full of bored children. "Tell me what you like and I'll have Chelsi track down a bottle for you."

"Just one bottle?"

Kari laughed. "Of course. You're going to be there for a week. I'll have her find as many as she can."

"Thank you, Kari. You're the best."

She disconnected the call, not exactly feeling like the best. She had clients she represented, but her boss still classified her as a junior agent. Kari glanced at an empty office at the corner of the room. That place should be hers. She'd earned it with hard work.

Kari stood and hung her purse on her shoulder. As soon as she started to head to Chelsi's desk, her boss stopped her.

"Kari, will you come in here, please?"

She turned and saw Frank Milliner standing in his doorway. He waved to her before turning around and disappearing into his office.

She took determined steps in her expensive heels as she went to see her boss. Hopefully, he would keep this impromptu meeting short. Then again, Kari wanted that position and the office. She glanced in that direction, hoping Milliner saw her. She'd been overt with him about her desires. She really needed him to get the picture.

"What's up, Frank?" Kari leaned against the doorframe. She crossed her arms over her chest, causing her massive saddlebag purse to swing and nearly knock her off balance.

"How's our friend Jean?" Frank sat on the edge of his desk and smiled.

As she stared at him, she saw the guy she'd admired when she started in sports representation. He'd gotten great deals for a lot of high-profile athletes, including Jarrod Townsend. Thinking of that name sent a shiver through her body.

"Temperamental as always, but I calmed him down." She pulled her keys from her bag to let him know she didn't want to stand around and chit chat.

Kari wanted Frank to get the hint that she had places to go. Unless the slick, mature man had her staying late to offer her a promotion to full agent, she didn't have time to sit around and gossip.

As though reading her thoughts, Frank blurted, "I want to put you in that office." With his manicured fingernails, he pointed in the direction of the empty space. Like she hadn't seen the darkened room before, Kari turned toward it to be sure he meant the same place she wanted. Before she allowed a smile to crack her hard countenance, she had a few questions. She'd learned not to take anything at face value.

"What more do I need to do to be a full agent?" She hoped he caught the underlying meaning in her question.

She'd worked hard for the business. He and everyone else here had to recognize that, as well as all her sacrifices. Making it as a full agent would allow her to represent a higher level of athletes that would get her more money. The extra money would afford her a better lifestyle for her and her son.

"Thane Wells." Frank stood and sauntered around his desk.

Kari blinked when he mentioned the name. Of course she knew the hot Major League Baseball pitcher with the golden arm. More like platinum arm…and a great body to go along with it. She didn't have to admit to her boss that she'd thought about the dark-haired, blue-eyed player in more than a professional way.

"The one that got away. Not for lack of trying though. I continue to contact him once or twice a month to make my sales pitch. Why did you mention him?" She shrugged to give a nonplussed appearance.

"I want you to represent him." Her fit boss sat behind his desk and adjusted his dark-rimmed glasses.

Inside, Kari screamed and did backflips. Then her reasonable self took over and started questioning everything. "That's a neat trick, but I know he's represented by Alec Fogel. I'm a great agent. You're a super agent. *That* man is God. I recalled the deal he got for Thane to play with the Wrens. I don't see Thane leaving him any time soon." She shook her head and took a step back.

Talking about Thane started to conjure up a lot of fantasies of Kari representing a man she wanted to strip naked and ride until the sun came up, or she killed him, whichever came first. Of course, she would only use the man for sex. Anything else would never work. It never did for her and athletes. Damn her taste in fit men who played their sports like champions.

"I've heard from a reliable source that Alec is looking to retire soon." Frank swept his large hand over his neatly coifed hair.

Although he could afford to have his clothes custom made, he wore suits that looked like they came out of department stores. He had to keep the top button of his blue-and-white striped button-down shirt undone because it didn't fit around his thick neck. She could hear the ticking of his Timex watch from across the room. His wedding band looked like the same one he'd gotten when he married his saint of a wife over thirty years ago. For that, Kari gave the man a pass for his other poor fashion choices.

"What source?" If this rumor could be substantiated, she would start cheering on the spot.

"Another agent at his firm." He leaned back in his chair and placed his feet on the desk.

Kari glanced at his scuffed shoes and had to look away. "Why would another agent at his firm tell you something like that? And why should anyone think that Thane wouldn't want to stick with the same firm and go with another agent there? That's what I would do if I were him."

"Because that agent also said that since Alec owns the firm, he plans on closing it when he retires. The old bastard never married and never had any kids, or any that he wants to admit are his, so he can't leave his business to anyone."

"So why don't you—"

Frank held up his hand. "I offered to buy him out and take all his agents. He told me—" He stopped and shook his head. "He gave me another option for my offer."

Alec had probably told Frank to eat shit and die. It wouldn't be the first time someone had given her boss that directive. Even with his plain clothes and accessories, Frank had battery acid coursing through his veins. She'd seen him reduce a junior agent to a puddle of tears and made an MMA fighter question his manhood. He kept in shape to keep up with the younger agents. Frank hadn't lost a lot of his hair and kept it cut short and neat, like his fingernails.

"What makes you think Thane Wells will even want to come over to me or this agency?" Kari also wondered why her tough-as-nails leader didn't have plans to go after this commodity himself.

Frank screwed up his thin lips and shrugged. "I don't know. I don't even know if they've put their other agents on him to pull some Jerry Maguire thing. Or possibly some rogue agent wanting to go out on his own with one key client. Only works in fucking movies." He stood. "You've worked hard here. It would be a cool feather in your cap if you can get this guy to come on over to us."

Kari knew what that meant. Frank would love to have an African-American woman as a full agent at his company. To him, he would look cool and trendy, instead of being fair and just.

"What else would I get besides a feather?" She took a step back into his office.

"What do you mean?"

Kari tilted her head, surprised Frank would play this cutesy game. "You mentioned the office. Would I be made a full agent?"

Frank's smile widened. "And then some." He came around his desk and faced her. "How would you like to be a partner at the Winning Edge?"

Now the cartwheels and flips started in her belly. Partner? Never in her wildest dreams had she thought something like this would happen for her. A partnership could get her everything she ever wanted—a better home, money for education, and maybe some respect.

That little voice in the back of her head decided to speak up now. Damn chatty bitch. Kari couldn't help but wonder if Frank thought this move scored him cool points or something. Even better than having a black agent would be having one as a partner, not that Frank ever came off a racist. He knew how to turn a good opportunity into an event.

"So you would take me from a junior agent to a full partner with this one deal? It sounds awesome. Baby steps. I'm a hard worker. I'm willing to go the right way to get what I want. Full agent first before anything else." She shifted her weight as she regarded him. "I wonder, though, if you recognize how hard I've been working, why haven't you made me a full agent before now? I'm representing a tennis player who barely cracked the top twenty, a new boxer, and a gymnast who couldn't make it to the Olympic team."

Frank put his hand on Kari's shoulder. "Because you got that tennis player the most lucrative endorsement deal I have ever seen. That boxer has had so many celebrities coming to see him fight that I think he's going to break into movies soon. And that gymnast is on that damn dancing show and plans to tour with them. You make things happen." He patted her shoulder. "Make this happen." He lifted his phone and hit a couple of items on the screen, which set off her phone. "I sent you Thane's information."

"I'm already familiar with his stats." *Among other things*, she wanted to add.

"Good. I sent you information on where he should be right now."

"Florida, right? Spring training. I would think—"

He cut her off. "Look at what I sent you. I'll give you a couple of weeks to work your magic."

"What? You don't trust I can do this in a day?" She cocked a smile at the corner of her mouth.

"I trust you can do anything. I wanted to give you time because of your son."

Hearing Frank bring up her child sent a nervous, creeping feeling to her stomach. She never brought up her personal life at work, fearing her colleagues would hold it against her.

"I'll be fine." She turned to leave.

"I'm sure you will be. I know basketball season hasn't started yet. Maybe you can let his father—"

This time Kari cut off Frank. "I'll report back with any news." She stepped up her pace. "Don't let anyone get that office space."

"You ready?" Chelsi held up her purse. "There's a new place they say is a hot spot for Redskins players."

"Rain check."

Too wound up to get in an elevator, she took the ten flights of stairs down to the basement garage and burst through the door. She hurried to her car. The entire ride she thought about several things—her job, the promotion, the money, Thane, her child.

By the time she got home, Kari felt like electricity pulsed through her body.

"You're home earlier than I thought." Reagan stood from the dining room table.

The affable Filipino woman who had been working for Kari for three years picked up her cup and plate. She carried them into the kitchen.

"You're home." Michael held up his hands.

"Hi, baby." She embraced her son, a great reason to skip the drink and rush home.

He smelled like cookies, milk, and grass.

"Been playing outside today?" She rubbed her hand over his head. She'd allowed him to grow his hair out a little.

Small, tight curls covered his head. Kari had convinced herself she'd let him grow his hair to a small Afro because of the cooler temperatures, not so he wouldn't look like his father. Too bad his hair couldn't cover up the similarities. Besides the same golden-brown skin tone, Michael's wide brown eyes held the same shape as his dad's, along with his button nose and full lips. Kari had to admit it. She'd birthed a miniature version of Jarrod Townsend.

"How did you know what I did?" The child glared at Reagan, who raised her hands in the air.

"I haven't talked to your mother today." Reagan shook her head.

"I can smell it on you, sweetie. You smell like grass and dirt and earthworms." Kari sniffed against his ear, which sent the child into a laughing fit.

"You can't smell worms." Michael giggled and tucked his chin down toward his tiny chest. When she stopped smelling him, he continued. "I was practicing."

"Practicing what?" Kari took off her jacket and hung it in the closet next to the front door.

"Basketball." He picked up a cookie from his plate and nibbled on it. "You think I could be as good as Daddy?"

Kari had to choose her words carefully. She never wanted to be the kind of bitter mother to talk ill about her child's father. At the time she'd conceived Michael, Kari had been in love with Jarrod—or what she'd thought had been love. What the hell did she know at sixteen? She knew that Jarrod had the best hook shot in their high school. She'd recognized back then he would go places. When he promised to marry her and take her with him when he made pro, she believed him.

Kari should have seen the writing on the wall. As soon as she told him she'd missed her period, he started distancing himself from her. When she confirmed her pregnancy on his eighteenth birthday, he questioned if the child could be some other man's, as though at sixteen she could be that free and loose with her body. By the time she gave birth to Michael, Jarrod had signed a contract with the Lakers and left her high and dry.

"Honey, I believe you can be anything you want to be." She smiled to mask her pain. When she glanced up at Reagan, she saw her shaking her head. "Did you finish your homework?"

"Yep." He held up his paper.

"Excuse me?"

"I mean, yes, ma'am." He turned to Reagan. "I hardly needed any help, right?"

Reagan nodded. "That's right. And they're teaching them a lot of stuff now. He had algebra. What teacher gives a ten-year-old algebra?"

"One who has a mother who insisted on it." She winked at Reagan. She returned her attention to her child. "Will you go into your room while Reagan and I have a chat?"

He nodded. "Yes, ma'am." Before leaving, he picked up another cookie from his plate then ran off, giving Kari and Reagan some privacy.

"What's up?" Reagan asked as soon as Michael ducked into his room.

"I need to go out of town for a while. I'm trying to secure a new client." Kari removed her gold hoop earrings from her lobes but left the small diamond studs in her second piercing.

"Really? Who?" Reagan gripped the back of one of the dining room chairs and stared at her with a look of childlike anticipation, complete with wide eyes.

Kari delighted in Reagan's excitement. Kari knew the day she interviewed Reagan to be Michael's nanny that she would get along with her. Reagan had answered almost every question with a sports reference.

"Thane Wells." Kari stared at Reagan for her reaction.

Reagan blinked. "Whoa. You swing for the fences, don't you?"

Kari smiled. "More like my boss does. He made the suggestion." She stepped out of her shoes and carried them. "I'd like to meet the man." This time she wanted to be face-to-face with him and not look at him from across the room and hope for more.

"I'm sure you would." Reagan winked.

"What do you mean by that?"

"You talked about him when he was still in the minor leagues. You knew even then that he was going to do something great."

Kari remembered her business infatuation with him years ago. She remembered thinking how great it would be to watch him train… among other things. Learning his brothers also excelled in sports had intrigued her even more. A family of athletes. The women in their town never had a chance.

"I'll need that enthusiasm when I try to convince him to switch to a new agent." She leaned against the wall.

"Not a problem. Wear something low cut with a high slit."

Kari sighed.

Reagan held up her hand. "Hey, I know you don't do business that way. But if the gossip magazines are right, he's a regular Casanova."

"I could care less who he beds each night as long as he wants me representing his interests." Kari swallowed hard to choke back the lie she told.

Curiosity plagued her like a lot of straight women and gay men when they looked at Thane Wells. She wanted to see what kind of game he had. She couldn't be selfish anymore. She had a child to think about now.

"Tell me what you would like me to do." Reagan wiped down the table where Michael had sat.

"Looks like he's in Virginia Beach right now." Kari still couldn't figure out why Thane wouldn't be down in Florida for spring training. Maybe he decided he didn't need to train. Her stomach lurched at the thought of him being that arrogant.

"That's good for you. Short drive instead of flying." Reagan nodded and headed back into the kitchen.

"You think you can stay here with Michael for a week? I'm hoping it won't take that long."

Reagan screwed up her face before she answered. "Can you give me a couple of days? I need to corral the home team to let them know what I'll be doing."

Kari nodded. "Of course. I need to break the news to Michael."

She hated spending so much time away from home. She didn't want to be so distant from her baby too long.

"And what if it takes longer than a week?" Reagan asked.

"Spring break is coming up. I'll bring Michael down to Virginia Beach with me. If I don't sign Thane, we'll make it a vacation." Kari would make sure to make every moment special for Michael.

"Does that vacation include me?" Reagan laughed.

"Of course. Someone has to watch Michael while Thane and I run around on the beach."

"I know you're joking now."

Kari padded over the hardwood floors to get to her room. Before she got there, she stopped at Michael's room. With his door partially shut, she peeked through to watch him at his desk on his computer. He had his back to her, and she hoped he wouldn't catch her spying on him. He usually did.

"Mom, what are you doing?" Michael didn't turn around in his chair.

She pushed the door open all the way. "Making sure you're not looking at anything dirty on the Internet, like anything to do with the Dallas Cowboys or the New York Yankees." She covered her mouth to suppress a laugh.

"Eww! Never." He pushed his chair back. "But look at this."

Kari walked into her son's room. It still looked like a child's room despite his rapidly advancing age. His racecar bed had been made as she instructed him to do each day. She knew when she turned off the lights, glow-in-the-dark stars and moons would radiate from his ceiling and walls. She couldn't bring herself to look at the posters of Jarrod Townsend covering her son's walls—*their* son's walls.

Michael looked up to the man who rarely visited him. When he did, Jarrod made a production out of it, offering expensive gifts and taking Michael to places she could only dream to take him one day. One iconic poster had Jarrod making a radical jump shot from what seemed like the half-court line and flying through the air to the basket. No doubt about it. Jarrod had become a legend…to fans and his son. Kari would never look at him as the man she thought she saw as a teenager.

"What is it, baby?" Kari stood behind Michael's chair and looked over his head to his computer screen.

When she saw Jarrod's image, she choked down her instant response to gag.

"Dad is going to be doing an exhibition show in New York in a couple of weeks." Michael pointed to the screen.

"Really? Did your father send that to you?" Kari stroked Michael's hair.

"No. I did a search on him and saw it."

She nodded. She wouldn't fill in the blanks for her child.

"He'll be here on the East Coast near us." He clasped his little hands together, almost in prayer form.

"He'll be working." Kari didn't want him getting his hopes up, especially if Jarrod had no plans of seeing him.

"Do you think he'll come by to see me?" His brown eyes held so much hope and innocence.

"I don't know, sweetie." She crouched down and placed her earrings in her shoes for a moment. She held her son's hands in hers. "Listen. I have to go away for work in a few days, so you'll be here with Reagan. I should be gone for about a week, maybe less. Is that going to be okay?"

Michael shrugged. "Sure. Where are you going this time?"

"Virginia Beach." She watched the excitement cover his face. "If I'm there longer than a week, I'll bring you down with me and we can make a vacation out of it. What do you think of that?"

"That would be so cool. You think Dad will come down with us?"

Kari's smile slipped down her face. "I'll ask, but you know how busy your dad is with the team and all." *And his other children and other women.*

Had Kari really been that blind and stupid not to see the snake she'd allowed to use her? She'd believed every one of his tired lines. Only half of them came true. He had become a basketball player for a professional team. He had become a millionaire from the sport. He *hadn't* married her and taken her and their son with him like he'd promised.

"But you'll ask him, right?" The expectation in Michael's eyes couldn't be broken.

She picked up her items. "Yes. I promise." Then she kissed the top of his head. "An hour on the computer and that's it."

"Aw, Mom." His little shoulders slumped down like his whole world had crumbled.

"I know. Your life is so hard." She got to the door and turned to him. "I love you, little slugger."

"Yeah, yeah. I know." He went back to the computer and fixed his stare on Jarrod's picture.

Yes, Kari would need to secure this deal with Thane. How else could she compete with Jarrod and his fame without bringing in his kind of money? She would have to convince Thane he needed change in his life. Kari would have to prove that he needed her. Time to get to work.

Chapter 4

Numb. For the last couple of days since Gunnar had flown down to Florida to break the news to Thane about their mother, Thane felt empty. He had immediately packed up all his belongings that he brought to the hotel and hopped on a plane with Gunnar. He waited a day to call the team's coaches and manager. In his conversation, he couldn't choke out the word *dead*.

The morning of her funeral, Thane stood off on his own. He didn't want to be there. Being there meant accepting the fact that Queen Elizabeth Sommerville, matriarch of the family, pillar of the community, and the best chocolate chip cookie maker ever would never talk to him again, would never give him sage advice to follow, would never embarrass him with questions about his personal life. As he felt his throat tightening, he lowered his head and leaned against a back wall.

When he did manage to look up, he caught sight of his brothers, both with their fiancées. Thane remembered Eboni Danielson. He didn't know she'd cut her hair short. It made him wonder if she'd done it because Gunnar had shaved his head, or had Gunnar copied her?

Eboni gripped Gunnar's hand and stood by his side. She'd even picked them up from the airport. After giving Thane a polite greeting, Eboni had turned her full attention and love—evident from the way she looked at him—to Gunnar. In turn, his strong, pigheaded, older brother had felt comfortable enough later that day to cry on her shoulder, and she'd wept on his. Gunnar probably thought Thane hadn't seen him expressing his grief. His tough brother had gone out to the backyard at their mother's home to let loose his emotions. It didn't look like Eboni had said anything to him. She held him. Thane had wrapped his arms around his body, craving that same attention.

His gaze fell on Gideon. As usual, Gideon had tried playing peacemaker by offering Thane a bed in his home. Thane had turned down the offer, especially after hearing that Elizabeth had been at his house when she collapsed. He didn't want to see the place where his mother had been before her final trip to the hospital. It had been hard enough returning to her home. He only did that because Eboni had taken him and Gunnar there. As soon as he could, he called for a cab to take him to a hotel.

At a time like this, he would have thought being around family would help him. Instead, constant reminders of how they became a family hit him over the head. Elizabeth had loved them unconditionally. Thane didn't know if he could feel love of any kind again.

Thane could barely take in the church surroundings. His gaze returned to Gideon and his significant other. Like Gunnar and Eboni, Gideon and Janelle stayed by each other's sides. Considering his middle brother walked with a cane thanks to his recent knee surgery, he really needed the support. Janelle kept him propped up especially when Gideon broke down emotionally.

Elizabeth lay in an all-gold casket. She would have wanted it that way. Gunnar asked Thane to pick out her final outfit. Thane had stood in front of his mother's closet, looking through her extensive wardrobe and not being able to find suitable attire to bury his mother. How the hell could anyone do that?

Thane found a dress that their mother had made. Gunnar said she'd told him she planned on wearing it to an upcoming event. It seemed appropriate she be buried in the final garment she created.

Gideon had outfitted the entire church cathedral area with flowers. Calla lilies and roses surrounded Queen. The whole scene looked good enough for royalty. Janelle had helped him the entire time. She'd arranged a lot of the bouquets and carried many of them in from the delivery vans. Each time Gideon had tried helping her, she stopped him, no doubt afraid he would injure himself even more.

Thane wanted someone like that in his life, someone who would look out for him, someone who would be his partner.

Gideon hobbled over to Thane at the back of the church. Thane wiped his face and kept his arms crossed over his chest.

"How are you holding up, man?" Gideon raised his hand like he wanted to put it on Thane's shoulder.

No. Thane didn't want to feel anything from anyone right now. He moved away from his brother. The stabbing pain he felt in his stomach reminded him that this stress didn't help his condition. As much as he wanted to down some antacid to help calm it, he didn't need to do anything to alert his brother of his ongoing issue.

"Maintaining. You?" Thane nodded toward Gideon's leg. "Shouldn't you sit down?"

Gideon almost smiled. "Now you sound like Mom."

Thane swiped the back of his thumb under his nose. If he continued talking to Gideon, he wouldn't be able to stop the tears that threatened to erupt.

"Before they open the doors to let people in, the funeral director wanted to know if you want some time alone with Mom." Gideon nodded toward the front of the chapel.

Thane looked toward the area. It seemed so far away from them, like her body sat in another building, like it would take him an hour to walk to her and see her face one last time.

Thane hadn't shared with his brothers that last night he'd spent some time with their mother at the funeral home, talking to her still, lifeless body like she could hear him and respond. He talked to her like old times. He missed hearing her quick, witty responses, and her touching his hand.

During his visit, Thane noticed how the funeral home managed to give Elizabeth her trademark smile. He'd made sure to perfectly press the outfit he brought for her. He'd written a letter and managed to tuck it into her pocket.

Thane had already said all he wanted to say to the woman who raised him. He shook his head. "No."

Gideon furrowed his eyebrows for a moment. "Are you sure? Once people come in, you won't be able to—"

"I said I'm fine." He started to walk away but stopped. He turned back to Gideon. "Sorry for cutting you off."

Elizabeth would have appreciated that.

As Gideon had warned, the doors opened and a flood of mourners arrived. Thane remembered many of them from his childhood, from seeing them around his mother's various businesses and from church. He wondered if some had arrived only to see the three star athletes, if they hadn't come to pay their respects to a woman who could do no wrong. They wanted to see the MMA fighter, the NFL quarterback, and the MLB pitcher in tears.

Fortunately, this mega church had a grieving area for the family that also had a sheer curtain to obscure their appearances. Thane decided to make his way to that area and sit in the second row in the corner.

"No, you're here." Gunnar pointed to a chair toward the end of the front row. "Immediate family up front."

Thane took a deep breath and sauntered to the front row. He sat down but kept his gaze forward, staring at the casket, noting how the ornate decorations glittered under the overhead lighting.

Gunnar stood in front of Thane. In his black suit and tie, he looked like the grim reaper himself.

"Do you have your speech?" Gunnar patted his pocket.

Thane shook his head. "I can't. I can't talk about Mom." Besides, the speech he'd written now rested in their mother's pocket.

"We all said we would get up and say something about her." Gunnar's voice started to rise.

The volume got Thane's attention. He peered up and planted his feet to get ready to stand and square off against the giant. Today, no one could hurt him.

"Gunny, please." Eboni held Gunnar's hand. "Some people can't get up and talk about a loved one in this kind of setting. I don't know if I could do it. Give your brother a break."

Gunnar glared at Thane for a moment before regarding Eboni. He gave her a solid nod before going back to their seats. Like the gentlemen Elizabeth had raised them to be, both Gunnar and Gideon helped their ladies take a seat before occupying chairs next to them.

Thane felt a brush against his shoulder. He turned to see an older African-American gentleman he'd never seen before. The man took a seat next to him. With his straight posture and expensive-looking suit, he looked like a businessman, or worse, a politician. He wore a black suit with a complementing black-and-red tie. Elizabeth would have appreciated the colors, but Thane didn't like this stranger sitting in the family area.

"Sorry, family only here." Thane pointed to the general seating area in the church.

Gideon leaned forward. "Thane, that's Fred."

Thane stared at his brother for a moment while he let the name tumble around in his head. The confusion on his face must have been evident.

Gideon quickly said, "Fred and Mom were dating."

Thane turned to the gentleman, who now had tears in his red-rimmed eyes.

"I wanted to ask her to marry me after she got all better." He pulled a handkerchief from his pocket and wiped his eyes underneath his glasses. "Son, if you love someone, don't wait to tell them."

"I know." Thane also wanted to tell this stranger not to call him *son*.

Only one person had the right to do that, and she could no longer speak.

It didn't take long for the church to fill up. So many people arrived that they had an overflow section in the recreation building behind the church where they had a live video feed projected on a large screen.

Thane took a deep breath. When he caught the scent of the flowers, it almost broke him. It reminded him so much of Elizabeth that the tears he'd been struggling to hold back began to cascade down his face. He turned his attention away from his brothers. When he did, Fred offered him another handkerchief. Thane shook his head and turned from him. Keeping his gaze directed to the floor would be the safest bet.

The funeral started with their reverend giving a lovely eulogy about Elizabeth. Thane tried tuning the man out, but as usual, his booming voice kept Thane interested in what he'd said.

"We will truly miss this remarkable woman," the reverend said. "Now we'll have her sons get up and speak about the woman they knew."

Gideon stood first. Janelle kissed the back of his hand before he could make his way up to the podium to speak.

Thane kept his stare on the blood-red carpeting. He tossed the idea around in his head of the type of person who would approve of such a color being used in a church. Then Gideon spoke.

"I met Elizabeth Sommerville, my mother, when I was about six or seven. My brothers and I had it rough before we were blessed to be adopted by this incredible woman." Gideon sniffed and paused a moment before he continued. "The very first thing I recalled about her was that she was so incredibly beautiful. You have to remember, I was a little kid. I had never seen anyone, man or woman, wearing as many pieces of jewelry as Queen Elizabeth."

A ripple of laughter sounded through the chapel.

That got Gideon to smile. "Her face was all done up. Her lipstick was put on perfectly. I think I even asked her how she was able to paint in the lines because I couldn't."

The audience erupted in laughter. Thane couldn't muster up the gesture.

"As usual, my mom put her hand to my cheek." Gideon put his hand against his face as though feeling her now. "And she leaned down and she said, 'Dear, I practiced a lot to get this good.'" Gideon did laugh this time. "She was the one who put a football in my hand and allowed me to follow my passion, of course, while making sure I got my education. She also made me work in her flower shop." He shook his head. "At first, I wasn't too thrilled about that. What teenage boy wants to spend evenings and weekends sweeping up leaves and stems? As always, Elizabeth made me appreciate what plants and flowers had to offer. She showed me the life and beauty in each one." He smiled. "It also helped that teenage girls like flowers and would come in to the shop often."

Laughter filled the entire church.

He glanced off to the side. "Now I have my own beautiful rose in my life thanks to Elizabeth Sommerville." He winked at Janelle. "My mother was so strong and so smart. She gave us all a great life while keeping us grounded. I'm going to miss this wonderful woman." He gazed down at the now closed casket. "I love you, Mom. I know you'll make Heaven beautiful." He blew her a kiss and resumed his seat.

As soon as Gideon sat, he broke down, crying harder than Thane had ever seen him. Thane started to reach out for Gideon's hand when Janelle seized them both.

Gideon had someone. Gunnar had someone. As usual, Thane would be left out.

Gunnar stood and stomped up to the podium. He took a deep breath before he spoke. "Excuse my language, but I was truly a bastard when my mother found me."

A slight gasp sounded from the audience. Thane stared at Gunnar to hear the rest of his speech. So far, Thane had no reason to disagree with him.

"I had no idea what good love was. My birth mother treated us so poorly. The foster families we went to were no better." Gunnar shook his head. "By the time we got to Elizabeth Sommerville, I didn't think of mothers as protectors. I never thought they could be nurturing. I put Elizabeth through her paces." He turned to the reverend who sat behind him. "He can tell you. I was not a good kid, even in church."

The reverend chuckled and nodded in agreement.

Gunnar continued. "One day, it all changed. Queen Elizabeth did something that no one else had ever done for me. She showed me she cared about me. She didn't have to say it. She loved me even when I didn't love myself. That's what I'll always remember about my mother. She had such a big heart. She regarded us all as her own. She disciplined us when we needed it, but she always made us feel cherished." He pointed to Gideon. "Just like she made Gid work in her flower shop, she made me work in her hair salon." He shook his head. "Can you imagine the looks women gave me, a little punk, asking them if I could wash and style their hair? The ladies were not having it. My mother allowed me to style her hair first, in the privacy of our home, mind you. Once I did that and she was satisfied with the work, she told her customers how great I was. It was her endorsement that got the clients to trust me." He took a deep breath before continuing. "I can't forget how anxious she looked when I told her I was going to go off and fight for a living. She didn't like the idea, but she knew it was something I had to do." He held up one finger. "She made me promise one thing before I left. She didn't want me to hurt anyone's feelings."

The mourners erupted in laughter.

Thane stared at Gunnar and wanted to blurt out that he had failed in his promise with one person.

Gunnar paused and looked lovingly at Eboni. "She would have been a wonderful grandmother."

Thane sat up straighter and looked over at Eboni, who sobbed in her hands. Christ, had Gunnar announced that he would be a dad soon and hadn't even shared that news with Thane?

"I will always remember Elizabeth Sommerville, not as the business owner or the woman who wore all the jewels and makeup, and had the great clothes and shoes. I'll remember her as the one who liked teasing me. I'll remember the woman who could make me laugh. I'll remember the way her bracelets would jingle next to each other. Looking around today, I can see she was loved by more than just her family. I hope you all have great memories of her like we do. Thank you all for being here. Thank you all for loving her."

Gunnar returned to his chair. He kept his head held high as the reverend returned to the podium to conclude the funeral. Thane, Gunnar, Gideon, Tillman, an employee from Press 'N Curl, Victor, an employee from Pick 'N Clip, and Fred all served as pallbearers. They carried the casket out to the hearse.

It took all of Thane's strength to release the coffin to slide it in the back. He couldn't let his mother go. Going to the gravesite would be worse than the funeral.

As he suspected, sitting down next to where his mother's body would be lowered and kept, rattled him. Thane wanted to crawl out of his skin. He peered up, and through the crowd, he spotted a woman he hadn't seen before, which for today, meant nothing. He'd sat through a whole funeral service next to a man who'd professed undying love for his mother.

This woman captured his attention, not because she stood far back from the crowd. Her long, black hair held full curls. Her oak-colored skin tone looked golden in the March sun. Whereas everyone else wore sunglasses, she didn't. Her almond-shaped brown eyes had him sucked in without her even staring at him. She kept her gaze on the coffin, even as they lowered it into the ground.

At the conclusion of the service, Thane stood, trying to keep up with this mysterious woman.

"Are you coming back to the house?" Gideon tugged on Thane's jacket.

"What?" Thane broke from his stare to regard his brother.

"Mom's house. We're having family and a few close friends over. You coming?"

Thane turned back to where he'd seen the woman. She'd disappeared. Damn. "Uh, no. I'm going to—"

"I know what you're going to do." Gideon shook his head. "It's Mom's funeral. Can't you cool it for a day for her?"

"Christ, Gid, I wasn't even thinking about—" Thane stopped himself. He hadn't thought of anything inappropriate with the mystery woman until Gideon had put the idea in his head. "Yeah, I'll be there."

Gideon hobbled off with Janelle by his side. Gunnar had stayed behind with Eboni to talk to the reverend and the funeral director. As always, Gunnar made sure to take care of everything, leaving nothing for the rest of them to do.

Thane crawled into the stretch limousine and managed to get to a seat opposite Gideon and Janelle. The plush interior seemed out of place with what had happened. To match his heartache, Thane would have been happy riding in a broken-down pile of crap.

Thane ran his hands over the empty seats beside him. The darkened windows along with the black carpeting and black seats gave the space an eerie feel. Then Thane peered over to see a small bar. Although not a big drinker, especially during game season, he needed something to take off the edge. As he leaned over to grab a small bottle of whiskey, the door opened.

Gunnar helped Eboni inside before he hopped in and closed the door behind himself. They positioned themselves at the back row before the big car took off toward their mother's home.

The thought of going to Elizabeth's house again forced Thane to continue reaching for the booze.

"Mom's family and friends will be at her house." Gunnar's deep voice carried a harsh quality. His warning tone, directed at Thane, came with a complementing glare.

Thane cracked the top, breaking the silly paper seal. "Is that supposed to mean something?"

"It means you shouldn't be loaded when you talk to Reverend Rufus or Aunt Millie." Gideon stretched his leg in front of him as he draped his arm around Janelle. "Can you hold off until after everyone leaves?"

Thane scanned his brothers' faces along with the ladies, who both had problems connecting their gazes to his. He recognized shame and embarrassment. He didn't want the women to feel bad. He could care less what his brothers thought.

"I'll pop a mint in my mouth." He tipped the miniature bottle, pouring the contents down his throat.

The smooth burn oozed down inside like a tasty river of lava. Thane closed his eyes and leaned his head back against the plush seating. Once the liquid settled in his belly, he had to grit his teeth to endure the discomfort he'd caused himself. He squeezed his eyelids closed as the wave of pain crested and flowed away. Even with the ache, he wouldn't stop drowning his sorrows.

Take away all memories of today. Let me forget it all.

"Great." Gunnar shook his head. "Perfect."

Thane shook his head. "Nope. That's not me." He reached for another bottle, rum this time. "I'm not perfect."

"Mom's barely in the ground and you're—"

"Gunny!" Eboni tugged on Gunnar's arm. "Please."

Gunnar looked down at Eboni. "So he's allowed to make a fool of himself, and we all have to excuse his behavior?"

"Why not? We did it for you for years." Thane said what he'd been thinking for a while and felt no shame in his words, even as Gunnar shot laser beams at him with his stare.

"What? The alcohol makes you brave?" Gunnar started to get up like he wanted to get to Thane when Eboni's hand on his arm and Gideon's forearm across his chest stopped him.

"Chill, guys." Gideon pushed Gunnar back. "Can we get along for Mom's sake?"

"Yeah. After today, you won't have to deal with me anymore." Thane downed the second bottle and tossed it to the floor.

Gunnar took a deep breath and lowered his head. He put his hands together in prayer form. Had Thane reduced his brother to seek answers through religion?

"We're all we have now." Gunnar brought his head up and stared at Thane. "We have to stick together."

Thane wanted to have a smart comeback to Gunnar's statement. He wanted to blast his brother for wanting to bond as a family when Gunnar had taken off as soon as he could, running away from the only family he knew. Somehow, Eboni had learned to forgive him. Thane hadn't gotten to that place yet.

Thane reached into his jacket pocket and pulled out a tin of wintergreen Altoids. He showed the container to Gunnar, opened it, and popped two mints into his mouth. Without another word, he turned his back on the group. He wanted this ride and this day to end.

Thane recognized the landscape as they approached their final destination. Knowing his mother never drank, he collected as many of the small bottles of alcohol from the mini bar that he could. He heard a small gasp. When he turned in the direction of the sound, he found Janelle covering her mouth as she turned her head away from him. Gideon, however, kept up his stare.

"Don't do this, man." Gideon shook his head. "We're all hurting."

"Then come see me if you need something." Thane peeked at Gunnar, who hadn't raised his head since he'd last spoken to Thane.

Thane thought he would be okay not getting a judgmental look from his oldest brother. Being ignored, he found, hurt as much as the comments. His gut wrenched even as he stuffed the bottles in his jacket pockets. The glass clinked like a whisper of a promise for his salvation.

As the limo slowed to a stop in front of Elizabeth's home, Thane wasted no time in getting out of his seat and opening the door.

"You want to wait until we come to a complete—"

"No." Thane cut off Gideon and stepped out of the car that stopped abruptly.

More than likely, the driver had caught sight of the door opening and wanted to make sure his passenger didn't injure himself. Thane stumbled but managed to stay upright as he stomped up to the house. Inside, he found his mother's flower shop employee, Victor, putting the final touches to a lovely buffet table along the dining room wall. The place had flowers of all kinds everywhere—by the front door, under each window, over every surface, and even from the ceiling. A beautiful bouquet of daisies hung from the center of the room like a decorative but living chandelier.

"Hey, Thane." Victor pulled Thane into a hug.

Thane left his arms dangling on his sides at first, but he couldn't deny this old family friend. He patted Victor on his back, which triggered the waterworks. Victor embraced Thane harder and cried, which came with long, loud screeching wails.

"We all miss her." Thane continued rubbing Victor's back to calm him down.

The hug actually started to slow Thane's raging heartbeat. He found that he missed a personal connection like this, one his brothers had been offering to give him all day.

The front door opened. He saw Eboni and Janelle walk through before Gideon and Gunnar walked in behind them. Not wanting them to see him looking vulnerable, Thane released Victor. He handed the older man a napkin to wipe away his tears before going to the kitchen.

In the small space, he found a lithe African-American woman he remembered meeting one time before during his visits home, but he couldn't recall her name. She had her Afro slicked down in the front and trumpeting out the back in a huge puff. Her tight, black dress left nothing to the imagination. The tears in her eyes spoke volumes. She pulled out a tray of sliced ham and placed it on the table.

"You probably don't remember me." She grabbed a napkin and wiped under her eyes. "My name is Shay. I worked with your mom, I mean, I work at the hair salon."

Thane nodded. Now he remembered her. She'd flirted with him when he'd met her the first time. He didn't mind flirting back. The attractive woman could catch any man's interest. He didn't view her as a serious girlfriend. Had he only used her for a good time, his mother would have killed him.

"Thane." He pointed to himself.

She nodded while her face broke. She raised her arms and enveloped him in them. Her large breasts pressed against his chest as she cried. With each gasping sob, her body trembled.

Thane couldn't help but hold her. He wrapped his arms around her tiny waist.

"She let me live in the apartment over the garage when my boyfriend—" Shay stopped and cried even harder. "She saved me, her and Gunnar."

Thane released his hold as soon as he heard Gunnar's name. With his arms by his side, he jiggled his jacket pockets, which clinked the small bottles against each other. Shay pulled back from him and peered down.

"Glad my mother could be there for you." He moved back from her and returned to the living room, which now had filled up with bodies.

Some people he recognized from his mother's businesses, like Tillman and Tisha, also from the salon. The rest of the people came from Elizabeth's side of the family, like her sister, Millie, who looked nothing like Queen.

Whereas Elizabeth carried a statuesque height, Millie stood shorter than height-challenged Victor. Millie's eyes reminded him of autumn, full of light brown, green, and gray colors, depending on what she wore. Unlike his mother, Millie flaunted a fuller figure.

Thane had no problem hugging his aunt. "Hey, Aunt Millie."

She squeezed him like she wanted to absorb him into her compact body. Thane took a deep breath. His aunt didn't even smell like his departed mother. Millie always reminded him of spring and summer. She smelled like fresh-cut grass and honeysuckle.

She pulled back from him. Thane had expected to see tears filling the woman's eyes. Instead, she looked strong. She kind of reminded Thane of Gunnar, like she had to be the rock.

"Your mother loved all of you boys so much." Millie's voice remained steady as she spoke.

"We loved *her*. She will be missed." Thane's voice broke, but he took in a deep breath to keep from crying.

"You three are going to have to be like Elizabeth and I were when our parents died." She rested her hands on his shoulders. "You have each other. Lean on your family."

Thane put his hand on top of his aunt's. "If you need anything, you know you can call any of us. You're family."

Millie smiled. "I know, baby. But I'm more concerned about you three. I know what a force of nature my sister is…was." She shook her head like she couldn't wrap her mind around the concept of Elizabeth being gone. "She saw strength in each of you. You all are going to have to hold each other up for a while. There's no shame in asking for help."

Thane didn't see his situation with his brothers that way. He craned his head back and saw the back door by the kitchen, a way out. "Speaking of help, I think they might need some in the kitchen." He kissed Millie on her cheek. "Love you."

"Love you, Thane."

Thane made his way through the throngs of people milling around his mother's modest home to get to the back door. He bolted through it, needing space and air and a place to think. He paced in the grassy area next to the two-story two-car garage, the place Shay said she now lived.

He pressed his back against the garage wall and pulled his jacket around his body. When he heard the bottles in his pocket clicking against each other again, he wasted no time retrieving one and downing it in a swallow.

Thane grimaced and growled when he realized he'd drunk a bottle of vodka. He shoved the empty bottle into his pocket and pulled out another one. At this point, it didn't matter what he ingested. He needed the effects of the alcohol to kick in now.

An hour later and several bottles of liquor poured down his throat, Thane achieved what he wanted. He slid down the wall to sit on the cold ground under him. He'd buried his mother today. The thought of that hit him despite being too drunk to stand.

He bowed his head and covered his face with his hands. "It's not fair."

"Hey."

Thane felt a hand on his shoulder. He peered up and saw Gideon standing over him.

"We've been looking for you. Why are you out here?" He held his hand out to Thane.

Thane pushed himself up and stumbled as soon as he made it to his feet. Gideon held on to Thane's arm and helped him get straight.

"You really did it, huh?" Gideon held Thane's chin so he could look into Thane's face.

Thane grabbed Gideon's hand and pushed him away, which made him stumble back. "Why won't you all leave me alone? Everyone grieves in their own way. Can't I sit here and get shitfaced without you judging me? Mom's dead." He shook his head. "Mom's dead." He fell to his knees.

Maybe if he prayed for a different outcome to this day, it would happen. He wished for a miracle. He wanted some good to come into his life. Most of all, Thane wanted to stop the ache in his heart.

The alcohol provided the effect he sought. Besides being drunk, the pain he felt beat anything he had ever experienced. The sting rivaled the normal throbbing that struck his midsection on a regular basis. This would be his punishment for wanting to forget it all. He'd done this to himself.

"The people are starting to thin out in the house. Why don't you come back inside? You can go upstairs and sleep off your binging." Gideon reached for Thane again, but Thane stumbled back out of his grasp.

"Gunnar doesn't want me in there." Thane shook his head. "He hates me."

Gideon screwed up his face. "Now you're sounding drunk. Everyone in that house loves you. Come on in." He held his hand out to Thane.

Thane shook his head. "No, I'll be fine. I always am." He felt himself smile even though a riot rampaged through his body.

"You're not fine, man. Come inside."

Thane staggered around the backside of the garage, knowing he could easily outrun his incapacitated brother, even in his inebriated condition. "Is the limo still here? I'll take it back to the hotel."

"Yeah, it's here. But we don't want you to—"

"Your girl"—Thane stopped and nodded—"she's nice."

Gideon stood a few feet from Thane. "Yes, she is. The best."

Thane rubbed his hand over his face and laughed. "Funny about Gunnar and Eboni. Who saw that coming?"

Gideon finally smiled. "Yeah, it's great for them. If you stop sleeping around, you can find yourself a good woman."

Thane stopped. In his head, he stood stock still as he glared at his brother. Honestly, he felt like the world had shifted under his feet, which made him wave back and forth.

"Still judging me. Still assuming." He held up his two middle fingers to Gideon. "Fuck you." He turned and opened the gate that separated the backyard from the front area.

He made it to the limousine where the driver stood smoking a cigarette. As soon as the driver spotted Thane, he stomped it out and made it over to the back door.

"Ready to go, sir?" He attempted to hold Thane's upper arm to help him into the car.

"Been ready." Thane tripped into the car and didn't bother standing. He crawled inside and braced his back against a row of seats. "Take me back to my hotel, please."

"Yes, sir." He closed the door.

Thane rested his head on the seat. He couldn't wait to get away from this place and get home. Right now, getting to his hotel would be fine.

He hadn't realized he'd fallen asleep until the driver revived him. "Sir? Sir? Mr. Wells? We're here."

Thane felt a hand on his shoulder shaking him with enough force that it roused him from his alcoholic stupor. Drinking so much had been a mistake. Even at twenty-two, he shouldn't have knocked back as much as he had.

He pressed the heels of his hands against his eyes. This time, he accepted help and gripped the driver's hand to get out of the car.

"You need assistance getting up to your room?" the driver asked as he straightened up Thane's jacket.

An empty bottle fell out of Thane's pocket and rolled onto the sidewalk. "Fuck." He looked down at the small bottle and started to bend over to get it.

"No worries, sir. I'll take care of it. You need help getting—"

Thane shrugged out of the driver's hold. "I'm fine." He adjusted his tie. "Thanks for the ride." He reached into his pocket to get money out for a tip.

The driver held up his hand. "Mr. Wells has already taken care of that."

Thane felt his eyebrows draw together.

"Sorry, your brother, Gunnar."

Thane's stomach tightened and twisted again at hearing his brother's name. "Of course." He waved as he made his way up to the front door. "Have a good one."

A doorman opened the door for him and Thane continued through the lobby. He didn't expect to see flashes of lights as he tried going to the elevator.

"Thane! Thane! Are you coming from your mother's funeral?" one person shouted.

He turned to the jerk to give him a piece of his mind when another person started in on him.

"Are you going back to training camp now?" a woman asked him.

The voices came at him as fast as the flashing lights. Before he could answer, he felt and arm around his waist.

"No questions. This is a rough time right now for Mr. Wells. Please give him and his family some privacy." The woman guided Thane to an elevator and pressed the *up* button.

It didn't take long before the doors opened. The stranger pushed Thane inside and asked that no one else join them in the car. When the doors closed, he got his wits about him to gaze down. The woman he'd seen at the funeral stood next to him.

"You?" he slurred.

"I hit the top-floor button to give us some time. What floor is your room on?" Her voice sounded angelic if not commanding.

"Lucky guess. I am at the top." He pointed up. "Penthouse one."

The elevator stopped at the top floor. She helped him out of the car and propped him against the wall next to the bank of elevators.

"Your room key?" she asked.

Thane couldn't wrap his mind around the fact that this dream woman he'd seen at his mother's funeral had now appeared in front of him. When he didn't answer her, she started her own search. Her hunt began with his jacket pockets. When that yielded nothing, she went to his pants pockets. One errant exploration got him a satisfying stroke against his penis.

Christ. Was this woman some paid escort? It wouldn't be above his teammates or even his manager to do that for him, get him a woman to help him forget his pain.

She pulled out his wallet and found the card inside. "Bingo." She put her arm around his waist again.

She felt sturdy as she guided him down the hall to his room. After they reached their destination, she set him against the wall again.

She swiped the card and opened the door. "Can you make it in?"

Thane smiled. "Thought you would never ask." He fell on top of her and pressed his lips against hers.

Chapter 5

The scene seemed all too surreal. First of all, Kari hadn't stopped shaking since leaving Thane's mother's funeral. She hadn't expected when she'd come down to Virginia Beach that she would experience a family grieving the loss of a loved one.

Kari had no one to blame but herself. Before meeting any potential new client, she always did her homework and researched the hell out of him or her. So confident had she been of her knowledge on all things related to Thane Wells, she skipped that step and hustled it down to Virginia Beach only to learn the news about his mother's death. Even the local media had reported that Thane and his two equally famous brothers would be laying their dear mother to rest that day.

Wanting proof, she went to the church to get a standing position outside the recreation building telecasting the funeral. Following the procession to the cemetery had been a mistake. At the gravesite, she couldn't take her stare off Thane.

Gunnar and Gideon had looked grief stricken but stood strong. Thane appeared so alone and wounded. The vision of him standing by his mother's coffin brought Kari to tears. She barely knew this man. She knew he played baseball like a god. She knew he had athletes for brothers. She certainly hadn't bonded with him or his mother enough to be moved to tears. Yet she couldn't stop them from flowing.

Now she stood in a hotel room with the very man she wanted to represent, kissing her, albeit sloppily. Kari tasted the liquor on his tongue and lips. The acrid flavor confirmed the aroma surrounding him.

She braced her hands against his chest and felt nothing but muscle. What did she expect from a twenty-something-year-old athlete?

Kari broke from the kiss long enough to speak. "Mr. Wells."

He stumbled forward and pressed her back against a wall. She started to panic when she heard the door close behind him. Trapped.

"You're"—he hiccupped—"beautiful."

Sober, Thane Wells defined sexy. Right now, this all felt wrong, desperate, even though it would have been a crime not to touch his rock-hard body. When she'd gone through his pockets to find his room key, she'd created a happy accident of brushing her hand against his shaft.

Wow. She'd wanted to find out what kind of game he ran on women. Now he had her in his room and wanted to strip her naked.

Thane slipped his jacket from his shoulders and let it fall to the floor. "We have too many clothes on." He reached down and started pulling up her dress.

"Mr. Wells, please." Kari held the hem of her dress while keeping her stare directly on his hypnotic blue eyes. "I think you have mistaken me for someone else."

"My angel." He smiled. "I saw you at the funeral."

Kari blinked. She had made eye contact with Thane before she left, but she didn't think he would remember her, especially now.

"You've come to make me feel better." He nuzzled his face against her neck. He took one of her hands and placed it directly on his crotch. "Make me feel good." He brought his head up and looked at her in her eyes. "Make me forget today. Can you do that?"

Reluctantly, she removed her hand from his impressive yet flaccid genitals and started easing him back to what she suspected to be the bedroom. "Let's get you to bed."

He released an obscene laugh. "That's what I'm talking about. A traditional girl. I like that."

"Yeah? What else do you like?" She thought if she kept him talking, it would keep him from embarrassing himself even more.

"This." He put his hand on her breast and gave her a rough squeeze.

Too late.

Before she could stop his manhandling, she managed to position him with the bed behind him. She pushed him against the mattress and gave him a hard shove so that he would fall back. When he did, he lay on the bed with his arms outstretched, laughing the entire time.

"You've had a hard day, Mr. Wells." Kari bent over and removed his black leather shoes. She placed them at the foot of the bed. "You really need to get some sleep."

"No. I want to keep drinking." He raised his hands in the air.

"I don't think that's a great idea." She planted a knee on the mattress and hovered over his body. She undid the top three buttons on his shirt.

"And I want to fuck." He put his hand to his mouth. "Oops. I mean make love." He wagged his finger in the air. "No cursing in front of women, my mother would say. Used to say." His voice trailed off to almost a whisper. "Would have said." When he reached up to touch Kari again, she moved away.

"That's not such a great idea either." Even though the thought had tripped through her mind even before tonight. Kari couldn't take advantage of this man, not like this, not right now.

"If I drink, I won't remember anything. I don't want to remember anything about today." Thane became somber for a moment before he brought his legs up on the bed and placed his head on the pillow. "Come here. Lay down with me." He patted the mattress next to him while keeping his eyes closed.

"No. You have the bed all to yourself. But I'll be here in case you need me." Now that she had intimate access to Thane Wells, she didn't want to walk out the door. Plus, if he vomited in his sleep and choked, she would never forgive herself. Neither would Frank.

As soon as she heard Thane's heavy breathing, she turned off the light and backed out of the room. She kept his door open and left the light on in the living room so she could keep monitoring him.

Kari took a seat on the couch and exhaled. What luck that she would get this close to Thane this quickly. When the alcohol wore off, however, she would have to be fast on her feet to keep his attention. Then again, the man had called her beautiful. He had also touched her and kissed her. Truth be told, he probably would have done that with any woman helping him or even standing outside his hotel room.

She removed her shoes and glanced at her phone for the hundredth time. Thankfully, she'd called Michael before it had gotten too late. She liked talking to him before he went to bed.

Kari would have to think fast about what to do when Thane slept off his mistake.

She should have done her research. She should have at least Googled him to see what he planned on doing during his stay in Virginia.

One thing she did know. His behavior that night did not fit the person she admired. Kari had seen Thane in practice and on the field. He played with an intensity she hadn't seen in a young player. It impressed her enough that Thane had done so little time at Carolina Wrens farm team before making pros.

In past interviews, his coaches had described him as a solid pitcher, a good team player, a reliable member of the Wren family. A person like that wouldn't go on a bender like the lump she'd left on the bed. A part of her wanted to chalk it up to his young age.

No, his state tonight had to do with the funeral and the loss of his mother. She understood that. Kari had made questionable decisions herself after she'd lost her beloved grandfather.

Now that Thane slept soundly, Kari decided to get some sleep herself. The long drive down had zapped her of her strength. Wrestling with a drunk man, a sexy one at that, had drained the rest of her power. She padded over to the closet by the door and found a pillow and an extra blanket. Before going back to the couch, she crept over to the bedroom and poked her head inside to check on Thane.

He remained motionless as he slept. As she scanned his body, she wondered if she should have removed his shirt or socks, maybe loosened his belt. Kari figured if she jostled him too much, he would become that octopus again and want to continue what he'd started at the door.

Kari returned to the couch and removed her shoes. She curled her legs under her and put the pillow down before she reclined back and closed her eyes. She would have a lot of explaining to do in the morning.

* * * *

The pounding in Thane's head and the twisting in his gut woke him up and became more intense. Blinking hurt. Breathing pained his entire being. It felt like someone had beaten his midsection with a baseball bat all night long.

What the hell had he done? He sat up and scanned his clothes. As soon as he spied the black slacks, he remembered. The funeral. The drinking. Had he kissed someone? He ran his hand over his mouth. When he exhaled, he caught the scent of his stale breath. He winced.

"Never again." Thane removed his socks and tossed them to the floor.

He stood, but had to sit down almost immediately because he felt woozy. He took that moment to unbutton his shirt and remove his belt. He braced his hands on his knees. A hot shower would do him good if he could stand for that long.

Thane took his time getting to his feet again. He no longer felt any pain or unsteadiness. He undid his pants and let them and his jockey shorts drop to the tan-carpeted floor. He padded to the bathroom. As soon as his feet touched the marble flooring, his shoulders slumped down. The coolness eased his nerves.

He turned the shower faucet and allowed the water to heat up while he took care of his biological needs. He caught his reflection in the mirror above the sink. His pallid complexion told a tale of his bad choices. He needed a shave.

While the room steamed up, he brushed his teeth. He couldn't stand the feel of his tacky mouth. Even his tongue felt thick, like it had on a fur coat. Thane made sure to scrub it down and rinse his mouth with two capfuls of antiseptic mouthwash.

Now that he felt closer to being human, he jumped into the shower stall. He stood underneath the streaming water. He wanted all the bad memories from the funeral to be flushed down the drain. He scrubbed body wash over his flesh.

Later that day, he would need to meet with his brothers again for the reading of his mother's will. He could care less what he would receive from Elizabeth's estate. Moneywise, he had what he needed.

Thane shaved his face. Maybe if he looked presentable, his brothers wouldn't give him a hard time about overindulging. Hell, hadn't they made mistakes in their pasts?

He rinsed himself and turned off the shower. He stepped on the bath mat and wiped his feet while he dried his body. To see his reflection, he swiped his hand over the mirror to remove the condensation. Bits and pieces of last night started to come into focus. He remembered talking to Gideon right before he jumped into the limo to go back to the hotel.

He started remembering flashes of light once he hit the lobby. Cameras. Reporters. They shot questions at him about his career and his mother. The inquiries about his mother got his blood boiling. Now he understood why Gunnar chose to be a mixed martial artist. He probably released a lot of stress that way.

He couldn't discern if the next bit he recalled had happened for real or in his dreams. Either way, he'd enjoyed it. A sexy woman had pulled him into the elevator. His memory went fuzzy on whether or not they'd made out there. Then, when they got out of the elevator, she'd run her hands all over his body. Thinking about that now had his dick getting hard.

He couldn't remember what she looked like other than she'd been an African-American woman. She had skin like gold. That part he believed he imagined because of the alcohol. Her brown almond-shaped eyes had seemed like they could see through to his soul. Again, he chalked that feeling up to the gin, vodka, and rum he'd downed. Her lips and how they felt against his burned in his brain.

Damn, he wished he'd been sober if this woman had been real. Considering what he had going on in his life right now, he didn't need any complications. She needed to remain a dream woman.

Thane glanced at the digital clock on the wall. He'd slept a lot longer than he thought he would. He stepped out into his bedroom. Sunlight streamed through the curtains, bathing the room in a warm glow. He had time for some breakfast. He needed to call down to room service to see if they'd send him up some eggs with lots of hot sauce to combat his hangover.

He strolled into the main living area of his hotel room and stopped. He never suspected he would have a woman sitting on the couch staring at him while he stood there naked.

Chapter 6

Kari should have excused herself. As soon as she saw him getting out of bed and going to the bathroom—naked—she should have walked out of the room and knocked on his door a few minutes later, acting like she hadn't been there all night. No way would he remember seeing her last night, or that she'd helped him to his room.

Like with the funeral she'd crashed, she couldn't tear herself away. The reason this time had more to do with her work than her burgeoning fascination with his hard body and impressive lower half.

Either Thane felt comfortable with his nudity or he couldn't move from shock. He remained still, staring at her.

"Uh, hi." He ran his hand over his wet hair, which had transformed into an even darker shade, making his eye color stand out more.

Kari kept her stare directed on his eyes to avoid scanning him from the waist down. Looking at his muscular chest with complementing toned arms led her gaze down to his hard abdomen, and it didn't take long for her stare to gradually drop down to his genitals, the same ones she'd touched, both by accident and when he'd pressed her hand against him.

"Hi." She pushed the blanket she'd used to cover her body off to the side. "I hope you don't mind. I took the liberty of ordering coffee and something for you to eat. You probably didn't do a lot of that yesterday."

Kari stood. She hoped when he saw her in her black A-line dress that he would view her as a professional and not some groupie or worse.

"Um, thanks." He glanced around the room. He stopped when he spotted the dining room table full of food.

She'd thought he would search for it as soon as he came out of the bathroom. The hotel had given him a full pot of what smelled like hazelnut coffee. Since she didn't know what kind of appetite he would have, she'd ordered an assortment of food, including scrambled eggs, bacon, sausage, wheat toast, potatoes, fruit, and various breads and pastries. Something had to hit his fancy.

Trying to still be accommodating, she said, "I can prepare a plate for you if you like."

Thane regarded her for a moment, looked at the food, and brought his attention back to her again. "I don't know how this works. Do you need money or something?" He scanned the floor, probably looking for his wallet.

So much for appearing like a professional. To Thane, she apparently looked like a different type of working girl. Great.

Kari balled her hands into fists as she slipped her feet back into her black platform heels. "I can see you don't remember me."

He shook his head but kept direct eye contact with her. "I don't. Did I meet you at the funeral? Or was it down at the bar?" He scratched his head.

She could almost see the wheels spinning in his head. "I saw you at the funeral, but we didn't meet there." She cleared her throat. "Mr. Wells, would you like to put on some pants or cover yourself up with a towel or something?"

He furrowed his eyebrows that didn't look like they had been plucked or professionally shaped. "Why? Didn't we have sex?"

She brought her gaze up to the ceiling. As soon as he said the word *sex*, she wanted to look down at what dangled between his muscled thighs. His legs looked like an artist had carved them out of marble. "No, we didn't."

"Oh." He let that sink into his head before his eyes widened. "Oh. Excuse me." He went to a waist-high dresser and opened the top drawer. He pulled out a clean pair of underwear that he slipped on first. He then went to a closet and retrieved a pair of jeans.

Even in jeans, he looked good enough to eat. Kari loved seeing a man with a defined stomach and a set of muscles that trailed down to his pubic area. Thane had that. He had a lot of things she admired.

As soon as she felt her tongue snaking out of her mouth to lick her dry lips, she drew it back in and wiped the sides of her mouth.

She'd been in rooms with half-naked athletes before. This one shouldn't be different. Kari couldn't explain it, but something about Thane bucked every stereotype she knew.

"Sorry about that. I mean, I apologize." He slipped a pullover charcoal gray sweater over his head and padded back to the living room area. "Okay, so we didn't have sex and we didn't meet in a bar or at the funeral.

Who are you and what are you doing in my hotel room?" He crossed his arms over his chest as he stood a few feet from her.

Kari took a deep breath and smiled. Thankfully, she had mints in her purse that she popped in her mouth while he showered. She'd used her handy dandy morning-after kit she kept with her to freshen herself a bit. She had wiped off her old makeup and put on new eyeliner, lipstick, and blush. She'd combed her shoulder-length hair, trying to revive some of the curl it had yesterday. After she misted body spray over her bare legs and arms, she felt presentable, not perfect. She would have rather met him at the top of her game, but this morning would have to do.

She extended her hand to him. "I helped you to your room last night when you returned in the limousine."

He graciously shook it. Although his manners seemed welcoming, he hadn't smiled the entire time.

"Thank you. You work here at the hotel?" He stared at her.

For a brief moment, he dropped his gaze to their joined hands. Maybe he felt the electricity that ran from his hand into hers. She didn't want to let him go. Not yet. The touch along with his incredibly penetrating stare kept her transfixed.

"Ma'am?"

Damn it. She'd done it. She'd been drawn into his spell.

"Yes." She pulled her hand back. "I mean, no, I don't work at the hotel. I'm an agent."

He cocked his head.

"We've spoken before. My name is Kari Meyers. I work at the Winning Edge Agency. We understand that your current agent, Alec Fogel, is about to retire. I'd like to—"

"Wow, you have some nerve, lady." He turned his back on her. "Didn't mean to interrupt your speech. You go from constant calls to breaking and entering. I can't believe you tricked your way into my hotel room so that you can try and convince me to sign with you." He pulled out a pair of socks from a bottom drawer and returned to the living room where he sat on the couch.

"I didn't trick you." She sauntered closer to him, which didn't help.

He bolted to his feet and went to his bedroom area. On the way, he picked up the clothes he'd strewn over the floor last night.

"Word has gotten to all agents about you." She followed him as he deposited his dirty clothes into a makeshift hamper.

He picked up a pair of shoes from the closet and returned to the same location on the couch. "So you think that gives you the right to come here and ask me to sign with you? Do you know what I'm going through right now?"

"To be honest, I didn't until I arrived in town. I was kind of wondering why you weren't at training camp." She smiled, hoping to lighten the mood.

It didn't work. He snatched his wallet from the coffee table and peered through it, making sure she hadn't stolen anything. First he'd thought he had a call girl in his room. Now he'd practically likened her to a petty thief. Could she be humiliated any more than that?

"Ms. Meyers—"

"You can call me Kari."

Thane chuckled. "I guess that would make sense considering you've seen every part of my body." He stepped into his shoes. "Even if Alec was leaving, what makes you think I would sign with another agency instead of staying where I am?"

She crossed her arms over her chest. "For one, I would protect your interests more than your old agency." She squared off against Thane. "It took me no time to find you. I know you're new at this celebrity thing, but you should never ever check into a hotel under your real name. Always use an alias."

Thane gritted his teeth as he glared at her. He said nothing.

She continued. "When I got to the hotel, the lobby was full of reporters. So they did the same thing I did. They called the most expensive hotels and found you. I pretended to be one of them until I saw you stumbling in."

He dropped his gaze to the floor.

"You looked like a man in need of some help. So I wielded some authority and acted like I represented you to get you to your room." She took a step closer to him, encroaching in on his personal space. This time he didn't move. "Once I got you to your room, I found your key and I—"

"Did I touch you?" He lowered his voice.

Kari swallowed. "It doesn't matter what happened. I knew you weren't your true self yesterday."

"No, tell me. Did I touch you? Did I do anything inappropriate?" He scratched his head. "I can only remember bits and pieces from last night. Images of you come in and out of focus. One thing is clear. Something happened between us. I don't remember what."

She sighed. "Fine. You kissed me."

She heard Thane cursing under his breath. After years of becoming so jaded in her business, she found it refreshing to be with a man who felt some guilt after his questionable behavior.

Calm down, heart. He's hung over. He didn't turn into the pope.

"Although we didn't have sex, you offered it several times." She would leave out the part where he forced her to touch his package. "I guided you to bed, took off your shoes, and stayed here while you slept to make sure you would be okay. That's what a good agent would do, look out for your best interests."

Thane looked around and stopped when he saw a hotel phone on an end table.

"What are you doing?" Kari didn't want him calling hotel security or worse, the police. She hadn't broken in to his room. She'd helped him.

"Calling the police." He glanced at her. "On myself. I shouldn't have touched you."

She blinked. She had been hit on by all types of athletes. Some sober athletes had done worse things to her than what Thane had done. This man wanted to be punished for his crimes. Her heart pumped harder for his gentlemanly gesture. A true man would own up to his mistakes and try to make amends.

Kari rushed to him and attempted to take the receiver from his hand. "You don't have to do that."

He moved it away from her. "I can't remember what I did, but if you say I was inappropriate, I believe you. I wasn't myself yesterday for obvious reasons. That's no excuse for me to push myself on you." He put his hand to his chest. "I apologize. But I'm serious. I'm turning myself in. I wouldn't put you through a trial or anything. I would confess my guilt and suffer the consequences."

She stood stunned for a moment before she spoke. "Even if it meant it could ruin your professional baseball career?"

He nodded without even waiting to think about his answer. "Baseball is meant to be family entertainment. Kids should look up to the players. I wouldn't want a boy thinking that it's okay to get drunk and force himself on a girl. It's not right. So, yes, even if it meant I couldn't play a sport I love, I would still do the right thing."

Kari slammed her finger down on the phone cradle to disconnect the call. "Don't do this. I'm fine."

"I'm not." He attempted to release her finger, but she refused to be moved.

The sincerity in his eyes let Kari know that Thane hadn't given her a line. He hadn't said what he'd said to get into her panties. He truly believed in God, family, baseball, and apple pie. His genuine nature came off as refreshing and honest. It had been a long time since Kari had been with a man who willingly admitted his faults and tried to make things right. For a moment, she didn't know how to respond to him.

"I chalked up your behavior to the alcohol. I appreciate your readiness to do the right thing. I don't know many men who would offer to do the same thing, especially professional athletes. I would expect you to call your attorney or manager or try to pay me off."

"The men you're talking about aren't men." Relenting, he handed her the handset. "Look at me and be honest. Did I hurt you?"

Kari swallowed hard. "No. I told you. I'm fine. You even apologized for cursing in front of me at one point." She hung up the phone. "Trust me. Had you been the least bit inappropriate with me, I wouldn't be standing her talking civilly with you. The police would have you locked up already."

"I couldn't live with myself if I thought I disrespected a woman, especially—" He stopped. Thane went to the bedroom again and came back with his phone. "I'm grateful for all you did for me last night. Had I gone to the hotel bar, I can only imagine who I would be having a conversation with this morning."

"But?" Kari could hear it coming.

"However, I'm happy with Alec. When and if he retires, I'll make a decision about my representation."

"You know Alec plans on closing his agency. Did he tell you that?"

Thane slipped on a black leather jacket. "What my agent and I discuss is our business." He opened his door. "Thank you for everything you did for me."

"Nice jacket. Looks custom. You know I can get you a deal with a lot of designers to be the face of their brand."

"Thanks for the compliment, but I'll pass."

Kari picked up her purse and headed to the door. "I've left my business card on the coffee table, and you already have my number." She saw him opening his mouth to comment, but realization must have hit him that she had been calling him on a regular basis in the past, and he hadn't blocked her number. "If I were your agent, I would have asked for double what you're getting now. And, yes, I already know you're the highest paid baseball player out there." She regarded him for a moment. "You're worth it." She tucked her hair behind her ear and dropped her gaze for a bit to gather her wits. Thane had a way of making her feel vulnerable and defenseless. For a woman who had become an expert on the games men played, she couldn't get her head wrapped around that concept. "You would be in a house rental and not a hotel, or at least with your brother. I'm sure he has a well-protected place here. I also would have made it so that no one outside of family and friends could have gotten close to your mother's funeral."

"That means I never would have met you." He watched her as she strolled out the door.

"Good thing you have a subpar agent and a questionable manager." She smiled. "I'll be in town all this week if you would like to meet."

"I'm not going to change my mind, Ms.—Kari."

She turned to him as she walked down the hall. "Never say never, Mr. Wells."

"Thane."

"Thane, you know I'm very persistent. Hopefully, you'll come to realize I'm the best person for you." As Kari walked away, she hoped two things would happen. She wanted him to keep her number to call her soon. She also hoped she had intrigued him enough to keep him watching her every move. She turned and caught Thane standing outside his hotel room, staring at her.

Bingo. Now, would he call her? Time would tell.

Chapter 7

Kari Meyers's intrusion had kept Thane's mind off losing his mother. Getting an up close and sober view of Kari paled in comparison to what he'd imagined. Her light skin tone reminded him of golden honey. She had seductive eyes that captured his attention. Her full lips had him wanting to kiss her again, but this time he would remember it.

A ripple of embarrassment inched through his stomach when he thought about what he'd done to her in his drunken state. According to Kari, he had kissed her and propositioned her. He shook his head as he drove his rental car to the attorney's office.

Thane had meant it when he'd picked up the phone to call the police. He didn't tolerate teammates accused of similar crimes. He wouldn't be a hypocrite. He also wouldn't be getting drunk like that again. He would have to deal with the pain in his life in other ways.

He pulled up to an office building and backed into a space across from the front door. Now that his head felt better since he'd eaten a bagel and followed it with some strong coffee, he bounded into the office. He wanted to get this meeting done so that he could get back down to Florida to train.

His coaches and the team's manager had been very good to him. They'd shipped a large flower arrangement to the funeral home. It couldn't be missed. A large wreath with a wren in the middle. The head coach told him to take as much time as he needed. Thane didn't want to hang around town for very long. The faster he got back to work, the easier it would be for him to forget all this.

Thane walked up to the front desk. The receptionist blinked when she saw him. She smoothed her hand over her hair and flashed a bright smile. Too bad he couldn't reciprocate.

"My brothers and I are supposed to meet Mr. Ubo regarding Elizabeth Sommerville." He tapped his fingertips on the counter.

"Yes, Mr. Wells. Mr. Ubo and your brothers are already in the conference room waiting for you. I'll take you back there." She stood and came around her desk.

Thane glanced at his watch. "They're kind of early, aren't they?"

"No, the meeting was supposed to start at ten. They've been waiting for you." She opened the door.

Thane caught Gunnar's glare first. "I apologize for being late. I was told the meeting was starting at ten-thirty." He shook the attorney's hand before sitting down next to Gideon.

"I called you several times last night and this morning to let you know about the change," Gunnar said between gritted teeth.

Thane looked at his phone. He saw Kari's number first. He shoved the phone into his pocket.

"Guess you were too busy with your new female friend." Gideon cleared his throat and sat up taller.

"It's not like that." Thane shook his head.

"Let's not go into it now. I'm sure Mr. Ubo has other things he needs to do today." Gunnar directed his attention to the stately dark-skinned attorney.

The lawyer adjusted his wire-rimmed glasses on his nose. "Nice to meet you, Mr. Wells. Now that you're all here, we can get started." He opened a file and peered down. "Your mother drafted this a year ago. She contacted me a couple of months ago to confirm that she didn't want to make any changes to it."

Thane nodded.

"Each son will get controlling asset of a business." Mr. Ubo turned to Gunnar. "Gunnar will own Press 'N Curl, the hair salon." He faced Gideon. "Gideon will get Pick 'N Clip, the flower shop." Then he looked at Thane. "Thane will get Sharp, the clothing boutique."

"No surprises there." Gideon scanned Thane and Gunnar's faces.

"Yeah, I figured Mom would do that." Thane nodded. "As soon as I can, I'll sell the space."

Gunnar's face flashed to a dark crimson. "You'll what?"

Thane didn't understand Gunnar's anger. "Sell it. I've got a career, and I'm at the top of my game. I'm not going to retire like you and stay in town to run it." He turned to Gideon. "Are you giving up football to run your shop?"

Gideon shook his head. "No. But Janelle runs that for me, so it's still in the family. Don't you want to preserve Mom's legacy?"

Mr. Ubo cleared his throat before more could be said. "Elizabeth Sommerville included in her will that the only way one business could be sold is by having all three brothers sign off on the deal."

Gunnar crossed his massive arms over his chest and leaned back. "That settles it. I'm not signing jack." He glared at Thane. "You don't want to run it? Fine. I'll take care of it. Spring time is coming up and you know what that means."

Thane did, but he knew Gunnar would remind him.

Gunnar continued. "School dances. Mom always donated dresses to that underprivileged school in Chesapeake. You're going to let them down?"

Thane hadn't thought about them. He knew that his mother would take on interns and temporary help to assist her in running the place when she opened it after Easter each year. Unlike Gunnar and Gideon, he didn't have to worry about a full staff of employees. He didn't want to disappoint a group of school girls. He presently had other priorities.

"Can we move on with the reading, please?" Thane had a lot to think about now that he had something that tethered him to the community.

Mr. Ubo held up a piece of paper and continued. "Gunnar will get the house and Elizabeth's car."

"No surprise there either." Thane peered down at the table.

"What's that supposed to mean?" Gunnar asked.

"You're the oldest. Of course you'll get the lion's share of everything." *Along with love and attention,* Thane wanted to add.

"Boys, come on." Gideon tapped his knuckles on the table like a judge's gavel. "Hold it together."

To keep the session going, Mr. Ubo said, "Her assets totaled four million dollars."

Thane sat up taller. "You mean liquid assets? You're not talking about her home and the businesses?"

Mr. Ubo nodded. "Her accounts held that amount."

Gideon shook his head. "I'm not sure why we're all surprised. Mom was a smart woman."

"She wants that money going to the Oceanfront Community Center." The attorney flipped a paper over.

"Sounds like Mom." Thane smiled as he thought of his mother.

"Ms. Sommerville also had life insurance that totaled twenty million. That she wanted split equally among the three of you."

"My share can be donated as well." Thane waved his hand.

"To the center?" Gunnar asked.

"Sure. Or the American Heart Association." Thane wouldn't want another family to experience a heartache like this.

The lawyer removed an envelope from the folder. "Ms. Sommerville also had a safe deposit box." He slid the envelope toward Gideon. "Gideon gets the contents of it."

Gideon looked at Thane and Gunnar. "Did you know she had a safe deposit box?"

Thane and Gunnar shrugged and shook their heads.

"News to me." Thane looked over at Gunnar.

"I didn't know. But there's a lot about Mom that I didn't know."

"This may also shock you all. She owned a beach house in the Outer Banks, North Carolina." Mr. Ubo removed another envelope. "That she wanted it to go to Thane."

Thane didn't even touch the envelope. "What? Mom owned another house?" He volleyed his gaze between Gunnar and Gideon. "Did you guys know that?"

"No." Gideon shook his head. "She never told me about it or took me there. Gun?

Gunnar also shook his head. "No. I'm not surprised though. Mom loved the beach. She loved peace and quiet."

"I have all of the necessary paperwork for you all to sign to take over all of the assets, the homes, the car, the businesses, and the money." Mr. Ubo stood, revealing his full height.

"None of that will bring Mom back." Gunnar tapped his fingers on the table. When the attorney left the room to get the rest of the paperwork, Gunnar turned his full attention to Thane. "So what happened with you yesterday?"

"I was upset about Mom. I drank way too much. It was all a mistake." Thane shook his head. "I apologize for making a fool of myself. Trust me. It won't happen again."

"Yeah? And the woman who went up to your hotel room, was she a mistake?" Gunnar pulled out his cell phone, clicked a couple of items on his screen, and turned it around to Thane to view it.

Thane saw a video of him stumbling in the hotel and Kari coming to his side. As she'd told him, she had helped him into the elevator. Gunnar pulled his phone back, made a swiping motion over his screen, and showed Thane another video.

The black-and-white shot looked like it had come from a surveillance camera. The pulled-back image showed Thane leaning against Kari as she helped him to his room. Thane brought his face in closer to the screen in time to catch a view of himself kissing Kari and pushing her back into his room.

"Classy, dude. The day of your mother's funeral. Mom would be so proud." Gunnar slammed his phone on the table.

"Excuse me." Thane sprang to his feet and walked out of the meeting room.

He looked up and down the hallway for a bathroom. After running down one end of the hall, he found the men's room. Thane bolted through the door, pushed his way into a stall and purged his guts into a commode.

All he'd drunk last night hadn't made him nauseous. The idea that he disrespected his mother with his actions hurt him more than anything. Another good heave into the toilet and Thane felt a little better, until he saw spots of blood in the murky water.

He balled toilet paper around his fist and wiped his mouth before anyone could see it. He flushed away his feelings and turned around to catch Gunnar standing behind him.

"You want to talk about it?" Gunnar asked.

Thane washed his hands and splashed some cool water in his face. "You don't want to hear what's going on with me. You want to make judgments and comments." He ripped a couple of sheets of paper towels from the dispenser. "You don't have to pretend you like me anymore. I get it. The least we can do is be polite about it." He started to walk by Gunnar when Gunnar stepped into his path.

"Man, talk to me. What is it? Tell me. The last few years, I felt you pulling away from me, pulling away from the family." Gunnar wrapped his tree-trunk sized arms around Thane's shoulders and hugged him. "I love you. You know that, right?"

Thane didn't hug him back. His arms remained down by his sides. When Gunnar released his embrace, Thane threw away the used wad of paper towels he'd continued to hold after he'd dried his hands and face.

"We should get back to the meeting room and sign the paperwork." Thane made it around Gunnar.

One day he would reveal the real reason for his distance. Thane couldn't do that now.

After the meeting, Thane looked at Gunnar and Gideon. He really stared at them, studied them. Until Gunnar cut his hair, they could have almost passed for twins. Both dirty blond. All three had blue eyes, but Gunnar and Gideon's eye color matched a bit more.

"There's still plenty of food at Mom's house from the funeral yesterday." Gunnar stood. "The two of you want to come by for some lunch?"

"Sounds good." Gideon rubbed his stomach. It took him a bit to get on his feet. With the help of his cane, he started to move around a little better. "You coming, Thane?"

Thane thought about his actions the past few days, well, more like past few years. Like Gunnar said, Thane had been pulling away from them for a while. He could go to lunch and clear the air.

Thane started to open his mouth to respond when his phone rang. He glanced at the screen and saw his agent's name. "One sec, guys." He left the room and went down the hallway close to the bathroom. "Alec. How are you?"

"Hanging in there, kid." His agent's voice sounded a bit gruffer than normal. With Alec in California, the man had probably just gotten out of bed. "Sorry about your mother. I know that was rough for you."

Thane rubbed the back of his neck. "Very. But I'm dealing."

"Speaking of deals, I need to tell you something."

Thane paced. He hoped Alec wouldn't reveal what Kari had told him this morning. Deep in his gut, he knew she hadn't lied.

"Shoot," Thane said.

"I'm closing up shop, kid. Time to take it easy." Exhaustion laced every word.

"I hate to tell you, but I already knew." Thane leaned his back against the wall.

"What?"

"Yeah, a competing agent tried getting me to sign."

Alec snorted. "Bastards. The chum is already in the water and the sharks are circling. Listen, kid, I have plenty of agents here who can represent you."

Thane nodded. "That's what I thought. That's great."

"Yeah, competent guys. The good thing is that I've already established a great deal for you. Your new agent will have to make sure the team doesn't screw you." Alec coughed, not unusual for the pack-a-day smoker.

Of course, whenever he and Thane met, he never smoked around him. Alec protected his client. The idea reminded Thane of Kari and how she'd said she would look out for him if she represented him. It didn't seem possible. For one thing, he'd never heard of her. He had heard of her agency. Thane checked out East Coast businesses first in his quest to find representation. When he'd received the call from Alec Fogel himself, Thane's search ended.

"I knew you would look out for me." Thane started to head back to the conference room to see his brothers.

"Of course. Like I said, you should be content with what you have," Alec replied.

The hairs stood on the back of Thane's neck. "Are you saying no one else could get me a better deal than you?"

Alec paused before continuing. "I'm the last of a dying breed. I'm still hungry for making deals. Agents nowadays aren't like that."

Maybe one still fit that category. Persistent. Kari had described herself that way.

"I'll shoot over some names of agents. I personally like Jack Johannsen. He's been an agent here for fifteen years, but in the biz for twenty. He's developed a rapport with owners all over. The great thing about him is that he'll stay out of your business. You don't need an agent who wants to appear on camera with you or anything like that. A strictly behind-the-scenes kind of guy."

"Quiet."

"But powerful." Alec coughed again. "Let me know if you need anything, kid."

"Sure." Thane disconnected the call and returned to the conference room only to find it empty.

He snatched his jacket and personal items he'd left in the room. Thane stomped out to the parking lot where he found Gunnar and Gideon standing by Gunnar's Hummer.

"Everything okay?" Gideon hopped to the front of the vehicle.

"Yeah, yeah. It will be. Look, I need to take a rain check on that lunch." Thane held up his phone. "Some business stuff came up that I need to take care of."

"Like what? Are they asking you to come back to train now?" Gunnar planted his hands on his hips like he wanted to hit someone.

Thane missed Gunnar's protective nature. "No, nothing like that."

"Does it have something to do with your agent?" Gideon stared into Thane's eyes. When Thane didn't immediately answer, Gideon filled in the blanks. "Most of the stuff about you we read online. I heard your super agent is retiring. You might want to use my guy. He's good. I can contact him and set up a meeting if you—"

"No." Thane went to his car. "Sorry for cutting in. I have to go. I'll talk to you guys later."

"Okay. Coming over to the house for dinner at least?" Gunnar asked from over the hood of his truck.

"Maybe. I'll call and let you know." Thane ducked into his ride right when Gunnar and Gideon said they loved him.

Thane pulled out of the lot and down the street before he could answer any more questions from his brothers. He peered over at the passenger side car seat and spied the envelope with information and keys to his mother's beach house. He would have to check that out later. He didn't have the time or energy to make that journey.

Thane's mind tripped over Alec's words. He said Thane should be happy with what he had. Content. Nothing about that defined Thane. He'd always pushed himself, and he expected people around him to do the same thing.

He pulled into a shopping center parking lot and parked in a space. He picked up his phone and checked for messages first. He saw that Gunnar had called him about twenty times between yesterday and that morning and had left ten messages, both text and voice. Then he found Kari's number.

She'd labeled herself as Kari Your Next Agent Meyers. He almost broke into a smile when he saw it, but he remembered her invasion of his privacy. Had it not been for her, though, he would have ended up facedown in the hotel's lobby or at the bar, hitting on a woman or two or more.

Thane pushed the option to dial her number. If nothing else, he could apologize to her again. He heard a beeping sound, meaning his call would be interrupting a current call. This would be a test. Would she click over to talk to him, truly show him that he would be at the top of her list?

He heard a click.

"Kari Meyers." Her voice sounded professional if not clipped.

"Thane Wells." He kept his tone low and business like. "Did I catch you at a bad time?"

A pause lingered before she answered. "May I call you right back?"

He sighed and made sure to make it audible through the phone.

Before he could give her an answer, Kari spoke. "I'm dealing with an ongoing issue right now. I don't want to blow you off."

That statement alone got Thane imaging Kari on her knees in front of him. He rubbed his eyes in hopes of bringing back the gentleman Elizabeth Sommerville had raised.

"Don't bother calling me back." Thane put his vehicle in *drive*. "Meet me tonight at seven. I don't want to do business over the phone." Plus, he wanted to see if he still got that fluttery feeling in his belly like he had earlier in his hotel room. "We could meet at the restaurant at my hotel. Would that work for you?"

Kari cleared her throat. "Would we be able to get a private table? Talking business face-to-face is great, but I would like some privacy."

Damn, was she leaving it open that she wanted to go back to his hotel room...so close to his bed?

Thane swallowed hard. "I'll make a special request. So I'll see you later?"

"Yes. Thank you for the opportunity. You won't regret it." She disconnected the call as fast as she'd answered it.

He tossed his phone into one of the cup holders and thought about his decision to contact a competing agency. In his head, he wanted to get the best person to represent him. The rest of his body wanted to see what she would wear to their dinner meeting.

He needed to get his head out of the clouds. He had too many things going on, including a career that he needed to get back to eventually. Tonight would only be business...he hoped.

Chapter 8

Kari had barely gotten back to her hotel room when Reagan called her about Michael. Kari paced the floor after kicking off her shoes.

"Put him on the phone." She didn't mean for her voice to sound so gruff, but she felt so helpless being away from her child.

"Did you not hear me? He's locked himself in the bathroom and he won't come out."

Kari heard a knocking sound through the phone.

"Come on, Michael. Open the door. I have your mom on the phone right now," Reagan said.

After a beat, Kari heard, "No!"

She rubbed her forehead. She wanted to sit. She needed to sit, especially after her quick but surprising call from Thane. She couldn't believe he wanted to talk business, at least, she hoped he wanted that and not some sober repeat performance from last night.

She couldn't think about him right now. She had a child in crisis. "Reagan, slide your phone under the door."

"What?" Reagan pounded on the door. "Open up that door right now."

"Please don't raise your voice to him." Kari knew what had set off her son. "I know the gap under the door is big enough to fit your phone."

"Yeah, but what if he breaks it or flushes it? Are you going to buy me—"

"Yes. Put it on speaker. Please do it." Kari chewed on her lower lip as she waited. She heard a click and then a sliding sound.

Silence.

"Michael? Come on, little slugger. Talk to me." She sat at the edge of her bed and closed her eyes. She remembered when she brought her precious son into the world. What a wonderful gift.

She sang the John Fogerty song about baseball softly at first. She didn't care if the guests in the other rooms heard her. She raised her voice after the next verse and stopped after singing the chorus. Her throat tightened a little until she could hear confirmation that she'd gotten through to him.

"Mom?"

His tiny voice jumpstarted her heart again. "Yeah, sweetie?"

"Why did you stop singing?"

She smiled and slipped down the bed to sit on the floor. "I was waiting for you. Will you sing it with me?"

He sang the song from the beginning. When he got to the chorus, Kari joined him.

"What's going on there?" Kari spoke calmly and slowly.

"I tried calling Dad. He didn't answer me. I left him messages and he hasn't called me back."

Kari cursed under her breath and bounced the back of her head on the bed. "For one thing, you know you're not supposed to use the phone. What did I tell you about that?"

"I didn't use the phone...at home. I went to Kyle's house and used it there. You never said I couldn't use it at the Monte house."

Her clever child.

"Don't get smart with me, Michael. You know better. No calls from any phone, understand?"

"Yes, ma'am." He released a big sigh.

"That would explain why he didn't answer you. He probably didn't recognize the number." That sounded plausible. "And you know how busy he is. I'll contact him and make sure that he reaches out to you, okay?" She really couldn't make that promise.

Nowadays, Jarrod handled almost all dealings with her through his attorney. Jarrod took great pains not to see her or Michael by having his child-support payments directly deposited into Kari's account. Whenever she called him, he would speak to Michael for one minute. She could almost recite his questions to their child by heart. "What have you been up to now? How tall are you? You have a girlfriend yet?" Then he would end the conversation with a lie, always telling him he couldn't wait to see him again.

"I need you to open the door and let Reagan in."

She heard a clicking sound before she heard a whooshing noise like a door opening.

"That's it. From now on you use the bathroom with the door open," Reagan said.

"You owe Reagan an apology," Kari said.

"Yes, ma'am." A rustling noise sounded through the phone. "Sorry, Miss Reagan. I told her, Mom."

"Very good. Thank you. When Reagan can't get to you, it scares her and it scares me. She's an extension of me. She does what I would do if I was home." She didn't hear anything for a while. "Michael? Reagan? Hello."

Kari heard a brushing sound.

"I gave Reagan a hug. The hug was for her and you." Michael's voice sounded sorrowful yet sincere.

How could Kari be mad at her baby? "I love you, buddy."

"Yeah, yeah. I know."

He was such a boy.

"What you did was wrong. No video games at all until I get back." She would have said no computer, but she wanted to keep some sort of contact with him.

"Ah, Mom."

She imagined him with his cute little bottom lip pushed out. "I know. Your life is so hard. Will you give the phone back to Reagan? I'll see you in a few days, okay?"

"Yes, ma'am. Here you go."

After a pause, Reagan said, "I was cleaning up from lunch and I heard him scream and slam the door. I didn't know what was going on."

"Daddy issues. He called Jarrod and Jarrod didn't answer or call him back."

This time Reagan cursed. "I swear I never let him use my phone until now." Worry rose in Reagan's voice.

"No, I know. He used a phone at a friend's house." Kari wiped the sweat from her forehead. "I told him no video games until I get back. He's fine using the computer."

"You got it, boss. So how's it going over there?" Reagan asked.

"Not bad. As a matter of fact, the call that interrupted us was from Thane. He wants to meet tonight to talk business." She smiled.

"Way to hit it out of the park. That's great. I'll keep my fingers crossed for you. Good luck."

Kari would need more than luck to impress a player baseball analysts compared to some of the greats. If she wanted to be on better footing than earlier, she would need to get some good sleep in, and she would need to do some research. Did Thane need to stay with the Carolina Wrens? He would probably do better in New York or even Chicago.

Before she could think about any of that, she had something crucial to take care of right now. She punched in the speed dial to Jarrod, knowing, as usual, he wouldn't answer. He never did when she called him. He would return her call a day or more later.

On the fourth ring, the line clicked.

"Speak."

Kari closed her eyes and had to count in her head before she spoke. She didn't want to start a conversation with the father of her child with an argument. "You know it's me. Why would you answer the phone like that to the woman who had your first child?" Unfortunately, Kari couldn't help herself with confronting Jarrod.

"On the treadmill."

Lie. She didn't hear any fluctuations in his voice or the sound of a whirring tread. She'd spoken to plenty of athletes who worked out while they talked to her. She knew the difference.

"No, you're not, but it's better than the truth."

Jarrod sniggered. "Your spitfire edge hasn't softened at all with age. Maybe that's why you're still single."

"And your ability to lie will continue to help you bed as many women as possible. The last time I heard about you, you were up to five kids now. Or is it seven? I heard the last birth was twins." She reached behind herself to unzip her dress.

"Are you calling to remind me again that you have my number-one seed?" Jarrod's naturally deep voice dipped down lower.

Back in high school, she found that trait drop-dead sexy. Now the tone and the man producing it turned her stomach. How could she have been that stupid to have sex with him at such a young age and get pregnant? She would definitely instill in Michael the importance of waiting until marriage to even have sex.

"Enough about me. You're calling for a reason. You normally do." Jarrod chuckled.

"Yes, we are beyond the stage of having pleasant conversations anymore." She took off her dress and draped it on the back of a chair. "I'm calling about Michael."

"The greatest basketball player ever," Jarrod said with enthusiasm.

"The child we named him after." Kari had wanted to name him after her grandfather, the man who'd raised her for most of her life. She yielded to her man. Mistake.

"What's up?"

Kari heard some beeping sounds through the phone. Maybe Jarrod had been on the treadmill. "He said he tried calling you. He's ten, Jarrod."

"I know how old our son is. My fiancée thinks it's hot that I have a ten-year-old and I'm only twenty-eight." He released a grunt that sounded pornographic.

Kari shook her head. "Fascinating. Listen, Michael is getting to that age where he needs a male figure in his life. He wants to talk to you more. He wants to see you more. He had to look on your Web site to see that you're going to be on the East Coast in a couple of weeks. Are you going to be able to come by and see him?"

A pause lingered before he released a long, arduous sigh like she'd asked him for a kidney. "I don't know. I have an important game."

"Exhibition." She knew better than anyone that those types of games meant the players could phone in their performances.

"And I'm doing tons of press. Doing a couple of morning shows and all the New York late-night gigs. I'm only in town for a couple of days before I'm back out on the West Coast."

Kari sighed loud enough to show her displeasure to the man who'd helped create Michael. "He asks for very little. A call. A visit."

"What? The money isn't enough?"

Kari's temperature rose the more she had to explain to Michael's father about the role he needed to play in their child's life. "No, it isn't. He wants to see you."

"I sent him a poster. I even signed it. If I see it up on eBay, I'm not sending him anything else."

Kari could no longer bite her tongue. "Asshole. Pure and simple. I don't ask you for much. I really don't. I know ex-wife number one took half your money. And ex-wife number two took a couple of homes. I haven't done interviews about you. I don't talk about you. I don't ask you for money. I just want you to be a part of our son's life. Is that so hard?"

Again, he laughed. "Hard? You don't know anything about having it hard. You like that career you have? Thank me for it."

Kari bolted to her feet. "I earned my spot as a sports agent. I have the education, the background, and the passion for what I do."

"Yeah, having a kid by Jarrod Townsend didn't help you secure it at all, huh?"

The comment hurt her more than she wanted. It had been a niggling voice of doubt in her head for years. She'd never mentioned Jarrod in her interview and barely talked about the man at work.

Before she answered, before she ruined the fragile relationship she had with her son's father, Kari took a breath. "Jarrod, we have a son to raise. We have to work together to give him a fully united family unit. He loves you." Saying that took a lot of strength, but she managed to choke the words out. "Even though we're no longer together, we have to work as a team for our child. A phone call to your son would go a long way."

It sounded like Jarrod spoke to someone who must have been in the same room with him before he addressed her. "I give you plenty of child support. Use the money to bring him up to see me." He disconnected the call.

Kari threw her phone into her open purse that sat on a desk. Jarrod did provide a substantial amount of money to support Michael. That money shouldn't have to go to travel tickets to see his own father.

She would have to figure out something for Michael. Jarrod might feel comfortable disappointing their child. She didn't and wouldn't. For now, though, she needed a nap. She had a big night. Maybe if she could get Thane to sign a contract with her to represent him, she could be on the road and back home tomorrow. She could only hope.

* * * *

Thane didn't want to go to Sharp, his mother's clothing boutique. *His* clothing boutique now. After talking to Kari, he had planned on heading back to his hotel to get some more sleep before his date, well, meeting. Yes, meeting.

As he drove, he kept heading toward the Oceanfront area until he reached the boutique. The quaint spot reminded him of a typical beach cottage. It had probably been a vacation rental before his mother bought it and made it into a clothing store.

What attracted Thane to this place more than her other two businesses had to be the beach. Although the storefront sat on the other side of the street from the boardwalk, he could look out the front door and see the ocean in between the buildings. When Queen felt generous on the days she dragged him to work with her, she would allow him to go to the beach. She only asked that he return on time, and for him to not drag a bunch of sand back with him. Remembering that caveat brought a smile to his face.

He pulled his rental beside the small light blue building and sat in the car for a moment. With the chilly weather, the streets remained bare with the exception of some construction workers repairing the road for the upcoming season.

Thane couldn't stay in the car forever. It felt like it'd taken him years to get to this point. As he thought about it, using years as a timeframe could be classified as accurate. Once he went away to college, Thane rarely came home. When he did, he didn't visit Sharp.

He got out of the rental. The crisp sea air hit him first. The familiar fishy aroma wafted to his nose. The sounds of jackhammers and dump trucks replaced the usual beach noises. To escape the intrusive sounds, Thane unlocked the door and stepped into the place, then locked the door behind him.

Thankfully, his mother left the electricity on so the pipes wouldn't freeze in the winter. He flipped a switch on the wall. The fan started spinning, but the light didn't come on like he hoped. Great. He would have to replace the bulb.

So that he could see, he ripped down a sheet of newspaper that covered part of the front window. He didn't remove all the paper though. He needed enough light to move around, although he knew he could navigate through the place blindfolded.

He put his hand out in front of him to feel for the display table his mother had in the center of the room. As soon as he touched it, he shifted to the side to make a beeline to the office area. Once he found it, he felt around the wall for an alternate light source. He flipped the second switch and the office light came on, which offered a bit more illumination to the main showroom.

Thane looked around the place. Nothing looked different, yet everything had changed. His mother wouldn't be the one uncovering the display shelves and counters. She wouldn't be the one selling her designs. She wouldn't be here.

He went back into the office. The hardwood floors under his feet squeaked with each step. Thane felt odd taking a seat behind the desk. That had always been Queen's spot. As the new owner, he would have to get used to occupying this chair and taking over her duties, or at least part of them.

Gunnar and Gideon had already taken over their inherited businesses and had been running them for at least a month or more. It would be business as usual for them. Thane felt so behind the eight ball on everything.

Elizabeth's familiar floral scent immediately wafted up to his nose. In that moment, he felt like Elizabeth sat with him again.

Thane opened the desk drawer to see if he could find more clues about his mother. The slender top drawer offered nothing except for pens, loose change, stamps, and hard candy. He opened a side drawer. No surprise. It looked organized and straight.

He reached down for the first file and pulled it out. Instead of finding business documents, it contained sketches...*his* sketches. The first file had drawings he'd done at probably around age five or six. The crude drawings looked like he'd tried to sketch a man's suit. From the thick blue lines, it must have been a pinstriped one.

Thane laughed at his failed attempt. He pulled out the second folder and found similar drawings he'd done. Twelve additional files contained his artwork. The last folder broke him. Inside, it held not only his sketch of his future baseball uniform, it also had a photo he hadn't seen in years.

Tears filled his eyes as he stared at the shot of him and Queen sitting on the steps in front of her store. She had her arms wrapped around his shoulders as she kissed him on his cheek. He remembered taking that picture with his mother and had wondered where it had gone.

Thane dropped the picture and buried his face in his hands. He'd never imagined a life without his biggest supporter. There would be no way he could run her business. As soon as he could, he would have to figure out a way to sell it and go.

Chapter 9

Kari glared at her watch for the fifth time in two minutes. To be sure it hadn't failed, she picked up her phone and checked the time there. Yep, Thane Wells had officially stood her up. The restaurant confirmed they hadn't gotten a reservation from Thane or any special requests for a private table.

Twice in one day, she'd been disappointed by a man. Unlike her situation with Jarrod, she could rectify this circumstance face-to-face. She stormed out to the hotel's lobby. She wanted to go to Thane's room and curse him out to his face. She knew hotel security wouldn't let her go up. She had managed to skate by yesterday only because she had Thane with her.

She punched in the speed dial to call him. It went straight to voice mail.

"Damn it." She called Chelsi.

Even outside of work, the woman could work magic.

"Hey, Kari. How's our favorite baseball player? Sign him yet?" Chelsi asked with a playful lilt to her voice.

"No, and I'm pissed." Kari paced the marble floor.

"What's going on?"

"He called me. *He* called *me* and asked me to meet him at his hotel restaurant at seven to discuss business. Nothing. He's not here, and he's not answering his phone. I even used the hotel's phone to call his room phone directly. Have you heard any news about him going back to spring training? Anything online about him?" Kari knew if the man sneezed, Chelsi would hear about it and let her know.

"Let me check something." Chelsi remained quiet for a moment. "Nothing about him going back to training." After another beat, she offered more information. "Okay, I did a Google search on his mother, Elizabeth Sommerville."

"Why are you looking her up? She died." Kari felt bad enough that she'd intruded on the woman's funeral.

"I'm seeing if I can find out anything about her other than she had three incredibly hot sons. Ah-ha."

Kari stopped pacing. "What?"

"The mother owned a bunch of businesses."

Kari shrugged. "And?"

"A couple of months ago, Gunnar Wells gave up his illustrious MMA career to start his own hair care line. I'm assuming he has something to do with his mother's hair salon," Chelsi said.

The logic kind of made sense even though it still surprised Kari that this champion had given up his career to do hair. "Okay, what else?"

"Uh, looks like she also owns a flower shop. Wait a minute." Chelsi made a couple of clicking noises through the phone. "Ah, there are a ton of pictures on social media of Gideon in some flower shop. I would say he's got that place locked down."

"Makes sense. Anything else? Or are you saying I should check those two places first?" Kari headed to the front door.

"No. You need to check out a place called Sharp."

Kari blinked. "Did you say Sharp?"

"Yep. Supposed to be a clothing boutique down at the Oceanfront area. If I were a betting woman, I would say that Thane Wells is there." Chelsi sent the address of the store by text to Kari. "I'll keep digging. I'll let you know if I find anything else."

"Thanks so much. You're a life saver." Kari slipped on her coat as she walked out of the hotel.

"Does that mean you won't kill Thane when you see him?"

"Don't go that far." She would check out this boutique.

If she saw him there, she would give him a piece of her mind about standing her up for an appointment he'd made.

Kari tried not to speed down the interstate to the beachfront area. Anger more than embarrassment fueled her.

"Half a mile to your destination," her phone's mapping feature said in its robotic voice.

Kari looked ahead to see if she could see this business. If her phone hadn't told her that she had arrived, she would have passed it. It looked like a small house with a parking lot big enough to fit about ten cars.

One thing did catch her attention. A single car sat in the parking lot. Since she'd only seen Thane getting out a limo, she had no idea what he drove. She assumed the rented Lexus belonged to him.

Kari parked her car next to his and slammed the door after she got out. She stomped to the front door. She found resistance when she pulled on it.

Undeterred by this barrier, she pounded her fist on the door. Patience had never been her strong suit. She walked to the large picture window next to the door and peered inside. Her heart stopped when she saw Thane sitting in what looked like an office area.

He had his head down on his outstretched arm. He looked like he'd fallen asleep. If he'd done nothing but run around all day instead of going to bed like she'd done, he probably needed the rest. For that reason, she would give him a pass.

She saw him stirring. Kari backed away from the window to retreat to her car. She would have to try him again tomorrow. As soon as she unlocked her door, she heard another door opening.

"Who's there?"

Thane's unmistakable voice stilled her. She couldn't even turn around, an atypical response considering how angry she'd been when he missed their meeting. Kari finally turned to him.

He stared at her for a moment before a look of realization crossed his face. He cursed right after he glanced at his watch. "I apologize and I'm so sorry. I mean it. I'm sorry. I planned this date—"

"Meeting."

Had he actually called it a date? Kari's stomach rippled in excitement.

"And I oversleep. I didn't even know I had drifted off. You must think I'm the worst person out there." He climbed down the few steps to stand in front of her.

In the darkened parking lot she couldn't see much of his face, except for those hypnotic eyes. "I understand."

"No, it's no excuse." He turned back to the building. "Let me lock up here and then we can talk, that is if you still want to. I know I'm—" Thane glanced at his watch. "—an hour and a half late. Jesus. Please, let me make it up to you."

"By allowing me to represent you?" She smiled.

He finally smiled. "I'm embarrassed, not irrational. Nice try, Kari."

She started liking hearing him saying her name.

"Give me a minute." He raced up the stairs to the business.

Kari heard some knocking around before he extinguished the lights. Thane made sure to secure the front door before he bounded down the steps again.

"I still owe you a dinner. If you don't mind, we can go back to my hotel to have that."

Kari regarded him for a moment. She owed it to herself to see this through at least tonight. "Okay. I'll see you at the hotel."

Thane nodded. "Thank you."

She reached for her car door again. Thane surprised her by holding the door open. After she got inside, he closed it.

Some of his manners might have waned, but chivalry hadn't died in him. Thane got into his car. He pulled out of the lot first with Kari right behind him. She tried to stay close without being right on top of him. She didn't want to lose him or have him change his mind as soon as they arrived.

At his hotel, Thane parked on the side with Kari sliding in next to him. She walked beside him to the front door.

"I'm sure the people who work here will think that I'm some sort of stalker." Kari crossed her arms over her chest to ward away the chill in the air.

"Victims normally don't walk with their stalker." He smiled as he went up to the door.

Before the doorman could open it, Thane grabbed it for Kari. She could definitely get used to this type of treatment. When she headed toward the restaurant, Thane walked to the elevator.

"Do you need to change or something?" Kari asked as she stood outside of the restaurant's entrance.

"No. I thought we could eat in my room instead of the restaurant, which looks a little busy." He peered into the eatery, and so did Kari.

She saw what he meant. The waiting area now overflowed with patrons. "Come on up."

Kari suspected that going up to his room could be her downfall.

* * * *

Thane hoped that Kari didn't think he'd planned to get her into his hotel room. When he woke up to find her standing outside of Sharp, he felt like a jerk for making her wait.

The elevator ride up to his floor remained eerily quiet. He could only imagine what she thought of him. When the elevator stopped, she walked cautiously as she followed him to his room. He suspected she might be calculating possible plans to get out of being alone in his hotel room.

Although he hadn't arranged for this turn of events, he didn't mind the change in venue.

"I made a call when we left Sharp. I hope the room is set up." He unlocked his door and opened it for Kari.

She stepped inside and stopped. Kari glanced around with her mouth agape. As he requested, the hotel had set up a table with food for both of them. He did notice one thing he asked them to do that they'd neglected.

"Excuse me." He went to his bedroom door and closed it. "I took the liberty of ordering some dinner for us." He picked up one sterling silver cloche. "Ah, steak." He lifted a second one. "Chicken." He replaced the domes and picked up two more covers. "Fish and salads, in case you're a vegetarian or pescetarian. And"—he picked up the final one—"cheesecake."

His showing got Kari to smile finally. "Aren't you in training?"

Thane's smile melted. "I'm taking a little break."

"I don't think I said it to you, but I'm so sorry for your loss. I definitely understand."

He took her coat and hung it up in a closet before he pulled out a chair for her.

"Thank you." Kari draped a white cloth napkin over her lap after sitting.

Thane sat across from her. "I'm glad you mentioned that. You were at my mother's funeral." He felt his jaw getting tight as he thought about the intrusion. "Did you know my mother? Were you her friend? Although we've talked on the phone for over a year, I wouldn't consider us close."

Kari stared at him for a moment before she sat up taller. "Although I met and talked with Elizabeth one time before, I didn't know her. And even though I'm familiar with your brothers' work, I'm not friends with them either."

"So what were you doing there? You wanted to see a family on their worst day?" He gripped a fork to keep his hand occupied as he glared at her.

"Although I know your history, I should have done some research on you before I made the trip here. I don't usually work unprepared." She took a deep breath like she needed to steel her nerves. "When I arrived, I contacted my office assistant and found out about your mother. She told me where the services were being held."

"So you went out there thinking you could convince me to sign with you? You thought that would be a good time?" He balled his free hand into a fist.

Kari's gaze dropped down to the table, and for a short while, she didn't speak. She sniffed and shook her head. "I didn't believe my assistant. I went to the church, expecting to prove her wrong. When I saw it all, I stayed." She hesitated before she finished her thought. "I stayed through the service and went to the cemetery to pay my respects. As soon as I did that, I left." She brought her gaze up and looked him in his eyes. "I was at your hotel to apologize for being at your mother's funeral."

Thane sat back, stunned by her honesty.

"I'm sorry for the intrusion. That's not my style." She lifted her napkin to wipe under her eyes. "I would be mad if someone did that to..." She trailed off before she shook her head and picked up her glass of water to take a sip.

He loosened his grip on his fork. "You said you understand what I'm going through with my mother. Did you lose someone close to you?"

Kari brought her gaze up to meet his. "My grandfather." A small smile peeked through her hard countenance. "My grandpa raised me. He loved that I loved sports. It united us. Baseball, football, even hockey. We would sit and watch it all."

"Did you play any sports or were you only a spectator?" He couldn't help but stare at her plump lower lip.

"I played softball for a while. I did lacrosse until..." She stopped herself and let her gaze fall to the table for a moment before she reconnected her stare to his eyes. "I didn't do it for long."

"Not tough enough?" Without really knowing her, Thane wanted to raise her spirits.

He thought he kept his life private. Kari Meyers proved she could hold on to a secret better than him. A wall surrounded her, and she only allowed her eyes to be seen. Her intense need for personal privacy should be a plus for a potential agent. He didn't need to get involved in his agent's life. His agent didn't need to know his personal business. Yet Thane found that each time he looked into Kari's eyes, he wanted to know more about her.

"Where were your parents?" He didn't want his curiosity to become vocal, but while he had this woman captive in his room, he might as well explore all aspects of her life.

Her smile dropped. "They both died in a plane crash when I was a baby." She drummed her fingertips on the table with her free hand. "If you can believe this, they were flying to Seattle to attend a friend's funeral. They never made it. My grandpa told his son, my father, not to take me because at six weeks, I was too young to go on a plane. My dad agreed. If he hadn't..." She stopped her story. "That's why I don't take no for an answer. My life was spared to do more than be on the sidelines."

Her drive boosted up her attractiveness. Thane's lower half throbbed the longer he looked at her. Why the hell had he brought her back to his room?

Thane offered Kari some salad first before serving himself. "Sounds like your parents loved you a lot, even for the short time they were here. And your grandfather sounds awesome. The fact that you two were into sports is amazing. At least you had that. My mother wasn't into anything athletic, but she understood what it could do for me and my brothers growing up. It was the extracurricular activities that really bonded us with her, too. For me, it was the clothing store." Before taking a bite, he stopped and stared at her for a moment. "How did you know where to find me?"

"Google. My office assistant looked up your mother and found out she owned three businesses. By doing some logical deductions, we figured out that you would probably be at Sharp." She took a bite of her salad.

"Modern technology." He picked up his iced tea and took a needed drink. "So I take it you're an only child."

Kari nodded. "And I know you have two brothers. Any other siblings? More importantly, any siblings in sports without representation?"

Thane laughed. "Just two brothers. That's it." He stared at Kari. "Wow."

"What?"

"I think that's the first time I've laughed in the last week. Thank you." He exhaled. "I needed that."

Her golden skin glowed with a slight pink hue. "Not a problem."

Thane took that opportunity to check out her outfit. Tonight, she had on an all-black pantsuit. She took business attire to a new level. He noticed a lacy, red bra peeking out from her jacket, and dropped his gaze back down to his food to keep from staring at the garment.

"Your husband doesn't mind you traveling so much?" He would leave out the part about her being in a hotel room with a strange man. He didn't want to scare her.

"No."

Thane's heartbeat slowed.

"Because I'm not married."

His pulse accelerated again.

"And that was a tired way of asking me about my relationship status."

He shrugged. "Oldie but a goody. Boyfriend?"

"No, and—"

"Girlfriend?"

Kari placed her fork down on the table. "Thane, since you asked, I have three distinct rules regarding my dating life." She held up her hand and raised her index finger. "I don't date athletes." She raised her middle finger. "I don't date anyone younger than me." Then she raised her ring finger. "And I don't mix business with pleasure."

"Okay, so let's dissect each one of the restricting rules." So far he enjoyed learning about Ms. Kari Meyers.

"I don't find them restricting. They're my rules to live by." She shuffled lettuce around on her plate.

"So the athletes thing. You've loved sports all of your life. You work in an industry where you're around athletes all the time. Why wouldn't you consider dating them?"

"Oh, I did. Many, many years ago. It didn't work out for me." She shook her head.

"One bad apple, huh?"

She nodded. "Since then, I decided to stay away from them. They travel a lot. I would have to travel a lot. It wouldn't work. I need stability in my life."

"Why is that?" He offered her a roll from a basket covered with a napkin.

She shook her head. "Every woman wants a sure thing. If she says she doesn't, she's lying."

"Okay, fine. So let's talk about the age thing. You look about my age." Although her face and body made her look like she'd graduated from high school yesterday.

"Try four years older."

Thane's eyes widened. "You're twenty-six?"

Kari nodded. "I find that younger men are immature. They want to party and drink." She stared at him for a moment before dropping her gaze to her plate.

Thane knew she looked at him suspiciously because of his bad behavior the night of his mother's funeral. He hadn't been himself that day, and the alcohol hadn't helped.

Before she took another bite, she explained herself. "I don't blame young guys for acting crazy. But that craziness can manifest itself in other ways."

"Such as?" He stopped everything to hear her assessment of his entire sex and age group.

She cleared her throat before speaking. "Younger men are impulsive. They don't look before they leap. They don't stop to smell the roses."

"You're saying we don't take our time." He tried hard not to smile, but he felt his lips pulling to the sides. Then a subtle warmth washed over his body at the same time her face flushed a deeper rose color.

Kari smoothed her hand over the back of her neck. "This seems like an inappropriate conversation to have with—"

"A client?" he asked. "Or with a man?" Thane felt like he held his breath until she answered his question. When she didn't respond right away, he followed up with, "Take your time. I'm a very, very patient man."

Kari shook her head. "I can't talk for all women, but for me, I need someone who's going to be a partner in life. I have no interest in raising a man-child."

He felt his body go cold. "The day of my mother's funeral, I was in a bad place. I needed to forget about the day, so, yes, I overindulged. That's not me. I don't drink like that, and I'm disappointed in myself that I did. It still bothers me that I was rude to you." He wiped his mouth. "I saw the hotel's video of me kissing you and pushing you into my room. That was wrong and disgusting."

"There's a video of that out there?" She covered her mouth. "You need to sue the hotel and have whoever on the staff that leaked that video fired. You came here expecting a modicum of privacy, and they clearly breached that trust."

Thane blinked. He liked her fiery spirit, her fight and determination. He hadn't thought about the whole angle about the security footage being leaked. Again, he chalked it up to being a celebrity. She saw him as more. Kari saw him as a person.

"Oh, that reminds me." She stood and went to her purse that sat on the coffee table. From a side pocket, she pulled out a business card.

Thane stood as she came back to the table. Had he known she had planned on getting up, he would have stood up with her.

"Here's the name of a real estate agent friend of mine. She sells homes and does rental property. She would keep her mouth closed about any dealings with you. If you plan on staying here any longer, I would suggest you give her a call. Otherwise you'll be constantly bothered by reporters and photographers."

"And agents." He held out Kari's chair for her before taking a seat. "Thanks for the tip, although I doubt I'll be here for very long." He picked up his fork but kept his gaze down. "After my mother, um, she left me Sharp, her clothing business. But I won't be able to stay to run it."

"Wow. A clothing boutique. That's nice." Kari placed her hand on the table, dangerously close to his. "Too bad you can't keep it open."

Thane couldn't help but stare at the short distance between the two. It would take the slightest effort to twitch his little finger to brush against her hand.

What the hell was he doing? He and his brothers had buried their mother only yesterday. He should be mourning, not ogling some woman.

To cut down on temptation, he placed his hand on his lap, which also helped in easing his burgeoning erection. "I know my mother worked hard to get her boutique off the ground." He brought his gaze up to meet hers. "Are you familiar with the boardwalk area in Virginia Beach?"

Kari shook her head. "Can't say that I am."

"After Labor Day, the strip pretty much shuts down to tourists. Small businesses like my mom's close up shop through the winter and reopen around spring." Thane thought about how he and Queen would pack up all the items in the store and cover everything with sheets.

He would throw a sheet over his head and pretend to be a ghost. She would wrap one around her shoulders and act like a movie star. As he recalled those silly times, he chuckled to himself.

"What were you doing there?" Kari asked.

He shook his head. "Cleaning up a bit. Going through her things. I have to get back to baseball. I'm missing spring training. I worked hard to get where I am. I can't stop now to sell clothes."

"You can get someone else to do it. Hire someone to run it for you."

Kari's wide-eyed optimism almost weakened him. Almost. "As soon as I can, I'm going to try and sell the place."

"Oh." She picked up a glass of water and took a sip.

"What?"

"I didn't say anything." She shrugged.

"I feel like there's something you're not saying."

"It's nothing. You don't know me. I don't know you. Let's get back to talking about business." She sat her glass on the table and scanned the different dinners on the tray next to the table.

"No. I want to hear what you were thinking. You think I'm being selfish, don't you?" He crossed his arms over his chest as he awaited her answer.

Kari exhaled before she spoke again. "My grandfather passed away right after I graduated from college. Sometimes I even think that he held on long enough for me to get through college. While he was alive, he would tell me that I should always work hard and preserve the Meyers name to honor my parents because that's all they left me. Your mother left you a real, tangible legacy. She gave you a business that you two enjoyed together. Why would you get rid of that so quickly?"

Thane opened his mouth to answer, but he couldn't say anything. She'd echoed the same sentiments Gunnar and Gideon had. That same chill coiled around his spine again.

"Tell me something, Kari. After your grandfather died, did people tell you that each day it would get better, that the pain and hurt would lessen as time passed?" He sat back in his chair and studied her.

"Of course." Her eyebrows knitted together.

"And did it upset you when people tried to tell you the right way to grieve, like saying to visit his grave, or be sure to get rid of all his clothes and personal items, or tell you not to do anything on the anniversary of his death?"

Kari remained still.

"I don't know when your grandfather died. I'm not going to say any of those things to you. How you deal with his passing is your business." He picked up his fork. "Same should go for me. I need time to deal. Going back to a place that is the epitome of my mother is a bit tough to take right now."

She drew her hand back and placed it on her lap. "I know what you mean." She made the statement and squeezed her eyes shut like she didn't want to utter those words. "I'm sorry."

"Don't say you're sorry. Sorry is a state." He straightened up in his chair. "You're tenacious. I can tell you work hard at what you do. And you're compassionate. You helped me without really knowing me. There's nothing sorry about you. And you have no reason to apologize either."

"Wow." Kari dabbed her napkin against her forehead. "For a young man, you seem to have it all together. You're lucky. At least you have your brothers to help you get through this hard time."

"Yeah, well, sometimes loneliness is better than constantly trying to explain yourself to people who you thought really knew you." He didn't want to open himself up to her, a stranger, a beautiful one.

She stared at him. He returned the intense gaze with one of his own and couldn't break it. The heaviness in the room returned as his heart pounded hard and fast. He had once pitched a no hitter that went into double innings and didn't remember sweating as much then.

"Glad you brought up my age again." Thane needed to get this conversation back on her. "We need to get back to your list. So your last item. Last I checked, I haven't signed up with you, so we're not in business together."

"And that reminds me. What made you want to call me?" She crossed her legs under the table, obvious from the way her body shifted.

Although he thought about revealing that he loved the way she smelled and looked out for him, instead, he said, "I talked to Alec. He confirmed what you told me. He also suggested I go with one of his current agents, and told me I should be content with my deal. I never want to be complacent about anything. I want more. If you can get that for me, I'll consider signing with you."

Kari's eyes lit up. She looked so beautiful and excited. Before he could think about representation, he had to get more facts about her, more than her dating life, which interested him a lot.

"What clients do you represent right now?" He finished his salad, but waited until she finished hers before starting on the entrée.

"I represent tennis player Jean Rattineaux." She dropped her stare onto her frosty glass of water instead of looking him in the eye.

"I don't follow tennis that closely. I don't think I've heard of him."

She picked up her glass. "He's one of the top twenty professional tennis players in the world." She took a long sip.

"Is he number twenty?"

Kari paused before placing her glass back on the table. "Does it matter?"

"That's a yes."

She blew out an exasperated breath. "I also represent a couple of professional basketball players."

Thane blinked. "Wow. Now I do follow basketball closely. Who are your clients?"

She cleared her throat. "You probably won't know them."

He felt his eyebrows rut together. "Why is that? Are they out with an injury or something? Rookies?"

"No. They play for the WNBA."

A strange tickle crept up the back of his neck. He stood and went to the living room area where she'd left her business card on the coffee table. Thane picked it up and read all of the contents on the card.

"You've got to be kidding me." He leaned his head back and let out a chuckle. "You're a *junior* agent?"

Kari waited a beat before she addressed him. "For now. I've worked hard and I can secure you an awesome deal that's equal to or better than what Alec got you."

He returned to the table and sat down. "I have to admit, you have a lot of spunk for believing you can sign someone like me as a client." Thane didn't mean to sound arrogant. He knew what he earned and the kind of deal he'd signed.

He wouldn't say it out loud, but he liked her determination. That didn't mean that he needed to take a step backward in his career.

"If you give me a chance, I can show you what I'm made of." She glanced at the dinners. "Do you mind if I have the chicken?"

Thane picked up the chicken dinner and placed it in front of her. "Don't mind at all. I wanted the steak. Had you asked for that, we might have had to wrestle for it." He shook some pepper onto his vegetables. "Let me ask you something. Did you give that same speech to your WNBA clients about your dating preferences?"

She blinked. "Of course not."

"Why is that?" He cut a piece of his steak but waited before he ate it to hear her answer.

"Why would I tell my female clients something like that when I'm not a lesbian or bisexual?"

"So you felt the need to tell me as a potential male client." He took a bite of his steak.

"You asked me about my relationship status."

"I was making small talk."

She laughed. "You were checking me out."

"And I don't think you minded, not that much."

She picked up her fork and knife and cut into her chicken. "Let me ask you something. When Alec first met you, did you share your concern about his travel schedule and his relationship with his—"

"Husband?" Thane cut her off.

She stopped to regard him.

"Didn't mean to interrupt you. I thought it was the worst-kept secret in the industry that Alec Fogel is gay and married. You didn't know that?"

Kari shook her head.

"No, I didn't ask Alec about his relationship. But he had no problem sharing. Our first meeting, he brought his husband to dinner with him. Actually, I got along better with his husband than with Alec. When you have an agent like him, you laugh at his corny jokes and hope he takes you on as a client. He did." He popped a piece of steak in his mouth.

The beef melted as he chewed it. Since learning of his mother's death, he finally got to savor a meal. He glanced at Kari, who stared at him with her mouth agape.

"You're pretty, um—" She ate a piece of chicken like she needed something to occupy her mouth.

"I'm what?" Thane wouldn't let her off that easily.

"Nothing. Dinner is delicious. Thank you."

He looked at her free hand resting on the table. In that moment, he wanted to reach out and touch it, hold it. He hadn't held a woman's hand in a while. He hadn't done a lot of things with a woman since his break up with a Sri Lankan model a year ago.

After dinner, Kari piled her dirty dishes and pushed them off to the side.

"Ready for some cheesecake?" Thane rubbed his hands together.

"I am, but I have one request." She chewed on her bottom lip and leaned forward.

He wondered if she wanted to ask him for something salacious like taking a bath together or giving each other a massage. As quickly as the suggestions popped into his head, he pushed them right out for good reason. The longer he stared into her eyes, the faster his pulse raced.

"What's that?" he asked.

She turned to the living room area before bringing her attention back to him. "Mind if we watch the sports wrap-up show? I need to get some stats."

He exhaled. "Yeah, yes. Sure." He pointed to the couch. "Go get comfortable. I'll be in there in a minute."

She stood and sauntered to the couch. He had to break his stare from watching her slink away, otherwise he wouldn't be able to stand up at all pretty soon.

When he heard her turning on the wall-mounted TV, he stood and grabbed a small dessert plate with a slice of cheesecake. He rested his finger next to the silver coffee pitcher, which felt hot. He poured a cup for Kari and carried the dessert and coffee to her.

"You're not having any?" She looked at both items he placed in front of her.

"Someone reminded me that I'm still in training." He took a seat on the couch next to her but with a comfortable space in between them.

She picked up the plate. "Thank you. You didn't have to do this."

"Yes, I did. It's the least I could do for leaving you hanging like that." He stared at her until she broke first to bring her attention to the TV.

"Wow, what a shocker." Kari took a bite of the cheesecake and made an approving moaning sound.

"What's that?"

"Kurt Bodilasky is out with a shoulder injury. Right at the start of basketball season. That's horrible." She shook her head.

"You know who Kurt Bodilasky is?" He stared at this beauty with wonderment.

In high school and college, the girls he'd associated with only knew athletes with big endorsement deals or who appeared on reality TV shows or dance shows. Kari's knowledge impressed him, probably more than it should have.

"Of course." She turned to him. "I also know your ERA back when you were still on the Wren farm was three-point-two-one. You've already had almost a thousand strikeouts. And your batting average is point-two-three-four. You're a beast. I mean that in a good way." She stared at him.

This time Thane sat stunned. His blood pumped throughout his body so hard that it felt like his flesh pulsed. Had she touched him, she would probably be shocked.

"I'm impressed. Most fans don't know my stats like that, much less a—"

"Agent?" She cut him off, probably before he could say something stupid like assuming a woman wouldn't know anything about sports.

"Yes, an agent." The longer he stared into her eyes, the more he wanted to kiss her, a strange reaction to a woman he'd only met a day ago.

Somehow, in that short amount of time, she'd managed to worm her way into his thoughts. He enjoyed talking to her as much as he savored her beauty and the heavenly scent swirling about her that lulled into comfort and lust.

"You said you had talked to my mother before. When was that?" Thane leaned back on the couch.

Kari laughed a little before she adopted the same position, leaning back on the opposite end of the couch. "Shortly after I graduated college, I hopped on a train and came up to New York by myself in hopes of wooing this amazing college star athlete who was meeting with major baseball teams at the time. I was in the bathroom talking to my grandfather when this beautiful woman walked in. She asked me what I was doing. I told her that I was there to sign the next big thing in baseball, Thane Wells."

As she told the story, Thane sat up taller.

"I had on what I thought was my best dress. It was this red wrap dress." She stared at him. "It was one of those dresses that's kind of like a robe, and women—"

Thane held up his hand. "I know what a wrap dress is. Owner of a clothing boutique, remember? Pardon my interruption."

"That's okay. Anyway, she introduced herself as Elizabeth. Then she said although she admired my determination, she didn't think I would be the right agent for you." Kari looked down at her outfit. "She even accused me of trying to seduce you to get your business by dressing in what she thought was too risqué."

"My mother said that to you?" He felt his heart pounding hard.

Kari nodded. "She said it in a nicer way than that, but in a nutshell, she let me know that she was protecting her child and wouldn't let someone like me take you down." She smiled. "I must admit, even in that short meeting, she got to me. I don't know if you even remember me. I tried passing myself off as part of the Yankees' team that was there to meet you. You came out of a meeting room with a couple of Yankee recruiters and your mother. You looked at me and—" Kari stopped.

"What?" Thane went back through his memory bank to recall that moment.

He remembered the many trips he'd taken to meet with recruiters. His mother had never told him that she'd talked to an agent in the bathroom.

"You stared at me." Kari gazed at him. "Kind of like the way you're looking at me now. Before I could approach you, hotel security dragged me out. If you remember me at all from that moment, it'll be because I was pulled out like I was some hooker looking for a john."

Thane nodded. "That's why you looked familiar. I do remember that security took you away. But that's not what made you memorable. You told me to finish college. That sounded like something my mother would say."

She scooped more cheesecake onto her fork. "Elizabeth was powerful. I told you she got into my head. She asked me what I would tell my son if I were in her spot. She was right."

"I now understand why she never told me that she talked to you. You looked really good in that dress."

Kari stared at Thane for a moment. The action on the TV became background noise as tension filled the room.

Kari cleared her throat and broke her stare. "I have something else for you." She reached into her purse and pulled out some papers. "It's my standard contract."

Thane covered his eyes and leaned his head back. "You really do not give up, do you?"

"Not when I really want something." She held the contract up to him. "I really do want you."

That line had him thinking of all the ways he wanted her. As quickly as the sinful thoughts entered his head, he remembered his mother. What would she think about him lusting after a woman right after her funeral? He recalled the disappointed looks from his brothers when they viewed the video of him groping Kari outside his hotel room.

"I guess you and I have something in common." He accepted her paperwork. As soon as he saw Kari's eyes widen, he brought her back down to reality. "I don't call them rules, but I have a code for my dating life. Right now, I don't have one. I have to keep my head in the game. I can't do that if I'm in a relationship and have to think of someone else. It sounds selfish, but it's better than trying to start something you know you can't finish." He placed the contract on the coffee table. "I also don't mix business with pleasure."

Kari struggled to keep a cheerful expression on her face. "Looks like we're both speaking the same language as far as a working relationship. If I can get you to sign that contract, we could really talk some business."

"You're missing the show." Thane nodded toward the TV.

She picked up her plate and slipped off her shoes. Like a cat, she curled her legs up on the couch. Then she settled back as she kept her stare on the screen.

When she downed another bite, she turned to him. "Is that why you use women?"

"Excuse me?" Thane sat up straight. He felt his blood pressure rising for all the wrong reasons again.

"Wrong choice of words. Is that why you, um, date a lot? Word on the street is that you don't like to be tied down…to a relationship."

Kari's meaningful pause had the wrong effect in him. He knew she wanted to say that not only had she heard he liked to screw around, but that he also liked it kinky.

"I wouldn't believe everything you read or hear. My last relationship with Anjana ended almost a year ago." He'd started falling for the exotic beauty hard until she started questioning him every time he had any kind of association with another woman. Thane couldn't stay in a relationship without trust.

"Yes, and since then you've been linked with a Playboy Playmate, another model, a yoga instructor, and a couple of actresses."

He wanted to be angry with Kari, but she had some facts correct. After breaking up with Anjana, he and a buddy from the team had gone to the infamous Playboy mansion. He'd met a beautiful, leggy blonde. Although he had a great make-out session with her, he'd never slept with her, or with the model or the fitness instructor or even the actresses.

"Like I said, I wouldn't believe everything you read." Thane directed his attention back to the TV in hopes that Kari would do the same.

When she did, he felt a wave of relief. He didn't want to answer any more questions about his mother, his career, his dating life, or Sharp. What the hell would he do with the business?

After the show, Thane and Kari watched a college basketball game. She cheered the team he opposed, which didn't surprise him. Kari seemed to be all wrong for him. She'd come to him at the worst possible time in his life. She dared to disrupt his idyllic world. Yet, somehow she fit.

The more she hung out with him, the more he wanted to get to know this woman on every level. When he imagined himself kissing her, his body jerked up with a jolt. He'd gotten so comfortable with Kari that he'd fallen asleep.

When he looked down, he discovered that she probably felt as relaxed with him as he did with her. Kari rested her head on his chest and wrapped her arms around his waist. He had to smile when he heard a small snore come from her mouth.

Thane wriggled from under her so that she lay flat on the sofa. He tiptoed to his bedroom and pulled down the sheets and comforter. He returned to the living room and turned off the TV first. He didn't want her waking up prematurely.

He picked her up in his arms, amazed at how easily he could carry her. She nuzzled her face into his chest as he made his way to the bed. Thane placed her down carefully and covered her gently.

Thane stared at her for a moment. He brushed her hair back from her face. Had he been in a better place in his life, he could see himself trying to start something with her. Bad timing.

Chapter 10

Kari felt like clouds cradled her as she stirred awake. She rubbed her hand over the softest set of sheets she'd ever been on, better than what she had in her hotel.

Wait. She sat up and glanced around the room. From the four-poster bed to the Oriental rug on the floor and the luxurious comforter covering her body, she knew she hadn't woken up in her hotel room.

Kari peered down at her attire. She still wore her sensible black pantsuit. Everything remained buttoned and zipped up, thank God. Then again, after the amazing connection she made with Thane last night, she kind of wished he would join her in bed if only to hold her.

She liked that she surprised him by spouting his statistics to him. She knew her job. She'd done her research. Most importantly, she liked Thane Wells, the player, the man, everything.

Kari looked out of the bedroom door to see if she could find Thane. Maybe he'd taken a shower and would be walking around naked like he'd done yesterday morning. She blinked when she saw the multi-million dollar baseball pitcher on the couch with a blanket over his body.

He certainly could have left her on the couch and had his own bed. Or he could have slept with her. With how polite and gentlemanly he'd been with her in his sober state, she knew he would never do anything to make her feel uncomfortable, not on purpose.

The lingering stares they had given each other had stirred feelings within Kari that she'd hadn't felt in years. She shook her head. She had to get her mind back in the game. Thane meant money and prestige. She could become a full agent. She couldn't see anything else in Thane other than work.

Kari crept out of bed and padded to the living room. As Thane slept, she picked up her purse that held her precious morning-after kit. She padded to the bathroom and closed the door.

In a short amount of time, she cleaned herself up, managing to wash her face and brush her teeth while fluffing out her hair again. Her hair no longer appeared disheveled and tousled. Now she looked like she had regained some control. She glanced one last time at herself in the mirror before she opened the bathroom door and released a bloodcurdling scream.

Thane stood on the other side of the door. Even half asleep, he looked hot. His heavy-lidded gaze liquefied her. His short, brown hair stood on his head in an odd, spiky manner. The five-o'clock shadow on his chin gave him a sexy and scruffy appeal.

Before she could say anything, he took a step closer. Kari peered down. Damn. Even his bare feet looked good.

"Thank you for letting me have your bed." She clutched her purse close to her body to create a barrier between the two of them. "You could have left me on the couch."

He shook his head. "Never." His voice sounded deeper than normal.

It didn't take long for Kari's knees to buckle. "And you definitely didn't have to carry me."

"How else could I get you into bed?"

Damn. Did he really have to ask that? Kari noticed right away how rapid her breathing had become.

"Done in there?" Thane pointed into the bathroom.

"Yes." She stepped around him.

Even in the early morning, he smelled like a man, all delicious and musky and heady. Her mind raced with thoughts of him rubbing his stubbly face against her bare skin.

Stop it, girl. He's a job. That's it.

Once Thane closed the bathroom door, Kari wasted no time in getting her stuff together. With luck, she'd be out of his room before he could reemerge.

She found her shoes by the coffee table. She remembered slipping them off while she watched TV with Thane. As she thought about how they cheered along to the college basketball game, she couldn't help but smile.

Kari froze when she spotted her agent contract pages flipped over. Had Thane seriously reconsidered signing with her? She hoped he had because of her sports knowledge and her passion, and not because of some sexual attraction.

When she heard the toilet flushing and water running in the bathroom sink, she quickened her movements. Kari slipped into her shoes. She scanned the place to find her coat and remembered that Thane hung it in the closet by the door. She rushed to it and pulled out her coat. As soon as she slammed the door, she felt a tug.

Kari turned around and saw Thane standing behind her.

"Let me help you with that." He secured it from her grasp and held it up for her. "I was hoping you would at least stay for breakfast."

"You don't have to do that." She kept her back to him, afraid that if she looked at him again, she would make a stupid mistake.

"I feel like I owe you. You did the same for me. I'd like to return the favor."

"That was different."

"How?"

Kari turned around. She had to look up to stare him. "You were in need."

He closed into her personal space. "I still am." Thane dropped his gaze for a moment before reconnecting with her again. "I appreciate your tenacity to get my business."

"I saw you reviewed my contract." Kari nodded toward the living room area. "I would protect your interests. I could make sure to set you up for the rest of your life."

"That's a big promise to make. I'm not sure if I'm the right"—he paused as he sought his words carefully—"client for you."

She nodded. "Thanks for dinner. Most athletes would have stood me up and not felt sorry about it." Maybe she meant some men, or rather her child's father.

Kari approached Thane, stood on tip toes to kiss his cheek. She didn't know what had come over her to do that instead of shaking his hand. After the night they'd had, she wanted to show him that she had listened to him. She understood the pain he felt right now with the loss of his mother. She appreciated the way he cared for her.

Her lips brushed against his stubbly face. The tiny, prickly hairs tickled her sensitive flesh. When she pulled back from the kiss, she made the mistake of connecting her gaze to his. A strong magnetic pull forced her to plant another kiss on his other cheek. Pure selfishness ruled her senses. She'd wanted to bond with him again, take in his manly scent, touch him.

Kari lowered herself while still maintaining her close proximity to his body. Before she knew what happened, Thane swept her hair away from her face. Then he framed her face in his hands, pulled her in close, and pressed his lips against hers.

Kari's breath caught in her throat at the idea that Thane Wells had her in his hotel room. His kiss made her feel lightheaded and grounded all at once, like a fantasy that became realized.

She dropped her purse to the floor with a thud and put her hands on his chest. His muscles flexed under her touch. In turn, he lowered his hands to her waist and pulled her against his body. When he slipped his tongue into her mouth, she accepted it. She wanted it. She wanted him. Everything about this connection felt right, like they should be together. Kari imagined where this passionate moment would take them.

Maybe he would ease her back to the door and have his way with her there, ripping off clothes and imprinting himself in her mind and on her body. Or maybe, like last night, he'll lift her into his massive arms and carry her to his bed.

As he kissed her, letting his tongue touch and tease hers, she imagined the sex. She pressed her body against his harder. She didn't have to dream about the size of his penis. His erection pushed against the zipper of his jeans and her stomach.

Juices oozed from her core into the red panties she'd worn specifically for Thane, even though she hadn't thought there would be an opportunity for him to see her undergarments. Wearing them gave her a sense of sexiness and the confidence she needed to deal with this A-list athlete.

Like she had imagined, Thane eased her back so that her back hit the door. He moved his mouth over her jaw and toward her ear. The tickling sensation had her curling her toes in her shoes.

"Don't go," he whispered.

Kari wanted to stay in the room with him. She wanted to see where this moment would take them. If she stayed, would that mean he would sign with her? If he did, would she want him as a client, knowing why he'd signed? Would he accept Michael?

Michael. The thought of her child sobered her to the situation. She hadn't mentioned him at all to Thane because she didn't want her clients involved in her personal life. Kind of hard for her to support that rationale when this man had his tongue in her mouth. She pushed him back as hard as she could.

"We can't do this." She shook her head and secured her coat around her body.

"Why not? You felt it last night, didn't you? We have chemistry?" He put his hand to her chin and lifted it so that she would look at him. "I haven't felt this way since—" He stopped. "Stay."

She stared at him. Besides thinking about her son, she also recalled the stories about Thane. His love-em-and-leave-em tales had become stuff of legends. Although he'd refuted them last night, the thoughts lingered in her mind. Did he want her, or did he need someone warm next to him to ease his ache. She wouldn't allow herself to be a pacifier, a placebo for love.

Kari shook her head again. "No." She knelt down to get her purse. "I'm not going to be a notch on your headboard."

The comment had Thane taking a step back. His eyebrows furrowed. "What did you say?"

"It's no secret that you love the ladies. I think even Leonardo DiCaprio feels inferior to you when it comes to the women you've bedded." She hung her purse from her shoulder.

When she stared at Thane, she got a return glare that felt like he'd punched her in the gut. He took a few more steps back from her.

"I told you the truth last night. I know we haven't spent a lot of time together, but have you ever gotten the impression from me that I would treat any woman like that?"

Deep down, Kari knew what he'd said held some genuineness. He'd damn near begged her to call the police on him for actions he hadn't remember doing. He opened doors for her. He pulled out chairs for her. When she stood, he jumped up to his feet. All those gentlemanly traits seemed perfect, but Kari had been fooled in the past by men who promised her the world and treated her like a queen until they got what they wanted.

Kari took a deep breath. "I'm sorry for falling asleep here. I didn't mean for you to take care of me. I should have gone home sooner."

Thane dropped his gaze to the floor and shook his head. "I can't catch a break, can I?"

She gripped her purse strap and attempted to regain her professional countenance. "I'd still like to represent your interests."

He snickered. "Of course. You have standards. I'm a young baseball player you want to do business with. That's a cocktail for disaster for anything else, right?"

Kari didn't respond. She didn't know what she could say to salvage the moment.

"Did you ever think that you're not the only one who might be afraid of all this?" He moved in close to her only to grip the doorknob and open the door for her. "Good day, Ms. Meyers." Thane wouldn't look her. "If you'll excuse me, I have a lot to take care of before I leave for Florida."

Damn. She'd lost him. Frank would be pissed. She saw her chances at getting made a full agent going right out the door with her.

Kari walked by him into the main hotel hallway. The slam of Thane's door behind her expressed his anger. What could she have done in that moment? Slept with him? Kari wouldn't have been able to look herself in a mirror, let alone be a role model to her son.

After this gigantic stumble, she would have to do some serious regrouping if she hoped to still get his business. She couldn't give up, not when she had gotten so close to getting her man.

* * * *

Thane hung his head under the streaming water in the shower as he allowed the last few minutes to roll around in his head. He'd been determined not to get close to Kari. She'd wowed him when she'd spouted his stats. He never thought he would meet a woman he'd have so much in common with so quickly.

It didn't help that she smelled so good and looked even better. Had dear Queen Elizabeth been alive, she would have popped him on the back of his head had she caught him looking at her luscious backside. Even in her somewhat conservative pantsuit, he'd seen the hellcat lurking underneath.

When she kissed his cheek and he felt her body brushing against his, his will had shattered. He hadn't had a full connection like that in months. The bond went beyond the sexual chemistry. He'd enjoyed talking to her, until she'd accused him of being a player.

Thane had heard the stories about himself before. Then he hadn't minded being known as a lover boy. Hearing it from Kari snapped him into reality. He didn't want to be that guy. Right now he didn't have time to do any damage control. Thane had to get back to what he knew.

After his shower, he dried himself off and secured a towel around his waist. He'd learned his lesson from the last time he paraded around naked. Before he did anything, he called his coach.

"Hey, man." Jermaine spoke in a low and slow tone as though he had to talk Thane off a ledge.

To bring his head coach back around to business, Thane made sure to talk like he wanted to come back to work. "Hey, Jay. I'm going to tie up some loose ends here. I should be back down for training by this weekend." He glanced at his watch.

Thane would need to go back to Sharp to pack up some personal items he wanted to keep, then he would arrange for his flight back to work.

"Are you sure you're ready to come back? If you need more time to—"

Crystal B. Bright

"No, I'm ready." Thane paced. "Didn't mean to interrupt you. I'm ready to get my mind on something else."

"Yeah, I can understand. We want you back."

That same strange tickle crept up the back of Thane's neck. "But?"

Jermaine sighed. "We want to make sure you're ready. You're dealing with a lot right now. First your mom, and now switching agents."

Damn, did everyone know Thane's business? "Work will get me back into the game, pun intended."

"Cool. Besides your mom, we know about your other issues."

Thane rubbed his hand over his stomach. So far, he hadn't felt any pains yet. The day had only begun.

Jermaine continued. "If you're not ready, we have Witt waiting in the wings."

Thane gritted his teeth. He knew about the young player groomed to take over the pitching spot when Thane couldn't perform. This wouldn't be Witt's moment. Thane had to get back. If he didn't, he could spend his upcoming season riding the bench.

"I'm fine. I'm ready. See you this weekend." Thane disconnected the call.

He would have to figure out what to do with Sharp. He needed an ally. The best person for that would be Gideon. Always the peacemaker, he would be able to sway Gunnar to see things his way.

Now dressed, Thane left his room and drove to Sharp. On the way, he called Gideon.

After the third ring, his brother answered. "What? Did you oversleep again?"

Thane felt a knot bunching between his shoulders. "What are you talking about this time?"

"Christ, really? Yesterday, before you left the attorney's office, you said you were going to come over to Mom's for dinner with us. We didn't hear from you at all."

Thane pulled into the Sharp parking lot and parked his rental. "No, I said maybe. Something else came up."

"Really?" Doubt filled Gideon's voice. "Was it another woman, or were you on a bender?"

"I went to Sharp and came across some pictures and stuff." Thane covered his eyes with his hand. "It was a lot, you know."

A pause lingered before Gideon spoke. "Where are you now?"

"Here at Sharp. I'm going to pack up some stuff." Thane stopped before admitting what he had planned. He still needed Gideon to be on his side.

"You're close enough to my house. Why don't you come by for lunch? I should be done with physical therapy by then." Gideon's voice lightened. He started to sound like the protective older brother Thane remembered.

"I don't want you to rush on my account. How about dinner?" Thane suspected that after the events of that morning, he wouldn't be seeing Kari again. "I promise I have nothing else on my agenda. I really need to talk to you."

"Seven sharp. If you're late or don't call, I'll come find you and beat your ass." Gideon completed the threat with a chuckle.

"Duly noted. See you later." Thane disconnected the call.

His mind immediately went to Kari and what she must be thinking now. Did she really believe he had bedded countless women? Hell, even his brothers believed it.

Brothers. It had been a while since Thane had truly thought of them that way, especially Gunnar. He would keep that secret buried deep, at least until he could get out from under his familial obligations, the business, and the house he had yet to see.

Thane entered the boutique again and locked the door behind him without glancing around. Despite his brothers' wishes, he wouldn't be reopening the place.

He stepped into the office, and found an empty box in the corner. Had he truly been prepared, he would have brought one with him. He knew his plan.

He slammed the box on the desk, which blew some stray papers around and onto the floor. Until then, he hadn't noticed the flashing red light on an answering machine next to the desk phone. He had to laugh at his mother's reliance on an old-fashioned machine. Thank goodness she had. He wouldn't have known her voicemail password.

Thane hovered his finger over the *play* button and stopped. If he listened to the message, he would be investing time and energy into the business, more than he'd planned. What if he could hear his mother's voice again? Queen used to call herself all the time to leave herself reminders.

Curiosity got the better of him and he punched the silver button.

"Three new messages," the female computerized voice said in a monotone fashion.

"Queen, make sure you order those silk fabrics for the dance season."

Thane smiled as soon as he heard his mother's voice. He took a seat as he absorbed each word. She sounded so strong, so healthy. He wanted to remember her that way always.

Elizabeth continued her message. "Call the boys to get them over for Christmas."

The smile slipped down Thane's face. He had no idea his mother even came to the business during the holiday season after she closed it for the year. His heart stopped when he realized how wrong he'd been to avoid his mother, especially during the holidays. Actually, he hadn't been dodging seeing her. He hadn't wanted to chance confronting his brothers. He'd done a great job of steering clear of them. By doing that, he also missed a lot of time with Queen.

He balled his hand into a fist and pounded it on the desk. So many mistakes.

"Message two."

Thane directed his attention to the small, rectangular machine.

"Hey, Ma."

The sound of Gunnar's voice bristled Thane. He scooted the black box closer to him to find a way to skip the recording.

"Got your message about coming home for the holidays. I'm not sure if I can get away. I'm in training for a fight coming up in January. Hopefully Gid and Thane will be there. I talked to Gideon. Still can't get in touch with Thane. Think he's avoiding me." Gunnar sounded a bit down at the tail end of his message.

Thane leaned back in the chair. Maybe he needed to let the past go. If it didn't hurt as much as it did, he would have.

"Final message."

Good. Thane didn't know how much more of his past mistakes he could take in one sitting.

"Hi, Queen. It's Arlene Sortoberg calling about the girls. I'll be there around the first or second week of March with the girls to try on dresses. I appreciate that you do this for the Rosa Parks Middle School students each year. You don't know how much it makes their day." The woman's bubbly voice echoed in the small office.

Thane pulled out his phone and glanced at the date. With it being the middle of the second week in March, maybe this woman had forgotten.

As though he'd cued it, a knock sounded at the door. He thought about avoiding the person on the other side. He could sit still in the office and act like he hadn't heard it. He made the mistake of peeking through the doorway from his seated position to view the front door. A corner of a newspaper that hung in the window remained pulled down, allowing the person at the door to look through and spot him.

"Oh, hello!" A plump woman beamed as soon as she made eye contact with him. She waved at him and pointed to the door.

"Great." He lumbered to his feet and made a slow trek to her.

He unlocked the door but blocked her entry.

"Oh, my. Aren't you a—" She fanned her face. "I don't remember you here at Sharp."

With the chill of the spring air down at the Oceanfront, no way could she be hot. He shivered thinking that he could have elevated her temperature.

In her purple top and matching pants and purple suede boots, she looked like a grape. It didn't help that she'd topped her look with a green hat. Her light brown skin tone almost matched his mother's, but she looked a bit ashen. The piles of makeup she used to cover a multitude of sins didn't help her cause.

Her eyes widened and she pointed at him. "I know you."

Thane had expected her to talk about his baseball career.

"You're Queen's boy, the one who helped her around here. I haven't seen you here in years." She opened her arms and pulled him in for an unexpected hug.

The large woman caused Thane to stumble backward into the store.

"Thane Wells. I'm Elizabeth's son." He pried himself out of her grasp.

"Arlene Sortoberg. I'm a counselor at Rosa Parks Middle. You and your mother have done great things for the girls at the school." She smiled and patted him on his shoulder. "Where is Queen? I was hoping to see her."

Thane felt like a waterfall of ice water had dropped on him. He had assumed everyone who knew his mother knew about her passing. "My mother passed away about a week ago. Her funeral was earlier this week."

Arlene covered her mouth with her chubby fingers. "Oh, no. I had no idea." She fanned her face again, but for a different reason.

"Let me get you a chair." Thane darted to a dressing room and pulled out a wooden chair. He placed it next to Arlene and helped her take a seat.

"Thank you." She shook her head. "It sounds silly, but I never thought Queen would ever die." She pulled out a couple of tissues from her large red purse. "When kids come to me when they experience death in their families, I tell them how death is a part of life. I need to give myself that pep talk." She dabbed under her eyes, careful not to remove any of her caked-on makeup. Then she peered up at Thane. "It's great that you're continuing your mother's work."

He sighed. "That's the thing, Ms. Sortoberg. I'm—"

Arlene cut off his speech. "Your mother did such great things. She was so generous and giving." She dove into her purse again.

"Yes, she was. I know you getting these dresses is important to you."

"And the girls."

Thane nodded. "Yes, but—"

"I need to give you this." Arlene pulled an envelope from her purse and held it up to Thane.

He didn't want to take it until he looked at the outside and recognized his mother's handwriting. He didn't mean to, but he snatched it from Arlene's hand.

"I got that in the mail earlier this year from Queen with a note saying not open it, but to bring it with me when I came to get the dresses. She said to give it to whoever was here if she wasn't."

Thane tore into the envelope and read the letter.

If you're reading this, that means I'm no longer here. I'm either enjoying myself at my beach house or I'm at that big beach house in the sky.

He smiled at the reference.

Whoever is here when Arlene comes in, be sure to help her and those girls. They don't have a lot. These dresses give them some self-worth. Stand up straight. Always say please and thank you. I love you.

Thane stared at Arlene. "You got this earlier this year?"

She nodded. "It was in my Christmas card, but I didn't open it until January. I spent my two weeks' vacation from school visiting my oldest boy in Michigan."

Elizabeth must have known about her failing health before she went into the hospital the first time. The fact that this woman had kept the letter in her purse all this while amazed him. It could have been a check for a million dollars. It wouldn't be out of his mother's character to do something like that. He crumpled the letter and ran his free hand over his head.

"So I'll be back here on Friday with about twelve girls, okay?" Arlene nodded.

"Great."

Chapter 11

Kari hadn't stopped thinking about the kiss since it happened that morning. She wanted to push it and Thane's disappointed expression out of her mind, chalk it all up to bad decisions. Now she had to think about her next step. She couldn't go back to work with her tail tucked between her legs. She'd promised Frank she could sign Thane to their agency. If she didn't, she could kiss her chances of a promotion good-bye.

She would have to avoid catching up with her boss and Chelsi on her progress. She had other priorities.

As Kari sat in her hotel room, she picked up her phone and called Reagan.

"Hey, boss." Reagan's voice sounded light.

Must be a good day at home.

"Hey. How's my little man?" Kari crossed her legs.

"Excellent and exceptional, of course. How are you doing? How's the headhunting going?"

"Okay." She peered up and caught her reflection in a mirror over the dresser. She wondered if her lips looked different than before. Had the kiss made them swell?

She touched them, brushing her fingertips over the thin skin. It brought her back to memories of the man who had possessed them without apology. Her skin tingled like it had only a few hours ago. Kari ran her hand up her arm and averted her gaze from the mirror.

"Hey, I was thinking maybe you two can pack a bag and come on down to Virginia Beach to hang with me for a week." Kari twirled her hair around her finger, a habit she thought she'd long outgrown.

"Whoa. Really?" A pause lingered before Reagan spoke. "What happened with the pitcher? Did he sign already?"

Kari kicked around the idea of lying to her friend, but she could barely look at her reflection now. She couldn't imagine avoiding Reagan's stare. "Let's just say that I want to enjoy a week with my family and friends before I get fired."

"Holy crap. That bad? Are you sure? Maybe it's—"

"Michael's out of school on Friday, right?" Kari stood from the bed and strolled over to the desk in her room where she had her tablet. She kept a constant vigil over all gossip sites to see if any of them reported information about Thane.

"Yes, half a day tomorrow and off on Friday and all next week for spring break."

Kari smiled. She couldn't wait to see her baby again. He would give her balance. "Good. Drive down here on Thursday after he gets out of—"

"Hey, stop on third. Don't slide on home. You know me and driving long distances. Not a good thing."

Kari imagined Reagan shaking her head and tightening her already thin lips.

"Okay, fine. I'll pay for a one-way flight down to Virginia Beach. I'll pick you two up at the Norfolk Airport and bring you over to my hotel. Will that work for you?" She moved off the tabloid site to make travel arrangements for Reagan and Michael.

"First class?"

"Don't push it. Michael's passport is in my desk drawer. Be sure to pack his bathing suits and plenty of underwear. The hotel has an indoor pool. And it's chilly here so lots of hoodies, long pants, and socks." Her son would hate to hear how much she fussed over him.

She also imagined that he wouldn't be too happy to hear about him going so far away from New York when his father would be there. Kari would have to make it up to him somehow.

"You got it, boss. See you later."

Kari disconnected the call. She stared at her phone. She reviewed the calls she'd recently received. When she saw Thane's name and number, she almost smiled. Again, that passionate kiss filled her thoughts.

His scruffy beard felt better against her skin than she'd imagined. In his hands, she'd felt safe and desired all at once without him having to touch her breast or her ass. She brushed her ear when she remembered how he'd whispered, *"Stay."*

Her body screamed for her to drop her silly rules and give this man a ride. She couldn't. She had more at stake than her job. A man like Thane Wells could damage her already fragile perception of men and relationships.

Kari threw her phone on the bed and made the reservations for her child and his nanny. She didn't care that they would get in late on Thursday. The sooner she could get them down with her, the better.

When her phone rang, she immediately thought it would be Reagan complaining about the time of the flight or the seat assignment. When she saw her boss's name across the screen, she shoved her phone into her purse. Kari didn't know how to explain to Frank that she hadn't gotten her client because she'd decided to be ethical and not sleep with him.

A walk. That would help her clear her head. Kari slipped on her trusty white Keds and grabbed her purse and room key. Even though tourist season hadn't officially started, she could still enjoy a peaceful stroll on the boardwalk.

The crashing waves along with the seagulls' call offered her some peace. She filled her mind with thoughts of what to do with her child while he visited her. Where would she take him? What would he like to see? When she passed the closed fun house, she had to smile. Michael would have loved something like that. Maybe she could bring him back down to Virginia Beach in the summer when the Oceanfront area came alive.

After walking a couple of miles down the boardwalk, Kari bought herself a coffee from a small diner and headed back to her hotel room. She heard her phone chime in her purse again. For a split moment, she thought about not looking at it. She knew it would be Frank calling a second time. Then she thought about Michael and realized it could be Reagan.

She dove into her purse and pulled out her phone. When she saw Thane's name across the screen, her heart thrummed.

Going against her better judgment, she answered the call. "Kari Meyers speaking." If she kept up the professional tone, he would get the hint that she had no designs on slipping her standards.

"I need to apologize for this morning." His husky voice rumbled through her phone.

"No, you don't. I shouldn't have kissed your cheeks. I wouldn't have done that with anyone else. I crossed the line. I'm sor—" She stopped herself when she remembered what Thane had told her last night. "I apologize."

"I would like to see you again...to talk about business, of course. I have a dinner date tonight."

Kari's heart slowed. "Oh. Okay."

It hadn't taken Thane long to find someone to put in her place.

"I'm having dinner with my brother Gideon. Nothing else," he quickly supplied.

She smiled and continued walking. "After you asked me to leave this morning, I didn't think you would want to see me again. I definitely didn't think you would want to do business with me."

"Only an impetuous young man would turn down a potential business relationship because of a misunderstanding. I told you, I'm patient." Thane's voice dipped down lower. "I have some time right now. Are you able to meet me?"

Kari's insides did cartwheels. Before she could allow herself to say yes, she blurted, "I can't. I have to go to the airport tonight."

"What? You can't—"

"You have my contract. If you're serious about signing with me, do it and send the contracts to the address at the bottom of the last page." She threw her coffee cup in the trash can outside of her hotel's front door.

As soon as she stepped inside, an employee said, "Welcome to the Cavalier."

Kari smiled and went to the elevators. "Unless you need me for anything else, I don't think it will be wise to meet again, at least not in hotel rooms. Good day, Mr. Wells."

Before he could mount any kind of argument, Kari disconnected the call and put her phone on mute. She didn't need the interruptions or the distractions. If Thane really wanted to do business with her, he had all her information. She would wait and see what he had in store.

* * * *

Thane thought about flaking out on Gideon on purpose this time. He couldn't get that close to perfection only to lose her. He couldn't believe after the kiss they shared that morning that she wanted to hop on a plane and leave.

He came up to the guard shack into Gideon's complex. An Asian woman occupied the small space.

She smiled at him. "How can I help you?"

"I'm here to see Gideon Wells." Thane smiled back only to be pleasant.

His agreeable expression waned as soon as she scowled at him.

"What's your name? What is your business with Mr. Wells?" She picked up a clipboard and scanned it.

"I'm Thane, his brother. I'm here for dinner. That's all. Do you need to see my ID?" He started to reach in his back pocket for his wallet.

By that time, the woman had picked up a phone and punched in a series of numbers. Good Lord. Had she called the police on him? He knew Gideon lived in a secured area, but this seemed extreme.

"Hi, Mr. Wells. I have a—" She leaned her head out of the guard shack window. "Your name?"

Thane sighed before he answered. "Thane Wells."

"A Thane Wells here to see you." The woman kept her gaze down as she listened intently. "Really? He doesn't look like you or Gunnar."

Thane settled back into his seat and waited for this humiliating moment to be over.

"Okay. Yes, sir." She disconnected the call. "Put this on your dashboard. Be sure to discard it in the box on your way out." She lifted the gate. "Have a good night, sir."

Thane powered up his window and rolled through the barrier. By the time he got to Gideon's home nestled in the back, he had calmed down from hearing the guard's comment. He parked in front of the house and strolled up to the door.

He didn't need to ring the bell or knock. It opened as soon as he approached. Janelle smiled as he strolled toward her.

"Janelle, right?" He remembered her from the funeral but wanted to make sure he didn't mess up her name.

She nodded. "Yes, Thane. Great to have you here." She wrapped her arms around his shoulders for a big hug.

She smelled like the outdoors, but in a floral sense. Not like grass or wood. Like violet and lilac. No wonder Gideon had fallen for her.

She pulled back from him and ushered him into the house. "Let me get your jacket. Your brother is in the kitchen. He refuses to sit down and let me cook." She closed the door and headed to a closet. "Will you please talk some sense into him?"

"Impossible. Gideon is a Wells. That means he's headstrong and stubborn." Thane headed toward the kitchen.

He saw Gideon hobbling behind the counter, going from one pot on the stove to the refrigerator. Gideon had his blond hair pulled back in a ponytail, a look Thane recalled Gunnar having not too long ago. Today Gideon wore a simple black T-shirt and long gym shorts. The shorts allowed Thane to get a good look at the brace around his knee.

"Should you be doing that much moving around?" Thane strolled into the kitchen and gave his brother a hug while Gideon continued with his mad rush to prepare dinner.

"Damn, you're on time for once." Gideon braced his hands on the counter. "A bit behind but no worries." He nodded toward the stainless steel fridge. "Will you get out the salad and put it on the table, please?"

"Sure." On the way to the professional-size icebox, he asked, "No, seriously. Should you be doing all of this? Janelle said she offered to help you."

"She did. I'm fine." He lowered his head for a second. "I promised I wouldn't say that anymore. My knee hurts. But it's okay. I feel good in the kitchen. Feel like my old self. Remember how Mom taught us all to cook?"

Thane pulled out a big wooden bowl filled with spinach leaves, cut-up tomatoes, cucumber slices, sliced mushrooms, and slivers of almonds. He carried it to the dining room table and placed it in the center. Thankfully, he only noticed three place settings. Thane didn't need any surprises like Gunnar showing up out of the blue.

"I remember Mom having to teach you and Gunnar how to cook because you were about to leave home. After you two left, Mom let me fix all the dinners. I think she got tired of cooking for us boys for all those years." Thane fondly remembered how much fun it used to be to prepare dinner. He missed doing that for someone.

"Yeah, I listened. Gunnar, well—"

"Is he still eating pasta and toast?"

Gideon laughed. "I think so. Probably not though. Eboni is really good to him. You remember her, right?"

Thane nodded. "Candy girl."

Gideon furrowed his eyebrows.

"So that she and Gunnar could do bad stuff together, she would feed me candy to keep me from telling Mom when Gunnar climbed out his window." Thane patted his belly. "Thank goodness he did leave the house. Otherwise I would be a butterball."

Janelle strolled into the kitchen. "Honey, will you please sit down and enjoy time with your brother? I'll get the rest of the dinner."

Gideon scanned the items on the stove. "The corn is done."

"Okay, dear." She put her hands to his chest and walked him backward out of the kitchen area.

"I put the rolls in the oven. They should be ready in about ten minutes." Gideon pointed to the oven.

"Got it, honey." She eased him back to the dining room.

Thane took a cue from her movement and pulled a chair out for Gideon.

"I took the roast out. It needs to rest a bit."

Janelle got him to sit. When he did, she kissed him. Thane liked seeing his brother so in love with a woman who truly adored him.

"I love you." She kissed his cheek. "I'll bring dinner out."

When she disappeared into the kitchen, Thane leaned forward. "Looks like she's good for you."

Gideon stared at her working in the kitchen. "Yeah, I got really lucky." He turned to Thane. "You'll find the one once you stop messing around."

Thane took a seat next to Gideon. "I'm not as much of a player as you all think." He felt the heat creeping up under his collar.

To get Gideon on his side, he would hold off trying to argue with him.

"Sure. Whatever you say." Gideon patted Thane on his shoulder.

This would be a long dinner. Thane hoped he could make it a quick meal. During his earlier phone conversation with Kari, he caught a hotel staffer saying the name of the hotel. Now that he knew how to find her and what she drove, he would be able to locate her. Now if he only knew when she planned on leaving.

Gideon truly outdid himself with dinner. The food reminded Thane of Elizabeth's cooking, even down to the amount of spices used. Gideon had proved to be a good student when Mom taught him how to cook.

As Thane watched Gideon and Janelle interact with each other, he understood why they worked so well together. Thane watched Gideon fighting the urge to get up and get things for himself. She waited on him but also stood toe to toe with him on issues.

"How did you two meet? Gideon never told me." Thane volleyed his attention between Gideon and Janelle.

"Gideon had won the Super Bowl." Janelle stared at Gideon as she told the story.

"My *team* did. I couldn't have done it without them." Gideon brushed his thumb over Janelle's cheek.

"Gunnar had been shot that night, and Gideon rushed home. As soon as he got to town, he took over your mother's flower shop. He came over to my flower shop to ask for help." Janelle giggled like she knew a secret. "Apparently, Queen Elizabeth told him that if he needed anything, to come see me."

"She refused to help me." Gideon's smile widened.

Thane blinked. "Really? Football hero and you didn't want to help him?"

"At the time, I really didn't know him. I was barely scraping by at Flowers Galore, and I didn't want to give up anything or ask for help. He wore me down." Janelle broke her stare from Gideon for a moment to address Thane directly. "I've never met a man like Gideon. I love him so much." She leaned forward to kiss Gideon.

"Wow. Nice. Sounds like you two belong together." Unlike he and Kari. Thane glanced at the clock on the wall. "So what's going to happen when your knee gets better?"

Gideon held Janelle's hand. "Training starts about June or July. Luckily, it'll be in Richmond."

"You're not going to commute, are you? That's a heck of a drive."

"Janelle will be running the flower shop. Otherwise I would have her stay with me in Richmond. I don't mind the two-plus-hour drive as long as I get to see her every day." He cupped her cheek.

"I told him he would be crazy to do that. I think Victor will be fine running the store for the week."

"Business has increased so much since I took over Pick 'N Clip. It's too much work for Victor by himself." Gideon shook his head.

"He'll have Penny with him." She squeezed his hand. "I hate the idea of you traveling so far each day."

"You make sacrifices for love." Gideon looked at Thane. "Mom did it for us."

Janelle stood. "Anyone want any coffee?"

Thane shook his head. "None for me."

"I'm good, honey." Gideon patted her hip.

"I'll clear off the table and clean up the kitchen." She picked up a couple of plates. As Gideon started to stand, she put a free hand on his shoulder. "Don't help me, please. You and your brother go in the den to talk." She kissed him on his cheek before going into the kitchen.

"Come with me." Gideon stood. "I'm afraid if I step into the kitchen, she'll take out my other leg."

Thane stood and followed his brother into a room Gideon kept dimly lit. "Look, I can't stay very long."

Gideon glared at him before taking a seat. "Really? I thought you would want to talk about Mom and the good ol' days. I didn't know you had an agenda."

Thane took a seat across from him. He glossed over Gideon's comments to say what he needed to express. "I loved Mom. I loved what she did for us. I appreciate all the sacrifices she made. No one gets that more than me."

Gideon's eyes widened. "You don't think Gun and I get all that Mom did? We were old enough to experience the difference. You were a baby. You had no idea how rough we had it."

"Mom taught us to fight for what we wanted and to chase after our dreams. You wanted to be a football player. Now look at you." Thane glanced down at Gideon's hand. "Nice ring."

Gideon kept his stare on Thane while he brushed his thumb over the underside of the ring.

"Gunnar wanted to do this ultimate fighting thing. He did that. And now he's choosing to step back from that career. You get to go on with yours when training starts. My training is going on now. My season will be starting soon. I can't run Sharp and play baseball. As much as I loved and appreciated Mom, I need to sell that business." He braced his elbows on his knees. "Ms. Sortoberg came by earlier today about the girls at Rosa Parks. She wants to come over Friday to get twelve dresses, and that's the day I had planned on going back to Florida."

"So this trip, the dinner, that was your way to convince me to sign some agreement so that you can sell the store?" Gideon propped his leg up on an ottoman as he continued glaring at Thane.

"It wasn't all about that." Thane dropped his gaze to the floor.

"Liar. I can always tell when you're not telling the truth." Gideon adjusted his seated position. "Have you even tried finding someone to manage it for you? You don't have to be there."

"I don't want the responsibility of owning it."

"You could have stopped that sentence at the word *responsibility*. Mom would be so disappointed if she knew you wanted to sell something that meant a lot to her and that she probably thought meant a lot to you." Gideon shook his head.

"You're one to talk. You have someone running your shop. You didn't have to interview anyone or change your life." Thane felt that same tickling heat engulfing his chest. The sensation took no time burning its way down to his stomach. He coughed and hoped nothing would come back up and allow Gideon to worry about him.

Gideon brought his injured leg down and leaned forward. "You don't think losing Mom changed my life?" He peered over his shoulder before he continued his conversation with Thane. "You selfish bastard. I love you, but I don't like you right now. While you're here in town, you're more than welcome to stay with me. And you can come over to my house whenever you want. But we will not talk about this anymore until you sit down and actually think about everything you're doing."

Thane had known convincing his brothers about his plan to sell would be hard. He'd thought Gideon would be an easier to persuade than Gunnar.

He stood from the couch and made his way over to Gideon. "Thanks for dinner. Be sure to tell Janelle good-bye from me."

"Think about your decisions, Thane. Do the right thing." Gideon brought Thane down for a hug.

Thane pulled back as quick as he could to get out of the house. He sped through the streets in Gideon's neighborhood before finally getting out to the main road. He drove a few miles down to Kari's hotel.

He rolled around the parking lot first to look for her vehicle. When he didn't find it, he parked and went inside. A few guests recognized him, evident from the way they pointed and whispered. Thankfully, no one stopped him.

He went up to the front desk. "I need to leave a message for one of your guests."

The clerk's eyes widened before he settled down and grabbed a pad and pen. "Yes, sir."

"Do you have a guest here by the name of Kari Meyers?"

The clerk released the pen to type something on the computer. "Yes, I still show she's registered."

Good. She hadn't checked out yet. Maybe she'd told him that story about going to the airport to throw him off.

"The message, sir?" the clerk asked.

"Will you please leave a note that says point two-three-four?"

The young man stared at Thane for a moment. "That's all?"

Thane nodded. "She'll understand."

He walked away from the desk to go to his car. From the corner of his eye, he saw a car that looked like Kari's pulling out of the lot.

Thane jumped into his vehicle to follow it. When the car headed toward Norfolk, he relaxed a little.

He made sure to keep a safe distance while keeping an eye on it. When it got off on the exit going toward the airport, Thane's heart pounded. He kept a tail on it all the way to the front area to pick up and drop off passengers.

The car stopped at the curb. Thane pulled up behind a car that sat behind the one he suspected belonged to Kari. When the door opened and Kari stepped out, he gripped his seat to keep from jumping out and grabbing her.

When she got inside the building, he wasted no time in getting out and following her.

* * * *

Kari scanned the baggage claim area for Reagan and Michael. Reagan had sent her a text as soon as they'd landed. She had hoped by the time she got to the airport the duo would be outside waiting for her.

"I guess you aren't going anywhere."

Kari turned around and nearly choked on air when she saw Thane walking toward her. "What are you doing here?"

"You found me at my hotel. I did my own detective work and found you. I thought you were leaving." He stood in front of her.

"I never said I was leaving. I said I had to go to the airport." She crossed her arms over her chest.

She wanted to be angry that he'd found her. Instead, she felt bubbly inside like a lovesick girl. The closer he got, the more her bubbles turned into searing coals, eating away at her insides.

"So who are you waiting for?" Thane scanned the area.

"That's none of your business." She peered over the carousel and spotted Reagan coming out of the women's bathroom with Michael. "I need you to leave."

"Why? Who are you hiding?" Thane started to follow her. "Are you waiting for your husband?"

"No. I told you I'm not married. Please go." Kari started to head toward Reagan.

"Is that your sister?"

"No," Kari growled. Then she stopped and faced him. "I get it. You feel I've invaded your space, so you're paying me back."

"You're partially right." He moved in closer to her. "You've invaded my thoughts."

Kari swallowed hard. "I'm not an oddity."

"Yes, you are. You fascinate me. I want to know more about the woman who likes watching sports, knows all of my stats, and kisses like you invented the act."

Talk about bad timing. She didn't want Thane meeting or even seeing her child. When Michael spotted Kari, he ran right to her.

"There's nothing fascinating about me." Kari turned back to her son.

"Mom!" Michael ran into her arms.

"Mom?" Thane stopped in his tracks.

Michael looked over Kari's shoulder. "Is this your surprise? Whoa, Thane Wells from the Carolina Wrens. Awesome!"

Chapter 12

Kari didn't want Thane this involved in her personal life. She only wanted to sign him on as a client and have a normal life with her child. Now she stood with Michael in front of her, Thane staring at her like she had tentacles growing from her shoulders, and her friend, Reagan, loving every minute of it.

"You are an awesome pitcher." Michael pointed to Thane.

"You think so?" Thane strained to be polite to Kari's son by looking down at him, but his focus kept getting redirected back to her.

"Yeah. Mom and I watch your games on TV all the time." He looped his thumbs into the shoulder straps of his Teenage Mutant Ninja Turtles backpack.

"Really?" That made Thane keep his stare on Kari.

She wanted the floor at the Norfolk International Airport to open up and swallow her. Kari patted Michael on his shoulder. "Honey, let's not hold Mr. Wells up. I'm sure he has better things to do than talk to us."

"Whenever we watch you play, Mom says she likes when you start to pitch." Michael nodded and crossed his feet. "She says you have a great form."

Reagan snickered. Kari, not caring if Thane caught her, jabbed her employee with her elbow.

"Good to see that your mom appreciates my…form." Thane gave Kari a quick wink. "Excuse my manners. We have not been properly introduced. You know who I am, but I don't know your name." He bent over and extended his hand.

Michael looked at Thane's hand before gazing up at Kari, who still hadn't wrapped her mind around this entire situation.

"This is my son, Michael." Kari patted her young child on his head, which signaled him to shake Thane's hand.

"Nice to meet you, Mr. Wells." Michael beamed.

"You can call me Thane."

"No, he can't. He knows to call adults by their last name." Kari didn't need her child to get too comfortable with Thane.

"But, Mom, I call Reagan by her first name, and she's an adult." Michael pouted as he pointed to his nanny.

When Kari looked at Reagan, she noticed the woman's shoulders shaking from her failed attempt to hide her laughter.

"She's barely an adult." Kari shook her head.

"Hey, I resemble that remark." Reagan looked at Thane. "I'm Reagan Amaba. I'm Michael's nanny." She shook Thane's hand.

"Thane Wells." He nodded.

"I don't need a babysitter. I'm old enough to take care of myself." Michael crossed his arms over his chest. "She mainly helps me with my homework."

"Is that right?" Thane regarded Michael seriously. "So you must be really smart."

"I like this guy already." Reagan laughed.

"You might like this even more." Thane reached into his pocket and pulled out a key. "Why don't you and Michael ride to the hotel in my Lexus, and I'll catch a ride back with Kari?"

When Reagan said, "Hell yes", Kari said, "Absolutely not" at the same time.

"Wow! Your Lexus?" Michael jumped around Kari. "So cool. So cool." He repeated the phrase as he hopped.

"Will you excuse us for a second?" She managed to grab Thane's arm to pull him away from Reagan and Michael.

"I'm in trouble, aren't I?" he mused.

"What do you think you're doing?" Kari stood toe to toe with him.

"I think I'm trying my best to get to know you and you're fighting it. Why didn't you tell me you have a son?" Thane stared at her and didn't move.

"Because I didn't want you to know. I want you—"

He cut her off. "You do?"

She took a breath before she continued talking. "I want you as a client. You don't need to know what's going on in my home."

"What if I told you that I want my agent to know what's going on with me beyond what I do on the field?" He lowered his voice when he made the query.

"I'd say that this isn't Jerry McGuire. You should want me—"

"I do."

Kari's breathing increased as she looked at the man in front of her. To break the spell, she turned to her family only to see empty spots where they once stood.

She headed to the front of the building where she'd parked her car. "We can talk about this another time. Right now, I have my son here with me to show him a good time during spring break."

By the time she got outside, she saw a silver Lexus rolling by her. It slowed down to almost a stop.

When the window rolled down, she spotted Reagan in the driver's seat.

"Reagan, what are you doing?" Kari rushed toward the vehicle.

"Enjoying Virginia Beach. This ride is sick." She nodded her head.

The backseat window rolled down and Michael popped his head out. "This is so cool. Mom, I'm having a great time."

"I have the Cavalier address programmed in the mapping system. Use that to get to the hotel." Thane pointed toward the dashboard. "We'll meet you there."

"Don't you dare pull off." Kari grabbed the passenger side door and glared at her soon-to-be-fired friend. "Get out and get into my car."

"Sorry. This is a once-in-a-lifetime opportunity. I'm not going to pass this up. I suggest you take that advice yourself." Reagan winked and nodded toward Thane. "See you at the hotel." She sped off.

"Damn." Kari turned to Thane. "How did she get your key?"

Thane smiled. "When you pulled me away from them, I threw it over my head to her. I am a great pitcher. Your son even said so." He held up his bent arm to her. "Can we leave now? We don't want them waiting for us too long."

* * * *

Thane knew Kari protected her privacy. He'd also suspected she hid certain aspects of her life. A child. He hadn't seen that coming. It made sense. Her protective nature over him when he'd had too much to drink. Her drive and determination. Those qualities reminded him of his mother. Kari had something extra.

On the drive back to the Virginia Beach hotel, Kari remained quiet. She kept her stare on the road. Thane couldn't believe she even let him in her car. He suspected she would have been happy to let him stand on the curb without a ride.

"How old is Michael?" he asked to break the ice.

She remained quiet. Her lips tightened, a bad look considering the lusciousness of them.

"Come on. You can share some things with me. You did crash my mother's funeral."

Kari turned to him. "I didn't. Not on purpose." She huffed. "Ten."

"Wow. You were sixteen?" Thane thought taking on three youngsters had been hard. He couldn't imagine trying to be a parent at a young age. "Where's the father?"

She shook her head. "We're not together."

"Is that recent? The breakup?"

Kari remained silent for a beat before she answered. "No. He was out of the picture as soon as I told him I was pregnant." She took a deep breath before she continued. "He made a lot of accusations about me. For the longest time, I thought it was my fault. If I loved him more or stayed by his side all the time, he wouldn't have…" She trailed off.

"What?"

She shook her head. "Never mind. It took me a long time to understand that I can't control anyone else. My mistakes are my mistakes."

"You're not calling your son a mistake, are you?" He couldn't imagine Kari could be that cold.

"Of course not. Michael is the best thing that has ever happened to me." She got a faraway look in her eyes before she started smiling. "When Michael was a baby, he was so happy. He laughed at everything. He is so smart. He definitely keeps me on my toes."

"You didn't do him any favors with his name." Thane chuckled.

"What are you talking about?"

"Michael Meyers? Come on. Kids into horror flicks are going to tease him."

"He has his father's last name." She glanced at Thane briefly before returning her gaze to the road.

Thane considered everything she'd said. "You gave Michael his father's name, and he still didn't come back."

Kari shrugged. "I wanted us to be a family. I hadn't had that. I lost my parents. My grandfather lasted long enough for me to get through college and find a job, and then he died."

Thane couldn't help himself. He put his hand on Kari's, which caused her to gasp and turn to him.

"I think you've done a great job." He stroked his thumb over the back of her hand.

Kari pulled into the Cavalier parking lot and parked her rental in a darkened area. Thane heard her breathing increase. She slipped her hand from under his to turn off the lights and the car. Even in the dark, he saw her eyes.

"My family is inside, waiting for me." She said it in a way like she needed to convince herself not to do something foolish.

"Okay. Let's go." Thane didn't make a move.

Sitting still gave Kari the opportunity to place her hand on his leg. She brushed her thumb over his knee.

"I'm here for my son."

"Nothing has to happen." He placed his hand on hers.

The longer he stared at her, the more he wanted her. He brought his face closer to hers. The motion prompted her to action.

Kari backed away from him. "I need to get my child in the room so he can get some sleep. It's late." She unlocked her door and bolted from the car.

Thane had to be as quick. He slammed the door and followed her to the front of the hotel. He spotted his rental vehicle parked in a space close to the door. Once inside, Kari darted toward her family.

"Ready to go to the room?" she asked breathlessly.

Reagan's eyebrows furrowed. "You can give me the room key if you have other plans." She put her hand on Michael's shoulder. "This guy is tired. He fell asleep on the way to the hotel."

"I did not." Michael rubbed his eyes and leaned his head against Reagan's stomach.

"Thanks for letting us ride in your car." Reagan tossed the key to Thane.

"Not a problem. Anytime." He turned to Kari. "You think you and I can—"

"Good night, Mr. Wells." Kari rushed toward the elevator, pulling Reagan with her.

"Um, nice meeting you." Reagan waved as she dragged a suitcase behind her.

"See ya, Mr. Wells." Michael gave Thane a sleepy wave as he trotted alongside his mother.

"Kari?" Thane began.

Kari waited until the elevator doors opened and she stepped inside before she looked at him.

"You know where to find me." Thane winked.

Chapter 13

"What the hell was that?" Reagan didn't wait for Kari to close the bedroom door after tucking Michael in to tear into her. "It was so obvious that Thane Wells wants to get to know you better, and I mean in the biblical sense."

"Will you stop it? You know his reputation." Kari sat on the couch and picked up a remote.

Reagan snatched it from Kari's hand and slammed it on the coffee table. "Don't deny yourself. Even if you don't get his business, you can get into his business, if you know what I mean."

Kari let the thought roll around for a moment before she shook her head. "I've been burned by an athlete before. I can't go through that again."

"Stop. Just because Jarrod was an asshole, doesn't mean every athlete you meet will be like him." Reagan sat next to Kari. "I'm here. Michael will sleep through the night. You will not be a bad mother if you steal away some time for yourself."

"But I brought you two down here for all of us to be together."

"No. You brought Michael to Virginia Beach to show him a good time. That good time could be had with me or with you."

Kari chuckled. "Now you sound like Thane."

"He makes a lot of sense." Reagan held Kari's hand. "Do you know where he's staying?"

Kari waited a beat before she nodded.

Reagan stood and went to the bathroom. She came out with Kari's personal hygiene bag and handed it to her.

"Why are you giving me this?" Kari accepted it while glaring at Reagan.

"I figured you would want to brush your teeth." She smiled and winked.

Kari stood. She padded over to her friend, brought Reagan's hand up, and plopped the bag into it. "Take it right back to the bathroom." She waited a beat before she smiled. "I keep a toothbrush and toothpaste in my purse."

"Go get your man. We'll be fine. If you're not back when little man gets up, I'll call you so we can all go out to breakfast."

Kari shook her head. "No. I don't want Michael getting attached. It's bad enough I'm even thinking of doing this."

"So don't think. Do." Reagan handed Kari her purse and keys. "I keep snacks in my purse so we'll eat something. I can take him down to the pool at least. Don't worry about us. Oh." She reached into her pocket and pulled out a small box of condoms. "I had time to stop at a convenience store before we got here. That car is really fast."

Kari shoved the box in her bag. "This is crazy. I'll go there to talk to him. That's it. We'll talk."

Reagan nodded. "Whatever happens, happens."

Kari hugged Reagan before leaving. She hoped Thane still wanted her like he'd seemed to only moments ago.

As soon as the elevator doors opened at the lobby, Kari darted out like a racehorse.

"Ms. Meyers."

She wanted to act like she didn't hear the guy behind the registration desk, but she couldn't ignore him. Kari attempted to smile but felt her mouth go tight.

"Yes?" she asked quickly.

"There's a message for you." He handed her a small envelope.

"Um, thank you." She accepted it tentatively.

Since she refused to answer Frank or Chelsi's calls, she had a feeling they resorted to leaving her notes at the front desk. She opened it and simply saw *234*. She had to go get this man.

She sped over to Thane's hotel and parked close to his Lexus. When she got inside, a night security guard stopped her. Where was this guy when the lobby had been filled with reporters? Maybe the hotel had hired him because of that incident.

"Room key, please." He stared at her in a way that would probably crumble a lot of people.

Kari had stared into the faces of tough MMA fighters and boxers and never flinched. "I don't have a room. I'm here to see a guest."

"Who?"

"That's none of your business. I know where his room is." She attempted to go around him, but the beefy guard blocked her path.

"No key. No admittance."

It shocked her that this muscle-bound wall knew such a big word. She went into her purse and pulled out her phone. She hit one key to dial Thane's number.

"Hey." Even over the phone, he sounded sexy.

"I'm in the lobby." Kari kept her stare on the guard.

"Come on up."

"Can't. This guard said, wait, what was that again? No key. No admittance?"

"Hold on." A pause lingered.

Kari heard a phone ringing behind the front desk. She kept her attention on the clerk who answered it. He glanced at Kari and the guard. When he hung up the phone, he took no time in running over to her.

"Excuse me, Ms. Meyers. I apologize for delaying your visit." The young man split his attention between her and the guard, who didn't look happy to have his authority usurped. "Right this way."

Kari listened in on her phone. "Thane?"

"Are you on your way?" he asked.

"Yes. Getting escorted to the elevator."

"Good. See you in a bit."

The clerk called the elevator for her and hit the button for Thane's floor. "If there's anything you need, please don't hesitate to ask."

"Thank you. I think we'll be fine." She wished she could convince her knees of that. Since calling Thane, they hadn't stopped knocking together.

When the car stopped on his floor, she took a deep breath before stepping out. She strolled down the hallway, the same one she had walked down when she helped him get to his room.

She almost expected to see Thane standing outside his room waiting for her. When she got to his door, she knocked and waited. After a moment, he opened it.

Thane had removed his shoes and socks, and taken off his jacket and sweater. He stood in bare feet wearing a T-shirt and jeans.

"Come in." He stood off to the side to allow her to pass.

Kari tried to look confident as she walked inside. She figured the way she wrung the strap on her purse betrayed her cool front.

"Would you like something to drink?" he asked from behind her.

She shook her head, unable, or rather unwilling, to speak.

"Are you hungry?"

Kari turned to him. "No."

Thane slipped the purse strap from her shoulder and placed her bag on the dining room table. Then he eased his hands over her shoulders to remove her jacket. With it off, she only had on a long maxi dress and her Keds, not sexy at all. The way Thane stared at her, it looked like he viewed her in a sexy corset and thong panties.

"I don't know what I'm doing here." She whispered the words.

"No pressure." Thane shook his head. "We don't have to do anything."

His normally bright blue eyes darkened as he spoke.

"I haven't done this in a long time."

He stopped moving as he looked at her. "Seriously?"

She nodded. "I dated a guy a few years ago. I never introduced him to Michael. We did it a couple of times and that was it. I was content to remain single until Michael graduated from college."

"And now?"

She stared into his eyes. "I'm scared. I don't do fear very well."

He lowered his head and brushed his lips over hers, slow at first, never putting his full pressure on her. Kari felt the motion seemed fitting for what he'd said to her. No pressure. He didn't want to push her to do anything she didn't want.

Kari's breathing increased. She backed away from him. "I think I need to sit down."

"Are you okay?" He helped her to the sofa.

"It's all a bit too much to take." She stared at her purse sitting on the dining room table.

Kari had condoms inside in preparation of bedding this man. When the fantasy started to come into focus as reality, it hit her hard.

As she looked at him, the same hot feelings she felt earlier flooded her body. She stroked the side of his face. "I do want you." With that admission, the heaviness escaped the room. Kari could take in a deep breath.

"Let me take care of you." Thane spoke like a man who knew what to do with his woman. He held up his index finger. "Rule number one. I only want to hear you say one word. Yes."

"But I—"

He put his finger over her lips. "Say yes."

He kissed her cheek and dragged his lips down to her neck while he caressed her face. Shivers ran up and down her spine as he sucked on the sensitive flesh.

"Yes," she moaned.

He moved down to her clavicle as he made his way over to the other side of her neck where he licked that area.

"Mmm, yes." Kari wrapped her arms around his broad shoulders, letting him lave her neck area until her body trembled.

Thane pulled back from her and stood. When Kari started to stand, he surprised her by picking her up in his arms and carrying her to his bedroom.

"Yes." She held on to his shoulders until he placed her down next to the bed, and even then, she didn't let him go.

Thane swept his lips over hers and this time, he introduced his tongue, brushing it over her bottom lip and darting it into her mouth. As he teased her with it, Kari only wanted more. She moved in closer.

At that point, she realized that he had pulled up her dress, gathering it in his hands that he rested on her hips. With the dress around her waist, he slipped his index fingers into her panties and pulled them down, but only halfway so that they now rested in the middle of her cheeks.

She reached down to push her panties down all the way.

"No. Leave them right there." Thane released her dress on one side.

He used his other hand to grip her ass cheek.

"It feels weird to have them down only part way. Let me—"

"Say yes." He wrapped his free arm around her waist and pulled her against his body. "Say it."

Kari loved feeling his hard body brushing hers. "Yes."

A knock sounded on the door, which sobered her to their situation. She backed away from him like a teenager caught with a boy in her room.

Thane gave her a quick peck before he lowered her dress. "Don't pull your panties up, and don't push them down. Leave them right where they are."

She opened her mouth to argue with him, remind him that she had a few years on him and had a child. Instead, she simply said, "Yes."

He went to the door, leaving Kari in his darkened bedroom. She could hear him talking to someone. In the meantime, she scanned the room. It hit her that she hadn't brought her purse. She would need the condoms inside.

As she started to leave the room, she met Thane.

"Where are you going?" He carried a tray of strawberries with a bowl of frothy whipped cream and another bowl of grapes.

"I need something in my purse." She pointed behind him.

He set the tray on a dresser and turned to her. He shook his head. "You don't need anything right now. Let me take care of you." He kissed the side of her face. "Say yes."

She nodded, feeling the sandpaper grit on his cheek.

"I took the liberty of ordering some food." He nodded back toward the tray.

"I'm not hungry."

Thane removed his T-shirt and smiled. "You might work up an appetite later."

He faced her. Kari approached him and reached for his jeans. He arrested her hands and eased her back toward the bed. Before allowing her to sit on it, he pulled her dress over her head and tossed it aside.

Kari didn't care where it landed. She stood in front of the sexy Thane Wells wearing a plain white cotton bra, matching white panties, and Keds. She should have worn her sexy red bra-and-panty set tonight instead of the night she had dinner with him.

With her panties still at half-mast, she felt off balance. Thane probably wanted her that way. He controlled this moment. Usually the idea of giving someone else power over a situation would bother her. With Thane, it didn't.

Nothing about him felt like an impetuous young man. He didn't grope and grab at her. He didn't kiss her like he wanted to chew off her face or devour her. He didn't dive his hands into her panties and finger her until it felt good and painful at the same time.

Thane reached behind her and unfastened her bra while keeping his stare directly on her eyes. This man knew what to do. Again, he didn't take off her bra. He allowed it to hang loosely over her breasts, still covering them.

He held her shoulders and gently eased her back so that she sat on the bed. Then, without a word, he put his hand on her chest and nudged her so that she would lie down.

Kari stared up at the ceiling. She felt Thane removing her shoe. When he did, he kissed the top of her foot.

Sexy.

She exhaled when she felt his lips touch her. He did the same for the other foot, kissing it after removing her shoe. Then he hooked his fingers into the sides of her panties and finally pulled them down her legs.

"Do you mind if I eat something?" he asked.

Kari's heart pounded. She would not be uttering the word *yes* at this moment.

Thane parted her thighs. She felt cool air blowing over her inner thighs up to her throbbing core. When the mattress dipped down like he braced his hands on it to stand, she brought her head up to see his actions.

She felt her eyebrows furrowing before she realized what he'd done. She caught him standing and getting the tray of food. He placed it on the floor next to him.

Thane resumed his spot, picked up a strawberry, and bit the tip. "Mmm, so good." He presented the bitten berry to her. "You sure you don't want one? It's really good and sweet."

She shook her head but watched him carefully. He slowly ate the fruit and licked his fingers when he finished. Then he picked up another one, this time he dipped it in the whipped cream, evident from the fluffy tip. Instead of eating it like he'd done the other one, he dragged the cream-covered strawberry up her inner thigh, leaving a white trail up to the apex of her thighs.

Thane licked the whipped cream from her leg, dragging his tongue so slowly it felt like he controlled time. She dropped her head back and moaned. Even with her bra unfastened, she felt like it constricted her body.

Without shame or permission, she pulled her bra off and threw it to the side. "Yes."

Thane swept the fruit down her other inner thigh and licked the cream away like he'd done on the other leg. When Kari felt him painting her clitoris with the tip of his tongue, her body constricted.

"Yes!" She gripped a handful of the comforter as her body writhed.

The air filled with an aroma of fresh fruit and cream along with her own essence. What a scintillating smell. She reached down and ran her fingers through his hair as he continued licking her, loving her, caring for her like she hadn't felt in a long, long time.

Like he did with his kisses, Thane took his time. He made slow, easy passes over her hardened nub and occasionally dipped his tongue inside her vagina, which made her twitch each time. When he covered her clit with his mouth and pressed his tongue against it while massaging her thighs, Kari broke.

She felt her body trembling before she grumbled a guttural moan, a sound she didn't think she could produce. He pressed his tongue against her and brought her over the edge.

"Yes! Yes! Yes!" She jackknifed up from the bed and held the back of Thane's head.

When her body eased back down, she couldn't believe he had so much more to give. She surrendered to him. He twirled the tip of his tongue around her clitoris.

Kari felt the familiar tightening in her gut the longer he worked on her. Thane moved one hand up to her chest. He held her breast, massaging it like he'd done her thighs. He matched the motion of his tongue by swirling his thumb around her hardened nipple.

She gripped his hand, not wanting him to stop, nor willing to let him go. Thane gave her nipple a slight pinch, causing another orgasm.

Thankfully, Thane removed his hand and pulled back from her, giving her a chance to catch her breath. When she looked up, she watched him placing the tray on the dresser. He turned to her and kept his gaze on her eyes as he undid his jeans.

He pulled them down along with his underwear. Although Kari had seen Thane completely naked, seeing him now, his erection jutting from his body, gave her a new appreciation of his form.

Before she could protest again about having to get her purse to retrieve her stash of condoms, he opened a nightstand drawer and removed a box.

"I told you I would take care of you." He smiled as he opened it.

He removed a string of condoms and tore one away from the lineup. He ripped the package open and rolled the prophylactic over his long, thick cock. Thane crawled onto the bed and over her body.

Instead of immediately sliding himself inside her, he positioned his body next to hers. He dragged his fingertips over her chest between her breasts to her belly, barely touching her flesh with his fingers. The sensation drove her crazy with desire. She writhed on the bed in anticipation of more of his handling.

From the way he controlled this session, he made it obvious this would be an intense and slow experience. He brushed his fingertips over her hips and right over her clit. Kari curved her hips to get him to touch her more intimately.

Thane wouldn't be tricked into doing anything he didn't want. When she moved her hips, he raised his hand up to her stomach. Then he went down her thighs.

With his face next to hers, Kari couldn't wait to show him what his treatment did to her. She put her hand to his cheek and kissed him. She tasted sweetness from the berries and cream, and the saltiness of her own juices on his mouth. The concoction made her want more. She drove her tongue into his mouth as he continued tickling her body, bringing her sensitive nerve endings up to the surface.

Thane broke from the kiss long enough to roll on top of her. He positioned himself at her opening. While keeping a direct stare on her eyes, he entered her ever so slowly. After so many years of not being with a man and not even taking care of her own needs, she didn't take long to adjust to this introduction. She released a small cry, her stomach contracted, and her heart drummed. Kari coiled her legs around his and gripped his shoulders as she arched her back.

He surprised her by still taking his time. She half expected him to pound in her like an overeager frat boy. Thane controlled his strokes in a methodical manner that drove her crazy in the best way possible.

She reached down and gripped his firm ass. Perfect.

"You're so beautiful, you know that?" Thane kept his stare on her until she answered.

"Yes." Kari didn't want to sound arrogant.

When she answered, she didn't feel conceited. The way he looked at her throughout the night, and even before, made her feel sexy.

Thane kept his pace steady, occasionally surprising her by pulling so far back she thought he would remove himself completely, but then he would thrust hard and deep. She felt her body shaking again. No way could this man make her climax again so soon.

As the thought entered her mind, her intimate inner walls tightened around his shaft. He must have felt it. He smiled and nodded.

Before she could stop herself, Kari leaned her head back and released a scream that probably the entire floor heard. Thane pulled out of her long enough to slip behind her, positioned on his side, and eased himself into her again. He held onto her hip as he continued with his commanding thrusts.

Kari reached and held the back of his head. Her fingers slipped through his hair. He didn't sweat even though he'd been working hard for her pleasure. Thank God for youth. She smiled.

"You like it?" he asked and kissed the side of her face.

She nodded. "Yes."

Thane slipped his arm underneath her body and held onto her breast, massaging it and circling his thumb around her sensitive nipple. He used his other hand to rest on her hip at first. Then he eased it down, moving it between her legs to find her clit.

She gripped his hair in her fist and undulated her body to match his movements. The motion seemed like they had been together before. Everything about Thane felt so comfortable to her, which worried her. She'd gotten so relaxed around Jarrod that his leaving had blindsided her.

She had to stop thinking that way. As Reagan said, this one slip would be her vacation treat. When she got back home without a contract, she would be out of work.

Thane pulled out of her again to take her in another position. Kari surprised him by pushing him onto his back and straddling him. The man proved he could take control of a situation. She needed to show him that she could be just as powerful.

She rode him slowly at first. She grabbed his hands and placed them on her breasts. As soon as he began massaging them, circling her nipples with his thumbs, she increased her speed.

Thane coasted his hands down her body to her waist and over her ass. He palmed her cheeks, squeezing them occasionally as though letting her know he had her. She almost thought he would spank her. He never did. He didn't need to resort to tricks to coax an orgasm.

Kari gyrated her body faster and faster. She rested her hands on his chest and he raised his hips in the air to meet her motions. She let out a curse as her body tightened. This time, she finally felt Thane cracking. His muscular thighs started to tremble. He interlaced his fingers with hers and squeezed his eyes shut until she came.

"Yes!" she exclaimed.

He gritted his teeth and his body froze for a moment before he relaxed against the bed. "Incredible."

Kari smiled. "Yes." She gave him a kiss and placed her head on his chest.

Now she would have to figure out a way to tactfully leave while still trying to get his business.

Chapter 14

Thane stared at the woman in his bed. He knew the sex would be great. What he had with Kari couldn't compare with anyone he'd been with in the past, including Anjana. Whenever Kari looked at him, the connection deepened.

He wanted her again. She'd slept in his bed after a second marathon session, and now he wanted to experience her flesh one more time. Thane couldn't remember when his body had felt this alive and healthy and satisfied. As Kari lay on her side, he wrapped his arm around her waist and gently tried rolling her onto her back.

He wanted to see her face, watch her expression when she came again. Thinking about that moment raised his pulse. As soon as he got her on her back, and before he could climb over her, she moaned with her eyes still closed.

"Easy," she whispered.

Thane moved back from her as she resumed her deep, heavy breathing. Christ, he had become that guy Kari had said she didn't want. He'd taken his time with her last night for a couple of reasons. He didn't want her thinking this young man couldn't slow down for her. He'd also wanted to enjoy every curve and swell of her beautiful body.

I got to get out of here, he thought. He threw on some workout clothes and wrote a note to Kari to let her know his whereabouts.

Working out some of his pent-up anxiety would help him calm down… he hoped. He crept out of the room and went down to the fitness center. At five in the morning, he hoped no one else would be there. He didn't need a bunch of fans bothering him. He wanted to run and think about last night's events and Kari.

Would she want to be in his life? How did he feel about her having a kid? No, better question. What did *she* think he thought about her having a child? Thane had come from a broken home and into an adopted family. He understood the power of blended families. If only his own family could meld together.

He stepped on the treadmill and did his run. The small gym had an all-glass wall and door that faced out into the main lobby. Although the treadmill allowed him to have his back to people walking by, the large mirror in front of him let him see who stopped to look into the room. For that reason, he covered his head with a hood, hoping to block out his identity.

The large wall Kari had around her had come down last night, but not all the way. She'd hid her child from him. Why hadn't she wanted him to know? Then again, he hadn't told her everything about his checkered past. She knew about all his former relationships, what had been reported in the media. He had more to tell, more to share. Could he trust Kari with those types of secrets?

* * * *

Kari curled her body in bed and felt soreness between her legs. This time she smiled. She'd had incredible, mind-blowing, hot sex with Thane Wells. No, he hadn't been the guy she knew from the media or even the man she suspected from her research. He had been patient, kind, creative, passionate, and, damn it, lovable.

She wanted to be here with him. She wanted more of him. Kari slid her ass back to brush against Thane. When she didn't feel anything at first, she continued moving back until she finally decided to open her eyes and look behind her.

Kari blinked a few times before the realization hit her that Thane had left her alone. She leaned to the side to peek into the bathroom, the darkened, quiet bathroom. No way he would be in there.

She clutched the comforter to her chest and scooted to the edge of the bed, hoping beyond hope to see him in the living room or dining area. Maybe he wanted her to sleep longer. She briefly glanced at the digital clock next to the bed. Almost six in the morning.

Kari stood while continuing to keep her body covered. She looked into the two areas and found nothing. Maybe Thane had gone out to get her breakfast. A man that compassionate and considerate wouldn't have sex with her and leave. That move came out of Jarrod's playbook.

One weak moment shortly after her grandfather had died still haunted Kari. She'd lied to Thane last night when she told him the story about a random boyfriend she had sex with years ago. Not so random. Jarrod had said the right things to her at the wrong moment, and she'd fallen for his lies. The topper had been the impersonal note he'd left.

"Thanks for the memories, babe," had been the sentiment Jarrod left for her after she'd opened herself up again.

As she yanked the covers from the bed, she noticed something fluttering to the floor. Kari peered down. By her foot sat a folded piece of hotel stationery. A note. Another fucking note. She wouldn't be played again.

Kari stomped into her panties and yanked them up her legs. She put on her bra and hooked the back. Only after fastening it did she realize that she had the undergarment on inside out.

"Screw it." She didn't care about what she had on underneath. She had to get out before she had another embarrassing encounter with Thane.

Kari slipped on her shoes but didn't bother tying them. Then she put on her dress and grabbed her jacket and purse. She wouldn't be coming back to this hotel or seeing Thane again. She knew that for sure.

She yanked the door open and stormed down the hallway as fast as she could. As she waited for the elevator, she put on her jacket. She knew it would be chilly outside. Yes, she would use that excuse to explain why she couldn't stop shaking. When she felt her throat tightening, she swallowed and blamed the reaction on pollen. The hotel did have fresh-cut flowers everywhere.

The elevator doors opened. She got in the empty car and pushed the button to take her down to the lobby. The smooth ride gave her too much time to think. She'd awakened from dreams of a life with Thane, him being in her life and in her child's.

Kari shook her head. No way. She would never let him near Michael. If she hurt this badly from this disappointing experience, she couldn't imagine how Michael would react.

The elevator doors opened and she practically ran from it. She kept her pace brisk but still ladylike.

"Hey!"

Kari heard the shout and assumed the exclamation had come from a concierge or maybe that nosy guard.

"Kari, wait."

At the sound of her name, she couldn't help but stop and turn. She saw a hooded man approach her. When he revealed his identity, she turned and headed to the door.

"Where are you going?" Thane touched Kari's arm.

"Don't touch me." She backed away from him and balled her hands into fists like she wanted to fight.

In a look of surrender, he raised both hands in the air. "I'm not going to hurt you. I wanted to know why you are trying to leave so quickly. Did I do something wrong?"

She huffed. "No. I did. I let my guard down. I got soft." She looked into his eyes, the same ones that had melted her heart whenever he'd stared at her during sex. "I should have stuck to business. No one gets hurt that way." She started to head to the door again, but Thane blocked her.

"Will you wait one minute? Did you read my note?" Thane crouched down a little to meet her gaze face-to-face.

"I didn't need to. I can guess what it said. 'Had fun last night. I'll call you. Take care.' I would have more respect for you had you told me up front that all you wanted was sex. Don't play with my head and my—" She stopped before she could reveal more of herself.

"Come back up to the room." He stepped forward, which forced her to take a couple steps back.

"For what? You want to hit it again?" She didn't realize the volume of her voice until she noticed the desk clerk's uncomfortable expression.

"Please. I won't touch you. I need you to see something." Thane took a couple more steps toward her.

So that she didn't look ridiculous walking backward, Kari turned and walked in front of him to the elevator. Thane hit the *up* button and the doors opened immediately. Inside the quiet car, Thane kept his stare on her but didn't speak.

Kari didn't look at him. Not directly. His reflection showed on the mirrored elevator doors. When she looked at him, she noticed sweat around the collar of his T-shirt under his hoodie. Perspiration also dotted his forehead and down the sides of his face. When she took a deep breath, she smelled that familiar sweaty aroma that she'd already grown to adore.

At the top floor, the doors opened. Like a gentleman, Thane waited for her to step out first. After he got out, he walked ahead of her to his hotel room door. He opened it for her and allowed her to go in first.

"I was in the gym downstairs," Thane said. "I left you a note to let you know where I was." He picked up the paper on the floor and came back to her. "Please read it." He held it up to Kari.

She studied his face for a moment. That same sincere look returned. She snatched it from his hand and opened it. "This won't change anything."

Kari read the note:

To my honey badger. I need to get a workout in. Please don't leave until I get back. Order whatever you want for breakfast. Can't wait to see you. Thane.

Damn. The game had changed.

No, no, no. Kari wouldn't fall for his charms.

"Seems awfully strange that you would need to do a workout after last night. Are you saying I wasn't that exciting to you?" Kari ground her teeth as she awaited his answer.

Thane shook his head. "I needed to get away."

She blinked. "Really? Get away from me?" She tossed the note to the floor. "Fine. I'm out of here."

He held her arm without apology this time and stopped her. "Don't you get it?" He looked down at the hand that held her. His thumb brushed over her arm.

Thank goodness, she'd put her jacket back on. To feel him touching her actual skin would have broken her.

"Get what?" she asked in a lowered voice.

"I don't know what it is about you, but you've invaded my soul." He let her arm go and moved back. "I looked at you this morning and I wanted you again. I wanted to feel you, taste you, make you scream again."

Kari's legs buckled. "And?"

"And I thought if I did that, you would think of me as that horny teenager you didn't want in your life instead of the man that I am. I wanted to be a gentleman because I knew I wouldn't be a *gentle* man." He crossed his arms over his chest as though he needed to corral himself.

"How do you know I wouldn't have wanted that?" Kari wanted to seem like she had control of this situation when really she had fallen for his genuineness and power. She'd never been with a man like Thane.

"Earlier this morning, I rolled you on to your back. I was prepared to wake you up with kisses all over your body. Then you stopped me with one word."

She swallowed. "I did? I don't remember saying anything."

"You said 'easy.'"

She swallowed. Sure he'd pushed her body to its breaking point, but in a great way. She didn't want him to stop. Maybe he had been too much for her.

He put his hand to his chest. "I can't help my age. I'm young. I have a lot of energy. I can't stop my needs." He removed his hoodie and tossed it to the side. "I ran to work out some sexual tension."

She peered down and saw a distinct bulge in his track pants. "Did it work?" She knew the answer, but she wanted to hear it from him.

He shook his head. "Not even close." He took a step closer to her and stopped. "I'm not that man you read about online or in magazines. My last serious relationship was with Anjana, and even with her, I waited before we got physical. I know the media portrays me as some Casanova. I'm not that guy."

"Who are you then?"

"I'm Thane. I am my mother's son. I'm honest and faithful." He put his hand to her cheek.

Kari heard his breathing increase. She licked her lips. As soon as she did, he let out a low groan.

"I like you a lot." He smiled. "Have you showered yet?"

She shook her head. If he undressed her right now, he would see her bra on inside out. Hell, her panties could be the same way for all she knew. She didn't remember.

"Why don't we shower and change and go to breakfast? I don't want to scare you off." He lowered his voice. "I want to get to know you."

"Even though I have a son?" As great as all this sounded, she didn't need him trying to infuse himself into her life if he only wanted one thing. She couldn't disappoint her child, not again.

"*Especially* because you have a child." He kissed her forehead.

"You seem a lot older than twenty-two." She gazed up at him.

He chuckled. "Patience has never been my virtue. I'm learning that when it matters, it helps." He walked by her and headed to the bathroom. "Will you wait here while I take a shower?"

Kari glanced down at her watch. "I really should get back to my hotel. I want to be there when Michael wakes up."

Thane held his hands up. "Please. Give me a couple of minutes to shower and change. Don't leave, okay?"

She nodded.

"Good. I promise I won't be long. Whatever you do, don't go. I don't mind chasing you down the hall wet and naked, but I'd rather not. Then again, you could join me. Plenty of room for the two of us."

When Kari didn't answer, he ducked into the bathroom but didn't shut the door.

Kari heard the streaming water before she heard the shower door close. She glanced around the room. She looked into the bedroom and saw the remnants of last night's activities. The disheveled bed, the half-eaten bowls of fruit, the condom wrappers on the floor. She'd been that woman who gave in to her desires. So why hadn't she wanted to do that this morning when Thane desired her again? Why was she always putting the brakes on having fun?

She dropped her purse on the floor and slid her jacket down her arms as she strolled to the bathroom. She stripped out of her dress and kicked out of her shoes. As she stood on the cool tile floor, she reached behind her and unhooked her bra. She stared at Thane, who had immersed himself under the water and looked like he was trying to take the fastest shower possible. She could slow him down and speed him up in one motion.

Kari pulled her panties down and opened the shower door, which must have surprised Thane. He whipped his head around as soon as she stepped inside. She closed the door, enveloping them in a fragrant fog of his musky-scented body wash.

"I decided I do need that shower." She put her hands on his chest. "I don't want you changing yourself for me. All you have to do is say yes."

He framed her face in his hands and kissed her. Kari slid her hands down his slick body to his waist. Because she liked touching his skin, she eased her hands behind him to his ass. Thane stopped kissing her and released a growl as soon as she squeezed his cheeks.

"You are really letting the beast out." He kissed her cheek and moved down to her neck. "I should have brought the condoms in here with me."

"There are other ways to get relief." She wrapped her hand around his steadily hardening shaft. "This time let me take care of you."

Kari kept her stare on Thane's hypnotic blue eyes until she brought her hand up to his mushroom tip. Then he squeezed his eyes shut and planted his hands on the shower stall wall over her head.

She kept her hand tight as she stroked him, slow and easy. With each pass, he became harder. Kari couldn't resist him. She leaned forward and licked his small nipple.

Thane sucked air between his gritted teeth. He stomped his foot on the floor as though trying hard to keep himself contained. When she covered his nipple with her mouth and sucked him, he surprised her by cupping her breast and twirling her nipple with his large thumb.

It still blew her mind that this man had used that hand to throw a no-hitter game. Kari moved her mouth over to his other nipple and worked on it as she continued to manipulate him below. She felt his body shake and heard his breath become ragged.

Kari kissed his chest before descending to her knees in front of him. While she still had him in her hand, she licked the tip, tasting his salty goodness.

Thane cursed, apologized, and cursed again. Good. Now he could experience what he'd done to her last night, experience the sweet, sweet torture that had reduced her to a puddle. While keeping her hand wrapped around the base, she used her other hand to cup his balls. She massaged them as she brought her mouth down as far as she could go and back up again.

She dragged her tongue underneath his pulsating shaft and moaned, knowing how good the vibration would feel to him. After a few more passes, Kari heard the shower water stop. A few drips came from the head as the remaining water swirled down the drain.

"No, no." Thane held Kari's shoulders and brought her up to her feet. "Not this way. Not in your mouth."

He crouched down and lifted her so that he slung her over his shoulder.

"Thane!" She didn't mean to squeal, but she'd never had a man manhandle her like that. Too bad she really liked it.

He wiped his feet on the rug outside the shower stall and carried her across the room to his bedroom. After depositing her on the mattress, Thane opened the last of his condoms. He probably didn't know she had some in her purse thanks to Reagan.

Thane sheathed himself and got into bed.

"No, no, no." Kari scooted away from him.

"What?" He could barely contain his breathing as he glared at her.

Not willing to torture them both for very long, she got on her hands and knees in front of him. She turned and smiled. "Yes."

He held her hip with one hand and used his other to help guide himself inside her. She curled her toes at the introduction and had to grip the headboard. Like last night, he controlled every aspect of this session. He pulled back almost to the point of removing himself before slamming himself back in her.

He did that over and over again, driving her wild. When she didn't think he could do anything else to push her over the edge, he reached under her body and slipped her clitoris between his index and middle fingers.

"Yes!" Kari clawed the wall behind the headboard.

Thane checked off every box from her perfect-man wish list. He not only thought about her needs, he made sure she stayed satisfied as well. He leaned down and kissed her shoulder, even taking a little nibble, which made her scream.

Before she could catch her breath, Thane pulled out of her, turned her around, and had her on her back. She gripped his shoulders before he entered her again.

His incredible strength and stamina had her wishing she had taken him up on his offer to sleep with him that first night when she saved him. No, she liked him better this way. Sober, lucid, aware, sexy. He also reminded her that at twenty-six, she hadn't become a blue-haired old bitty yet. She needed to embrace her fun side.

By the time Thane twisted her body to the fourth or fifth position and Kari had come three times, her nerves felt banjo tight like the right touch would shatter her. With her on his lap, he cradled her ass with his large hand and held the back of her neck with his other. With her stomach tightening and her legs wrapped around his body, she felt another orgasm building.

He kissed her neck. He coiled his muscular arms around her and held her as her body trembled. When she came, he followed shortly after.

"Thank you," Kari said and kissed him all over his face.

"What are you thanking me for?" He grinned.

"You reminded me that I'm more than just an agent and a mother. I'm a woman. Sometimes I forget that."

He patted her backside. "I'm more than happy to remind you. Two or three times a day if you want."

She laughed. "I'm sure."

"Tell me who it was."

Kari leaned back to look Thane in his eyes.

"Tell me the jerk who wrote you some whack note after having sex with you that you thought I was like. I'm in a fighting mood."

She saw the fire in him. He wanted to defend her honor. Her heart started pounding again for another reason.

Her defenses down, she felt compelled to come clean with him. He'd already seen her son. No use hiding anything from him. "It was Michael's father." Kari saw Thane's jaw flex.

"The father of your child dismissed you like that. That's what you're telling me?" He cupped her cheek and brushed his thumb over her face. "Who is he? Does he still live near you?"

She shook her head. "No. He mainly lives in California unless he travels for work." She took a deep breath. "You said you know basketball."

He paused before answering. "I do."

"My son's last name is the same as his father's. Townsend." Kari braced her hands on Thane's shoulders before she pushed herself off his lap and stood. "Jarrod Townsend is Michael's father."

Chapter 15

It all made sense now. No wonder Kari didn't want to date an athlete. She'd gotten pregnant by one at a young age, and he disappointed her on more than one occasion.

After Thane and Kari took real showers without getting entwined in each other's arms, they got dressed. Silence had filled the room after she'd dropped the bomb about Michael's father. It amazed Thane that he hadn't heard this story. He knew Jarrod had a string of ex-wives and had a boatload of children. As he looked at Kari, he didn't want her and her child to be a part of his casualty list.

"I still want to take you to breakfast." Thane reached for her.

She glanced at her watch as she moved away from him. "We don't have to do this."

"Do what?" He kept after her, not wanting her to leave.

She spoke, keeping her gaze averted. "I need to get to Michael."

"You don't want me to join you?" He watched her shoulders slump. His stomach knotted.

"This was nice."

"Nice?" He cocked his head.

Kari continued. "I don't want to confuse—"

"Who? Michael? Me? You?" He moved in closer to her. "You've come too far to go back now. Talk to me."

She shook her head. "I came out here for a job. I didn't come here to…" She stopped herself before she exposed any more of herself.

"Wow. Put that in a note and I'll know how you felt with Jarrod."

Kari's bottom jaw unhinged as she glared at him. "That's so unfair." She headed to the door.

Feeling like a heel for what he said, Thane came up behind her and wrapped his arms around her waist before she could touch the knob. "You're right. You didn't deserve that."

"If you think I don't feel something after last night and this morning, you're crazy." She turned around in his arms and stared into his eyes. "But if you think I'm not afraid of what this all means, then I must be one hell of an actress. I'm scared. I can't say that enough."

Thane pressed her back against the door and held her hips. "I'm telling you that you don't have to be. I came home to bury my mother. I didn't expect anything else. But here we are." He kissed the tip of her nose. "Here we are." He pressed his lips against hers. "Let's explore this. I'm not going to call your friend about rental properties." He shook his head. "I'm going to be checking out of this hotel."

"You're leaving?" Fear laced her inquiry.

"Just the hotel. My mother left me a home I didn't know she had down in the Outer Banks." He interlaced his fingers with hers. "Come down there with me." When he saw her open her mouth to protest, he stopped her. "You, Michael, and Reagan. I have no idea what the house looks like. We can explore it together. We can explore a lot of things together."

She shook her head. "No. You are a young—" She stopped as she put her hand to his chest and felt him. After a sigh and licking her lips, she continued. "You are a young man. You have your whole life ahead of you. You don't need to saddle yourself with a woman with a child."

Thane put his hand on top of hers and pressed it to his chest. "For one thing, I'm a man. Don't mistake that. I make up my own mind and make my own decisions. Remember that. Not since my mother cut the crusts off my sandwiches have I had a woman try to tell me what I need. I know what I want. You may know my stats, but you have no idea what drives me."

"And what is that? What pushes you to get out of bed?" She swallowed hard as she awaited his answer.

"Family. That has never changed. I appreciate a good woman who loves and respects that." He held her hand and brought it up to his mouth to kiss her palm. "I'd like to get to know you and your family more. Join me down in North Carolina."

"That sounds interesting and exciting." She put her hand back on his chest. "There's something you need to do first."

He grabbed the sides of her dress and started inching it up. "Again? And you call me insatiable."

Her face remained stoic as she pulled her dress down. "Your career."

He leaned his head back and rolled his eyes. "Come on with this. You're like a broken record. You're still on the agent kick?"

Kari shook her head. "No. I wanted to know if playing baseball is still something you want."

He blinked. "Of course. I love the game. I'm on a great team. I'm paid a crazy amount of money."

She put her hand to the side of his face. "No doubt. You are an incredible player. Where there's smoke, there's fire. Stories about your questionable health have been plaguing you and your career this year."

Thane jerked back from her. "What is this? You've been after me for a while to represent me. Now that I won't give you an answer, you want to say that there's something wrong with me? Is this some mind game?"

She shook her head. "No. The agent side of me wouldn't have said anything to you. But as a woman who has gotten to know you better, I'm concerned about you. Your stats, although impressive, have slipped. At your age and experience, usually numbers would be getting better."

"Are you kidding me? One player hits one of my pitches and all the sudden I'm a loser?"

"I'm not saying that." Kari moved in closer to Thane. "Are you okay? I mean health-wise."

"You've been with me all night and this morning. Did I act like a man in poor health?" Thane's stomach tightened after he asked his question. He refrained from clutching his midsection.

"Like you, I noticed some things while *you* slept." She kept her stare on his eyes. "I wrapped my arm around you, at least I tried. You flinched and turned away from me. Maybe I said easy for you, not me."

Thane exhaled. "I'll walk you to your car." He retrieved her jacket.

Thane couldn't think straight after her accusation. Had he really been that obvious about his medical condition? He thought about his mannerisms on and off the field. Had he held his stomach too much? Had he slipped and said something in an interview?

He had to squash her assumptions now before she spread the word to her colleagues, not that he really thought she would do that to him. After helping her with her outerwear, he put on his jacket.

"You don't have to walk me to my car." She grabbed the doorknob.

He stepped in and seized the knob from her grasp. "Yes, I do. If you hadn't driven here, I would have taken you back to your hotel. Now I'll just have to follow you there."

Kari shook her head as Thane opened the door for her. "No, you won't. You know there are going to be reporters downstairs and following you."

He shrugged. "So?"

"Do you really want them asking you questions about me, especially when you're supposed to be in Florida?"

He punched the *down* button beside the elevator doors. "You let me worry about myself."

She shook her head. "Thank God I'm not your publicist. I would be pulling my hair out."

"Don't do that." He ran his fingers through it. "I kind of like your hair."

She swatted his hand away from her as she got into the elevator. "Don't do that. There are cameras everywhere."

"Why are you so panicked about being on camera? You worry too much." As soon as he said it, his belly compressed again. He gritted his teeth as the pain crested and then subsided like a crashing wave.

"I can't help it. I'm a mother. It's what mothers do." She glared at him as though trying to warn him again about trying to start something with her.

He leaned down by her ear. "No need to worry about me. Let me take care of you for a change." He placed his hand down at the small of her back. "I apologize for cutting you off when we talked. I can't tell if I'm talking to Kari the woman or Kari the agent."

She turned to him.

"Can you give me a sign? A signal? Let me know who I'm dealing with?" He moved in closer to her to kiss her succulent mouth again when the doors opened. Before he knew it, she bolted from him and headed to the front door.

Thane kept up behind her until she stopped abruptly before the doors.

"No." Kari shook her head.

He didn't know what made her freeze in place until he spotted the source of her apparent fear.

"Mom! Reagan said you would be here. We took a cab and everything." Michael beamed as he hugged Kari around her hips.

"What are you doing here?" Kari glared at Reagan.

"I tried calling you several times. I guess your phone is off." Reagan peered up at Thane and smiled. "So I came here, hoping to find you. Make sure you're okay."

"Really?" Kari cocked her head away from her son's line of vision.

"Good. Now that we're all together, we can do that breakfast." Thane beamed. He couldn't have planned this even if he'd tried.

* * * *

Instead of venturing out to a pancake house like Thane and Michael wanted, Kari begrudgingly agreed to dine in the hotel's restaurant. She hung back with Reagan and followed Thane and her son to a back table.

"Worried about me, huh?" Kari said between clenched teeth.

"Yes. I thought you would be back to the hotel earlier. When you didn't answer, I had all these different scenarios running through my head." Reagan flailed her hands around as she spoke, expressive as usual.

"So if Thane had beaten me up or killed me, you thought that would be a sight for my child to see?"

Reagan pursed her lips. "Did you really want me to leave your ten-year-old son alone in a hotel?"

Her friend had a point. It still angered her that they'd intruded on her like that when she hadn't figured out her true feelings for Thane yet. It didn't take a mother's intuition to know that Thane kept a portion of himself hidden. She'd touched on a nerve when she brought up his health. Instead of getting him to trust her more with his secrets, she felt like she pushed him away.

She watched the waiter point to their table. Michael ran to a chair and plopped himself down like he did at home. Then she watched Thane lean over and whisper something into her child's ear.

Michael jumped up. Then, like Thane, he stood behind a chair and pulled it out. Kari didn't want to look shocked, but she knew her open mouth and her frozen stance showed her surprise.

"Always hold a chair for a lady." Thane patted Michael on his back. "Ladies."

"Reagan, this is your chair." Michael pointed to chair he held. "Mr. Wells has Mom's chair."

"Thane." He tapped Michael on his shoulder.

"No, Mr. Wells. He had it right." Kari stood in front of the chair Thane held. "You aren't the only one who can teach him good manners."

Instead of coming back with a smart remark, Thane nodded. "I see. He's a good kid."

Thane skillfully slid Kari's chair under her as she sat. He surprised her by taking her napkin and draping it across her lap. The careful attention caused her heart to pound wildly. When she peered over at Reagan and Michael, she noticed that Michael had been watching, and he quickly snatched Reagan's napkin, balled it in his hand, and threw it on Reagan's lap.

"Um, thank you?" Reagan subtly smoothed the white cloth over her thighs before Michael occupied the chair next to her.

"Yes, thank you." Kari had to step up her game with Thane.

He bucked every stereotype she had about him.

"You're welcome." Thane sat next to Kari. As he faced her, he gave her a quick wink.

"Mom, why were you here instead of with me and Reagan?" Michael picked up his glass of water and downed it as he awaited Kari's answer.

"Uh—"

"She spent the night here." Thane quickly supplied. As Kari prepared to snatch her child from the table and leave, Thane finished his statement. "Your mother and I have been talking business over the last week. We're still working on a deal."

Kari tried to contain her anger as she smiled to her son. "Yes. That's why I came down here in the first place."

"So are you going to let my mom represent you?"

For that question, Kari wanted to give Michael a bonus and a bump up in his allowance. She had to hear how Thane would answer. She hadn't been able to pin the man down after all this time. Would he finally answer a child?

"Not sure yet." Thane dropped his gaze to his menu, probably as a way to stop the conversation.

Kari should have felt some reassurance that he at least hadn't said no.

"I think it's great that you two are spending so much time together." Reagan bit her bottom lip.

Reagan always looked pained when she tried not to laugh. If Kari knew she wouldn't come in contact with her child's legs, she would have kicked her employee under the table.

"I'm glad you think so, Reagan." Thane took a sip of his water before he continued. "I asked Kari if you three would like to spend the rest of the week at a place in the Outer Banks. I think she's still deciding."

Kari shook her head. For as sweet as Thane looked, he had a sneaky side.

"Whoa, Mom, we have to go." Michael's eyes got wide.

From the way he wiggled in his chair, Kari imagined him kicking his little legs under the table out of excitement.

"That does sound awesome, way better than staying in a hotel in Virginia Beach." Reagan's eyes rolled to the back of her head.

"Yes, the offer is very generous." Kari forced herself to smile to look pleased by the suggestion even though she hated feeling manipulated. "However, we cannot intrude on Mr. Wells's time and home."

"No intrusion at all." Thane faced Reagan. "My mother gave me the home in her will. I never knew it existed. I have no idea what it looks like. It would be a great trip for all of us to visit it."

"Wouldn't you rather do that with your brothers?" Kari glared at Thane. He didn't hesitate before he answered. "No."

An uncomfortable silence hung over the table until the waiter came back to take their order.

Fortunately, the conversation flowed smoothly during the meal. The awkward tension that had existed when Kari had first seen her son and his nanny disappeared as soon as the food arrived. She also found Thane even more charming and appealing.

He managed to split his time and attention among the three of them while expertly remembering small details and keeping up with all conversations. It made her wonder why he couldn't tell her the truth about his health. She didn't believe him when he said he had no problems.

At the end of the meal, Kari retrieved her wallet from her purse. Thane's large hand covered hers.

"I have it." He shook his head as he grabbed the check from the waiter.

"No. I'll pay for myself and my family." Kari attempted to snag the bill, but Thane handed it back to the waiter before she could touch it.

"Great conversation with you all is payment enough for me." Thane looked sincere. He cast his eyes down and left his hand on the table a sliver away from Kari's.

She felt the heat coming from it. She longed to touch him again. In front of her son and Reagan, she had to refrain.

Kari stood. "Thank you, again. You're very generous." She looked at Michael. "Did you thank Mr. Wells for the meal?"

"No, ma'am." He faced Thane. "Thank you. Those pancakes were awesome."

"You're welcome." Thane smiled at him.

"Come on. Let's get you washed up and we'll get out of Mr. Wells's hair." Kari held up her arm to signal Michael to come to her.

"Mom." He twisted his little mouth to the side as he went over to her. "Can I go to the men's bathroom by myself?"

"Absolutely not. People are crazy. I'm not having some nut-job snatch you from the bathroom or worse." Kari would never tell Michael what would be worse than getting kidnapped. He didn't need to have the nightmares.

She knew that he would get to an age where going into the women's bathroom with his mother or his nanny wouldn't work. She had to protect him as long as she could.

"I can bring you all up to my room if you want to use that bathroom," Thane offered.

Kari quickly did a mental inventory of his bedroom, whether or not she'd left anything behind that would give away what they had done. She couldn't be sure that Thane had discarded all the condom wrappers.

"His room might be a mess, sweetie." Kari shook her head.

"I don't mind taking him." Thane looked at Kari. "If it's okay with you."

"I couldn't ask you to do that." Kari wrapped a possessive arm around her son.

"You didn't. I offered." He looked down at Michael. "Are you okay with that?"

"Are you kidding? Washing my hands with Thane Wells? The kids at school will never believe me." Michael turned to Kari. "Please, Mom?"

Looking at the two of them, she relented. "Okay, wash and dry your hands. Don't play in there."

"Yes, ma'am." Michael looked like he wanted to skip to the bathroom.

"In and out. We'll be right back." Thane put his hand on Michael's back. "Will you two be right here when we get out?"

"Here or by the car." Kari couldn't stop staring at her little man. "Be good."

Michael rolled his eyes. "I'm just washing my hands."

"I know. I love you." She blew him a kiss.

"Yeah, yeah. I know." Michael gave her a dismissive wave and started to go toward the bathroom when Thane stopped him.

"Always tell people you love them, especially family." He looked at Kari. "Especially your mother. You never know when you might not see them again." Thane stared at Kari for a long moment before dropping his gaze to her son. "Say it. It doesn't make you less of a man to be open and honest."

Michael blinked before turning to Kari. "Love you, Mom."

Kari smiled and nodded. Before she knew it, Michael ran to her and wrapped his arms around her. Her steadily tightening throat completely closed as she held him.

Michael gazed up at her. "Don't tell my friends I did this, okay?"

Kari released a chuckle. "Our little secret." She kissed the top of his head before sending him off with Thane.

Reagan draped her arm around Kari's shoulders as Kari watched the duo go into the men's room.

"Hold it together, mama." Reagan nudged her hip against Kari's. "Don't let him see you crying."

Kari waited until the door closed before she broke down. "He's growing up so fast."

"I know. You knew this was coming. I knew it was coming when he complained about going to the bathroom with me." Reagan patted Kari's shoulder.

"And did you see him with Thane? And how Thane was with him? He's such a good man. Polite and respectful and—"

"And you couldn't wait to get away from him, right?"

Kari turned her back to the bathroom, afraid to show her son her vulnerable side.

"Come on. Let's get some air." Reagan led Kari to the door.

"No. I have to be here when he comes out of the bathroom." She turned back around, but Reagan continued pulling her toward the door.

"He'll be fine. It's you I'm worried about."

The doorman opened the door as Kari and Reagan walked forward. The morning sun warmed Kari's face. She closed her jacket around her body.

"What do you mean?" Kari walked toward her car.

"I've never known you to work a client this hard."

"Hey." Kari jerked her shoulder back from Reagan.

"I don't mean it that way. I've never known you to work so hard to get a client. You've been on this guy for years. So now it looks like work has turned to pleasure, which I think is great. But you're still hung up on work. Give that up and go with your heart."

Kari wiped under her eyes. "Give it up? So are you okay with not having a raise? You think Michael will be okay with vacations to locations I can drive to? His father can give him so much more. I have to compete with that."

Reagan shook her head. "No. You think you have to for whatever reason. You don't. Michael loves you. He said so." She nodded toward the hotel.

When Kari remembered him telling her he loved her and hugging her, the flood of tears returned just as Thane and Michael walked out of the hotel.

"Hey, give your mom a minute." Reagan put her arm around Kari. "She's on a call."

With her head down and her hands to her face, Kari did look like she had a phone to her ear. She had to admire Reagan's quick thinking. No way could she face Michael and Thane like this. She didn't want Michael to worry. She didn't know if Thane would even care, or how he truly felt about her. Then again, could she admit to him or herself how she felt about him?

Reagan had hit the nail on the head when she said that Kari's pursuit of Thane had changed from business to personal. Maybe she needed to drop the pretense.

"This is the most I've ever cried since my grandfather died, do you know that?" Kari dug through her purse for some tissue or napkin or something to wipe her face.

"I know this whole story about you being on the phone won't work for very long, especially with both hands in your purse. And I know I deserve a raise for this." Reagan laughed.

* * * *

"Mom is always busy with work." Michael stared at Kari, who still had her back to them.

Thane hadn't bought Reagan's story. He wouldn't worry Michael. That didn't stop him from wondering what had made Kari so emotional. He hoped he hadn't overstepped his bounds by offering to take Michael to the men's room or correcting him when he dismissed his mother's proclamation of love.

He'd been Michael's age once. He remembered the moment Queen Elizabeth had given him the same speech about the *L* word. He hadn't understood it back then either. Now he wished he hadn't missed a moment to say it to his mother more.

"Sounds like your mom works hard to provide you with a good life. You have to respect that." Thane headed to his car with Michael tripping next to him to keep up the pace.

"I do. I would like to see her more. But at least I see her more than I see my dad. He's always on the road and so busy." Michael gazed down at the parking lot.

Thane wouldn't allow this great kid to wallow in any misery. "You play baseball?" He touched his trunk to unlock it.

Michael shook his head. "Mom doesn't let me play sports. She wants me to be smart."

Thane had to smile at the child's unintended dig.

After a moment, Michael's eyes widened. "I didn't mean it that way. I don't mean that you're dumb or anything."

"I know what you meant. No offense taken." Thane removed two baseball gloves and a ball from the trunk area. "Your mom must want you to be a doctor or lawyer."

Michael shook his head. "Astrophysicist. Is it bad that I don't know what that is?"

Thane laughed. "No." He handed Michael a glove.

The child looked over at his mother before accepting the well-worn glove.

"That was the glove I used when I was in high school." Thane slipped his hand in the other glove. When he noticed Michael struggling to wear the oversized, padded leather mitt, he stopped to help him. "Put these fingers inside here and your index finger outside in this pocket." He positioned Michael's tiny fingers until he had it right. "Feel okay?"

Michael looked at his hand in the glove. "It's heavy. But this is so cool." He smiled.

"I thought the same thing when my mother bought that for me." Thane slammed the trunk hood down and led Michael to a field between the parking lot and the hotel.

"Your mom let you play sports when you were a kid?" Michael stared at Thane like the concept made no sense to him.

Thane nodded. "She didn't want to deny me or my brothers the opportunity to try things, and that included sports."

"She won't even let me play basketball, which is crazy because—" Michael stopped himself.

Apparently, his mother had trained him not to talk about his famous father to strangers. For that reason, Thane wouldn't let him know that Kari had already enlightened him to the situation.

"Baseball is America's favorite pastime." Thane tossed the ball in the air and caught it with a thud into his mitt. "Do you know how to catch a ball?"

Michael furrowed his eyebrows and did his best to scowl. "Sure I do." He held his glove open sideways next to his face.

Michael reminded Thane so much of himself at that age.

"If you catch a ball above your waist, hold your glove like this." Thane held up his hand so that it faced outward and kept it by his chest. He waited until Michael mimicked the position. "Good. If you catch a ball below your waist, hold your glove like a scoop, like this." He turned his hand over and squatted down. It reminded him of the training he'd missed in Florida. "And if a ball is rolling to you, you get down low and put your glove right on the ground." He sunk his body lower and put his hand on the grass. "And for someone like you, whenever you catch a ball, always use your other hand to secure it."

"I can do it with one hand." Michael nodded confidently.

"I'm sure you can with enough practice. Want to try to catch a few?"

Michael squatted down, mirroring Thane's position. Thane tossed the ball lightly. The young child shocked him by catching the ball the correct way, and he placed his hand over the ball with his free hand as Thane had suggested.

"Great job. Toss it back." Thane held up his glove below his waist, expecting a low toss.

Instead, Michael surprised him with a pretty sweet throw that would make some minor league pitchers jealous. When the ball smacked against Thane's glove, he felt the sting against his palm.

"Nice throw. Are you sure you haven't practiced that?" Thane smiled as he tossed the ball in his hand.

Michael giggled. "No. I told you. Mom won't let me play."

"Then you, my friend, are what we call a natural. You have a great throwing arm, and you're not bad at catching. It's a shame your mom won't let you play. If you were my—" Like Michael had earlier, Thane stopped himself from saying more.

Thane continued tossing the ball to him and giving him tips on what he could do to improve. As he did, he got lost in his thoughts about his fate with Kari. He saw something more with her, even with her child. Although he'd never thought of himself as a family-man type at such a young age, the more he hung around Michael, the more he imagined himself with a wife and more kids running around him.

"Stop what you're doing."

Thane heard Kari's voice behind him as soon as he caught another one of Michael's ball tosses. He turned and saw her storming up behind him. She no longer looked like an emotional wreck. Now she appeared angry.

"He's not hurt or anything. I only threw underhanded with him." Thane held up his hands in surrender. From talking to Michael, he knew Kari's stance on sports for her child.

"That's not the problem." She marched by him to Michael. Once she got to him, she pulled off the glove and took his hand. When she made her way back to Thane, she said under her breath, "Look around you. People are taking your picture and getting video of you."

Thane blinked. "That's it? So what? Why would that bother me?"

"You're not practicing with your team right now." She moved in even closer. "And you're throwing a ball to Jarrod Townsend's son." She slammed the glove into his hand. "Think about it."

"I could care less what Jarrod thinks. I only cared about what he thinks." Thane pointed to Michael. "And what you think. So tell me how you feel."

She looked down at Michael. "Thank Mr. Wells for his time. I'm sure he's busy with work. We won't hold you up."

Thane pounded his forehead with the back of his glove. So lost in thought, he hadn't even noticed the bystanders watching him and Michael. Now that he scanned his surroundings, he saw people everywhere watching him, all holding up their rectangular phones to get his image.

He turned and watched Kari walk away from him. Had he been thinking, he wouldn't have put Michael in that position. He hoped nothing came about from an innocent game of catch. He also hoped he hadn't ruined his chances with Kari.

Chapter 16

Kari didn't want to bring her anxiety with her throughout the day with Michael and Reagan, but her body showed her unease. She'd wrapped her arms around herself most of the day to contain emotions. She only realized she'd been gritting her teeth when a headache stabbed her brain.

"Mom, did you see the stingrays?" Michael pointed inside of a shallow tank that housed a few slate-gray kite-shaped fish.

Taking Michael to a living science museum had been a great idea. It kept him occupied while giving Kari time to mull over her decisions.

"Yes, they're cool. I think the handlers will let you touch them if you want." She nodded toward one of uniformed attendants standing by the waist-high water tank.

Michael scampered off, leaving Kari time to sulk, or so she thought.

"Okay, boss, what's the deal?" Reagan got in Kari's space. "One minute you're boo hooing over Thane taking Michael to the bathroom, and the next minute you're flipping out because they're playing catch. What gives?"

"Did you notice all the people recording that? What if Jarrod sees it?" Kari moved away from the tank so that Michael couldn't hear their conversation. "He sees Michael so very little now. I don't need to give him a reason to cut him off completely."

"Is Jarrod really worth all this energy?" Reagan shrugged. "Thane was showing Michael some attention that he's needed for a long time." She lowered her voice. "Sound familiar?"

Kari didn't want to admit out loud that being with Thane had given her new life and hope for the future, and she didn't mean her career.

"I didn't even ask. Did you have a good time last night?" Reagan raised her eyebrows.

Kari felt her face get hot before she answered. "Whether I did or not, it doesn't matter. I can't do that again with him."

"Why not? You amaze me sometimes. You have great vision and insight when it comes to picking people to represent. In them, you see a complete future. With your love life, you act so clueless."

"I don't want to see anyone get hurt, least of all Michael."

"Stop worrying. You're a thoughtful and considerate mother. And judging by the way Thane looked at you during breakfast, I would say you must be a very skilled and giving lover as well." Reagan nudged Kari's side with her elbow.

"Will you stop it? Life isn't all about"—Kari checked to make sure Michael stayed occupied—"sex."

"I know. It's also about work. So what are you going to do about Thane, as a client this time?"

With everything that had occurred between the two of them over the past few days, Kari hadn't thought about work. At that moment, her cell phone rang in her purse. She retrieved it and saw Frank's name and number flashed across the screen. She couldn't keep avoiding him.

"Keep an eye on Michael. I'll be right back." Kari stepped over to the starfish exhibit. "Frank. How are you?"

"Cut the pleasantries, Meyers." Frank's voice sounded gruffer than what Kari remembered. "Is Wells signing on or what?"

"He's still mulling it over. I've spoken with him several times, and I've given him my contract terms. Although he hasn't said yes, he hasn't said no either. So I'm still hopeful he wants me." She thought about her choice of words and amended her comment. "And our agency." In her heart, she'd meant what she said.

Fear had kept her from opening herself up to men. She'd gotten burned way too early in life and love. To go through that pain again would crush her, especially if Michael somehow got attached and felt his own disappointment.

She had to admit that seeing Michael throwing a ball back and forth with Thane had made her want to cry all over again. She longed to give Michael a complete home. She couldn't assign that role to Thane.

"You have until the end of this week."

"And then what?" Kari's brazen attitude could only save her, not hurt her. "If I don't land Thane Wells, will I lose my job?"

A long, uncomfortable pause lingered before Frank spoke. "See you back here next week." He ended the conversation before she could come back with a response.

What could Kari say? She'd lived her life counting on Plan A. She never had a Plan B, hence the failed relationship with Jarrod, and her unexpected surprise with Michael, and the loss of the only support system she'd had in her grandfather. At this point, she would feel like she would be using Thane if she signed him instead of being the best person to represent him and his interests. More than anything, she wanted to be by his side as his woman.

Michael ran over to Kari with a huge grin and a starfish sticker on his jacket. "You ready to see the sharks?"

"I work with them, so why not?" Kari took her child's hand.

"What does that mean?" He scrunched his button nose.

"Never mind. Lead me to the finned ones."

Michael pulled Kari through the colorful museum that reminded her of being inside of a fish tank herself. Blue walls and carpeting helped with that effect.

"Can we come back here tomorrow?" Michael asked once he got Kari to the large glass wall that held back the multitude of sharks.

"Honey, we're still here. We can see everything you want today and do something else tomorrow." Kari swept her hand over her son's head.

"I know. But I don't think Thane, I mean Mr. Wells, has been here before. Can we bring him here?"

Kari stared at her child. Damn it. He'd gotten emotionally involved.

"I'm sure he has other things to do. He's here because his mother recently passed away."

Michael's face became solemn. He squeezed Kari's hand and leaned his head against her arm as he looked into the tank. "He needs family now."

"You're right. Good thing he has two brothers who are also here."

"He does? He didn't talk about them. He said he liked hanging out with us." Michael pointed to one of the sharks in the tank. "He said he likes you."

"When? While you two tossed the ball back and forth?" Kari held her breath while she waited for Michael to share his news.

"No. When we were washing our hands." Michael moved in closer to Kari. "Now I understand why he said I should tell you I love you all the time." He looked up at her. "I love you."

Kari's throat felt scratchy. Although she wanted to tease her son by giving him his standard "yeah, yeah" line back, she said, "Love you."

Reagan stood next to Kari. "Time's ticking." She punctuated her statement with the sound of a clock.

No one knew more about losing time than Kari. She had to be smart about what to do. For now, she had her son by her side.

* * * *

Thane had tasted a small morsel of familial bliss with Kari and Michael. He'd seen how she crafted her life around her family. It still surprised him how instantaneous his paternal instincts kicked in when it came to Michael. Although Thane hadn't grown up with a positive father figure, he knew good parenting thanks to Queen Elizabeth.

Although he didn't want to, Thane went over to Sharp. He had no plans to open the place, but he needed to have the dresses ready for the gaggle of girls coming over in a day. He ducked into the storage room and removed the sheet that covered them. His mother hadn't lost her touch. Each dress looked appropriate for a young girl, yet hip enough for the girls to actually want to wear them.

As he admired the workmanship, colors, and styles, a spark ignited in him. He went into his mother's office and pulled out a sketchpad. Everything for him started with a plan…with the exception of Kari. He never saw her coming.

Although she had been hounding him for a while for work, when he really looked at her and touched her, he wanted more. He desired more.

Thane put Kari's full image in his mind. He thought about her style, both conservative and relaxed. Then he recalled her naked body. His fingers tingled as though touching her smooth, velvety skin again. He closed his eyes and her full, brown eyes appeared in his thoughts.

He picked up a pencil and rested his hand on the notepad as he awaited inspiration. It didn't take him long. As soon as he remembered her perfectly rounded breasts, her nipped-in waist, and her full hips, he opened his eyes and started sketching.

Thane thought about something low-cut but not too revealing. Then he remembered her long legs and how she wrapped them around his body. He made sure the dress had a high slit on the side. When he imagined his hand gliding up her thigh and under the dress, he bolted from his seat and went to the showroom.

Fabric. He would need something appropriate for her. Thane put his hand on a bolt of black velvet. Although the snow had melted a couple of weeks ago, velvet seemed too heavy to wear going into spring weather.

He pulled out a roll of gold satin. The gold reminded him of Queen Elizabeth. He and his brothers had buried her in a gold dress. For that reason, he shoved the fabric back into place.

He rested his hand on a roll that first appealed to his touch. The silky fabric felt smooth. He could only imagine what it would be like against skin. When he saw its vibrant red color, he knew he'd found his material. He already had his muse.

It had been a while since he'd made a dress. Because he had continued making clothes for himself, his construction skills remained intact. No one knew his body better than him, although Kari probably came a close second. She'd touched him, physically and emotionally, more than any woman he'd ever dated.

The fact that she'd run off with Michael and Reagan after a simple game of catch concerned him. Had she really been that worried about Jarrod or had something else spooked her? Had he gotten too close too fast?

Feeling like a contestant on *Project Runway*, Thane cut and sewed his heart out, determined to make a dress made for Kari. At the end of the day, he stared at the garment on the form, feeling both proud and deflated. He had no idea if he would see Kari again. She seemed to have given up her pursuit to get him as a client. Her disappearing act earlier proved his theory might be correct.

Thane couldn't be called a quitter, which reminded him about his career. He needed to do some damage control in case someone had seen a video of him throwing a ball around. For all of her paranoia, Kari might have been right about one thing. His manager and coaches could look down on him for not coming back sooner. Mentally, he couldn't step on that mound yet.

Thane called one of the coaches. "Hey, I wanted to bring you up to speed."

"Yeah, I'm all ears." The tone in Jermaine's voice sounded doubtful.

"I need another week and then I'll be back. I have to fulfill an obligation for my mother first and then I'll be ready."

"Take your time. Witt is doing a great job. He can start if you're not ready." Jermaine's voice sounded light, like he'd already made up his mind. "You can practice with the rest of the team when you come back."

Thane heard a hard pounding on the front door before he could make his argument. Jermaine disconnected the call as Thane walked toward the door.

With the power behind the knock, he knew it couldn't be Arlene Sortoberg. He saw the large shape of a person through the taped-up newspaper on the glass front door before the realization hit him who stood on the other side. He stopped right before opening it.

"You know I can see you, right?" Gunnar said.

Thane sighed before unlocking the door. "What are you doing out here?" He held the door and kept his body in the frame to block his brother's entrance.

"I took Gideon to his therapy appointment. Figured since I was in the neighborhood I would come by and see you." Like a steamroller, he walked through the doorway, forcing Thane to move aside.

To prevent anyone else popping into his space, Thane locked the door and followed Gunnar into the showroom.

"You haven't opened." Gunnar scanned the boutique before locking his stare onto Thane.

"I have and I haven't." Thane leaned against a table away from Gunnar. "I haven't opened the doors to the public, but I at least have one customer." He watched his brother furrow his eyebrows at his statement, so he clarified. "Mrs. Sortoberg from that school Mom helps—helped—each year came by a couple of days ago. She's bringing the girls by tomorrow to pick up the dresses."

Gunnar nodded. "Good. At least you're fulfilling that promise. After that, you can open this place up, get it going again." He put his hand on Thane's shoulder and even offered a smile.

A knock sounded on the door before Thane could retort.

Gunnar beamed. "See. Now you have two customers." He pointed to the door.

"Probably some surfer looking for a bathroom." Thane stormed to the door and snatched it open.

A short African-American man with a tight Afro stood on the other side. He smiled when he looked at Thane. Then he craned his head to look around him and damn near jumped for joy when he spotted Gunnar.

"Oh, shit. What are the odds?" The stranger burst into Sharp.

"Excuse me." With the way Thane felt, he didn't mind grabbing this little dude by his collar and pushing him back out into the streets.

"Guns, I didn't know you would be here." The man went in for a hug, but Gunnar held his hand up.

"Ant, what are you doing here?" Gunnar shook his head.

"You know this man?" Thane strolled over to them.

"Old classmate." Gunnar nodded toward him. "He came over to Press 'N Curl when I came back to town. He thought it was a gym."

Ant chuckled. "Yeah. My bad."

"And Gideon told me that you thought Pick 'N Clip was a flag-football team league."

Ant put his hand to his chest. "Again, my mistake. You have athletes running businesses, you automatically think it's going to be sports related."

"So are you following Gunnar, or did you think Sharp was a knife store?" Thane cocked his head.

"Funny." Ant pointed to Thane while he showed off his megawatt smile. "This is still a clothing store, right?"

"Yes, but—"

Gunnar interrupted him. "You need something?"

Thane glared at his brother. He didn't need any extra business. After outfitting the girls, he planned on heading back down to Florida.

"Yeah, I need a really sexy dress made." Ant waved his hands in the air to simulate an hourglass figure. "It has to be about a size six, black, and for someone shorter than me."

Gunnar blinked. "Really? So you really do have a girlfriend? It wasn't all just talk before?"

"Not exactly."

Both Thane and Gunnar furrowed their eyebrows.

Ant continued. "I want a dress for a future girlfriend. My dream woman will be able to fit into that dress. It'll be like Cinderella and the glass slipper."

"Unbelievable." Thane went to the front door. "Nice to meet you, Ant." He opened it. "Unfortunately, I'm not in the business to make custom clothes for imaginary people."

Gunnar chuckled.

Ant grimaced and pointed at them both. "Fuck you, guys. You never want to help me out." He stomped out.

As soon as he left, Thane locked the door again. "Another great reason not to reopen. I can't have crackpots like that as customers."

"They wouldn't all be that way. You will have serious people in there. That's no reason to keep the boutique closed."

Thane pulled away from him. "What is your obsession with me opening Sharp? I keep telling you that I have a life and a career that doesn't involve me running a boutique. If Mom were here, she would understand. She was the only one who got me."

Gunnar blinked. "You don't think I understand what you're going through? Mom's death affected all of us. Coming home forced me to make some decisions about my career and my relationship."

"There you go." Thane chuckled and shook his head. "Not everything is about you."

Gunnar grabbed Thane's arm and turned him around. "That's it. For once and for all, you're going to tell me what the hell you have against me. What did I do to you? Did you have some little-kid crush on Eboni, and now you're pissed that we're together?"

"Give me a break. I like Eboni, but I would never go after your girl." Thane turned his back on Gunnar and braced his hands on the front counter.

"Then what? And don't you dare say nothing." A pause lingered before Gunnar spoke again. "You remember when we were kids and how in the summer we would catch fireflies in our hands? You would keep yours in a jar but forget to poke holes in the lid."

Thane barely recalled that memory. He didn't remember a lot of good times with Gunnar before he went off to train for his fighting career. He started to look behind him at his brother.

"You sure that wasn't Gideon?" Thane turned when he didn't hear Gunnar responding.

Gunnar shook his head. "Nope. It was you. The next morning, Mom would find the jar with the dead insects inside. She would get so mad, first because she hated bugs of any kind."

Thane cocked a smile at the corner of his mouth.

"Then she was upset that we had harmed something. She blamed me for it."

Thane turned around to look at Gunnar. He hadn't remembered that. "She did?"

Gunnar shrugged. "I told her I had done it. Had I been a good brother, I would have poked the holes for you or told you to set the fireflies free. I was screwing up then anyway. One more punishment didn't hurt me."

Thane stared at his oldest brother for a while. "Mom would have hated you lying to her like that. She was all about accountability. You could have told her the truth."

"Wouldn't bring those fireflies back to life. You were too young then. I didn't mind protecting you. But I wished I had taught you this one thing back then. I should have told you to open that jar to let them fireflies go. You liked holding on to them. You need to learn to let things go." He glanced off to the side. He smiled before bringing his attention back to Thane. "I see you haven't forgotten everything from the past. Nice dress. Doesn't look like it'll fit Arlene Sortoberg."

Thane walked to the room that held the gown he wanted to give to Kari. He closed the door before turning back to Gunnar. "You're looking for me to thank you?"

Gunnar approached Thane. "No. I want you to remember that we're family. We always will be family."

"Even if I sell this place?"

Gunnar's face went pale before he stepped away from Thane. "I'm not signing any paperwork for you to sell Sharp." He headed to the front door. "Figure something else out so you can keep it going." He unlocked it and glared at Thane before leaving. "Family always looks out for each other." He slammed the door behind him.

Thane locked the door again but looked through a tear in the newspaper to see Gunnar driving away in his Hummer. Gunnar remembered a lot from their past. Thane wondered if Gunnar recalled the line he had said to their mother a few years before he left the family home. Thane would never forget.

Chapter 17

Even being separated from Thane for only a day, Kari felt like she missed a part of her body, like an appendage had been removed without her knowledge and she had phantom pains to remind her of its existence. She felt a pressure on her inner thighs that reminded her of when Thane had been nestled between her legs.

Not talking to Thane felt like a punishment. She couldn't bring herself to call or see him. After only a day, Michael missed him. No matter what they did during their mini vacation, he asked about Thane, more than he asked about his father. As hard as Kari tried being both mother and father to Michael, he started to show signs that he needed a male figure in his life.

She couldn't understand it. Kari hadn't missed a female figure in her life when her grandfather had raised her on his own. Who was she kidding? She'd joined every team she could as a teenager to have a semblance of sisters. She'd watched female-centric talk shows to hear other women's views on life and careers and men, especially men.

She didn't want to deny Michael a complete family. That didn't mean she needed to find a substitute. Thane wouldn't be a replacement for Jarrod.

"You're getting that faraway look in your eyes again." Reagan draped her arm around Kari's shoulders while they walked down the quiet boardwalk.

"Dreaming stuff I shouldn't be considering." Kari patted Reagan's arm. "I screwed up so badly. Not only am I confused, but I allowed Michael to get sucked into my mistakes."

"You keep saying that, but you haven't considered the idea that what you've done isn't a mistake." Reagan lowered her voice when they got close enough to Michael for him to catch their conversation. "Has he called?"

Kari shook her head.

"Don't sweat it. Like you said, he's in mourning."

Kari nodded and felt something next to her hip vibrating. She reached into her purse and pulled out her phone, hoping it wouldn't be Frank. When she saw Thane's name across the screen, she stopped.

"What?" Reagan released her hold and stared at Kari. Then her eyebrows rose to her hairline. "Thane?" she whispered.

Kari didn't respond to her friend. She swiped her finger over the screen and answered the call. "Kari Meyers speaking." She had to regain some professionalism in this relationship in the slim chance Thane actually wanted her as an agent.

"I need you." His gruff voice powered through the phone and it felt like his words alone stroked her skin.

Kari's breath hitched enough that she had to put her hand to her chest. "Excuse me?" She wanted him to repeat himself.

Before he spoke, she listened to the noise on the other end and the clamorous sounds grabbed her attention. Had he gone back to Florida to train? He could be standing in the center of a locker room.

"The girls." Thane seemed out of breath.

Heat rose up Kari's body until he spoke again.

"I can't handle all of these little girls. Will you please come to the shop and help me with them?"

She exhaled. She'd forgotten Thane had promised dresses to some middle school children. "I'm with my son."

"Bring him and Reagan. The girls are about Michael's age." Thane grunted. "Don't climb up on that, sweetie."

"They didn't come with a teacher or parent?" Kari crossed her legs to keep her excitement contained. She didn't care in what capacity Thane wanted to see her. He could have contacted anyone in his family, but he'd called her.

"One guidance counselor. She can't handle them either. No, no. I'm on the phone."

Kari heard giggling on the other end and couldn't help but laugh herself. She'd been the sole adult during a field trip and sleepover. For someone who hadn't been around a lot of small children, Thane did show some patience.

"I can't stay very long." She heard Thane sighing.

"Hopefully, it won't take very long. I know this is not a young boy's dream. I appreciate you coming by to help. Trust me. I'll make it worth your while."

Kari couldn't hide the beaming smile that split her face. "An hour. That's all."

"Thank you."

The screaming in the background got louder.

"Um, can you hurry?" Thane asked.

This time Kari couldn't help but laugh. "Let me corral the team. We'll be right there." She disconnected the call before she could say anything else. As she put her phone back into her purse, she looked at Reagan and Michael. "We have to go."

"Aw, Mom. Back to the hotel already? It's not even night yet." Michael stomped his way over to Kari.

"Oh, no. Walk correctly and take that attitude out of your voice right now or we will go back to the hotel." Kari glared at her child, who quickly adjusted his gait to something lighter.

"Sorry, Mom."

"Don't say that you're sorry. Say you apologize." She bit the inside of her cheek when she realized she had quoted Thane.

"Yes, ma'am. I apologize." He stood in front of Kari with his head down.

"Thank you." Kari kissed the top of Michael's head. "Mr. Wells called."

Michael snapped his head up and beamed. Kari glanced at Reagan, who winked at Kari.

Kari continued. "He needs some help and asked that we come by his boutique."

"Boutique? What's that?" Michael asked.

"Probably somewhere you don't want to be. But we won't stay very long. I promise." Kari would play it cool with Thane. Even though she knew that all bets would be off as soon as she looked into his eyes.

* * * *

With all the newspapers removed from the glass and door, Thane split his attention between the front door and the line of quiet, but excited, girls standing in front of him. Each time he glanced at any of them, a wave of chirpy giggles followed.

He had to thank his mother for his ease in dealing with children. Each time she'd had an event where she had to be around a lot of kids, she brought him and his brothers along. He learned not only patience from her, but also control that commanded respect.

In the past few years, he'd gotten used to being around little boys when he mentored students at baseball camp. When Mrs. Sortoberg had brought the girls to his shop, they had all squealed like little piglets as they hopped around him. Thane had stopped that quickly.

"I need you all to act like the beautiful young ladies you are," he told them.

That statement had halted their excited behavior. However, he did use those first chaotic moments to call Kari, thinking if she heard the ruckus, she would offer to come over and help him. At least he'd hoped she would. She hadn't disappointed him. Now he hoped that when she saw the girls behaving, she wouldn't be too shocked.

Thane didn't subscribe to the antiquated idea that a man should wait a certain number of days to contact a woman. He hoped Kari appreciated him being a man that stood on his own two feet. He certainly liked the fact that she worked hard and made time for her child and friends.

"Isn't this fun?" Arlene, wearing all red this time, smiled as she waddled around the showroom.

"A blast." Thane tried keeping his attention on Arlene while watching the girls and the door. "I'm glad to be able to continue this tradition my mother started."

Until he saw the looks on the children's faces, he hadn't realized how important this moment meant to them.

"You have to admit that this is something special. They get a pretty dress for a dance tomorrow." Arlene patted Thane's cheek.

"Mr. Wells, why do you keep looking at the door? Do you want us to leave?" A blond girl with the biggest brown eyes kept her head down while still casting her eyes up to look at him.

A chill crept up the back of his neck as he regarded her. In his quest to spot Kari as soon as she arrived, he had neglected his guests. Queen Elizabeth would be so disappointed in his behavior.

Thane crouched down in front of the child. "What's your name?"

She glanced at Arlene before answering. "Gayle."

He held up his hand to her. "Nice to meet you, Gayle."

Again, she paused before accepting his well-intentioned handshake. "Nice to meet you."

He pulled his hand back. "You are absolutely right. I'm being a rude host by not giving you all my full attention. Thank you for calling me on my bad behavior."

Gayle turned her head up to look at Arlene, who simply smiled.

"For that reason, you can be the first one to look at the dresses." He waited until she acknowledged his statement before he moved.

The girl beamed and jumped around before Thane stood.

"I don't think it was right how you were treating us either. Can I go to the front of the line?" A chubby African-American girl said from the back of the line.

"Sometimes you get what you get because of how you act. Come at me respectfully, and you'll get my attention." He approached the girl and put his hand on her shoulder. "Think about that from your current spot in the line."

He felt her shoulders slump down. "Don't worry. There will be plenty of great dresses to choose from." He patted her shoulder, which she firmed up.

He peered up when he saw sunlight reflecting off a windshield and gleaming through the door. His heart pounded when he noticed that Kari had pulled into the lot.

Thank God.

"Excuse me." Thane strolled by Arlene and went to the door.

Before Kari exited the car, he had the door open, ready for her to come inside. As soon as he saw her in her tight jeans, he forgot about the girls and the dresses and even his name. Her clingy T-shirt had him jealous of the fabric that got to cover her soft skin.

Kari opened the back door and helped Michael. He bolted by her to run up to Thane.

"Hey, Thane. I mean, Mr. Wells." Michael hugged him and then peered in the store. "You have a lot of girls in there."

"I know." Thane patted Michael on his back. He glanced at Reagan first. "Hi, Reagan. Thanks for helping."

"Hey, kids are my thing. I'm like a child whisperer." Reagan smiled.

"You yell a lot though." Michael scratched his head.

"You are such a joy to watch." Reagan peered down at him and stroked his head.

"I know sarcasm when I hear it." Michael screwed up his little mouth.

The banter between the two had Thane laughing until he looked at Kari again. "Hi."

Kari smiled. "Hi."

Silence lingered between the two of them. Thane didn't break his stare from Kari until he got hit from behind. He turned and found Gayle holding up a light blue dress.

"Can I have this one? Ms. Sortoberg said I have to ask you first." She looked like a million dynamite fuses had been lit in her tiny body and would detonate soon if he didn't answer her.

"Have Ms. Sortoberg help you in the dressing room to see if it works for you." Thane nudged the child toward the guidance counselor.

"Wow. I was kind of expecting a train wreck in here." Reagan walked into the store. She turned to Thane. "You seem to have everything under control."

"Yes, they do seem to be falling in line." Kari screwed up her lips, but not out of anger. She looked like she was trying not to smile.

"It was selfish of me to demand so much of your time, especially now with your family here." He moved closer to Kari. "I wanted to see you again no matter the situation. Is that okay?"

Kari's mouth opened but she didn't say anything. Thane didn't want to render the woman speechless. He liked hearing her talk.

Michael shrank back against Kari. "So many girls." He looked up at Kari. "May I wait in the car, please?"

Before Kari could answer, Thane spoke. "Hey, I have a quiet office in the back. There's even a computer in there." He looked at Kari. "That is if your mother doesn't mind."

"That's very kind of you, Mr. Wells." Kari's light voice floated to his ears and caressed them.

"*You* call me Thane." He put his hand on Michael's shoulder. "Come on. I'll get you to the office. Then your mother and I will get these girls out of here. Sound good?"

"Sounds great."

Once Thane got Michael situated in his office and closed the door just enough to block the girls but still let Kari see inside to keep an eye on her son, Kari took Thane's arm and pulled him into the corner.

"Before you get ahead of yourself, I want to tell you that I don't like being manipulated into doing things." Kari crossed her arms over her chest. "Don't use me."

Thane had hoped she wanted to steal a kiss when she pulled him to the side. Her speech brought him back down to earth. Knowing what he knew about her, he understood her stance.

"I would never use you, well, except for one thing." He held up his index finger. "You are still a sports agent, right?"

Her hard countenance cracked and she laughed. "You think you're cute, don't you?"

"No. *You* do." He traced his index finger over her heart. He felt it pounding through her thin shirt. "We can stand here and talk more about my appeal, but I have a whole room full of young girls looking for dresses. Will you help me?"

She nodded. "Yes, I will. But I have to ask you a question first."

Thane stared at her.

Kari asked, "What's the surprise you have for me?"

"Oh, yes. I want to invite you to a dance at the Oceanfront Community Center." He saw Kari's eyebrows knit over her eyes.

"Is this the same dance you're outfitting the girls for?"

He nodded. "Besides donating dresses, my mother also chaperoned the event. I would love it if you would come with me."

"As your date?" Kari lowered her arms to her side.

"Yes." No games. He liked this woman. He wanted her to know his serious intent.

"Hmm, me at a middle-school party."

"You and Michael and Reagan, although I'm sure Michael won't like it. Girls and all." Thane ushered her to the main showroom where the students stood obediently in line until he returned. "I remember being his age and my mother dragging me to these events." He shook his head.

"You don't sound like you enjoyed it. Why would I subject my child to this?" Kari asked.

"Because going there taught me how to appreciate the opposite sex." He leaned down. "I also learned how to kiss, but that happened years later." He winked. "You ready?"

* * * *

Kari worked alongside Thane, helping the girls find dresses that fit their bodies and personalities. After learning that Thane had gotten her there under false pretenses, she wanted to be angry with him. He did something that no other man ever had: He came clean with her even though he did it without apology.

He didn't need to feel sorry. She wanted to see him as much as he said he wanted to see her. Each time she walked by him, she brushed her arm against his or touched his back or hand.

He responded by giving her knowing looks and occasional winks. With each expression, her pulse raced. Damn. She shouldn't have started something she couldn't finish.

As expected, Reagan handled the children like an expert. She corralled them to try on dresses and made sure they settled down in seats when finished. Michael remained quiet in Thane's office. Kari poked her head in every once in a while to make sure he didn't feel slighted or ignored. Each time, he broke his concentration from the computer to smile at her.

Kari really did have a great child. She owed him an awesome vacation.

She turned to Thane. "Is that everyone?"

"I think so, although I hope you don't have to run." Thane rubbed his hand across the back of his neck. "I have another surprise for you and your family this time. The Norfolk Tides is a minor league baseball team. They heard about me being in town and invited me and my guests to see them play tonight. I would love for you all to go with me."

Michael bolted from the office. "Oh, wow, Mom! Can we go? Can we?" He grabbed Kari's arm and tugged on it.

"Excuse me." Kari pried her child's fingers from her arm. "Were you listening in on our conversation?"

Michael's flushed to a dark crimson, and chewed on his lower lip before he answered. "I heard a little bit, but not on purpose. I'm sorry. I mean I apologize."

Kari caught Thane's surprised expression before she regarded her child again. "You shouldn't have done that. Adult conversations are private."

"Yes, ma'am." He lowered his head. "It would be great to see an actual baseball game with *the* Thane Wells."

"Are you saying you wouldn't enjoy the game if you didn't go with a famous baseball player?" Kari crossed her arms over her chest as she looked down at Michael.

Michael volleyed his attention between Kari and Thane. "No. He's a nice man. I would enjoy watching the game even if he was my math teacher."

That got Thane to burst into laughter. "Too bad I don't teach algebra. As long as it's okay with your mother, I'd be more than happy to have you all as my guests."

"Even if Kari says no, I would like to go." Reagan stood next to Kari. Her wide eyes held excitement. "I haven't heard a real crack of a bat against a ball or had bad stadium hot dogs in a long time."

Kari sighed as she gazed at Michael's expectant face. "How can I deny them a game and greasy meats? Okay, let's go." She looked at Thane. "Take me out to the ballgame."

"No, Mom, sing the other song about baseball. You know. Our song."

Kari felt heat creeping up her neck. Singing that song usually meant Michael felt hurt or sad. She couldn't equate it to mean something good or joyous. Before she could sing a note or explain her silence, she saw Arlene walking toward them.

Arlene came up behind the group and tapped Thane on his shoulder. As soon as Thane turned around, the plump woman wrung her hands.

"There's a problem." Arlene wiped her forehead.

"What's wrong? Did one of the girls rip a dress or something?" Thane scanned the group of children.

His stare stopped on a girl the same time Kari's did. The girl sat in a chair with nothing in her hands.

"She couldn't find anything that fit her." Arlene fanned her face. "Now she says she doesn't want to go."

Thane headed toward the child without a word. As soon as he got to her, he sat in a chair next to her. Kari went to the duo in case Thane needed help, but she stood far enough back to give the child some privacy.

"Did you enjoy your day here?" Thane kept his voice low.

The girl shrugged and kept her chin resting on her fist.

"Hey, I didn't get your name earlier."

"Leona," she mumbled.

"Leona. That's a pretty name. I heard you might not be going to the dance tomorrow. Is that right?"

A single tear rolled down from the child's eye and over her nose. The young girl wiped her face with the back of her hand. Seeing that broke Kari's heart. She wanted to envelope her in a hug.

"I couldn't find a dress that fit my—" She glanced at Thane before she continued speaking. "My style."

Thane nodded. "I understand." He sat back and studied her. "I bet your style is more the Beyoncé or Jennifer Lopez. Am I right?"

Her eyes lit up as she sat up straighter. "More like my girl RiRi."

"Hmm, you don't think her style is a bit much for you? She shows a little too much skin."

As though he had a pin and had popped her balloon, Leona melted back down to her same defeated stance she'd had before. "It doesn't matter. I'm not going. My mother can't afford a dress for me, and I'm not going there looking busted." She shook her head.

Kari started to move toward the duo to offer to buy the girl a dress when Thane surprised her.

"Tell me what kind of dress you would like." He sat up taller. "I'll have it made before the dance tomorrow."

Kari and Leona blinked as they stared at him.

"Are you serious? You're going to have someone make me a dress?" Leona put her hand to her chest.

"Yes, and not just anyone. I'll make your dress." He stood and marched to his office. He came back with a pad of paper and a pencil. As soon as he sat down, he looked at the girl for a moment before he started drawing something over the paper. "What's your favorite color?"

"Purple. No, red." Leona clasped her hands together and watched Thane work.

Kari did the same. She wondered if Thane could pull off what he'd proposed.

"How about a combination of the two?" He turned the pad over to reveal his creation.

Kari couldn't see it, but from the girl's excited expression, she suspected he'd created something pretty spectacular. Now could he deliver?

"If you can make that, I would be the best-looking girl there." She bounced in her chair.

"Consider it made. I'll get your measurements and get started tonight." He turned to Kari. "Unfortunately, that means that I won't be able to go to the game with you tonight."

Damn.

Chapter 18

Thane didn't want to back out of going to the game with Kari and Michael, but as soon as he'd seen Leona looking so disappointed, he knew he had to do something. He hoped Kari understood. From her saddened expression, he guessed she didn't.

He wanted nothing more than to spend time with her outside of business and sex, which he still couldn't get out of his mind. She stimulated him like no woman had before.

With the shop empty and closed, he turned to Kari and her group. "I hate to back out of the game, but I need to do something important that requires a lot of time."

"For the girl that was crying?" Michael asked.

Thane nodded. "I'm like Superman. I have powers and I have to use them for good." He glanced at Kari and smiled.

"I understand." Michael nodded. "Can I stay and help you? Maybe if I help, we can all go to the game together."

Kari stroked her son's head. "You're such a good boy."

Michael rolled his eyes. "Mom."

"Your mom is right. Good kids deserve great rewards. You three go to the game. If I get out of here early enough, I'll join you. If not, I hope to see you all tomorrow." He stared at Kari to see how she'd answer.

"Thank you so much for the tickets. I hope you can make it." She put her arm around Michael's shoulders and grabbed Reagan's hand.

Thane nodded. "I'm a little rusty in the dress-making department, but I should be okay." He walked them to the door.

"Thanks for the awesome day. I actually had fun." Reagan got on her tiptoes and kissed Thane on his cheek.

"Sorry you're going to miss the game." Michael screwed up his lips.

"It's okay. I'm sure I'll catch the next one." Thane winked at him before Reagan pulled Michael out to the car.

Kari stood in the doorway staring at Thane, not saying a word.

"It's okay to go. I appreciate you all coming here to help me. Enjoy the night on me." He reached for his back pocket. "You need money?" Then he winced. "I need to stop saying that to you, don't I?"

Kari smiled. She glanced at her family, then back to Thane. "Will you wait here a second?"

"Sure." He assumed she had to go to the bathroom before they drove to Norfolk to enjoy the game.

She spoke to Reagan, who looked at Thane over Kari's shoulder. The last time she glanced at Thane, a strange smile hitched up the side of her mouth. Then Reagan nodded and hugged Kari.

Kari ducked her head into the car to speak to Michael. Before Thane knew it, he saw Reagan getting in the driver side and pulling away without Kari.

Kari ran back up to the door and stood in front of Thane. "Let me help you. We could go to the game together."

Thane stepped aside as he ushered her inside. "You don't have to do this. I know spending time with your family is important."

"It is. Michael was okay with me staying. I think he likes you." Kari stood behind him while he locked the door again.

"Good. I'm glad. In a lot of ways, he reminds me of me." Thane walked by her to go to the wall of fabric bolts.

"How's that?"

"He's smart. He's handsome."

Kari laughed.

"And he loves his mother." Thane pulled out a roll of lavender tulle and set it next to him. "It's been a hard trip coming back home. Hanging around you and your family has made it tolerable." He shook his head. "No, that's not the right word." He stared at her. "You've made me happy."

He watched her breath hitch at his admission. Thane meant every word. In a world where everyone wanted something from him, she'd managed to break down his defenses and be that rock.

"Really, you don't have to stay." Thane grabbed a purple satin fabric and some bejeweled trim.

When he didn't hear anything from Kari, he turned to see her approaching him. She framed his face in her hands and kissed him hard enough to make him forget his manners. He released the fabric and wrapped his arm around her waist.

As soon as he slid his tongue into her mouth, Thane pulled back. "If we keep this up, I won't make that dress. You are addicting and distracting." He held her tighter.

"I promise not to get in your way. I wanted to thank you for everything you've done for me and Michael."

"You really want to show your appreciation?" Thane pulled out a roll of red satin fabric. "Carry this for me and follow me to the work room."

She accepted the roll and trailed behind him to a room next to the showroom. He used his elbow to turn on the light and placed the fabrics on a table.

Kari put her roll next to his. "So you were serious about making this dress?"

Thane felt his eyebrows draw together. "Why would I lie about that?"

"I know. I should have known better." She went over to his sketchpad and picked it up. "Not bad. How long have you been making clothes?"

Thane kept his concentration on his work, afraid if he looked at Kari again he would do more than kiss her. "Making clothes? Since I was about Michael's age."

"Get out."

"True. When I was little, I used to draw clothes because I saw my mother doing the same thing. As I got older, she would show me more and more about how to make clothing. First is the pattern. Then you put it all together like a puzzle until you get your design. Once I learned the ins and outs of making clothing, I started making them for myself. That leather jacket I wore that you said you liked was actually one of my creations."

"Wow. You're really talented."

Thane smiled. "Thanks, but I haven't made a dress for a little girl, not even when I was her age. Mom always made the girls' dresses. I helped."

"Now I'll be your helper." She stood next to him. "It'll be the one and only time I'll let you use me."

He measured out the pattern on muslin first. With each move, he caught Kari's heavenly scent. When he looked at her, he saw her staring at him. He wondered if she regarded him in awe or lust...or both. He glanced up and saw the dress he'd made for her covered under a sheet. He hoped she wouldn't go snooping. When he saw her starting to turn around to look behind herself, he distracted her.

"So Michael likes baseball?" Thane started to cut the thin, gauzy fabric as he awaited Kari's answer.

"He loves all sports, even golf. I think he likes the athletes more than the sport itself. He sees them as superheroes almost. It's cute." She smiled and sidled up next to him.

When her arm touched his, Thane's body immediately reacted. Every hair stood on end and his pulse pounded hard enough that it sounded in his ears.

"Here. You cut out more of these patterns for me." He showed her what he wanted and then moved over to his mother's sewing machine.

"Not a problem." She started to cut while he threaded the machine.

It felt good to handle the same equipment his mother had used to teach him how to make clothes. The classic piece of equipment didn't have all the digital bells and whistles like new machines. That didn't matter. He knew what to do on this one.

"Will you tell me something?" Kari began as she cut ever so slowly.

"Depends." Thane had always been honest, even as a kid. That didn't mean he didn't have a guarded side.

"Why don't you get along with your brothers?"

He started to open his mouth and spout the same story he used to tell his mother whenever she brought up the topic. When he looked into Kari's eyes, he couldn't hold back.

He concentrated on the work in front of him as he spoke, too apprehensive to look at her now. "Gunnar was a bad kid when Queen Elizabeth first adopted us. He used to steal and lie and do drugs."

"He's certainly not like that now, right?" She put down the scissors to give him her full attention.

"No, of course not. He straightened up when he was about fourteen or so. But one night he and Mom had this big blow out. He was trying to hang out with a bad bunch of kids, and she knew it. She'd told him not to go out. He'd said some pretty awful things to her that night. He'd said she wasn't his real mother." Repeating that had him stopping the rhythmic stitching of the sewing machine. He balled his hands into fists. "I was only six or seven at the time. I remember always trying to hang out with him and Gideon. I'd wanted to be like them. I'd wanted to be with their friends. When Gunnar argued with Queen that day, it scared me. I'd never seen him that angry." He shook his head as he kept his gaze down to the floor. "Sure he would tell me to get lost when he tried to be with boys his own age. But I thought all older brothers did that."

"I wouldn't know. Only child." Kari moved around the worktable and sauntered toward Thane.

"That's right. Anyway, during that argument, Gunnar dropped another major bomb." Thane brought his head up and stared Kari in her eyes this time. "He'd said 'I don't care about you or Thane. He's not my real brother anyway.'"

Kari blinked and took a couple of steps back. "That's not true, is it? I always assumed the three of you were biological brothers when your mother adopted you."

"I always thought that, and Elizabeth never made us feel any differently. My brother"— Thane stopped himself before he continued his story— "Gunnar said some horrible things that night. I never thought he would lash out at me, and that I wouldn't be related to him and Gideon by blood. When Gunnar left, Mom went to the kitchen to call over a neighbor to watch me and Gideon so that she could go after Gunnar. When she saw me and realized that I had heard the whole fight, you know what she said?"

Kari shook her head but remained silent.

"She said that Gunnar was a lost soul and needed love and strength to find his way back." Thane shoved the dress through the sewing machine to finish off the hem.

"Those sound like wise words. Why would that make you angry at him?"

He stood. "She never once said that what he said was a lie. I wanted her to tell me that Gunnar and Gideon were my blood brothers. To know that Gunnar, Gideon, and I weren't really brothers made me feel like a loner. It was just me and Mom against them."

Kari shook her head. "That's not true. Whether the same woman gave birth to you or not, Elizabeth Sommerville adopted the three of you. All of you made up a family. Gunnar and Gideon are your brothers in the same way Queen was your mother. With your mother gone, you shouldn't push family away. Trust me. I know. I wish I could find someone else in my family to talk to and rely on."

Thane wanted to agree with every word she'd said. He'd allowed this pain to plant itself in him, and the roots had gone deep. Chopping the tree of deceit and anger down wouldn't eliminate the buried portion.

"Gunnar apologized to my mother, but he never said a word to me." He tossed the skirt portion of the dress onto the worktable and kept his back to Kari. "Gideon has always been good to me. He doesn't deserve me ignoring his calls or avoiding him. Whenever I look at him, I see Gunnar. I don't see me in any of them."

Kari came around him to face him. "You have to be the bigger man here. You can't keep going on ignoring them and thinking it's okay. I'm sure they love you." She put her hand to the side of his face. "Please."

He wanted to make this all right for himself. He couldn't. Not right now with everything still so raw and open.

He turned his head and kissed the palm of her hand. "I'll finish this up."

"The dress or the rift with your brother?"

Thane didn't say anything. At this point, he didn't know if he could repair what had been broken so long ago.

* * * *

When Kari asked Thane about his relationship with his brothers, she hadn't known he would reveal something so painful. She couldn't relate to him being adopted. She could only imagine the hurt a young Thane must have felt when he heard someone he considered to be his brother say they didn't have a blood bond.

The idea that Thane could be so dismissive of Gunnar and Gideon worried her. If she started a relationship with him, would he see Michael as more than her and Jarrod's son? Would he become as aloof with him? She wanted to think he wouldn't because he'd been so close to his mother. In this situation, she didn't know. Her head told her to treat this fleeting fling as nothing more than that. Her heart though kept reminding her that she wanted more, ached for more, felt more from Thane.

Kari didn't realize all that went into making a dress. It seemed so easy on that designer reality TV show. Once Thane got to work, he remained serious. She knew to stay out of his way as soon as he constructed the dress on the form. Before she knew it, he had the finish product in front of him.

Thane had made a pretty purple dress with a glittery belt and a bow in the back. "What do you think?"

Kari took a step back to admire the work. "Very nice." She bumped into another covered form behind her. She hadn't noticed it at all until now. "What's this?"

"Another surprise for you." Thane placed the dress down and sauntered to her.

"Another one? I don't know how many more surprises I can take from you." She stood off to the side while Thane slipped the sheet down and uncovered a stunning yet simple red gown.

"Oh my God. Did Queen make this before she passed away?" She stroked her hand over the sumptuous fabric and fell in love with it.

"No. I made it."

Kari turned to him.

"For you," he added. "I had this plan to do a big dress reveal tomorrow, but it's good that you saw it now. You can try it on and see if it fits."

"Are you serious?"

"Very. I'll go to the office and shut everything down. You try on the dress."

Kari couldn't take the garment off the form. She felt like she would be disturbing a museum piece or something. "This is too much."

"And you, my dear, are wasting time. Try it on." He glanced at his watch. "We've probably missed the game. Give your family a call. I'll wait for you."

"Reagan and Michael have been texting me since they got to the game. According to Reagan's most recent text, they're in the last inning, and Michael has eaten three hot dogs."

Thane laughed. "You're going to be in so much trouble when he becomes a teenager."

Kari couldn't help but laugh with him. "I think you're right."

"Try on the dress. Let me see if I've lost my touch." He backed out of the room and closed the door behind him, leaving Kari to contemplate the entire scene.

She touched the silky fabric again, allowing it to slip over her fingertips. Thane had made this gown with her in mind. For that reason, she couldn't wait to see how he saw her. She kicked off her shoes while she removed her shirt. As soon as she removed her jeans, she approached the expensive-looking garment again.

Kari unzipped the back of the dress and pulled it over the form. After she had the dress pulled up to her breasts, she realized her black lace bra ruined the look. Before removing her undergarment, she attempted to zip up the back of it but could only get it up part of the way.

She turned to the closed door and exhaled. Kari wanted to see the entire look of this dress. She removed her bra and tossed it on the table. Then she opened the door and went to Thane's office, all the while holding up the top portion of the gown to cover her naked breasts.

"I need a little help." Kari stood in the doorway of the office.

As soon as Thane spotted her, he stopped moving. "Whoa. I didn't think—"

She felt her pulse thumping the longer she stared at him. "Um, could you zip me up?" She turned her back to him.

From behind her, she heard him walking toward her. Before zipping up the gown, he placed his hands on her shoulders. The warmth melted her. She started to tilt her head to brush her face against his hand but stopped herself. She didn't want to start something again. Of course putting on the gown hadn't helped her cause.

He slid his hands down her arms, leaving a trail of goose bumps. She tightened her hold around her body until he finally zipped up the back.

"How does it feel on?" he whispered into her ear.

She nodded. "Good."

"Turn around. Let me see you."

After taking a deep breath, she pivoted. She lost herself as she stared into his eyes.

"You are absolutely beautiful." He held his hand up to her.

She accepted it and allowed him to lead her to the main store to one of the dressing rooms. He opened the door and stood behind her. Except for her socks and her casual hair, the dress made her look like a million dollars. The deep V neckline showed off enough cleavage to be both sexy yet appropriate. The slit on the side went up her leg but not too high.

"What do you think?" Thane asked from behind her.

"It's wonderful." She turned. "But I can't accept this. It's too much."

He shook his head. "I made it for you. No other woman can wear this dress." He rested his hands on her hips. "Looks like I had your measurements down."

"The backside feels a little tight." She tugged the front of the dress.

"I did that on purpose." He winked.

Kari playfully slapped his arm. "You are so wrong."

The stare between them lingered for a while before Thane broke the stillness, leaned his head down, and pressed his lips against hers. To maintain her balance, she held on to his shoulders. To feel more of him, she moved one hand up and raked it through his hair. When she felt him moving her back, she had to stop him.

"Wait." Kari put her hands against his arms.

"What's wrong?" Thane seemed out of breath. He panted as he maintained his hold on her.

"Not in this dress. I don't want to mess it up." She turned her back on him again. "Will you unzip it for me?"

Kari felt his hot breath by her ear before she heard him speak. "Depends," he began. "Do you still have condoms in your purse?"

She smiled. "Maybe."

Before she could come back with another teasing remark, Thane lifted her in his arms, which made her squeal.

"What are you doing?" She wrapped her arm around his shoulder and couldn't erase the smile from her face.

"Getting you out of that dress." He placed her on top of the worktable. "Unless you have to go." He spread her legs apart and positioned himself in between her knees. "I don't want to keep you from your family." He cupped the side of her face and kissed her neck.

"And yet you do things like that. So unfair." She started to wrap her legs around him and it hit her again about her attire. "Get me out of this dress." Then her phone chirped, signaling that she had another text message. She looked over to the side where her purse sat. "And maybe I need to go." She started to slide down from the table, but Thane held her thighs.

"I understand that you need to go." He gave her a gentle squeeze. "I need more of you."

"You could let me represent you." Kari said it as a joke, but after all this time, she wanted to hear what Thane had to say.

"You wouldn't want my business." He shook his head.

"And why is that?"

"I don't know if I can continue in baseball for much longer."

Chapter 19

After Thane confessed his concern about his career, he shut down. He unzipped her and retreated to the office while she got dressed again. Then he took her back to her hotel.

"Are you going to tell me what's going on with you?" she asked before getting out of his car.

"I have a lot to think about." He looked at her hotel. "Go be with your family." He put the car in *park* and got out. He strolled to her side and opened her door.

"We can talk if you—"

He interrupted her. "Come with me to the Outer Banks." He kissed her lightly. "Sorry for cutting you off. I can talk to you there."

"You can tell me now. Agent hat off. I want to help."

He took her hand and walked her to the door. "Are you still coming to the dance?"

"I have my dress." She held up the gray dress bag containing the couture gown Thane had created for her.

"I can pick you three up around five."

She nodded. "No, we'll meet you there."

Thane opened the lobby door for her. He kissed her cheek. "Thanks for everything."

As she stood in the lobby, she watched Thane go back to his car and drive away. Now that she understood him, she had to do more for him.

Kari went up to her hotel room. As soon as she walked into the hotel room, Michael surprised her with a tackle.

"Mom! Mom! Mom! You missed everything." Michael hopped around the room like he contained the energy of a million and one bunnies.

"It's after midnight." Kari closed and locked the door. "What are you still doing up?" She glared at Reagan, who looked like she wanted to pass out on the couch.

"Damn Cracker Jacks." Reagan shook her head. "And ice cream and cotton candy and soda."

"Reagan, you gave him all that sugar?" Kari draped her dress bag over the back of a chair and held Michael's tiny shoulders. "You, young man, need to take a shower, brush your teeth, calm down, and go to bed."

"I can't sleep. I feel like it's Christmas and my birthday all rolled into one." He ran to the other side of the room with his arms outstretched.

If Kari couldn't get this bundle of energy down, she would be too exhausted to go to the dance or do much of anything. She owed it to her child to be present and give him everything he deserved.

"Honey, if you don't go to sleep, then I won't sleep. If I don't sleep, I won't be a fun mommy." She glanced at Reagan. "And poor Reagan is trying hard to get some sleep herself. I know you had an exciting day."

"Yeah, you missed it. Where were you and Mr. Thane?" Michael managed to slow down to ask that probing question.

"Mr. Wells." Kari straightened her back. "Like we said, we made that little girl the dress." As though she needed to prove it, she went into her purse and pulled out her cell phone. She went to her photo gallery and turned the screen to Michael. "See. That's the dress."

Michael studied the picture for a moment. "Purple." He screwed up his lips for a second before he brought his attention back to Kari.

"Yes, the color she liked." She put her phone back in her purse.

"Why does she need a new dress? It looks too fancy for school." Michael wrinkled his little nose.

"She's attending a dance." Kari paused. "Mr. Wells invited us to go. Does that sound like something you would want to do?"

Michael never went to his school dances. He always had a reason to skip them, like a school project or a paper he had to write. If her son didn't want to go, she wouldn't make him. She was conflicted. She did want to spend more time with Thane. He had made her an absolutely gorgeous dress. She also wondered what he would look like in a nice suit.

"As long as I don't have to dance, I would like to go. But I don't have anything nice to wear. I brought shorts and my bathing suit. Is that okay for this party?"

Kari exhaled and smiled. Michael did want to go, although she hadn't thought about what he and Reagan would wear. "Go to bed right now, and we'll go shopping after breakfast."

"With Mr. Thane—uh, Wells?"

Kari stood behind Michael and held his shoulders as she led him to the bathroom. "I don't know what he his plans are for tomorrow other than the dance. We'll see him at the community center."

Truth be told, she wanted to see Thane earlier than that. She wanted to keep talking to him, especially since he had shared some incredible news, first about his brothers and then about his baseball career.

As soon as she heard the shower start, and when Reagan dragged herself to bed, Kari sat on the couch in front of the TV. She thought about calling Thane but decided against it. Then her phone vibrated and chirped in her hand. She looked at the screen.

"Thanks for the help & the tease. I like Kari the agent almost as much as I like Kari the woman. Go to bed. T."

Kari read the message ten times before she decided to respond. She started off typing a long message and then stopped herself.

"Good night, Mr. Wells."

She stood and headed to her bed when her phone vibrated again.

Thane. *"I knew you would still be awake."*

She smiled. Every time she thought she could pigeonhole Thane into one category, he surprised her. After tucking her son into bed after his shower, Kari went to sleep with a smile on her face and a heaviness in her heart.

* * * *

No matter how long Thane worked out that day, or what activities he did to occupy his mind, Kari filled and flooded his thoughts. He liked being open with her. Each time he shared some news about himself, he felt lighter. The pains in his stomach started to go away.

Thane stayed away from social media and the Internet that day. It didn't matter. His teammates and friends kept texting him articles and posts about him throwing a ball to Michael. Thane truly didn't think what he did would be newsworthy or interesting. The rest of the population didn't feel that way.

He hoped that Kari hadn't caught wind of any of this. He remembered how panic stricken she appeared when she found him keeping her son occupied. If she did see all the online attention, he didn't want it to keep her from attending this dance event. He didn't want to attend it alone. He needed the support.

Thane finished getting dressed in black slacks, a red button-down shirt, and a matching black jacket that he'd made himself. He glanced at his watch.

"Shit." Thane hurried out of his hotel room.

He hated being late, especially when he had something important to do. He rushed over to Sharp in time to see Arlene and Leona walking back to Arlene's car. Thane didn't bother doing a perfect parking job. He left his car sideways in the lot and hopped out of it.

"Sorry, ladies." He unlocked the door to the store. "I apologize for getting here late." He ushered the two inside and locked the door after them.

"We thought maybe you were kidding about the dress yesterday." Arlene struggled to smile.

"I would never make light of a promise." Thane crouched in front of Leona. "Are you ready to see your custom-made gown?"

The child shrugged. "I guess."

Thane could understand her disappointment. He'd almost ruined it for her by being late. He stood and opened the door to the workroom where he'd created the dress. "Tah dah." He held his hand up to show off the garment on the dress form.

When he didn't hear anything, Thane looked down at Leona. He found her mouth agape and tears streaming down her cherubic face.

"It's so pretty." She moved toward it but stopped before touching it. "I can't pay you for this."

"I know, sweetie." Thane nodded.

"I can return it right after the dance. My mama can clean it."

Thane crouched down again. "This is yours. From me to you. A one-of-a-kind original. A gift."

She didn't say anything when she hugged him. Thane wrapped his arms around her. When he looked up, he noticed Arlene Sortoberg crying. She turned her back on the scene.

Thane released the child. "There are changing rooms out there." He took the dress off the form. "You can put this on in there." Then he glanced at his watch. "You don't have a lot of time. The dance will be starting in an hour."

"Thank you so much." She ran out of the room.

Good thing. Thane looked down and noticed a condom package on the floor. Damn. One must have fallen out of Kari's purse. He casually stepped on it to keep it out of Arlene's view.

"This was really a wonderful thing you did." Arlene patted Thane's arm.

"It was nothing. I hope it fits. If it doesn't, it's going to take me a bit to make adjustments." He shifted, which caused the packaging to crinkle under his foot.

Arlene looked down.

"Ms. Sortoberg, I need help with the zipper," Leona said from the dressing room.

"Be right there, dear."

As soon as Arlene walked out of the room, Thane picked up the condom and shoved it in his pocket. A fleeting thought hit him that he might be able to use it that night. He shook his head to push the idea from his mind. Kari would be there with her family…in that dress.

Damn.

Thane's cell phone rang in his jacket pocket. He retrieved it, saw Gunnar's name across the screen, and put the phone back in its place. He didn't need this night ruined with an argument with his brother.

Thankfully, Leona's new dress fit her perfectly. He hadn't lost his touch. With Leona changed into her new dress, he escorted the two out of the store. They followed him to the Oceanfront Community Center.

Due to good manners, and to heighten Leona's special moment, Thane made sure to open the door for her into the center. He went to the basketball court area, which now had streamers trickling down from the ceiling and walls, balloons, and flashing colored lights.

Children already filled the space. Like typical kids, they screamed and jumped around with their friends. A few of them ran across the room, which put Arlene Sortoberg on high alert. She made the rambunctious children stand in front of her as she spouted the rules for their behavior during the event. He remembered almost verbatim her speech from when she'd given it to him when he'd attended these dances as a child.

Thane's shoes clicked over the shiny hardwood floor as he crossed the room to Drew, the center manager. As soon as Drew saw Thane, his face lit up.

"Hey." Drew held out his hand. "Thane Wells. I can't believe you're here."

Thane smiled and his stomach started to tighten.

Easy. Come on. One night. Give me one night.

"How are you doing?" Thane shook the older man's hand.

"Great now that you're here." He put his hands to his hips.

"I'm doing this for my mother. She would have done this if—" Thane stopped, unable and unwilling to say out loud that his mother had passed away.

"I know. She was good people." Drew nodded. "She raised good boys." He looked behind Thane and his smile widened.

Thane turned and his heart sank. Gunnar walked across the floor holding Eboni's hand. As usual, Eboni looked like a regal queen with her short hairdo, impeccable makeup, and a form-fitting black sheath dress. Wearing all black, Gunnar looked like a hit man for the mafia.

"You're here." Thane didn't try hiding his disappointment. He did manage to rest his hand on his stomach without the move looking suspicious.

"I called you to let you know we were coming. As usual, you didn't answer your phone." Gunnar glared at Thane.

"Honey." Eboni tugged on Gunnar's arm. "You promised to be nice."

"This is nice. I didn't call him a spoiled brat."

"Great." Thane started to walk by them. He leaned over and gave Eboni a kiss on her cheek. "Great seeing you again."

"At some point, you're going to have to talk to me." Gunnar growled his statement.

"Not tonight." Thane didn't need the aggravation. As soon as he thought that, he spotted another couple coming into the party area. "Jesus."

Gideon walked in without his cane and with Janelle by his side. She had her arm around his waist as they headed toward Thane. Could Thane's night get any better?

"You're here." Thane kissed Janelle on her cheek after addressing his brother.

"Of course. We're in town. This place and this event were important to Mom. It's a no-brainer that we would be here." Gideon tightened his hold on Janelle.

"It's been a long time since I've been back here and to this dance." Janelle shook her head.

"You came here? I don't remember you." Thane wracked his brain to recall if he'd ever seen Janelle during any of the events.

"I kept myself hidden back then." She leaned her head on Gideon's shoulder. "Someone special found me."

"Yeah, that reminds me. I'll have to keep an eye out for the bleacher areas. I'm sure I wasn't the first one to sneak a kiss back there. I know I won't be the last one." Gideon patted Thane on his shoulder as he walked by him to talk to Gunnar.

Music filled the room finally, making the place feel like a party. Thane started to turn back into the place when the world stopped around him. A long, succulent leg caught his attention first before he gazed up and saw the beautiful woman attached to it.

Kari sauntered into the room with Reagan and Michael flanking her sides. She had her hair up in a bun and wore nude, strappy sandals. She looked damn sexy.

"Hi, Mr. Wells." Michael ran up to Thane.

"Hey, Michael. How was the game?" Thane kept his attention on Michael as he spoke to him. As soon as Kari got into close proximity, he smelled her intoxicating scent.

"It was awesome. I ate everything and the Tides won." Michael pumped his fist in the air.

"Cool. That's always good when the home team wins." Thane glanced up to the two women. He addressed Reagan first. "Thanks for coming." He kissed her cheek.

"Wow. You are so nice." She hugged him. "And you really smell good." She turned to Kari. "Smell him."

"Get off him, please. He's not a plant." Kari talked between her teeth.

"Nope. I'm more like a weed." He pulled Kari in for a hug. "Thanks for coming."

He felt her heart pounding through her chest. Every part of him wanted to kiss her. He had a feeling she wouldn't want that in front of her son.

"I haven't gone to one of these in years. Michael won't go to his school dances." Kari embraced Thane but kept him in hold for a beat longer than expected.

Thane didn't mind. If he could keep holding her all night, he would. When he pulled back from her, he looked down at Michael. "Why don't you go to your school dances?"

Michael dropped his gaze to the floor. "You know why," he mumbled.

"I do?" Thane had to hear this. "Could you remind me?"

Michael scanned the area. Thane looked around the room. When he saw the boys all lined up on one side and the girls grouped on the other side of the room, he understood Michael's dilemma.

"Ah, the dancing." Thane nodded. "Is that it?"

"I don't know how to dance. I don't want some girl laughing at me." He shoved his hands in his pockets. "Especially—" He stopped.

Thane scanned the young man's outfit. He noticed then that Michael wore a nice pair of black pants and a purple shirt. "Nice shirt." He crouched down next to Michael. "You would probably look good next to her." He pointed across the room to Leona.

Michael tried hiding his smile. "I don't really know her."

"So you introduce yourself." He brushed the young man's shirt. "Compliment her new dress."

"Because you made it?"

Thane shook his head. "Because she looks cute in it."

Michael screwed up his lips. "Cute?"

"Fine. Don't say cute." He stood. "Get her a cup of punch and introduce yourself."

The child fidgeted. "Are you sure?"

"Positive." He pointed to the table. "I'll watch your back."

Michael nodded and darted over to the refreshments table.

"So now you're playing matchmaker?" Kari leaned into Thane.

"Only when it's obvious that he has a thing for someone." He looked at her. "Did you pick out that shirt color or did he?"

"He did." She lowered her voice. "He insisted on it. I thought it was adorable."

"Oh, don't tell him that. You'll take away all of his cred." He swiped his hand over his neck. "By the way, you look absolutely gorgeous."

"Are you saying that because you made this dress?" Kari held her arms out and twirled in front of him.

"Of course not." He slid his arm around her waist. "You look really, *really* good." He put his mouth by her ear. "Any chance I can take you out of that dress later on tonight?"

Kari laughed. "We're here chaperoning a children's function. You need to behave yourself."

Too bad Thane didn't want to be a gentleman. Seeing her made his heart pump hard. Although the pains in his stomach hadn't subsided, he'd forgotten about them as soon as she arrived.

"By the way, nice shirt. I see you and my son are playing from the same playbook." She nudged his side with her elbow.

"Does my shirt match your dress? What a coincidence." Thane put his hand to his chest and feigned surprise.

"Yeah, right. I see your brothers are here." She smiled harder. "That's good, right?"

His heart stopped for a moment as soon as she brought up Gunnar and Gideon. "They're here because Mom would have wanted them to be." He pointed to the center of his chest. "This has nothing to do with me."

She stood in front of him. "They're trying. You need to do the same."

Thane refrained from saying that to try meant that he cared. He'd stopped caring a long time ago.

"I'm in a great mood. I don't want to ruin that by talking about them." He held her hand and strolled with her across the gym.

The sounds of little feet running over the glossy floor brought him back to a time when he used to scamper around the place. Thane looked up in time to see Michael darting toward him and Kari.

"The punch worked." Michael hopped around Thane and Kari.

"And did you tell her she looked pretty?" Kari asked.

Michael looked sheepish before he answered. "I said I liked her dress. Is that good enough?"

"Depends. Did she smile?" Thane held Kari's hand tighter.

The child nodded. "She thanked me. That's good, right?"

"Very good." Kari kissed her son's forehead.

"Mom. Not here." He quickly wiped his head and even scanned the area to see if anyone had seen her sweet expression.

"So what are you doing with us?" Thane pointed to Leona and the group of girls surrounding her. "Shouldn't you be over there talking to her?"

"I would but—" Michael glanced behind himself before he continued. "The girls were talking about dancing."

Thane waited to hear more but Michael offered nothing else. "And?"

"I can't dance." He shook his head. "She'll laugh at me."

"It's easy." He held Kari around her waist to pull her toward the dance floor.

She remained cemented like a statue. "No way. I already feel overdressed. I'm not going out on the dance floor."

"If you don't, you're letting Michael know that it's okay to succumb to his fears." He held out his hand to the most beautiful woman in the world.

She hesitated for a moment before she asked Michael to give her purse to Reagan. As soon as she touched his hand, Thane smiled.

He held her delicate hand and led her to the middle of the room. When Kari faced him and attempted to hold his other hand so that they could dance, he held up his finger to her and jogged away from her to go to the DJ.

"Play any line-dancing song." Thane removed his jacket and placed it on a chair next to the DJ table.

"Anything, man?" The young man hit a couple of buttons on his console.

"Anything." Thane went back to a very bewildered-looking Kari, who now had her arms crossed over her chest. "How are you at line dances?"

"What?" She shook her head.

A beat to a popular song started.

"Come on, baby. Wobble with me." He winked at her as he started to dance.

From the way Kari stared at him, she looked like she had no idea how to do the dance. Thane thought for sure she would leave him on the dance floor alone. After watching him do one rotation, she joined in and caught on pretty quickly.

He glanced off to the side when he noticed someone coming toward him. Gideon, moving around a lot better than before, held Janelle's hand as he made his way to dance area.

"Even with a bum knee, I've always been a better dancer than you." Gideon beamed as he patted Thane's shoulder.

It didn't take Gideon and Janelle long to fall in line. Thane would have rather seen the kids join him. Each time he turned and caught his brother smiling and laughing, he couldn't help but join in the revelry.

He looked across the room and saw Gunnar sulking against the wall. Eboni tugged on his hand to get him to join her, but he shook his head and settled back in his place like a stone gargoyle.

Thane couldn't blame him. Gunnar had never been a great dancer despite being a champion fighter.

Reagan ran toward the group and joined in the line.

"Great. Almost all the adults are on the floor, but no kids," Thane said to Kari.

"Keep smiling and laughing." Kari beamed and twirled around.

As Kari had predicted, children started creeping to the dance area, starting with Michael. He planted himself between Thane and Kari and fell in line with the dance. Pretty soon, children filled the dance area. They all laughed as they did the synchronized dance in time with the music.

As soon as the song ended and went into another popular song, Gideon threw in the towel and left the floor with Janelle. Thane remained in the middle of the group of children. It brought back great memories of him showing off his moves to girls back when his mother chaperoned these events.

Thane felt a hand on his arm. He turned to see Kari.

"I'm going to get a drink." She waved her hand in her face like a fan.

"Can't take a little shaking?" Thane winked at her.

"You move around in four-inch heels." She laughed as she made her way off the floor.

To be a gentleman, and because he truly liked watching her in that dress, he followed her over to the refreshments area.

"You didn't have to leave because of me." Kari picked up a cup that Thane quickly took from her hand. "With you looking like that, no way can I leave you alone." He poured some punch in a cup and handed it to her. "I know this is not what you envisioned for a great night out drinking and dancing, but—"

"This is perfect." She got on her tiptoes and kissed Thane on his cheek.

With her body pressed against his, he couldn't help but wrap his arm around her waist and hold her closer. "Thank you for doing this." He glanced at the kids all skipping around and having a great time. "Mom would have loved this."

"I didn't know her that well, but I have a feeling she would have loved *you* doing this." Kari exhaled. "You're a good son." She looked over his shoulder. "Be a good brother and talk to Gunnar and Gideon. It's obvious they love and support you no matter what."

Thane didn't want to talk about them, not tonight. "Now is not the time."

"If not now then—"

"Check out of your hotel tonight." He eased her away from the preteens to have a private conversation with her.

"You want me to leave?" Kari blinked.

"Yes, with me. Come down to the Outer Banks tonight." He reached into his pocket and pulled out a card. "Here's the address. Follow me down there in your rental."

She shook her head. "My family—"

"Can come with us."

She stared at him for a while. "No, I shouldn't. You've been great with Michael, but I don't want him getting attached to you. " She crossed her arms. "I came down here for one thing. Going away with you would complicate things."

"More than the sex?" He took a step back. "I've made you a dress. You're here with me. You've met my family. Are you still trying to get me to sign with you as an agent? None of this means anything to you?"

Kari remained quiet. The silence between them lasted too long for Thane's taste. His stomach tightened and continued to a painful extent. He rested his hand on his midsection, something that looked like it caught her attention. She glanced down before she regarded him again.

"Excuse me. I need some air." Before he could walk away, she grabbed his arm.

"Thane, are you okay? Wait. Let's talk."

He shrugged out of her grip. "I'll be back. Enjoy the party."

Thane made it across the room to go toward the door closest to the bathroom. He couldn't believe that after everything they had been through, Kari still had her guard up. She still didn't get that she'd caused him to open up to her more than he had with anyone.

Before he could get out of the gym area, a man blocked his path at the doorway. Thane glanced up to see Jarrod Townsend standing in front of him. Ordinarily, seeing this basketball giant would have made him happy. As Jarrod glared at him, Thane knew this wouldn't be a pleasant exchange.

"What are you doing here?" Thane put his shoulders back and chest out as far as he could while his stomach compressed even more.

Chapter 20

Thane didn't have time for another confrontation. First his brothers had intruded on this special night. Kari had refused to join him at the house in Outer Banks. Now Jarrod Townsend had showed up looking like he wanted a fight. Thane balled his hands into fists.

"What? You think you're not that hard to find?" Jarrod crossed his arms over his chest. "I see you all over the Internet trying to play daddy to my son. *My* son." He pounded his chest. "I knew you were in Virginia Beach. I waited until one of these snot-nosed brats posted a picture of you and your location. Easy." He moved in closer to Thane. "Now that I'm here, you can stop trying to act like my kid's father. He has one."

"It's not even like that." Thane kept his stare on Jarrod's cold, brown eyes. "It was just a game of catch. Michael loves you."

"Don't tell me about my boy. You don't know anything about him." He pointed into the gym. "That's my kid. You go out and father a kid of your own."

"Dad!" Michael ran up to the duo, but Jarrod kept his laser-like focus on Thane.

Pretty soon, a few more little boys ran up to the trio. They stared at Thane and Jarrod, admiring them like gods. For this exchange, Thane preferred not to have an audience, especially with children. He waited for Jarrod to tell his son to go back into the gym, but he kept his full attention on Thane.

Thane couldn't be that uncaring. "Michael, go back to the party and have a good time while your father and I have a talk, please."

"Don't tell him what to do." Jarrod shoved Thane's shoulder.

As Thane started to charge toward Jarrod, a crippling pain stopped him. He bent over and had a coughing fit that didn't stop even after he spat up some blood.

"Shit, man. What the hell is wrong with you?" Jarrod jumped back before a mixture of blood and saliva could land on his expensive-looking sneakers.

Thane crumbled to the floor and curled into a ball as he heard the kids around him gasping.

Shit, not now.

"Mr. Wells, what's wrong?"

Thane heard Michael's voice, but he couldn't answer. He wanted to tell the child to go to Kari, but he couldn't speak.

"I think Jarrod Townsend stabbed Thane Wells."

Thane glanced up and noticed a boy snapping a picture and typing something on his phone. Great. He didn't need this getting out now, not with his brothers here and everything going on in his life.

"You hurt him. I hate you." Michael stomped his foot, evident from the sound next to Thane's head.

Thane growled through the pain. "No." He turned his head in time to see Jarrod grabbing Michael's small shoulders and shoving him back hard enough that the child stumbled to the floor.

Seeing this brought back memories of seeing Queen Elizabeth's ex-husband doing the same thing to him and his brothers. Fire filled Thane's chest when he noticed the disappointment in Michael's eyes.

"No." Thane raised himself up enough to get to a kneeling position. "Don't you touch him like that."

By that time, Michael had run away. He disappeared in the mass of moving bodies in the middle of the gym. Thane wished he had enough strength to stand and go after him. This attack had him thankful of the cool floor. So that he didn't worry anyone, he needed to stand.

"Thane? Thane!" Kari ran toward him and crouched down next to him. "What did you do to him? What's all this blood?" She stroked his head.

"Don't worry about me. You need to be worried about you. Don't be bringing no dude around my son." Jarrod pointed to Kari as he loomed over her. "Especially some sick sucker."

Kari looked into the gym. "Help! I need help." She looked at the boys around them. "Get an adult."

Finally, one child ran from the group. Thane couldn't wait to see who he would get. He hoped the boy would retrieve Drew.

* * * *

Kari wished she had her purse so that she could call an ambulance for Thane. To see him with blood trickling out of his mouth scared her. She'd had no idea that Jarrod would make the trip down to Virginia Beach to confront Thane.

Before she could scream for assistance again, Gunnar ran over to her and Thane with Eboni behind him.

"What the hell is going on?" Gunnar kneeled down next to Thane. "You okay?"

Thane took a deep breath before he shook his head. Kari trembled at his response. She hadn't known him to admit when he needed help. To see him in so much pain rendered her immobile.

"You son-of-a-bitch." Gunnar stood. "What the hell did you do to my brother?" He got in Jarrod's face and refused to back down.

A small part of Kari wanted Thane's brother to punch Jarrod's lights out for whatever he'd done to Thane. Violence at this event wouldn't be good.

"I didn't do shit to him." Jarrod's raised voice rumbled the floor. "We were talking and he started spitting up blood."

"I'm calling 9-1-1 now." Eboni had her phone pressed to her ear.

"What happened?" Gideon came over to the group.

Kari kept her concentration on Thane. Although she wanted to question why Gideon had his shirt out of his pants and looked out of breath, she figured he had gone back on the dance floor. When he glanced down at Thane, he immediately glared at Jarrod.

"What did you do to my brother?" Gideon rolled up his sleeves.

"Pump your breaks, man. Don't make me fuck up that other leg." Jarrod pointed down at Gideon's knee.

"Please stop this." Kari volleyed her attention between Jarrod, Gunnar, and Gideon. "Think about where we are and what we're doing here."

Thane squeezed Kari's hand and put his full focus on her. "Michael. Get Michael."

She glanced over her shoulder. When she saw Reagan running in the opposite direction, Kari bolted to her feet and chased after her.

She hated leaving Thane, but she had a child here. If Reagan looked worried, Kari knew she should be concerned. Plus, she didn't want Michael seeing Thane in his condition or his father in such a rage.

"Reagan. Where's Michael?" Kari managed to catch up to her friend, a feat considering her heels.

"I saw him crying and running this way. What's going on with Thane? Was he on the floor? Did I see Jarrod Townsend here?" Reagan spoke in between panting breaths.

Kari didn't have time to answer or sort out the whole situation. She saw her world falling apart in front of her.

When she hit the back hallway, she heard a slam at the far end. She moved so fast to get to the location that she overshot her destination and had to double-back to get to the door.

"Michael, honey, are you in there?" She pressed her hand against the wood as she waited for his answer. As soon as she heard quiet sobs from in the room, her heart accelerated. "Open the door, baby."

"He-he pushed me," Michael said from inside the locked room.

"Who? Thane?" She couldn't imagine him putting his hands on her child in anger, especially since he'd implored her to go after him and not concern herself with his wellbeing.

"Dad. Never seen him so angry." Michael cried harder.

Kari had seen Jarrod in a worse mood. She'd never known him to be physical outside of a basketball court. With all the hurtful things he'd said to her, he'd never put his hands on her out of anger.

She took a deep breath. "I need you to be a big boy and come out of the room. I can't help you if you keep yourself locked up." She looked over her shoulder and wondered if Thane had gotten some help by now. "Thane needs me, needs us."

She didn't know if her statement held any merit. He had his family around him, defending him fiercely. When she saw him on the floor at Jarrod's feet, her protective nature had kicked in.

When Michael didn't answer, she continued her plea. "He's hurt and they're going to take him to the hospital."

"I don't want to see Dad ever again." Anger filled each word. "Don't make me see him. Please."

Kari longed to make that wish happen. She hated the reasoning though. It took all of her willpower not to go back into the gym, go to Jarrod, and kick him squarely in his nonexistent balls.

"I'll sing to you, baby, if that will help." As the silence lingered, Kari started to open her mouth to sing his favorite baseball-themed song when the door finally opened.

Michael peered up at Kari as he stepped out of what looked to be the janitor's closet. "I don't need you to sing to me." He shook his head. "Sorry for making you worry."

"You apologize. You're never sorry." She wrapped her arms around him and held him close to her chest. Then she pulled back from him, held his shoulders, and crouched down to face level. "Are you hurt?" She did a quick scan of his body to look for scrapes or blood.

Michael's lips started to tremble, but he firmed them up to a tight line. "I'm okay."

"I'll talk to your father. He should have never touched you like that." She embraced him again. "I should have been there for you to keep that from happening."

This time, Michael pulled back from her. "I'm fine. I know you're always here for me." He smiled. "I love you."

Kari had to keep herself together to not cry in front of her child. Thane's influence showed in Michael's response.

"I want to see Mr. Wells. He tried to help me but he was hurt." He pointed toward the gym.

"Let's see how Thane is." She held his hand as she led him back to the gym.

By the time Kari made it the location, she watched the group of children breaking up around the doorway where Thane and Jarrod had been. She weaved through the throngs of people to get to that area. She found an older gentleman wiping the floor and Jarrod pacing.

Michael cowered behind Kari.

"Take him to the car." She nudged Michael toward Reagan.

"Don't take my boy from me." Jarrod started to move toward Michael when Kari blocked his path.

"Reagan, take him. I'll meet you all outside in a minute." Although she smiled at her son and friend, Kari wanted to scream and kick the jerk she'd once loved.

Once her family moved out of earshot, she let Jarrod have it.

"Michael told me what you did to him." She got in his face and said between gritted teeth, "If you ever put your hands on him again, I will kill you. I won't call the police."

"The police? I barely touched him. I took worse hits than that when I was—" He stopped.

Kari had always had a feeling Jarrod's home life hadn't been idyllic. He'd never shared anything with her, not then and not now.

Jarrod said nothing as he tried to return her stare. He ended up averting his gaze. "I didn't mean to shove him. I got caught up with arguing with your dude." He shook his head. "It's your fault. If you hadn't—"

She cut him off before he could say anything else damaging. "Stop it. Be a damn man for once and accept some responsibility." Kari had wanted to say that to Jarrod for years. "I can't believe you came all the way over here not to see your son. You wanted to confront a man who has been more of a father to Michael in the short time I've been with him than you have for Michael's entire life. Our son idolizes you." She shook her head. "At least he did before you showed up here. Go home. Get some professional help. You've done enough damage."

"Professional help?" He chuckled. "You think I need a shrink? Are you calling me crazy?"

Kari shook her head. "No. Damaged. You're not going to continue this cycle with Michael. If you truly want a relationship with him, you'll get yourself sorted out first. My child is my first, last, and only responsibility. I'm not going to stand by and watch anyone hurt him, especially you."

She went outside and met with Reagan and Michael in her rental.

"I asked a couple of people who saw them take Thane away where they took him." Reagan put the car in gear and sped off as Kari slammed the car door. "Virginia Beach General." She waved her phone. "Got it programmed in here. Should take us ten minutes to get there."

"Good. Drop me off at the hospital and you and Michael go back to the hotel." Kari didn't need Michael mixed up with any adult drama.

"No. I want to make sure Mr. Wells is okay. Please?" Michael's voice sounded mature, like he'd skipped the whole little-kid phase.

She didn't like that. Michael deserved his innocence. "I'm going to visit with him first and see how he is. If he's okay, I'll bring you to check on him tomorrow morning."

Michael slumped back and crossed his little arms. "Fine."

Reagan pulled up to the emergency room entrance of the hospital. "Are you sure you don't want us going in with you? What if you can't see him right now?"

Kari opened the door. "I'll take a cab back to the hotel." She opened the door to the backseat. "I love you, Michael." She leaned in and kissed her son. "I'm so sorry about what happened tonight."

Michael held Kari's hand. "You're not sorry, Mom. You apologize." He smiled. "And there's nothing for you to apologize for."

"When you get back to the hotel, I want you to order room service and get the biggest and best dessert they have." For his rough night and his amazing attitude, he deserved a treat.

"I'll see you when you get back. If I'm asleep, wake me, okay?" He squeezed her hand.

"I'll see you two later." Kari closed the door and ran into the hospital. She forgot about her flashy attire until the security guard and triage nurse scanned her from head to toe. "Hi, I'm looking for someone who was brought here."

"Name?" The surly nurse hovered her hands over the computer keyboard.

Kari leaned forward and lowered her voice. "Thane Wells."

The nurse didn't bother typing. "Nice try, lady. Unless you're family, you're not getting back there and you're not getting any information."

"You don't understand. I'm his—" Kari didn't know how to complete that sentence. What did she mean to Thane? Better yet, what did Thane mean to her?

"Hey."

She felt a hand on her shoulder. She turned and saw Janelle behind her. "Thank God." She moved away from the window and went to the waiting area with Janelle. "Can you tell me what's going on with Thane?"

Janelle shook her head. "Not yet. Gideon and Gunnar were able to go with him when they took him to the back." She sat down next to Eboni. "They said they would be out when they know something."

Kari took a seat in between the women.

"Can you tell us what happened? Why was Jarrod Townsend here and why was he confronting Thane in the first place?" Eboni shook her head.

Kari had to steel her nerves before making her confession. "Jarrod is my son's father. I'm sure he saw video or pictures of Thane playing catch with him recently. It made him angry enough to come here."

"Are you two still dating?" Janelle asked.

"No." Kari shook her head. "He's moved on with his life. He needs to realize that I'm going to live my life."

The doors going to the back area swung open. Gunnar and Gideon strolled through them and headed straight to the women.

Kari stood and the other two ladies followed suit. "How is he? What's going on?"

Gunnar glared at her for a beat before he spoke. "Did you know about his bleeding ulcer?"

She blinked, glanced at the women before returning her attention to Gunnar. "No." She shook her head. "He mentioned something about not being able to play. I thought it was a mental thing, like he didn't enjoy the sport anymore. He never told me about his medical condition."

"Maybe you two aren't as close as you think." Gideon draped his arm around Janelle's shoulders.

Kari understood Gideon's anger. To him, he probably saw her as the catalyst for all the drama. Gideon had no idea that Thane had asked her to go with him to the house in the Outer Banks and that he'd planned on confessing some news about himself. Perhaps he had planned on telling her about his ulcer.

"So now what?" Eboni asked.

"He's getting prepped for surgery." Gunnar smoothed his hand over his head.

Kari gasped and covered her mouth. "Surgery? It's that bad?"

Gunnar nodded. "The confrontation didn't help. Why would Jarrod Townsend show up to a dance at a community center?"

Eboni wrapped her arms around him. "I'll tell you later."

"One thing I do know is that Thane doesn't need any stress in his life." Gideon took a step toward Kari. "That includes you."

She took a step back. "What are you saying?"

"Maybe you shouldn't be here."

Kari scanned the faces of his family. "I would never, ever hurt Thane. I care about him deeply."

"As an agent?" Gunnar asked.

The dig stung. Kari suddenly felt cold and alone. She thought she would have allies. Instead, Thane's family gave her suspicious stares.

"No. As a woman." She sat down in the waiting area. "I'm not leaving until I know he's okay." She crossed her legs. "You can choose to sit with me or go as far away from me as possible. It won't change the fact that I..." Kari hesitated. The first time she confessed her true feelings for Thane, she wanted to do it to him and not his brothers. "I'm just as concerned about his health like you all."

Gunnar held Eboni's hand. "Good luck trying to get in to see him." Then he walked to the other side of the waiting area and took a seat.

"Go back to your hotel room." Gideon put his arm around Janelle's waist as he stared at Kari. "I'm sure you'll get updates on Thane on some social media outlet or something." He followed Gunnar and took a seat next to him.

Kari didn't care what they thought of her. She wouldn't be leaving until she found out Thane's condition.

As the time went by, she kept herself occupied by constantly checking her messages and ignoring calls from Frank and Chelsi. She didn't care how long she would have to wait to hear news about Thane.

Kari felt someone sitting in the chair next to her before she turned and saw Eboni. She gave Kari a sweet smile.

"Coffee?" She held up a cup.

Kari shook her head. "No, thank you." She peered over to the other side of the room and noticed Gunnar still glaring at her. "Should you be talking to me? I don't want to get you in trouble."

Eboni took a sip of her coffee first. "I've been in the exact same spot as you. Gunny was not happy with me and refused to talk to me right after he was shot."

Kari blinked. "Really?" She glanced down and noticed an impressive engagement ring on Eboni's finger. "But you two are getting married now."

Eboni nodded. "I know. It's because, like you, I refused to give up on the man I love."

"I never said that I love Thane."

Eboni patted Kari's hand. "You didn't have to. Your actions say it all." She leaned forward and lowered her voice. "Hang in there. The Wells men are stubborn, but they have good hearts. If they see your commitment, they'll let you in. Even if they don't, I will."

Kari smiled. "Thank you." She stared at the large hospital doors. "It's killing me not knowing what's happening to him."

As though she'd willed it, a doctor came through the doors. Her gut told her this woman in scrubs had operated on Thane. When Kari saw her heading toward Gunnar and Gideon, she bolted to her feet along with Eboni.

"Let's go in the conference area to discuss Thane's condition." The doctor led the group to a room behind the waiting area.

Not to be left out, Kari followed them along with Eboni and Janelle.

"You shouldn't be here." Gunnar pointed to Kari.

"Yes, she should." To make sure she didn't get kicked out, Eboni held Kari's hand. "She cares about Thane as much as we do." She turned to the doctor. "What's going on with Thane?"

"It looks like your brother allowed his ulcer to bother him for far too long. Ordinarily, you don't need surgery for these things. Thane had a tear in his stomach."

Janelle gasped and covered her mouth.

"Will he be okay?" Kari could care less what Gunnar or Gideon thought of her inquiry.

"Yes. With a lot of rest and some medication, he'll be fine." The doctor removed her surgical cap and threw it in the trashcan behind her.

Gideon exhaled. "Good."

"Can we see him?" Janelle held Gideon's hand.

"Yes. He's sleeping right now. If you want him responsive, come back in the morning. He should be awake by then." The doctor shook each of their hands before leaving.

"Some good news finally." Janelle exhaled.

Kari said nothing as she started to leave.

"Where do you think you're going?" Gunnar approached her.

Even without holding Eboni's hand, Kari felt powerful enough to face off against this giant. "I'm seeing Thane. I want to make sure he's okay, and I promised my son that I would check on him."

"You don't think you've done enough?"

"Gunny. Please." Eboni held her fiancé's arm. "It's obvious she cares about him." She pulled Gunnar toward her. "It wasn't so long ago that I was in her same position...with you."

Gunnar stared at Eboni for a beat before he cupped her cheek and planted a soft kiss on her forehead and lips. "This is different." He opened the door to the conference room.

Camera flashes bathed them in sporadic lights. Kari held her hand up to block the blinding beams.

"Christ, when did they get here?" Gideon held Janelle close to him.

"How's Thane?" one nosey reporter asked.

"Is this the reason he hasn't returned to spring training?" another blurted.

"Any truth to the story that Jarrod Townsend stabbed Thane?"

Gunnar glanced at Kari. "You're an agent. You've been chasing Thane for his business. You take care of this. Let us take care of our family."

As Kari watched Thane's brothers and their fiancées leave her with the den of wolves, anger swelled in her. She understood Gunnar and Gideon being scared and upset. She wouldn't be the fall guy for this situation. She also wouldn't be leaving. She made a promise to Michael, and she couldn't discount her feelings. Damn it, she loved Thane.

Chapter 21

Thane blinked so slowly it felt like years in between each time he opened and closed his eyes. He heard the heart monitor that registered each of his beats first before he finally focused and noticed the all-white room. For a moment, he transported back to the final call he'd had with Queen. He remembered hearing the same sounds through the phone.

He rested his hand that had tubes coming from it on his midsection. He felt the stiff puke-green striped gown he wore. He tried sitting up to get a better view of the room. Who was he kidding? He wanted to see if Kari had stayed here with him.

"Easy, Mr. Wells." A thin, young man placed his hand on Thane's shoulder. "Let me help you." He picked up a corded remote and adjusted the bed to elevate Thane's head. "My name is Orion. You can laugh."

Thane could barely muster a smile.

"I'll be your nurse." He glanced behind him. "I have to say, this is the first time I've been in a room with so many famous folks."

Thane looked beyond the nurse to see Gunnar and Gideon on two different couches, both fast asleep.

"Anyone   else?"   Thane   knew   his   abbreviated   question wouldn't be understood.

"What do you mean?" As he spoke, Orion took Thane's vitals.

"Besides my brothers." Thane nodded toward them.

"There were a couple of women here with them for a while. They made them go home sometime late last night."

Thane nodded. He had a feeling the nurse would say something like that. He'd had hoped for a different outcome. He'd wanted Kari to care beyond him being a star athlete.

"There was some woman in a smoking-hot red dress who was answering questions after a group of reporters showed up. She seemed to handle them well until security kicked them out."

"Really?" Thane noticed a pitcher on a raised tray. He started to reach for it when Orion stopped him and poured a cup of water for him.

"Yeah. She took care of those folks like a pro." He positioned the straw to Thane's mouth and patiently held the cup until Thane took his needed drink. "Is that your manager or something?"

Thane shook his head.

"Whoever she was, I wouldn't let her go." He set the cup back on the tray. "What's your pain level? One for tolerable and ten for the worst pain ever, like the kind of pain if you ended up in the ring with him for ten minutes." He pointed to Gunnar before chuckling.

Thane felt a little sore, but nothing he hadn't felt before while training. "Five."

Orion nodded. "Drugs are still in your system from the surgery."

"Surgery?" He glanced down at his body.

"The doctor will be in soon to talk to you. Until then, you get some rest." He placed the remote by Thane's hand. "If there's anything you need, you hit this button. Are you comfortable?"

"For now."

"I'll take that." Orion smiled. "What about food? You hungry?"

Thane shook his head.

"They're still coming by with breakfast. I think you're on the ultra-bland diet. Oatmeal." Orion shivered. "The perks of having gastric problems." He went to the door. "Like I said, if you need me, hit the call button."

Thane nodded. "Thanks."

He placed his head back on his pillow and closed his eyes.

"At some point, are you ever going to get out of bed?"

Thane opened his eyes and turned toward the voice. He saw Gunnar standing from the couch and heading toward him. He noticed that his oldest brother still had on the same all-black ensemble from the dance. Hell, what day was it?

"What happened?" Thane rubbed his eyes. He turned his wrist to view the time and date.

"They had to take off your jewelry before the surgery." Gideon stood from the couch and sauntered toward the bed. "Everything's in there. We checked." He also wore the same clothes from the dance.

"What day is it?" Thane raised his head a bit more to regard his brothers.

"Sunday." Gunnar cleared his voice. "The doc should be in soon, but you had a pretty nasty ulcer. Did you know?"

Thane remained quiet.

"That's a yes." Gideon nudged Gunnar's arm. "Why didn't you tell any of us? Did Mom know?"

"I didn't tell Mom or anyone that my stomach hasn't been right for a while. I didn't think it was that bad." Thane pushed the white, stiff blanket from his body and pulled up his hospital gown.

"Hey, easy there." Gunnar slid the curtain that blocked the view of anyone that might come into the room. "You don't want to show the whole hospital your business."

Thane didn't care who could see his dick. As soon as he saw five small incisions held together with surgical tape across his stomach he cursed. He plopped his head back on the pillow.

"So this is the lesson here." Gunnar put his hand on Thane's shoulder. "Stop holding things in. Let everything out."

"Yeah, that's always been your problem." Gideon shook his head.

"That and being a sickly kid, right? Isn't that what you've always said about me?" Thane glared at his older brother.

"Yeah. You were. Every week, Mom was taking you to see a doctor or a specialist. It surprised me that you even went into baseball. I thought you would have gone with the whole clothing design thing." Gideon ruffled Thane's hair.

Not wanting his touch, Thane pushed his hand away from him. "Where's my—" Thane didn't know what he should call Kari.

Did she qualify as a girlfriend now? He hadn't signed on with her as an agent, but that didn't seem to matter to her. She'd handled his business regardless. Hell, why hadn't he signed on with her?

Before Thane could finish his question, his hospital room door opened. The person who walked in pulled back the curtain. Thane blinked as soon as he saw his current agent, Alec. Although he talked to the man often, he hadn't seen him in over a year.

The short timeframe hadn't been kind to him. His now all-white hair stood over his head like the man had slept on the roughest flight over from California. Unlike a lot of agents, Alec wore an old-school track suit, complete with thick white lines down the sleeves and the sides of the pants. His purple-rimmed glasses covered half his face.

"You look like shit, kid." Alec patted Thane on his shoulder. "If I wasn't already retiring, you would push me there." He looked up at Gunnar and Gideon. "Christ, how did your mother do it? Raise a family of champions."

Thane didn't want to talk about his brothers. Or maybe his problem had to do with being lumped together with them in the same category.

"How did you get back here?" Gunnar pointed to Alec.

Alec snickered as he adjusted his glasses. "Nothing is off-limits for a man like me." He held Thane's hand like a nurturing father. "I told them I needed to see my number one client." He gazed down at Thane. "Client for now. Boy, news gets out about my retirement and the freaks come out of the woodworks."

"I don't think talking about business right now is the best thing." Gideon shook his head.

"Probably right, but it has to be done." Alec raised his hand in the air, showing off a stack of paperwork. "With your forced time off, you'll have time to read over these." He placed the papers on the raised tray by Thane's bed. "It's the contract to dissolve my representation."

"You've got to be kidding me." Gunnar ran his hand over his head. "He just had surgery, and you're talking business."

Alec shrugged. "It's the way of the world. Real life doesn't stop because you want it to." He faced Thane. "The other contract is for that agent I was telling you about."

"I haven't met him yet." Thane learned from his mother that if you do business with someone, you should be able to look that person in the eye, especially before signing a contract.

"You don't need to. He's handling your money." Alec laughed. "I'm trying to save you a headache. I was contacted by Frank Milliner with the Winning Edge Agency."

Thane recognized Kari's agency's name. He perked up at hearing it. "What did he say?"

"Thane, don't worry about any of that now." Gideon made his way to the other side of the bed where Alec stood. "You need to rest and get yourself better."

"Yeah, you need to do that. But whatever you do, don't sign with that agency." Alec shook his head and grimaced.

"Why is that?" Thane stared at Alec.

"The owner said he was sending over someone you wouldn't be able to resist. I think they're trying to get you with some groupies or worse, a hooker or something. That guy always seemed shady to me."

"Is that where your girl works?" Gideon tapped Thane's leg.

Thane didn't answer. He had to process all this information. His heart told him that Kari had been more than bait from an unscrupulous sports agency. She hadn't pushed for a relationship or physical contact. That had been all him. None of this could be true of Kari, his woman, his savior.

"Read over the terms." Alec looked around. "You should be getting some flowers or something nice soon."

"You're here. You couldn't bother to bring them yourself?" Gideon cocked his head as he regarded Thane's agent.

Alec tapped his chest. "Bad ticker. I probably shouldn't have made the plane trip over." He smiled at Thane. "But as soon as I heard the news, I had to come here myself and see him."

It warmed Thane's heart that at least Alec's main motivation to see him had more to do with Thane's wellbeing than business. His brothers stayed by his side, but the act felt more like familial obligation rather than genuinely caring for him. Or maybe his judgment had been clouded with hate for so long, he couldn't tell the true difference. When he caught Alec glancing at his watch, his heartbeat slowed.

"Got another meeting?" Thane's voice sounded stronger the longer he stayed awake.

Alec rubbed the back of his neck. For the first time since having the man as his agent, Thane noticed Alec's face transforming into a ruddy color.

Alec leaned down closer to Thane's ear. "There's a little get together happening down at the Oceanfront for, um, otters."

Thane felt his eyebrows rut together. Had he really come over here to look at animals?

"Otters are young, thin, sleek men." Alec stood up straight and gave Thane a knowing look.

Thane nodded. "Okay. Your husband is here with you?"

Alec took a couple of steps back to the door. "You can scan and e-mail me the paperwork whenever you're ready. Nice seeing you, kid. Call me anytime." He escaped before he could answer any questions.

"That's a strange dude." Gideon shook his head. "But he got you a sweet deal."

"Is Kari here?" Thane reached for his remote.

Gunnar shrugged. "Don't know. She said she would stay here until she could see you."

"Wait. She was here and you refused to let her come in and see me?" Thane pressed the nurse's call button.

"She's the reason you're here. If she had told you about Jarrod—"

Without apologies, Thane cut off Gideon. "No, *I'm* the reason I'm here. I've let things bother me and fester in my gut for far too long."

Orion came back in the room. As soon as he saw Gunnar and Gideon standing next to Thane's bed, he beamed. "Hey, gentlemen." He slapped palms with them both and pulled them each into a half hug before addressing Thane. "You rang?"

"I'm really tired." Thane glanced at his brothers. "They're about to leave."

"Oh, so it's like that?" Gunnar's voice boomed.

"You said that there was a woman last night in all red that was answering questions to reporters?"

Orion nodded. "Yeah. I think she's still out there."

Thane pulled his blanket up higher on his body. He glanced at Gunnar and Gideon. "Thanks for helping me last night and staying with me today. You two need to go home and get some sleep." Then he turned to Orion. "If she's here, will you get her for me?"

"Unbelievable." Gunnar shook his head and stormed out of the hospital room without a word to Thane.

It didn't surprise Thane that Gunnar had gotten angry about his decision. Gideon hugged Thane even after being politely booted from the room.

"You need us, you call." Gideon stood. "This changes nothing between us, understand?"

Thane found it hard to embrace his brother. Eventually, he raised his arms and held him. "Thanks for coming. I mean that, man."

"I know. Sometimes you have a funny way of showing it." Gideon strolled out of the room.

A couple of minutes later, the door opened again. From behind the curtain, Kari appeared. Her disheveled hair and wrinkled dress didn't take away her beauty. As soon as her gaze connected to his, she wiped under her eyes and smiled.

The smile nearly broke him.

* * * *

Kari didn't care that she looked a mess the first time she got to see Thane. She promised Michael that she would see him before she came back to the hotel. It hurt her that Gunnar and Gideon had refused to let her see Thane. Even Eboni couldn't get the big man to budge.

As she stood next to his hospital bed seeing him with his eyes open, she felt a wave of relief wash over her body. She wanted him to smile at least, but she understood. He had surgery. Who would be happy about that?

"Hey," she said as she approached his bed.

She leaned over to kiss him and he turned his head so that her lips landed on his cheek. His reaction sent a shiver through her body.

"How are you feeling?" Kari stroked his hair. She liked feeling his silky tresses through her fingers.

"Seen better days." Thane exhaled. "How's Michael?"

As soon as Thane mentioned her son's name, she replayed an image of her ex pushing him down. She shook her head.

"He'll be fine. Thank you for asking about him." She smiled. "He asked about you. He didn't want me coming back to the hotel until I saw you and talked to you." She held Thane's hand. "Thank you for allowing me to come back here. Your brothers are very protective."

Kari hoped that Thane understood what their actions meant. They looked out for him. It meant they loved him.

She gently coasted her hand over the blanket that covered his midsection. She saw Thane twitch before he settled down.

"I know," she began. "Easy. Is this what you wanted to tell me down in North Carolina?"

Instead of answering her question, he hit her with one of his own. "Did you see Alec Fogel?" He removed her hand from his stomach.

The motion caused her body to go cold. "Um, yeah. I saw him walking through the lobby. Did you see him?"

"Yes," Thane answered flatly.

"So they let him go through but not me." She shook her head.

"There's a difference. He's my agent. You're not my agent, but you're willing to do anything to represent me, right?" Thane glared at Kari.

She took a step back. "I've been trying to secure your business for years. You know this."

"I know. I'm wondering how far you're willing to go."

She cocked her head. "Where is all this coming from?"

Thane took a deep breath before he positioned his head higher. "Alec said he got a call from a Frank Milliner. You know him?"

Kari's insides froze as she regarded Thane. She could only imagine what her boss had said about her and her efforts to get Thane to sign.

When she didn't immediately answer, Thane continued. "He said that Frank told him he sent his best agent to come after me for my business, and that this agent would do anything to sign me. I don't want to believe that you would do anything and everything in your power to get me as a client."

She took a big step back. "You think I seduced you to make you sign? I've been after you since you started college. I knew your stats. I knew your worth on a team." She crossed her arms over her chest. "If I remember correctly, you kissed me first."

Thane rested his hand on his stomach. "I was at my most vulnerable when I met you. Tell me you didn't take advantage of that."

Her stomach lurched like she wanted to hurl the few contents she had in her belly. She hadn't felt this bad with a man since being with Jarrod. For how gentlemanly he'd treated her and how wonderful he'd been with her son, she'd never thought she would hear these vile words from Thane.

"I should have stuck to my rules. No athletes. No one younger. Never mix business with pleasure." She jerked the curtain back. "Good luck with your recovery. Sorry we couldn't do business together."

Kari ran from the room. Even in her heels, she felt like she barely touched the floor. Once she got outside, she remembered she didn't have her car. Thankfully, a row of cabs sat in front of the hospital. She snagged one to get her back to the hotel.

Along the way, Kari chewed on her lower lip to keep from screaming. How had she let herself get so involved? She remembered. Thane had charmed her. Never again.

As soon as she arrived at her hotel, she took the stairs up to her room. As soon as she burst through the door, Michael tackled her.

"Is Mr. Wells okay? What did Dad do to him? He's been calling Reagan's phone, but I told her not to answer." Michael tugged on Kari's dress.

The dress. She couldn't get out of it fast enough. Every stitch had been made with distrust and doubt.

"Pack your bag, baby. We're going back home." She pulled her suitcase from the closet.

"What's going on?" Reagan came from the bedroom.

"Mom says we're leaving." Michael pointed to Kari. "And she won't tell me about Thane."

"Mr. Wells. What did I tell you about his name?" She knew she had raised her voice when she caught the fear in her child's eyes.

Michael blinked and retreated from her.

She had to calm herself down, for herself and her son. "Go get your suitcase, please." She tried to smile but it felt wrong.

Michael crept to the bedroom to the other closet.

Reagan took that time to approach Kari. "What the hell happened? You were gone all night. Is Thane going to be okay?"

Kari slammed her clothes into the open case. "I don't want to talk about him or his brothers again."

"Oh, okay." Reagan held her hands up. "You're the boss."

Kari pulled off her shoes and threw them in the case on top of her tousled clothing. "That's something else I'll need to take care of when we get back home."

"What's that?"

"Where I work." Kari had to make some drastic changes.

Chapter 22

"You can't do this to me," Jean said with a slight French whine in his tone. "You know what I like."

Kari sat at her desk in her cubicle for the last time. She crossed her legs. "You don't have to leave me. Come with me." She smiled. "I'm branching off on my own. I'd still like to represent you."

The fight with Thane had one great result. She strengthened her backbone. Never would she fall for a man against her type. On top of all that, she would wait until Michael married and had children of his own before she even thought about a relationship.

She regretted getting Michael involved in her personal drama. He deserved to have a happy childhood. She owed him a normal upbringing. Then again, when would she get her happily-ever-after ending?

"You will give me the same representation as before? No changes?" Jean asked.

"No changes. What do you say? Take a chance with me?" Kari glanced up and saw Chelsi signaling her. She hadn't forgotten about her meeting with Frank.

"A chance? Leaving Winning Edge is a risk?" Now worry laced the tennis pro's voice.

"Staying in a den of snakes is a risk." She stood. "I'm a sure thing. I'll send over a termination contract and a new one to be solely represented by me."

"Okay. I'll read over it carefully."

"Good. Do it with your attorney. I look forward to hearing from you soon and working with you." Kari disconnected the call to end on a strong note.

If Jean signed the contract, he would be her one and only client. She had to start somewhere.

Before heading into Frank's office, she scanned her desk area to make sure everything had been packed. Kari wanted to leave nothing behind.

On a large head of steam, she sauntered to Frank's office. She kept her face straight and stoic.

"Have a seat." Frank pointed to a chair in front of his desk.

"No, thank you. I won't be here that long." She pulled out her phone and forwarded an e-mail she had written and ready to go. "I'm quitting."

Kari heard a ping from his phone signaling that he had received her message.

"You know when I said that you may not have a job if you didn't secure Thane Wells, I wasn't really serious. It was just to light a fire under you." Frank typed something on his laptop and stared at the screen before he regarded Kari.

"A fire has been lit under me, but it wasn't your veiled threat." She put her fists to her hips and felt like a superhero. "Did you really tell Alec Fogel that I was sent to Thane to seduce him into joining our agency?"

Frank laughed. "He is a true gossip."

"So you did say it." She nodded and paced next to a chair.

"As a joke. I never thought he would take me seriously." He stood from his desk.

"And if you feel comfortable making a joke about my professionalism and performance, then I guess you don't take me or my work seriously either." She held her hand up to him. "Good-bye."

He regarded her for a moment. "*You're* joking, right? You can't leave."

"I can, and I am." She took a determined step toward his desk. "I've worked hard to make a good reputation for myself. I can't imagine you giving the same story about one of your male agents if he was trying to secure a female athlete."

Frank went to the office door and closed it. When he faced Kari again, he wore a monstrous scowl.

"You ungrateful bitch."

Kari refused to be swayed from her position. She matched him stare for stare.

Frank continued. "I gave you a chance when you were getting your ass thrown out in the street." He marched to her. "And let's not be pious here. The fact of the matter is that you did fuck him."

She blinked and hated herself for reacting. She shouldn't have let her former boss see her crack.

"Thank you for the opportunity." Attempting to leave with some dignity, she kept her head held high as she tried to move around him.

He lashed out at her again, grabbing her arm and pulling her to him. "Fine. You want to go, try to do this on your own?"

With all the force she could muster, she yanked her arm from his grasp and managed to get to the door.

"You will fail. If I have anything to do with it, I will make sure of it."

"That's a shame." She shook her head. "I wish that you get exactly what you deserve."

Frank's threats meant nothing to her. The same hollow feeling she had for Thane she now had for her former boss. No, those feelings didn't match. A small part of her heart still smoldered for Thane.

"Jesus, Kari. Are you really going?" Chelsi stood from her desk.

"Wow. News travels fast." Kari glanced over her shoulder at Frank. "I've got to spread my wings. I'm sure I'll stumble. But I need to try. If I don't do it now, I never will." She hugged the person who'd had her back as much as Reagan. "Take care." She held Chelsi's shoulders. "Know your worth. Never settle."

Chelsi nodded, glanced at Frank, then looked back at Kari again. "Hope to see you around."

On her way out, Kari picked up the box with her personal items and her purse. Whether she made it or not, she wouldn't be back in this office, and she definitely wouldn't be working for a boss who didn't respect her.

Before heading home, she stopped at a park. Kari craved the crisp spring air that reminded her so much of sports and her youth. As soon as she got out of her car, she headed to her favorite playground attraction and the one least crowded—the swings.

She sat on the wide, thick leather platform held up by charcoal-gray chains. Below where she rested her hands, she noticed how worn the chains looked. Kari imagined all the children over the years who had used the swing before her and worn out the finish on the links. She added to that by gripping them and pushing herself back and forth.

It had been a few days since she, Michael, and Reagan had come home from Virginia Beach. Although she'd tried keeping a strong appearance for them, the whole situation had left her feeling drained. Every time she closed her eyes to go to sleep or even when she blinked, Thane's image popped in her head. If she couldn't stay at a job where she didn't feel trusted and respected, how did she think she could be with a man who valued her just as little?

After a few swings and some strange stares, Kari felt relaxed enough to go home. Thankfully, she could park in her garage. Reporters and photographers had become a new staple outside her home since pictures of her and Thane had surfaced. Even telling them she'd only wanted to represent Thane didn't calm the ravenous crowd.

After pulling into her garage, Kari quickly shut the door behind her. She didn't get out of her car until it closed completely. Then she emerged and went into her home.

Reagan stood in the kitchen cleaning up from lunch. "So you did it?"

Kari nodded. "I quit. I'll have to dip into Michael's support to pay you. But that's what that money is for anyway."

Even with Jarrod's temporary suspension from the team while the heat from the video of him pushing Michael died down, he still made his support payments. He'd contacted Kari to assure her he would do whatever he could for Michael.

"Why would you still need me around? You'll be home with Michael until you get your business going, right? You won't need me." Reagan shrugged, but the tough woman's eyes started to have a glossy sheen over them. When she blinked, one tear escaped and rolled down her cheek.

"Reagan, you're like family." Kari embraced her. "I will always look out for you."

"You don't have to." Reagan wiped her eyes.

"I know. I want to." Kari smiled. "Is Michael with the tutor?"

Another new change since coming home. After seeing reporters standing on the sidewalk trying to take pictures of Jarrod Townsend's son at school, Kari had to regroup and protect her child.

"Hi, baby." Kari smiled as she strolled into the office area where Michael met with his tutor.

"Hey." Michael's deflated answer matched how Kari felt inside.

She wouldn't show that to him. "You two had lunch already?"

Michael nodded. "Chicken sandwich and chips." He threw his pencil down and looked at Kari. "When can I go back to school? I miss my friends."

Kari glanced at the older man sitting next to her child. "Mr. Hashni, will you excuse us for a moment, please?"

The man nodded and arranged the papers they used on the desk. Kari put her hand on Michael's shoulder as she led him to his bedroom. It hadn't escaped her notice that Michael had removed all the posters of Jarrod from his wall. He'd replaced all of them with pictures of Thane, which made it difficult for her to go to his room. She closed the door for privacy.

"I know all these changes are a bit much for you." Kari sat next to Michael.

"It's all happening so fast. First, the thing with Dad, and then doing school at home, which I thought would be fun. But Mr. Hashni is as bad as my teachers." Michael shook his head. "And now I don't even get to see Mr. Wells anymore."

Kari had to come up with a good story, not a lie. "You know Mr. Wells was only in town for his mother's funeral. Spring training is going on right now."

"But he's not doing that." Michael sprang from the bed and retrieved his tablet from the desk in his room. "See. He's been put on the injured list. What's a bleeding ulcer?"

Probably something the Carolina Wrens didn't want to hear right now, Kari wanted to say. She'd avoided looking up stories about Thane to keep from being sucked back into caring again.

"An ulcer is when the acid in your stomach eats the lining in your belly and it makes you sick." Kari understood Thane's worry. First his mother, then the issues with his brothers, and now his job. For a young man, he had a lot riding on his shoulders.

"They said he's spending time in North Carolina." He turned the tablet around to show her the gossip site where he had found the information.

Kari took the tablet from his hands. "You know I don't like you going to these sites. They're not for kids."

"Sorry." He hung his head down.

"And Thane—Mr. Wells—has a right to his privacy just like we do. Stop following him online. It's creepy."

"But I miss him. You won't let me go outside to play, and I can't throw a baseball in the house." He leaned his head on Kari's shoulder. "Until he got sick, we had fun in Virginia Beach." He laughed.

"What's so funny?" She stroked her hand over his back.

"Before everything happened with Dad, I got Leona's contact information. I wouldn't have done that if it hadn't been for Mr. Wells."

Kari blinked. She didn't think she would need to have "the talk" with Michael so soon, although she found it adorable that he liked a girl already.

"I thought you liked him."

"I do, as a baseball player." She couldn't say as a friend. Not anymore.

"Did you two have a fight or something?"

She leaned back to look at her son's face. He still looked innocent, but the questions he asked made her wonder if he had aged ten more years since leaving the beach. "Why would you ask me that?"

He shrugged. "You seem different now."

"Different how? I still dress the same. I still eat the same foods. I still love giving you kisses." To illustrate her final point, she kissed his forehead, complete with the kissing sound she knew drove Michael crazy.

"Mom." He wiped his forehead.

"See. Still the same Mom."

"Yeah, but you seemed, I don't know, happier before." He patted her leg. "It's nice to see you smiling again."

It felt good to show some happiness. "Okay, I've kept you from your studies long enough." She helped Michael to his feet and nudged him toward the office. "Get back to work, mister."

"Aw, Mom." He schlepped toward the office.

"I know. Life is so hard for you, isn't it?"

He nodded.

"I could sing to you if you wanted." She paired the singing with some dancing.

Michael shook his head and waved his hands in front of her. "No, no. I'm fine."

Kari held back her laughter. With Michael gone from his room, it gave her the opportunity to scan the pictures on his wall. Thane's blue eyes drew her in to every shot, that and his incredible ass.

She shook her head. She had to stop. No way would he be pining over her. In her mind, Thane had moved on. In her heart, she hoped he felt the same as she did.

* * * *

"Are you sure this is what you want to do?" Jermaine asked for the seventh time over the phone.

Thane smiled as he drove down to the Outer Banks vacation house. "I haven't changed my answer each time you've asked me." He shook his head. "The surgeon has told me to take time off. The team doc won't clear me right now to even practice, let alone play. My body is telling me I need to take a little break. I'm hoping sixty days will do the trick, but we'll see."

"And then you'll be back?"

Thane heard the anticipation in Jermaine's voice.

"Yes, then I hope to come back." His contract covered another year. He owed the Wrens that much.

"Take care of yourself, man. Hopefully, we'll see you in a couple of months."

The call ended as soon as Thane's navigation announced his arrival to his destination.

Jesus, Queen Elizabeth had good taste. He drove up the brick-paved drive to the three-story house that sat on the beach. Thane had imagined owning this type of home when he saw retirement in his horizon.

He stayed in his car in front of the house for several minutes while he compared the address on the paperwork he'd signed at the will reading to where he sat now. Thane surveyed the place. He had arrived before tourist season so he didn't see any cars.

Before he lugged his suitcase up the stairs to the brown house with white trim, he went up to the door with the key. Even after opening the door, he still couldn't believe he had come to the right place and that his mother had owned this home without telling any of them.

Thane heard the telltale beeping from the alarm by the door. He entered the code the attorney had given him.

He walked into the living room first. The great open view of the ocean behind the house greeted him as soon as he entered the home. He clearly saw the picturesque beach through the glass wall at the back of the house. No wonder his mother had bought this place.

Thane explored the downstairs area first. He stepped into the kitchen with its all stainless-steel appliances and granite counters and bars. He half expected to find the refrigerator fully stocked. The nearly empty refrigerator only held a box of baking soda and a couple of bottles of champagne. However, in the freezer he found Tupperware containers filled with cookie dough, his mother's homemade chocolate chip cookie dough.

"Yes." Thane pumped his fist as he closed the freezer door.

He strolled around the home until he came across a strange-looking door. He opened it and found it went to an elevator. The idea that Queen would outfit her vacation home with an elevator tickled him. Thane laughed as he got inside and went up to the second floor. He would need this when he moved some things into the place.

He rested his hand on his stomach when the doors opened and he felt a slight twinge. The doctors had advised him to get a lot of rest and relaxation. This house would accomplish that goal...but not much of anything else.

As Thane explored each room, he found the furniture to be oversized and comfortable looking. The home reminded him of Elizabeth's house in Virginia Beach, or rather Gunnar's house now, except it didn't have an abundance of doilies.

Thane reached the top floor and walked around the open space with pitched ceilings. In every part of the house, he thought about Kari and how much she would like this place. He'd wanted Kari to be with him the first time he came here. He messed up that relationship. As much as he wanted to blame his misguided conclusion on the drugs, he knew what he had said. He knew what he'd done. To make it all right, he knew what he had to do.

Thane started to leave the house when he noticed an envelope sitting on a coffee table. He picked it up and opened it, thinking that maybe Mr. Ubo had left him other instructions regarding the home. The attorney had been extremely helpful in getting the utilities placed in his name.

He opened the envelope and instead found a handwritten letter from his mother. He recognized her writing. For this, he had to take a seat.

If you all are reading this, it means that I have gone to that great garden in the sky.

Thane smiled at her terminology, but he felt his throat getting scratchy and tightening up the more he read.

I know this home is a surprise. I had to have my secrets. You all shouldn't. I hope this home brings you all closer together as a family. It's all I dream of...well, that and grandchildren.

Thane laughed at that line. Queen would have made a wonderful grandmother. She'd always been a great mother to the three of them.

Be good to one another. Love each other. I will always, always love you all. Love, Mom.

He read over the line about being good to one another. Before leaving, he pulled out his phone. As soon as he started to call the first number, he instinctively put his hand to his stomach. Usually, a call to Gunnar twisted his gut. Not this time.

"Yeah," the gruff man said after only the first ring.

"Hey, Gun. How are you doing?" Thane rested his free hand on his leg as he talked to his brother.

"You mean since you kicked me and Gid out from your hospital room? Great. Just great." Sarcasm filled his voice.

Thane couldn't blame him. He had been a rotten brother to both of them.

"What are you doing? I read online that you were released from the hospital. Thanks for telling us."

Thane could now hear his brother pacing through the phone. "Yep, I got out yesterday. I checked out of my hotel. As long as I remain relaxed and take my meds, I'll be fine." He glanced around the space. "So I'm at Mom's house in the Outer Banks."

Gunnar chuckled. "You called to gloat? You want to rub it in my face that you're in a beach house?"

"No. I'm wondering why the hell you and Eboni aren't here."

The silence on the other line had Thane wondering if Gunnar had disconnected the call.

"You what?" Gunnar asked.

Thane sat at the edge of the couch. "Why don't you and your girl come down here? The house is beautiful, man. But it's too much for me." He glanced at the letter Queen left. "And Mom would want it that way." He stopped. "No. *I* want you here. I want to see you all here."

"Really?"

"You have something to write with? Let me give you the address." As soon as Gunnar said he could write, Thane spouted the address and gave some basic directions to get to the house.

"Eb and I have to make sure the salon is okay before we can go." Excitement filled Gunnar's voice.

"Good. I was thinking maybe you all can come down this weekend. Maybe stay a week or two or more. Whatever you want." Thane stood. "I need to get some food and stuff in the house. It's all furnished at least. I'll make sure there are enough towels, blankets, sheets, and stuff."

"Come on. It's Mom's house. Of course she would make sure it was stocked with everything we would need." Gunnar laughed, which prompted Thane to join him.

"Yeah, I suppose." Thane nodded as he headed to the elevator. "I'm calling Gid now and see if he can make it."

"Thanks, man. It'll be good to see everyone again under one roof without it being a funeral."

"Or a community center dance."

They laughed together. The elevator dinged and Thane got inside.

"I thought you said you left the hotel. Did I hear an elevator?" Gunnar asked.

"You have *got* to see this house. It's incredible." He reached the bottom floor and made sure to lock all the windows and doors.

"Can't wait. Love you, Thane."

Thane stutter stepped to the front door and stopped in place. "Love you." He did. Despite his pent-up anger and resentment, he did love Gunnar and Gideon.

Too bad it took losing their mother, having a surgery, and missing out on the best woman he'd ever been with in his life for him to realize the importance of family.

He turned on the house alarm and locked the door behind himself. As soon as he got into his car, he called Gideon.

"Hey, Thane. Are you back in the hotel? You know you can stay with me and Janelle while you recover." Gideon barely took a breath as he spoke.

"You are always opening your home to me and the family." Thane ran his hand over his head.

"Of course. That's what family does." He grunted like he'd stood from a sitting position.

"You're right. So how about you and Janelle come down to the Outer Banks this weekend and stay with me at Mom's house?" Thane looked up at the house through his car window. "I'm here right now. It's incredible. And I've already called Gunnar."

"You did?"

Thane nodded like his brother could see him. "He said he's coming down with Eboni after he makes sure the salon is all straight. What about you? Can you take some time from the flower shop to hang out? I need to do some things first and get some food in here. All that was left was a frozen container of Mom's chocolate chip cookie dough."

"No way." Gideon laughed. "I'll come down there now just for that."

Thane gave his brother the address of the house.

"I'll get up with Gunnar so that we can come down together. Thanks, Thane. This'll be good for all of us."

Thane thought so too. "See you all in a few days." He had to make a special trip first.

What he needed to do couldn't be done with a call. He glanced at the clock on his phone. By the time he got to where he needed to go, it would be eight or nine at night. He didn't care.

Thane made sure to gas up his ride before hitting the road to go north. He kept a laser focus the entire drive. Until he drove to the place where Kari worked, he didn't remember listening to the radio or hearing anything else. His mind stayed on Kari.

He started to head up to the building when a blonde strolled out. As soon as she saw him, she dropped the coffee she held and cursed.

"Are you okay?" Thane struggled to bend over to pick up her cup.

"Um, yeah. You would think after working here for so long that I would get used to seeing good-looking athletes." She put her hand to her head. "I'm so glad I agreed to work late tonight. Sorry. My name is Chelsi."

Thane accepted her hand and shook it. "Thane Wells. I'm here to see Kari Meyers. I'm hoping she's as dedicated as you. Can you tell me where her office is?"

Chelsi looked like she wanted to say something, then she stopped herself and reached into her saddlebag purse. "I'll do you one better." She scribbled something down and handed it to him. "You can find her there."

He glanced at the address. "Thanks." He headed back to his vehicle.

"Oh, no. Thank you."

Thane looked behind him and caught Chelsi taking a picture of him. She had her camera aimed down at his ass. He had to shake his head.

It took him no time to get to the other address. It surprised him to discover that Chelsi had given him Kari's home address. He hoped she didn't do that with every client looking for Kari.

A few vans lined the street in front of her townhouse. Thane pulled into her driveway and got out, which incited a feeding frenzy. The few remaining photographers jumped out of their vehicles and started snapping away.

Thane paid them no mind as he walked up to the front door and pushed the bell. He heard someone inside screaming about the nerve of the photographers approaching her home. When the door opened, he lost his breath as he stared at the beauty before him.

Kari's mouth hung open as she gazed at Thane. "You're here. What are you doing here? How did you find me?"

"Someone named Chelsi at your office gave me your address."

He heard Kari grumbling over that bit of information.

"Can I come inside to talk?" When Thane saw her screw up her lips, he knew this wouldn't be an easy conversation. "I promise I won't take up too much of your time. Please."

Kari glanced behind him before she nodded and took a step to the side. "You had better make this quick."

Thane didn't know about quick. He would have to make his plea good.

Chapter 23

Kari's heart hadn't stopped pounding since she opened the door and found Thane. She hadn't talked to him since that fateful day in his hospital room. Now her head and heart warred with each other. Her head had the lead.

She allowed him into her home but kept him standing by the front door. She would be kicking him out as soon as he finished whatever he had to say.

She glanced at her watch. "Hurry up and say what you have to say. I have to put Michael to bed."

Thane moved in closer to her. She remained where she stood. The hell she would run from anyone inside of her own home.

"I am sorry." He put his hand to his chest.

"Don't you mean you apologize?" She kept her stare on the front door. When he didn't respond, she connected her gaze to his.

Damn those blue eyes.

"I never meant to hurt you." He eased into her space more.

At this distance, she caught his heady, musky scent. She had to lock her knees together to keep from swaying.

"You did." Kari raised her chin. "You made me feel worthless. I can't be with a man who doesn't respect me."

Thane opened his mouth to continue his plea when he smiled and looked behind Kari. "Michael. How are you, buddy?"

Michael beamed and ran up to Thane.

"No, no. Easy. He had surgery." Kari held up her hands to her enthusiastic child.

Michael wrapped his arms around Thane's waist. Thane didn't grumble or grunt in any pain. He hugged the child back.

"Mr. Wells. I can't believe you're here." Michael pulled back from him. "Are you okay?"

Thane placed his hand on his stomach. "I will be. Turns out I was holding a lot of stuff inside and it was making me sick." He stared at Kari. "I'm learning to be more open and honest."

"Mom is always telling me to tell the truth." Michael rolled his little eyes.

"That's right." She held her son's shoulder and pulled him toward her. "Honesty is the best policy. Everyone knows where you stand."

"As usual, your mom is right." Thane looked at Kari. "I trust you with every part of my being. That day at the hospital, I wasn't questioning your integrity. I was wondering about my own. You have done nothing but be professional and straightforward and truthful. I've held back. I've made it difficult for you to get close. But you, you've made it so easy to love you." Thane moved in close to her, wrapped his hand behind her neck, and pulled her in for a kiss.

Kari immediately closed her eyes and let herself be transported to a life that included this hunky man and her child. She'd missed the feeling of his full lips against hers.

"Oh, wow. Looks like I walked in on something good."

Kari broke from the kiss and noticed Reagan standing behind them. Reagan smiled as she stared at the three of them.

Thane pulled back from Kari to give Reagan a hug. "Good to see you." Then he brought his attention back to Kari.

"I believe you were apologizing to me." Kari had to bring this back to reality.

"What?" Michael worried his little eyebrows. "You hurt my mom?"

Thane gazed down at the boy. "Not on purpose." He returned his stare to Kari. "I accused her of trying to get my business in an unscrupulous way."

Michael thought about the word for a moment before he spoke. "That means something bad, right?"

Thane nodded. "Some not-so-nice folks said some things about your mother that I believed. I can't blame it on being drugged or in pain. I should have known better. I know her. I know her as a woman, as a friend, and as a mother. She saved me. In every sense of the word, she saved my life." He looked down at Michael. "I wouldn't be here without her." Then he connected his gaze to hers. "I love you. I think I loved you from the moment I saw you in New York."

Kari finally broke. She smiled. "I love you."

"Because of his pitching and how he plays?" Michael asked.

She shook her head but kept her stare on Thane. "Because you're man enough to apologize when you make a mistake. Because you came back to me. You make me feel worth it."

Thane wrapped his arm around Kari's waist and kissed her cheek. "I will never doubt you again. If you give me another chance, I will treat you like the queen that you are." He started to go in for another kiss when Michael put himself in between the two of them.

"You made my mom get upset." He shook his head. "She wasn't the same after she saw you. I don't like that." His little mouth turned down.

"I know. If she'll let me, I'll apologize to her every day for the rest of my life." Thane put his hand on Michael's shoulder. "If you're really sorry and you apologize, you can repair most relationships."

"Like with my dad?" Michael split his attention between Thane and Kari.

"That's up to you." Thane tapped Michael on his chest. "You have to feel it in here." He looked at Kari. "Do you feel anything for me?" He put his hand on her chest over her heart. "In here."

The connection broke her. "Yes. I love you." She cried and embraced him.

Feeling him hold her gave her a sense of security she hadn't felt in years. No man, except for her grandfather, had been so open and honest with her. From his kisses to his stares, she knew he loved her. She loved him. Beyond the stats and how he played, she loved the man.

"I got to capture this." Reagan held up her phone and snapped the picture of the family. "So now what?"

Thane gazed down at Kari. "I finally went to my mother's house in North Carolina. My brothers and their fiancées are coming down this weekend. I want you to come with me."

Kari stared at the man she thought she knew. "You invited your brothers to stay with you?"

He nodded. "It won't be complete unless you're there. You pushed me to open up to them. You've pushed me in a lot of great ways." He held her hand. "I want you there." Then he scanned the rest of her family. "And you all can come."

Kari shook her head. "Not this time. I've already had Michael on vacation once."

"Then you go, Mom." Michael smiled.

"Michael, I'm not going to leave you." Kari crouched down to get eye level with her child.

"You won't be leaving me. You'll be building our family."

Kari gasped along with Reagan.

"When did he get so smart?" Reagan wiped under her eyes.

"Besides, with you two gone, maybe the photographers will go away." Michael jutted his thumb over his shoulder.

Kari laughed. "As nice as you are to be so understanding, I can't—"

Reagan cut her off. "Yes, you can. I'll stay here with him and make sure he studies. There will be other times for us all to be together. I have a feeling that this trip is something that's strictly for adults only."

"What do you say?" Thane asked.

Kari gazed at Reagan and Michael. "You two are awesome."

Reagan pulled Michael to her. "We know."

"But I won't be gone long."

Michael rolled his eyes. "We know."

Kari hugged her son and her friend. "Thank you."

"Anytime. Now I can help you pack." Reagan rubbed her hands together.

"So can I." Michael started to head to Kari's bedroom.

"Oh, no, mister. Time for you to go to bed." Kari held Michael's shoulders as she headed him to his bedroom.

"Aww, Mom." He hung his head as he stomped to his room.

"I know. Life is so hard." She managed to get him back to bed before she went to her bedroom to pack.

She found Thane standing in the middle of the room.

"I was fine with Reagan and Michael coming along," he said.

"I know. I think you need some time with your brothers first."

Thane moved in closer to her. "I think the big question is what are we going to do alone in that big house until they show up?"

She wrapped her arms around his waist and held him gently. "I'm sure we'll figure something out."

* * * *

Kari turned over in the plushest bed she'd ever slept in in her life. She ran her hand over the sheets and moaned.

"Good. You're awake."

She felt a hard body snuggling up behind her. While keeping her eyes closed, she smiled. She didn't want to wake from this dream. After three days of being alone in a huge house on the beach, she knew she hadn't stepped into a fantasy.

Thane wrapped his arm around her waist. "I haven't touched you in the way that I want in three days." He kissed the shell of her ear. "The doctor said I can have sex now. The sutures are all gone." He eased his hand up her shirt. "And the blood is flowing everywhere in my body."

Kari giggled. "We shouldn't."

"Yes, we should. My brothers and their fiancées will be here today. This will be the only time I can make you scream." He flipped her on to her back, which did make her squeal.

"Thane, wait." She held his strong, broad shoulders. Damn, she wanted this man. "Look me in my eyes and tell me the truth."

"Always." He stared into her eyes even as he deftly removed his pajama bottoms while under the comforter.

"Did the doctor really say you can have sex now?" Although she wanted him, she didn't want to hurt him. It would be hard, but she could wait.

Thane nodded. "I could have had sex a week ago. I didn't want you thinking that I only wanted you here to jump your hot body. But every time you put on a bathing suit and got into the pool or hot tub, I had to find something else to do to stay away from you. It was bad enough sleeping in separate bedrooms."

Kari removed her sleep shirt, revealing her bare chest. "Not my fault. I wanted us to share a room."

"Honey, if we did, this would have happened multiple times by now." He opened the nightstand drawer next to the bed and pulled out a string of condoms. "Sorry, baby. I'm going to go all frat boy on you." He smiled as he placed a wrapper between his teeth to open it.

She pushed him over to get him on his back. "Not if I don't play cougar first." She snatched the condom from him and rolled it down the length of him.

"I like the sound of that." He held onto her hips as she grabbed the base of his shaft and aimed him at her core.

As soon as she slipped him inside, time stopped. Kari gripped his chest as she undulated her hips on him, up and down ever so slowly.

"Better than I remembered." Thane pulled her back and forth to help guide her.

She didn't need help satisfying him. She removed one hand from her hip and placed it on her breast. Her hardened nipple brushed against his meaty palm.

"I signed your contract." Thane gritted his teeth as he nodded toward the nightstand.

Kari broke her stare from him long enough to see the contract she'd given to him in his hotel room sitting on a nightstand. "Tear it up."

Thane blinked. "Why?"

She shook her head. "No longer at Winning Edge." She planted her hands on his shoulders as she rode him harder and faster. "On my own."

"Give me your new contract. I'll sign with you."

Hearing that prompted her first of many orgasms. Kari screamed and constricted her legs and arms around him. "Am I hurting you?"

"Only if you stop." He pulled her to him and kissed her.

Kari sat up on him. When she gazed down, she noticed his incision scars across his lower abdomen. "We should have done this days ago." Her insides tightened again like she wanted to come.

"Yeah, if we did, you wouldn't have respected me." He winked at her.

At his statement, she did something that she'd never done before. She released a combination laugh-scream when another orgasm hit her.

She stayed entwined with him for another hour. Kari didn't care about the beach or the big house or even the contract as long as she had this man in her life.

Thane plopped back on the bed. "So good."

Kari lay on top of him but kept him inside her. "When did you say your family was going to arrive?"

As though she'd cued it, the front doorbell chimed.

Thane cursed. "You take a shower." He gave her a quick peck before removing the used condom and wrapping his body in a sheet. "I'll go answer the door. I'll be back after I let them in."

"Good." She jumped out of bed. "You can join me." She winked before disappearing into the bathroom.

* * * *

Thane had never felt more alive than in this house. No wonder his mother had kept it a secret.

Instead of taking the stairs down, he went down by elevator. Kari had drained him of his energy, but he would do it ten times over if he could. As he headed to the door, he saw Gunnar and Gideon on the other side with their faces pressed against the glass to look inside.

Thane smiled as he approached the door and opened it. "Hey, you made it."

Gunnar scanned him. "Looks like you made something yourself." He hugged Thane.

"You'll have to excuse my attire. Late start to the day." He kissed Eboni's cheek.

"I'm guessing you're not here alone." Gideon hugged him.

"Kari's upstairs." Thane kissed Janelle on her cheek.

"Really?" Eboni raised her eyebrows. "Glad you two worked things out. I like her." She nudged Gunnar with her elbow.

"Yeah, she's good people." He tried looking hard, but every time he glanced at Eboni, he let a smile peek through.

"You all need help with your luggage?" Thane pointed to the cars in the driveway.

Gideon shook his head. "You go shower and get dressed. We'll be fine."

"Let me at least give you a tour first so you all can decide on your rooms. There's not a bad one in the house." Thane took them around to every part of the house with the exception of the third floor.

"What's up there?" Janelle asked and pointed up.

"It's the master suite. It spans the entire floor. And Kari is there getting ready." Thane gripped the sheets tighter around his body.

"And, of course, you're in it, right?" Gunnar stared at Thane.

Before his stomach could twinge, Thane spoke up. "Of course."

Gunnar waited a beat before he nodded. "Makes sense."

Thane exhaled. "You all pick the rooms you want. I'll get ready and meet you down in the living room."

He took the stairs up to the third floor. When he opened the door, he found Kari slathering lotion on her nude body.

"I thought you were going to wait for me." Thane dropped the sheet that covered his body.

"And I thought you were going to let them in and come back." She gave him a seductive smile before sauntering back to the bathroom.

No way could he let her go. Not right now. He followed her and stood behind her as she washed her hands. "Now I wished I hadn't waited so long."

Kari turned to him. "I'm glad we did. This morning was so intense." She gave him a quick kiss.

He wrapped his arm around her and pulled her close to his body. "You're still naked. Let's get in the shower and—"

She put her hand to his chest and gave him a gentle nudge back. "I'm going to get dressed. I'll see you downstairs."

Before he allowed her to leave, he held her hand. "I want you in every room in this house, including the elevator."

"Good to know." She winked before getting dressed and leaving the bedroom.

Thane could make this the perfect weekend. He had to get his whole family on board. To do that, he had to be honest.

After his shower and throwing on jeans and a T-shirt, he sauntered downstairs to find the group all eating lunch. It looked like someone had found the lunchmeat he and Kari had purchased along with the bread, cheese, lettuce, tomatoes, and condiments. He stood at the opening to the dining room and watched Gunnar making fun of Gideon, Gideon feeding Janelle, and Eboni chatting with Kari.

Thane wanted this. He'd always wanted a house filled with family.

"It's about time you made your way down." Gideon smiled. "Kari made you a plate." He pointed to a sandwich on a plate on the breakfast bar with a salad next to it.

"Thanks." He kissed Kari first before retrieving the plate.

When he noticed Gunnar looking away from him after he'd kissed her, he felt a fire in his belly. To extinguish it, he would have to address his brothers. Not now. Not in front of the ladies.

As soon as Thane finished his lunch, he stood from the table. No time like the present.

"Why don't you ladies go for a walk on the beach? It's a beautiful day." Thane started collecting the dishes from the table.

"I know what that's code for." Eboni stood.

"The guys want to talk." Janelle squeezed Gideon's hand.

"And not in front of us." Kari regarded Thane.

A silent conversation happened between them. As he stared at her, she raised her eyebrow and made a slight turn with her head. Thane nodded before going into the kitchen.

Kari stood. "Sounds like a great idea. Grab your cameras. The views are absolutely to die for."

After each woman outfitted herself with her jacket and phone, they each kissed their man and made their way out back.

Gideon barely waited for the door to close before he addressed Thane. "So what's up? I know this is more than you showing us the house, which is awesome, by the way."

"It is." Thane took a deep breath before he turned to his brothers. "I know I've been standoffish for the last few years."

"Yeah. More like a spoiled brat." Gunnar went over to the bar and sat on a stool.

"I've had a lot of things on my mind that I let get to me. It's that behavior that made me sick. I can't do that anymore." He glanced at Gideon first. "Gid, I did go to the Super Bowl."

Gideon blinked. "I thought you couldn't—"

"I could. I apologize for interrupting you, and for making it seem like I didn't care. I was there and I invited some folks to join me in the suite. That girl you heard was someone else's girlfriend. I said what I did to push you away. I was proud of you for that game and how you played." Thane rinsed off each plate before loading them in the dishwasher.

"Wow. I didn't think you cared about any of us. Why would you want us thinking that?" Gideon sat next to Gunnar.

They looked like a section of the Supreme Court gazing down on Thane and judging him.

"I figured the more pissed off you two got with me, the more you would leave me alone." Thane wiped his hands on a dishtowel.

He would have sat next to them, but he wanted to look them in the eyes as he spoke.

"Did you know Gid rushed home after the game when I got shot?" Gunnar planted his large hands on the counter.

Thane shook his head. "I saw him bolting from the field. I figured he was going home because of Mom. I had talked to Mom and she told me she was okay."

"Guess we all had our secrets." Gideon lowered his gaze.

"So you and the other women?" Gunnar pressed.

Thane shook his head. "More of me acting like a jerk to you all, but I never used women." He turned to Gunnar. "The day you flew down to tell me about Mom, I was set to be interviewed by a magazine writer who got drunk and begged me to stay with her until she slept it off. I never touched her. When I nodded off waiting for her to sleep, she unbuttoned my shirt and undid my pants. By the time I woke up, she had taken off her clothes and was coming at me."

Gideon wagged his finger at Thane. "Was she a tall blonde?"

Thane blinked. "Yes."

"Laughed like a donkey?" Gideon asked.

"Oh, shit. That's right. What was her name?" Gunnar snapped his fingers. "Lorelei? Loretta Lynn?"

"Lora Ann." Thane ran his hand over his head.

"That's it," Gunnar and Gideon said at the same time.

"She's a piece of work." Gunnar shook his head. "She's the reason I don't do interviews. She tried getting me with that whole drunk bit."

"Yeah, Gun told me about her. When she got to me, I was wise to her. I told her I would only do an interview at the Wolves training camp or at my old high school. No alcohol in either place." Gideon shook his head.

"Had you said something to one of us about being interviewed by her, we could have warned you." Gunnar's tone came out harsh. He glared at Thane.

"So why the cold shoulder?" Gideon rested his elbows on the counter.

Thane stared at both men before directing his full attention to Gunnar. "I was bitter and angry at something Gunnar had said."

Gunnar blinked. "Me? When?"

"You remember that day you wanted to hang out with your old group of friends and Mom tried stopping you?" Thane wrung the dishtowel in his hand. If he didn't get his feelings out now, it would kill him.

Gunnar rolled his eyes. "You're really bringing that up now? That was twelve or thirteen years ago. I apologized to Mom for every stupid thing I said."

"Yeah, you did. But what about me?" Thane pointed to himself.

He felt his blood pressure rising. He had to calm himself down. Making himself sick wouldn't do him any good.

"You? Why should I apologize to you?" Gunnar cocked his head.

"You told Mom that you didn't care about me because I wasn't even your real brother." Saying it felt like he had ripped a Band-Aid off a wound.

"What?" Gideon looked at Gunnar, who remained quiet and stoic. "That's bullshit."

"The story might not be true, but he said it." Thane pointed to Gunnar. "Mom never refuted it. So I started really looking at the three of us. You two look alike. Both tall, same body build, blond, blue eyes."

"You have blue eyes." Gideon raised his voice.

"Yeah, but not like your blue." When Thane noticed how quiet Gunnar had become, he kept on him. "After that, I started pulling away." He glanced at Gideon. "I'm sorry I did that to you. I saw you both as a package deal. Both of your names start with G. Mine doesn't. Hell, your businesses even sound the same. Press 'N Curl. Pick 'N Clip. I got Sharp. You two always were close. I always felt left out. When you both left home, Mom and I had this bond. We were a team. She had my back more than I thought you two did."

"Unbelievable." Gideon stood from his stool. "Excuse me." He went out the front door and slammed it behind him.

With only Gunnar and Thane in the room, the silence hung heavy in the air. Thane wanted to relay this story and move on. Now that he said it out loud, he still felt a weightiness in the air. If Gunnar had said something, maybe Thane wouldn't feel that way.

"You're right." Gunnar's normally booming voice became light, small. "I did say that to hurt you and Mom." He brought his gaze up. "I was a little shit back then. I can't believe you heard me."

"I did." Thane released the towel. "I was so hurt. I figured that with everything we'd been through, at least you two were my blood brothers. Now I don't know who I am." He chuckled. "You know why I got into baseball? You two had your own thing. You were on the wrestling team in high school and went off to become an MMA fighter. Gideon had football. I wanted so desperately to fit in with you two somehow. So I did baseball. Even that didn't seem to matter to you."

Gunnar nodded. "It did. I was so proud of you. Mom told me about all of your accomplishments." He cleared his throat. "I never meant to hurt you with all the stupid stuff I said and did. Before you were born, our biological mother would have every kind of lowlife in our trailer. They would bring stuff for her to get high, or they would get high and drunk and crash there. I remember there was one woman that we had to call Auntie Katie. I don't know what she was to our mother, but she stayed with us for a long time."

Thane hung onto every word. His heart started pounding as soon as he started the story.

"Auntie Katie was a thin woman, except for one time." Gunnar held up his finger. "Once I saw her getting out of the shower and it looked like she had a belly."

Thane had to brace his hands on the bar as he listened to Gunnar.

"I was a kid. I'm sure I was wrong. But I knew what to say to hurt Mom. I shouldn't have said anything then. In every sense of the word, you and Gideon are my brothers. Nothing will ever change that."

The front door slammed again. Gideon marched back to the breakfast bar where Gunnar sat. He carried a stack of papers in his hand.

"You remember at the will reading that I got the contents of Mom's safe deposit box?" Gideon waved the papers in the air.

"Yeah." Thane kept his gaze on the folder.

"As usual, Mom has made me the mediator." Gideon slammed the papers onto the bar. "I went there a few weeks ago and found some of Mom's jewelry and important documents. Then I came across this." He pointed to the papers. "It has your birth information. You really want to know if you're our blood brother? Take a look." He put his hand on top of the folder. "I haven't looked at it because it doesn't matter what it says. You're my brother. I love you. Even if what it says in there is that you're the long lost son of an alien, I wouldn't care. You will always be my brother." He pushed the documents toward Thane. "If you really want to know, open that up and find out. But you're going to have to ask yourself if this will make a difference in our family. I will always see you as that kid who ran around the gym at all the dances."

Gunnar stood. "And you will always be my baby brother who knew I was sneaking out to see Eboni but could be bought off with chocolates and candies." He glanced down at the folder. "If you need to know for yourself, go ahead. No matter what it says, you'll always be my brother."

"Same here." Gideon removed his hand.

Thane stared at the folder like it would grow legs and start dancing. All those years he had ignored Gunnar and Gideon because of his unanswered question. Now he could get the truth.

He looked up and really regarded the two men. All three had the same experiences. They all shared Queen Elizabeth as a mother. If he did find out that his actual birth mother had been someone else, he knew his brothers would still love him. He loved them just as much.

Thane put his hand on the folder, waited a beat before pushing it back to Gideon. "Lock that back up or burn it." He smiled. "As far as I'm concerned, I have my brothers here. Knowing or not knowing won't change that."

Gunnar nodded. He made his way around the bar to Thane. Without a word, he pulled him into a tight embrace. "You keep talking to me, okay?"

Thane nodded.

"No secrets from each other." Gunnar looked at Gideon. "Understand?"

"Crystal clear." Gideon scooped up the papers and tucked them under his arm.

"So if we're not keeping secrets, when were you going to tell us that Eboni's pregnant?" Thane glared at his brother, who now looked confused.

"Eboni's not pregnant. Why would you think that?" Gunnar asked.

"When you were giving your speech at the funeral, you mentioned that Mom would have made a wonderful grandmother." Thane scratched his head.

"She would have. But we're not at that point yet to bring kids into the mix." Gunnar put his hand on Thane's shoulder. "I would have told you if Eboni and I were expecting."

"One more thing." Thane held up his hand. "Be nice to Kari."

Gunnar rolled his eyes. "If she hadn't come into your life, all the bad stuff that happened to you wouldn't have happened."

"Bad stuff? You mean like me finding love? Having her tell me that I needed to make up with my brothers because she knows how important family is?" Thane took a step back. "Or me deciding to give up baseball?"

"What?" Gunnar put his hand to his head. "Are you serious?"

Thane nodded. "After the next season, I'm going to put my full concentration into designing clothes." He smiled. "It's something I've always wanted to do. I pulled away from it because you guys didn't give up your careers to be a hair stylist and a florist."

"Uh, yeah. I did. I have one more fight and that's it. My full concentration has been on the salon and the hair product line I've developed." Gunnar leaned against the bar.

"I haven't stopped playing football. But I love the store and I've already got plans to expand it and build a nursery. I never thought about doing that until I got with Janelle. She makes me better." Gideon nodded.

"Same with me and Kari. She's an excellent mother and has been a great woman for me. I love her." Thane felt more at ease than he'd ever felt.

"If she makes you happy, then I'm happy." Gunnar slapped Thane on his shoulder. "You old dog."

Thane laughed. He felt relief to finally get his feelings out. With his brothers back in his life and his woman by his side, nothing could conquer him.

* * * *

Kari couldn't imagine a more perfect day, unless Michael had been there with her. She sat next to Thane while they watched a fire in a fire pit erupt in a tall flame. Gunnar sat next to Eboni with his arm around her. Gideon sat on the other side of Thane with his arms around Janelle.

"Mom was a smart woman." Gunnar tapped his temple. "She knew what to do to bring us all together."

Gideon nodded.

"I miss her." Thane confessed. "I miss our talks."

"I miss the way she would give advice at inappropriate times." Gideon chuckled.

"I miss her teasing." Gunnar smiled.

"I hate to do this without her, but I have to." Thane stood up in front of Kari.

She stared at him before glancing at the other four in attendance. "What are you doing?"

Before Kari could figure it out, Thane dropped down to one knee. Eboni and Janelle gasped. Kari couldn't breathe. She kept her stare on Thane as he smiled at her.

"When I first saw you, I knew you were the woman for me. Strong-willed, smart, sexy. You are everything I want in a woman and more. The fact that you have a child already makes you even more appealing." He reached into his pocket and pulled out a ring. "I already asked the man in your life for permission. Michael approved."

Kari laughed. She'd wondered why Michael kept texting her and asking her how she was doing. Michael always cared about Kari's wellbeing, but this level of interest seemed out of place.

"Kari Meyers, will you make me the happiest man in the world by being my wife?" Thane opened up a ring box and showed off a large princess-cut, canary-yellow diamond in a platinum setting.

She couldn't speak. Nodding seemed to be the only thing she could do. As soon as she did that, he slipped the ring on her finger and kissed her.

"Three weddings," Janelle said from behind Thane.

"I know. Baby brother, you had better get to work." Gunnar nudged his foot against Thane's leg. "You have three wedding dresses to design and make."

Thane laughed. "I can do that." He held Kari's hand. "For my family, I'll do anything."

"I love you so much. I'm so glad I dropped my dating rules for you." She stood. "I need to see this ring in a better light. I think the bedroom has the best lighting."

Thane draped his arm around her. "I think you're right." He leaned down to her ear. "Be gentle."

Kari laughed. As long as she had her man by her side, she felt loved and invincible.

Epilogue

Seven years later

Thane allowed Kari to grip his hand as hard as she could as he guided her into a Virginia Beach elementary school auditorium. She rested her hand on her protruding belly as she waddled down the aisle.

"People are staring at me." Kari started to sniff.

Gunnar had warned Thane about the raging hormones. Thane learned how to deal with Kari's mommy brain and rage by talking calmly and agreeing with everything she said.

"You are the most beautiful woman in here." Thane took her to the front row of seats where Gideon said they would be. "That's why they're staring. You're too stunning for words."

"No, I'm not. I'm fat and too old to have a child. That's what they're thinking."

He saw the tears coming. "You're only thirty-three. You still look like you're in high school yourself. I'm worried I'll get arrested for taking liberties with a minor."

A group of people overhead the last portion of his speech and gasped.

"No, I meant her." He pointed to his wife. "Never mind."

Once they got to the front of the auditorium, he noticed right away that Gunnar sat at one end and Gideon sat at the other. Like guarding gargoyles, they refused to let anyone else sit in the row. Not that they had any room. With Gunnar, Eboni, and their two young children, and Gideon, Janelle, and two of their kids seated with them, it only left three seats.

"Where's Michael?" Gideon asked.

"He's finishing up his exams." Kari sat down with help from Thane. "He'll see us afterward."

Thane sat next to Kari. He held her hand, happy to be with his family.

"The costumes look great." Janelle gave Thane a kiss on his cheek.

"Yeah, stellar work." Gideon gave him a thumbs-up.

The lights in the room dimmed before an older woman in sensible shoes appeared in the middle of a papier-mâché forest, complete with large apple trees, low, fluffy bushes and a log.

"Not a problem." Now that Thane had a whole team to do his sewing, he could also get them to put together costumes for a kindergarten play.

"Thank you to all the parents, family, and friends who came here to see our kindergarten class's play about an enchanted forest. Before we begin, we would like to thank Thane Wells for creating the costumes." The educator pointed Thane out in the audience.

Kari kissed him before she applauded with everyone else.

"We would also like to thank Gideon and Gunnar Wells for their generous donations, which allowed us to have refreshments available after the play." She pointed to the two men.

Another round of clapping echoed off the walls.

"Without any further delay, let's now be transported into the enchanted forest." She made her way off stage just as the curtain opened.

A group of small children walked out and gave a simultaneous speech about love and friendship. The cute scene got Thane to smile, but he wanted to see his niece, the star of the show, according to her doting dad Gideon.

Within seconds, a golden-toned child skipped onto the stage. Thane beamed when he saw her in the pink, glittery dress he'd made for her. Her matching pink wings fluttered behind her. A curly ponytail topped her head to accommodate her tiara. It made Thane wonder if Uncle Gunnar had anything to do with the styling.

"I'm here to make sure all the forest animals are free and happy." Lizzie, as Thane called her, reached into her pocket.

She threw glitter in the air but stopped when some of it fell back onto her face. She balled her little hands into fists and rubbed her eyes. Like a shot, Thane, Gideon, and Gunnar bolted to their feet.

Lizzie blinked before looking out into the audience. "Hi, Daddy. Hi, Uncle Thane and Uncle Gunnar." She waved.

Thane and his brothers waved to the girl before they sat back down.

"Smooth." Kari tapped Thane's hand.

"I thought she was in trouble." Thane settled back into his tight, uncomfortable seat.

"You're going to make a great dad." His wife patted his leg.

Hearing that sentiment from her made him smile. He wrapped his arm around her shoulders as he watched a play filled with fairies, squirrels, magical elves, and an evil wizard. In the end, Lizzie cast a spell that made them all friends.

After the play, all the children ran to their families. Lizzie trotted to Gideon. Her curls bounced all over her head like little golden rings.

"Did you see me, Daddy?" She held her hands up to him.

Gideon crouched down and lifted his oldest child. "I saw you. You were magnificent."

Lizzie giggled before turning to Janelle. "I want to do that again, Mommy."

Janelle, who held their youngest girl, Ava, in one arm and held the hand of their middle child, Ella, smiled and gazed at Gideon. "She's going to be an actress. You know that, right?"

"Had a feeling." He nodded.

"Congrats on the win." A man nodded to Gideon. "Great game."

"Thanks." Gideon smiled, but Thane could tell he did not want to talk about his third Super Bowl win.

"Love your purses and shoes." A woman held up a burgundy handbag with Thane's signature *TW* emblem on the side. She kicked up her foot to show off her matching pumps, also from Thane's line.

"Thank you." He wrapped his arm around his wife. "I happen to love that Kari line of purses and shoes myself."

Gunnar and Eboni joined the group, each of them holding a twin.

"Hi, Cameryn," Thane said to the one Eboni held. "Hi, Jilly Bean," he said to the little girl Gunnar held.

"I'm Cameryn." The little girl in Gunnar's arms pointed to herself.

"I'm Jillian." Eboni's bundle of joy raised her hand.

In mock horror, Thane covered his mouth. "How do I keep getting you two mixed up?"

In actuality, he could tell the difference. Jillian, the older twin by two minutes, had a slimmer face. Cameryn, the baby of the duo, had chubby cheeks and a small freckle beside her mouth. Thane liked teasing the three-year-olds just to hear them giggle. He couldn't wait for his own child to be born.

"We need to get to the house." Kari held Thane's hand. "People will be arriving soon."

"Hopefully, Michael is already heading down there." Thane kissed Kari's forehead.

"We have to finish up here." Gunnar nodded to Gideon. "The perks of being PTA parents. As soon as we're done, we'll be right behind you."

Thane didn't wait for them. He helped Kari get into the car before leaving Virginia Beach and heading down to the Outer Banks house.

As soon as Thane reached the house, he helped his wife out of the car first. He unlocked the door and disabled the alarm before getting Kari to a nearby couch.

"I don't know if I can take another month of this." Kari shook her head. "I don't remember being this huge with Michael."

"It's been seventeen years in between pregnancies." He rested his hand on her stomach. "You're doing great." He kissed her before retrieving the bags from the car.

After dropping them off in the master suite, he came back down and joined Kari on the couch.

"We need to get this place decorated." She struggled to stand.

"We could. Or, while we're alone…" He kissed the side of her face and went down to her neck.

"How is it that you find me attractive now?" Kari laughed and tried pushing Thane off her.

"I don't care what you look like. You will always be sexy to me." When he kissed her again, he slid his tongue into her mouth.

This time, she did manage to push him away. "Doing that is what got me here." She pointed to her belly.

"So I can't do any more damage." He reached for her again, but this time she managed to make it to her feet.

"You remember when I said you would make a great father? You are also a damn good husband." She winked as she went to the kitchen and started placing trays of food around the breakfast bar and dining room table.

While she arranged food on the bar, he came up behind her. "Have I told you I love you today?"

Kari nodded. "You did."

He wrapped his arms around her. "Have I told you how much I love being married?"

"I think you mentioned it once or twice." She nuzzled her head under his chin.

"The rest of the family has got to be at least thirty minutes behind us. Why don't we go up to the bedroom and—" As soon as he started to make the suggestion, a set of headlights beamed into the house.

"They're here." She rubbed his arm.

"Damn." He kissed the side of her face. "I'll answer the door. You make sure everything is out."

"Gotcha."

Thane opened the door to Michael, his son. It didn't matter that Jarrod Townsend had fathered him. For the last seven years, Thane had raised him like his own.

Michael now stood a couple of inches over Thane and carried the same lean frame like his father. "Dad." He pulled Thane into a hug.

Thane had never stopped Michael from calling him Dad. He'd liked it back then and now. It helped that after Thane and Kari married, he'd legally adopted Michael, and Michael had had his surname changed to Wells.

"I thought I was going to be here alone." Michael's smile lit up the room.

"No, your mom and I managed to see Lizzie's play and get down here in time." Thane started to close the front door when Michael stopped him.

"Wait. I have someone here with me." He opened the door and beautiful, young African-American woman followed him inside.

Thane stared at her for a moment. Her big, curly hair framed her face. As soon as she got into the house, she reached for Michael's hand.

"You look familiar." Thane didn't mean to stare, but he couldn't help it.

"I would hope so, Mr. Wells. You made me my first dress." She smiled.

"Leona?"

"You remember me." She embraced Thane.

"Of course, dear." He hugged her back. "Great to see you."

Kari walked into the room. "Is this Leona from the dance?" She pulled the young woman into her arms. "I haven't seen you in forever. The last time I saw you, this one was wearing a purple shirt." She pointed to Michael.

"You had to bring that up again, didn't you?" Michael kissed his mother's cheek.

Leona laughed. "I lost all that baby fat, but I still have that dress."

"Good. Save it for a child of your own someday." Thane smiled.

"Just not right now," Kari quickly added.

Soon the house filled with family and friends. The children ran around, chasing after each other and laughing.

It didn't surprise Thane to see Gideon's friend, Dennis, coming in with Shay, a stylist in Gunnar's salon. The two had hit it off at Thane's barbeque last summer, obvious from the way they wouldn't leave each other's side.

Reagan, Michael's former nanny, had remained a close friend of the family, even after she'd stopped her nanny duties. She arrived with her newest girlfriend, an ice skater Kari represented.

Thane took a breather in the kitchen. He pulled a cake from the refrigerator and placed it on the counter when Gunnar walked in.

"You need help with anything?" Gunnar scanned the food on the counter. Before Thane answered, the doorbell chimed. He furrowed his eyebrows. "I thought everyone was here already." Gunnar turned to the entryway.

"So did I." Thane moved around the breakfast bar to head to the door.

"It's probably Penny. I invited her." Janelle ran to it with Ava in her arms.

She opened it, and Penny, her best friend, burst through to hug Janelle and Ava.

"So good to see you." Penny kissed Ava's cheek, which made the toddler giggle. "And I brought a date. I've been seeing this guy for a couple of months now." She turned. "Come on in, honey."

Gunnar and Thane's faces dropped when Ant strolled into the home.

"You've got to be kidding." Gunnar shook his head. "You're dating Ant?"

The diminutive man poked his scrawny chest out. "Yes, we've been seeing each other. And people don't call me Ant anymore. I go by my real name. Waldo."

Thane tried hard to hold back his laughter. "Welcome to my home, Waldo. You two, come in. Get something to eat and drink. Everyone is in there. Mingle."

Janelle hung her arm around Penny's shoulder and led her into the room with Ant following behind.

"Incredible." Gunnar nodded toward the party.

"I know. He's like a bad penny. He shows up everywhere." Thane laughed.

"You remember when Mom used to host parties like these at her house?" Gunnar stood next to Thane.

"She celebrated everything. If you got an A on your report card, that called for an intimate get-together with about a hundred of her friends and family." Thane laughed. He looked into the living room when he heard growling.

Gideon and Dennis made fools of themselves by crawling on the floor like dogs and chasing after the kids, barking at them. The twins squealed and ran away from them. Ava and Ella tried climbing on Gideon's back for a ride.

"How it should be?" Gunnar nodded to the packed house.

"Always." Thane and Gunnar strolled back to the living room. "Can I get your attention, folks?"

Janelle turned off the music and made her way to her husband, who still sat on the floor.

"First of all, thank you so much for coming down here. I know spring break has just started, and you all have vacation plans of your own." Thane kissed the back of Kari's hand. "We're thankful you've chosen to spend a little time with us. We have a lot of great news to tell you." He looked to his wife.

"Before you all share your news, I have something to say." Dennis strutted to the center of the room.

"You always do, man." Gideon shook his head. "They don't call you Dennis the Menace for nothing."

Dennis held his hand up to his friend. "I'll make it quick. I promise." He turned to Shay. "My woman. Will you join me, please?"

Shay glanced around first before walking to the center of the room. "You are so silly. What are you doing?"

"This." He dropped down to one knee.

The women all gasped. The kids giggled. Shay cried.

"You have shared so much with me." Dennis held Shay's hand. "I want to be the man who protects you. With me, you will never have to worry. With me, you will always be secure. With me, you will always be my queen." He pulled a ring from his pocket. "Will you do me the honor of being my queen forever?"

Shay screamed before covering her mouth. Then she nodded. "Yes. Yes, I will."

Dennis slipped the ring on her finger, stood, and hugged her. Then he looked at Gideon. "I want you to be my best man."

Gideon smiled. "You know it."

"You will be Mrs. Menace?" Ella asked.

The group laughed.

"Something like that." Gideon pulled his daughter onto his lap. "Congratulations, man."

"Yes, way to make an honest woman out of her." Gunnar held up his glass to toast the duo.

Eboni walked over to Shay and gave her a hug. With her arm still around Shay's shoulders, she glared at Dennis. "Shay is special."

"I know this." Dennis nodded.

"She's strong and hard working and beautiful." Eboni held her tighter.

Dennis stared at his fiancée and nodded. "Yes."

"And I won't stand by and watch anyone disappoint her again. She deserves the best in life. She's my friend."

"Eb." Shay kissed Eboni's cheek.

Dennis shook his head. "It will never happen. Not on my watch, although I might cause her a little pain."

Eboni's eyes widened.

"Mom said I was a twelve-pound baby." Dennis put his hand on Shay's stomach. "Sorry, sweetie. You are going to carry a little linebacker in there one day."

Shay pulled away from Eboni to put her hands on Dennis's shoulders. "How do you know it won't be a long, lean baby like me?"

"Doesn't matter. As long as it's ours, I don't care. I love you, baby girl." He kissed her tenderly.

"Now, can my brother and his wife tell us their news?" Gunnar asked.

"Of course. Of course." Dennis put his hand to the small of Shay's back and helped her over to the couch.

"Congrats again, Dennis. Thanks for sharing that special moment with us." Thane held Kari's hand. "Honey?"

"First of all, this is a gender reveal party." Kari put her hand to her stomach. "It shouldn't be a surprise what I'm having."

In unison, the crowd announced, "A girl!"

"Mom has a sense of humor, even on the other side." Gunnar laughed. "I can see her wanting us to have families of only girls after being the only female with all of us."

"Hey, I take offense to that." Michael stepped forward and nudged his elbow into Gunnar's side.

"Of course, my son." Thane put his arm around Michael's shoulders. "That's the other news. Michael has chosen a college."

"Oh, wow. So tell us. What is it?" Gideon got up on his knees. "UNC?"

"Go Tar Heels!" Dennis pumped his fist in the air.

"No." Michael waved his hand and shook his head.

"I know you're going to play football." Gideon pointed to him.

The guests in the room groaned.

"What? Look at those hands. And he's fast." Gideon clapped, which made Ella mimic him.

"What's wrong with wrestling?" Gunnar asked. "He could go to the Olympics with that skill."

"Stop. I've thrown a ball to him since he was ten." Thane regarded Michael. "I told him then and I'm saying it now. He's a natural. He's got a great pitching arm."

"Will you all stop it and let him talk?" Eboni shook her head. "Go ahead, Michael."

He looked at Kari first before regarding Leona. "I've gotten offers from five top universities including Yale, Harvard, and Columbia. I decided—"

Gunnar drummed his hands over his thighs, which got the rest of the guests in the house to do the same.

"I'm going to Stanford." Michael beamed.

Kari and Leona didn't. The rest of the guests hugged him and congratulated him on his decision.

"Stanford in California." Kari nodded.

"Honey." Thane squeezed her hand.

"I told him I wanted him to be an astrophysicist. I didn't think he would go to the other side of the country to do it." Tears rolled down her cheeks.

"Come on, Mom." Michael held her shoulders. "I'm going there to be a doctor." He glanced around the room. "Sports medicine."

"And you have to go there?" Kari wiped her face with the back of her hand.

Thane handed her a napkin. "He *has* to go there." He nodded to Michael. "He's growing up. He's a man now. We have to respect his wishes."

Thane heard some sniffling behind him. When he turned, he saw Leona crying.

"We just found each other again." Leona shook her head.

Michael framed her face. "We won't lose each other. I promise. And if we do, we'll find each other again."

As he watched his son kiss Leona, Thane saw Michael as an adult. When he gazed around the room at all the activity, he saw them all as a family.

Don't miss the first book in Cyristal B. Bright's Mama's Boys series!

The Look of Love

You can't fight love…

There's only one thing MMA fighter Gunnar Wells is more devoted to than his career, and that's his mother, "Queen" Elizabeth. An elegant African American woman who adopted Gunnar and his two white brothers, Elizabeth was there when they needed her, and they'll do anything for her. For Gunnar, that means running her hair salon when she suddenly falls ill. And if that's not awkward enough for the champion fighter, he'll have to work alongside Eboni Danielson, the other love of his life. The one he left behind to pursue his dream. The one he's never forgotten…

Between the salon and her volunteer work, Eboni keeps busy to keep her mind off the man who broke her heart. So when Gunnar shows up again, she does her best to stay cool—on the outside. But the more she watches Gunnar step up and help out, the less she can deny her feelings. Soon Gunnar is doing everything he can to convince Eboni to give him a fighting chance. Can she trust him again—even when old secrets and new dangers come between them once more?

On sale now! http://www.kensingtonbooks.com/book.aspx/31356

Chapter 1

The adrenaline coursing through Gunnar Wells's body needed some release. The muscles in his arms and thighs tightened, ready for activity, for combat. A good workout would ease his tensions. Tonight, his mixed martial arts match would have to do.

He paced the cramped dressing room that smelled like rose petals and bleach, too dainty and too clean for what he had to do. The delicate aroma and the rough sport he would be engaging in soon reminded him of his mother, always a lady in demeanor and look, but a tough taskmaster.

A smile tugged at the corner of his mouth before he could arrest it and pull it back down to a scowl. He needed to keep his mind on his match. Staying away from his childhood home helped keep him on track.

A mural of the famous Welcome to Las Vegas sign painted on the locker-room wall snagged his attention for a brief moment. The blue, red, and white neon sign full of diverse geometric shapes attracted tourists every day. Gunnar saw the city as a place to start another part of his life. He didn't need a reminder of the location he'd made his home for the past ten years.

The Silver Streak Hotel and Casino spared no expense in keeping both the crowds and the performers entertained. Gunnar had heard that hosting these mixed martial arts matches had afforded the hotel enough funds to add a new wing to the hotel with another two hundred hotel rooms. He guessed beating a man to a bloody pulp meant good business.

Gunnar tilted his head from one side to the other to stretch his neck and help clear his head. Even with the door closed to his dressing room, the sounds from the audience in the main arena area filtered through the walls.

With each chant of "Guns" from the crowd, Gunnar's heart pounded harder and harder until both the chant and his heartbeat became one.

"Guns! Guns!"

Thump! Thump!

He swiped the back of his hand over his sweaty forehead. The tape on his hand scraped across his skin, leaving a tingling sensation in its wake. Gunnar glanced at the tape to make sure he hadn't ruined its integrity. After doing this sport for so many years, he found that every little thing mattered. A loose binding on his fist would distract him. Like a hunter, he needed to keep his focus.

For his match against a fairly established mixed martial artist like himself, he didn't feel unnerved. In his ten-year professional career, he'd battled absolute monsters. Being six-foot-three and two hundred forty pounds, he fit in the behemoth category. Like his mama always taught him, it's not the dog in the fight; it's the fight in the dog.

Gunnar attempted to push thoughts of his mother from his mind. He couldn't help but think about her and his brothers before each match. One brutal fight could leave him broken, destroyed, or dead. After all his family had done to support him, he couldn't let them down. He fought for them as much as he fought for himself and his career.

Truly the only woman who had ever understood him, thinking of her would only turn him into mush. For what he had to do in a few minutes, he needed to be on his game, an animal. He needed to be Gunnar "Guns" Wells, the heavyweight International Ultimate Fighting champion that the spectators loved to hate. Or maybe they hated to love him since he hadn't lost a match since starting the sport.

As he marched in his bare feet, he closed his eyes and envisioned the entire match, a calming technique he'd employed for years thanks to his yoga-loving mother. He stomped on the thin carpet that covered the concrete flooring. The hardness reminded him that nothing came easy to him, and it shouldn't. Only hard work would get him the rewards he wanted. Fighting afforded him the lifestyle he'd only dreamed of as a youth. If only he could have shared the success with someone.

"No negative thoughts. No negative thoughts." Gunnar talked to himself a lot to get into the headspace needed for his match.

As usual, he'd made sure to clear out his locker room before his match. No one disturbed him or retrieved him until he got called to the ring. After each winning match, he did the same ritual. He called his mother and then his two brothers, Gideon and Thane. All three of them understood the mentality it took for him to psych himself up to perform.

His brothers, as professional athletes themselves, had their own pregame rituals. Their mother proved to be a bit harder to train. She would call to wish Gunnar luck every now and then, probably when she thought his opponent looked too gruesome or menacing. She'd gotten better lately about letting him have his space.

After this match, he really had think about going to visit her. It'd been far too long since he'd been down to Virginia Beach and seen his mama. As soon as the thought entered his mind, his gut wrenched like he'd already been kicked in it by his opponent. The usual cold sweat he would get anytime he ventured close to the East Coast covered the back of his neck and back.

Although his mother would welcome him back home, not everyone would. Time and distance hadn't cleared Gunnar's mind of his past mistakes. He had a feeling some other people he'd left wouldn't be as open to his appearance.

Gunnar squeezed his eyes shut and stopped moving, stopped marching. He allowed the moment to be real for him, this fight, his job. He squeezed his taped hands, allowing the tightness of the adhesive to stretch over his achy knuckles.

He gazed down when a sharp pain struck a nerve in his wrist. He shook his hands to relieve the ache. The discomfort would be temporary. Security would last forever.

A two-rap knock sounded on the door before his trainer, Chuck Wilhelm, poked his shaved head into the locker room. Gunnar's insides twitched as soon as he saw the man. He knew what the next step would be. Showtime.

On instinct, Gunnar raised his hands, readying them to have them outfitted with his trademark black gloves with an eye embroidered on the backs of each. He already had his hair pulled back into a ponytail, something Chuck hated.

"Shave it all off," his trainer would tell Gunnar.

"What? And look like you? No way." Gunnar never thought his shoulder-length hair caused him a problem, especially since he never lost a fight because of it.

As Chuck approached him, Gunnar noticed his trainer carrying a cell phone.

"Call." Chuck held up the phone.

Gunnar shook his head. "You know the rule. No calls. No interviews. Just fighting." He picked up a plain black T-shirt and slipped it over his head.

"It's Mama." Chuck smirked.

"What?" Gunnar stopped moving.

"Queen Elizabeth." Chuck snorted. "Still don't understand how a big, blond dude has a black mother who calls herself Queen Elizabeth."

Gunnar didn't answer Chuck's standard question. He'd heard that comment about his relationship with his adoptive mother since she'd taken him and his brothers into her home.

Gunnar snatched the phone from Chuck's hand and turned his back to him. "Mama, how are you?"

To anyone else, Gunnar would have bitten their heads off and yelled about calling him before his fight. For the woman who had given him more chances than he deserved and a better life, she'd more than earned his respect.

"Darling," his mother said her standard opening that she gave to everyone. "How are you?"

As much as he didn't want to, Gunnar couldn't help but smile. She'd done it. With her smooth delivery and tone, she turned his insides to pudding. "Kind of a strange time to call to ask me how I'm doing, don't you think? I have my match starting in a few minutes. Chuck is getting me ready." He turned back to Chuck and held up one hand so that his trainer could slip on at least one glove.

"Oh, you have that thing tonight, don't you?" Her enunciation of each word further solidified her Queen Elizabeth nickname.

This time Gunnar did laugh out loud. "You can call it work, Ma."

"Good luck at *work* tonight." Elizabeth coughed.

The way she coughed raised the hairs on the back of his head. A standard Queen Elizabeth cough consisted of something that sounded like a slight puff of air through her always richly painted lips. She would usually follow what she considered an impolite expression with an apology. This time, she said nothing.

"Ma, what's wrong?" Gunnar squeezed his now-gloved hand into a fist.

"Why do you always assume the worst? You, out of all of my boys, are the most pessimistic, and I don't--"

"Don't start with me on that. You know--"

"Did you just interrupt me?"

His mother's stern tone came through clear on the small cell phone.

"I apologize." Gunnar had violated rule number one from his mother. Always hear a person's complete thought without interrupting. He certainly wouldn't want someone to cut him off midsentence.

"That's better. I think you hanging around those, um, those--"

"Coworkers," he added.

Elizabeth released an exasperated sigh. "You've done this fisticuffs thing long enough. I think it's time for you to come home."

Gunnar blinked. In all the years he'd done MMA, his mother had never asked him to quit and come home. Goose bumps sprang over his arms and crept up to his neck to the top of his head. He swallowed hard as he digested every word in her request. Then he heard a high-pitched beeping noise in succession...like in a hospital. A stone dropped in his gut.

"What's that sound?" Gunnar grounded himself to one spot. "Where are you? Are you in a hospital?"

"Guns, you've got to go." Chuck grabbed Gunnar's other hand.

The hold forced Gunnar to brace the phone against his ear using his shoulder. "One second." Gunnar didn't care about the match or Chuck. He needed to know what Elizabeth had neglected to share at the start of the call. "Ma, what's going on with you?"

"I know you have to go. We can talk later." Her voice cracked a little.

Gunnar's heart snapped. "Ma, don't hang up."

"You will be disqualified if you don't get out to the ring now." Chuck pulled on Gunnar's arm.

Gunnar snatched his limb out of his trainer's grip. "One damn minute!" he snapped at Chuck.

"We will talk later. Go do your fighting thing."

Her light voice made Gunnar imagine his gorgeous mother smiling. He couldn't smile. At the moment, his chest felt like every opponent he'd fought in his lifetime sat on it and constricted his air. He couldn't get out from under the weight. Right now, with his mother across the country, an arena full of people waiting for him, a ravenous opponent in the ring, and his impatient trainer, Gunnar found obstacles everywhere he turned.

Gunnar heard another woman's voice in the background.

"Queen, you cannot be on the phone."

"Who is that? Is that a nurse?" Gunnar scratched his head.

His mother cleared her throat. "No, it's not."

Gunnar heard some shuffling on the other end of the line.

"You need to get your rest. You can make your calls tomorrow before your tests."

Gunnar strained to hear this stranger's voice through the phone. It sounded a little familiar, but he couldn't place it.

"I love you." Elizabeth made a kissing sound through the phone before it disconnected.

Not content with ending the conversation that way, Gunnar tried redialing his mother. As he'd suspected, the number went to the reception desk at Virginia Beach General Hospital. After demanding to get transferred to Elizabeth Sommerville's room, he waited through several rings before disconnecting the call. Then he tried calling her cell phone. The call went straight to her voice mail.

He tried calling the hospital again. Once he got the main desk representative again, he asked about his mother. At the word cardiology, he nearly dropped to his knees. How could a woman who opened her home to three strangers have anything wrong with her heart?

After being transferred to the nurses' station, Gunnar unleashed a verbal assault. "I need to speak with a patient on your floor." Before she could ask for a name, he spouted, "Elizabeth Sommerville. Get her."

"Okay, please hold, sir."

Listening to the easy-listening jazz that played when the nurse placed him on hold didn't help to calm his nerves. Gunnar marched back and forth this time.

"Guns, you *have* to go." Chuck held the doorknob. He must have thought better of his decision to touch Gunnar again.

"One second." Gunnar held up his finger.

The music stopped. "Sir, Ms. Sommerville's daughter has requested no more calls for this evening. You can call again in the morning after eight."

Gunnar felt like flames engulfed his body. "Daughter? My mother doesn't have a daughter. She has three sons, and I'm one of them."

"Sir, I'm sorry. Your mother concurred with the young woman in the room with her, and we did just give her medication to help her sleep. Please give her a call in the morning when she wakes up." The nurse kept her voice even and authoritative, and before Gunnar could keep up his argument, she disconnected the call.

"Keep trying to call her." Gunnar shoved the phone at his trainer before cursing.

He hadn't even found out why his mother had to go to the hospital. Had she had a heart attack or a stroke? Every scenario he thought about had him grinding his teeth in anger.

"You have got to go." Chuck opened the door to usher him through.

A wave of chants flooded the room. The support should have been like a warm blanket around his body. Instead, Gunnar likened the shouts to spectators in a coliseum waiting to watch a hapless gladiator get mauled by a lion. Little did they know, he had enough fire in his belly to crush a lion, a tiger, and a whole damn safari.

"Something is going on with my mother. I'm fine just walking away right now. Just hop on a plane and go all the way back to Virginia." Gunnar put his fists to his hips and glared at Chuck to get across his intent.

The idea of going back to Virginia brought a layer of cold sweat that dripped from his head. He chewed the inside of his cheek, a habit he hadn't done since childhood when he'd prayed in his head that the foster father he'd had before getting with Queen Elizabeth wouldn't come home drunk with his own need to fight...anyone. Gunnar had left Virginia for a reason. Returning to it would stir up more questions and problems than what he faced in the ring.

Chuck held his hand up as a way to calm Gunnar, but Gunnar couldn't be reasoned with, calmed, or reassured until he either spoke to his mother or, better yet, saw her.

"Tell you what. I'll keep trying her. After your fight, you can talk to her again." Chuck placed Gunnar's heavyweight championship belt on Gunnar's shoulder.

Gunnar nodded. "Get her on the phone after the fight." He adjusted the heavy metal belt on the thick black leather backing.

Without another word, Gunnar stormed out of the door and headed to the octagon. The cheers from the audience roared in the large auditorium. He kept his stare directed on the lit ring. Fans grabbed at Gunnar's shirt and his arms as he stormed to the middle. He paid no attention to them.

The closer he got to the ring, the more his surroundings got smaller until his competitor became the only thing he saw at the end of his tunnel vision. He stepped into the ring and didn't bother stomping around like Tony "The Shark" Palombo. With it being a championship match, Gunnar handed his belt to the referee.

He didn't like the entertaining part of doing MMA. He just wanted to fight. Right now, he had a lot of aggression to get out of his system.

Gunnar broke his attention away from Tony for a moment to check Chuck. From the side of the ring, Chuck held up his phone to Gunnar and shook his head.

Gunnar wanted to race to the side and scream at his trainer to keep trying to get his mother. Why the hell was she in the hospital? Why wasn't that the first thing she'd said to him? Whatever afflicted her, it scared her enough to want him to come home. That fact consumed his thoughts more than anything else. He attempted to look at Chuck again when Tony got in his view.

"You're going down!" Tony screamed and stood an inch from Gunnar's nose.

Gunnar gritted his teeth. Right now, this hefty man sporting a Mohawk and tattoos covering the vast real estate of his enormous, chestnut-colored body stood in between him talking to his mother.

Gunnar removed his T-shirt and tossed it to Chuck. The screams heightened, especially from the women. He didn't pay attention to them. He had a job to do. He kept women out of his personal life so as not to get diverted from his goals, a decision that haunted him since jumping on a Greyhound bus ten years ago.

The referee spouted the rules and regulations that Gunnar ignored. The sounds in the arena blurred into one muted hum. His laser focus remained on Tony, directly on his eyes. He called this feeling right before he threw his first punch the glaze.

Chuck had once told Gunnar at the beginning of his career that every time he would start to fight, he got this glazed-over look in his eyes like he couldn't see anything else but the opponent in the ring with him.

A single sweat droplet rolled down between his shoulder blades. He planted his feet on the hard mat as he shoved his black mouth guard over his teeth. He tasted nothing but the bitter plastic. The palms of his hands itched in anticipation of what would happen. He had a job to do.

As soon as the match started, Tony surprised Gunnar by landing a solid punch to his left eye. A whole fireworks display lit up in Gunnar's head with the contact. He didn't even notice the pain. The man did carry some power behind his punch. Gunnar had something on him that even Tony didn't have--a purpose.

As soon as Gunnar filled his head with images of his mother in a hospital bed with tubes coming from her nose and wires attached to her fingers and hand, a volcano erupted inside of him that he couldn't contain or control.

Gunnar gave Tony a roundhouse kick to his head. The contact of the hit against his foot stung. That first strike sent an adrenaline rush through his body that gave him the needed boost for the next move.

When the big man hit the mat, Gunnar leapt on top of him and pounded his fists in his opponents face and head repeatedly. He heard nothing. Crimson shaded his gaze. He felt Tony's tree-trunk thighs attempt to hook him under his arms to bring him down. Instead, Gunnar moved down to the mat, cradled Tony's head in the crook of his elbow and framed the top of his head with his other arm.

Gunnar squeezed and clamped his legs around Tony's waist to keep the man still. Whenever Tony moved, Gunnar tightened his arms and legs around Tony's neck and body.

For every match, Gunnar kept his mind focused on winning, on his next move. Now, his mind clouded over with thoughts of his mother. What would he and his brothers do if something happened to her?

Until he felt the referee tapping his shoulder, Gunnar didn't realize that he had rendered Tony unconscious. He blinked and peered down at the person in his arms. Tony's blood dripped from his forehead and nose and onto Gunnar's arm.

"He tapped out, son. Release him." The referee grabbed Gunnar's arm and attempted to uncoil his hold on the limp body. "Stop fighting."

Gunnar blinked and unraveled himself from Tony. He sprang to his feet and gazed down at his handiwork. Tony's body lay motionless, curled in an unnatural position like a discarded marionette, as his trainers and handlers attempted to revive him.

Gunnar wanted to run from the ring, leave his belt, and get on a plane. He had to wait until Tony's trainers revived him. In that time, he paced in the ring, waiting for his moment.

Once Tony rose to his feet, the referee raised Gunnar's hand as the winner. A bit of relief washed over him. He'd finished work, and in record time. Now he had to go.

"Did you get her?" Gunnar asked as he climbed out of the ring and headed back to the dressing room.

He ignored the interviewers who shoved microphones into his face right after the match. From their grunts and groans, he knew they hated his silence.

"Are you kidding? You just did that match in about seven minutes. I barely had time to breathe let alone make calls for you." Chuck ran alongside of Gunnar.

"Guns! Guns! Just a quick question." An interviewer tried stopping Gunnar's trek by stepping into his path. "That match seemed too easy for you. Are you ready for Seamus Flannery, the second-ranked contender?"

Gunnar didn't answer. He stepped around the suited man and continued to his dressing room. If he didn't have another man's blood on him, he would have just thrown on some shoes and caught the next red-eye flight.

"You can't just blow off journalists." Chuck slammed the dressing-room door behind the two of them. "They can make or break your career."

"They haven't so far." Gunnar stripped. "You talk for me. I'm going to Virginia."

"Virginia? You can't go right now. You need to start training for your match with Seamus." Chuck started pacing.

Gunnar couldn't think about how Chuck felt. As much as he loved his career, Gunnar loved his family even more. With the threat of losing his mother, he would brave going back home to be with her.

Until he saw his mother and could see that he'd overreacted to whatever he'd heard on the phone, he wouldn't be able to rest. Then he would find out what woman had posed as his sister.

"What am I supposed to say as far as booking your next match?" Chuck asked.

Naked, Gunnar stood in the doorway leading to the bathroom to take a quick shower. "Tell them I'm going home."

* * * *

Eboni Danielson stirred awake with a throbbing pain in her neck thanks to sleeping in a steel and barely padded hospital chair. She should have slept on the couch, but she'd wanted to be as close to her friend as possible. She blinked to get a sleeping Queen Elizabeth into focus.

Yesterday morning, when Elizabeth had fainted in Press 'N Curl, the hair salon Elizabeth owned where Eboni worked, Eboni had wasted no time getting her friend and mentor to the hospital. Ever the diva, Elizabeth had refused to go until her hair had been styled and her nails had received a fresh coat of deep red polish.

Elizabeth looked like she'd redone her makeup sometime during the night. Her light brown skin glowed, especially with the morning sunlight streaming through the hospital-room window. Bright red lipstick covered her lips. Even her fake eyelashes looked like they had been curled.

As a child, Eboni and her girlfriends had all wanted to grow up to be just like Miss Queen Elizabeth. Not only did the woman always look amazing and have the best clothes and cool shoes, she owned not one, not even two, but three businesses.

The hair salon, more than her flower shop and the clothing boutique, had the most customers in Eboni's eyes, and the most buzz. Although she didn't plan to work in a hair salon for the rest of her life, Eboni definitely wanted to be close to the woman who could guide her into being a success in business.

The morning Queen fainted, Eboni had planned on talking to her about doing a fund-raiser to help renovate the community center. Kids with nothing to do had a tendency of finding dangerous activities to pick up from other wayward souls. Eboni didn't know how, but she knew she had to break the cycle.

A nurse walked into the room. "Ms. Sommerville, time to get your vitals." She opened the blinds and allowed the February sun to stream through them. The morning rays reflected off the gleaming-white snow that covered the ground.

Eboni wrapped her camel-colored dress coat around her body. The businesslike apparel didn't give her a cozy feeling like the poncho her grandmother had made for her. Appearances meant everything for Eboni.

Eboni remembered being a child and watching her grandmother knit the whole thing. She couldn't wait until she got to a size to wear it. Of course, her grandmother made the garment large anticipating that Eboni would never lose that baby weight that plagued her for most of her youth.

She'd changed. Times had changed. Eboni had to give up childhood fantasies, including finding that one true love. Seeing Elizabeth in a hospital bed made everything real.

"Do you have to wake her now?" Eboni rubbed her eyes. "She just got to sleep."

The nurse glanced down at Elizabeth's face and chuckled. "Is she going to an opera later? When did she put on all this makeup?"

"*She* can hear everything you're saying." Elizabeth opened her eyes and glared at the nurse before cutting her gaze over to Eboni.

"Darling, you didn't have to sleep in that awful chair." She shook her head.

"I didn't want to leave you alone." Eboni stretched her arms over her head attempting to relieve some of the ache in her neck. "Besides, I would have slept on the floor if I had to."

Elizabeth smiled, showing off an impressive set of straight, white teeth. "You're silly. The staff here would have taken care of me just fine." She finally turned her smile to the nurse who had already placed a black cuff around her arm and pumped away to get her blood pressure.

As the nurse allowed the blood pressure cuff to hiss out the air she'd pumped into it, she said, "A very loud and angry man called the desk for you last night." She removed the stethoscope from her ears. "He claimed that this woman is not your daughter." She glanced at Eboni.

Eboni swallowed but continued returning the nurse's stare, hoping to convince her of the lie Queen had told. Eboni hadn't corrected her. In a lot of ways, she did feel like she belonged in Queen's family.

"That's ridiculous," Queen said when she no longer had a thermometer in her mouth. "This beautiful young woman is as much as my child as my sons are."

Eboni smiled. She stood from her chair and held her friend's hand. The warmth of it as well as Elizabeth's words hugged her heart.

"Did you already pick your breakfast items today?" The nurse held up a menu.

"Yes. The lovely woman from food services got my order about an hour ago."

The nurse nodded and exited the room, partially closing the door behind herself.

Eboni felt her eyebrows draw together. "I don't remember hearing anyone coming into the room."

"Because you were out cold." Elizabeth placed her soft palm against Eboni's cheek and then brought it down to cover Eboni's hand. "You will need to go home at some point today to shower and get some real sleep."

Eboni shook her head. "Until the doctors tell me what's going on, I'm not leaving."

"Oh, honey, I know what it is. Back in my day, we called it having the vapors. I just got a little overwhelmed with work and had a little fainting spell. That's it." Queen removed her hand from Eboni's and turned her face away like she wanted to watch something on TV.

Eboni knew better. "I know Virginia is the South, but we're not that far south. I don't believe in this vapors nonsense. Something's going on with you, and I'm not leaving until I know what it is."

Elizabeth shook her head. "Stubborn. You're just like Gunnar."

At the mention of his name, Eboni became quiet. Like when he'd walked away from her ten years ago to pursue his fighting dream, Eboni's heart stilled again.

She'd thought she and Gunnar would have a future together. Her being African American hadn't stopped him from pursuing her, not that Eboni thought it would. If he didn't have a problem with his adoptive mother being black, she knew he would date outside of his race.

Eboni had been surprised the day he'd given her the critical ultimatum--go with him while he trained as an ultimate fighter, or break up with him and stay home. It had broken her heart to turn down his offer, but she couldn't leave. Not just yet.

"You talked to Gunnar?" Eboni backed up to her chair.

"I called him last night before his thing." Queen huffed. "I told him he should stop that stuff and come on home."

Eboni collapsed in the chair. "You told him to come home? Why?" Would the man who'd had no problems running from her ten years ago come home because his mother asked him to?

"Darling, while I'm a touch incapacitated, I'm going to need someone to run the businesses."

At that bit of news, Eboni's spine crumpled enough for her to melt her back into the chair. "I thought you would let me run Press 'N Curl."

"You are running Press 'N Curl. Gunnar will do what I do there." Elizabeth waved her hand as though this aspect meant very little to her.

"So he'll have his nails and hair done?" She winked at Elizabeth. The little bit of levity helped her not think of Gunnar.

Elizabeth gasped. "I do more than just have my hair and nails done."

"I know."

"Don't forget eyebrow waxing." Elizabeth winked.

Eboni laughed. Queen Elizabeth wouldn't be a success if she'd been an absentee owner. The woman defined hands-on. When a stylist didn't show, she had no problem taking their clients.

"What in the world am I going to do without you at the shop?"

"You'll be fine, and Gunnar will be fine in my spot." Elizabeth nodded. "I'll eventually have to bring my sons in to the businesses. I was just hoping it would happen later than sooner." She sighed. "Besides, all three have signed power-of-attorney forms for the businesses in case something happens to me."

It made sense to have Elizabeth's sons to acquire the three businesses when something happened to her. Eboni just hoped Gunnar would stay away from her while she worked.

"Speaking of bad timing." Eboni made sure to make eye contact with Elizabeth. "Before you, um, caught the vapors, I was going to propose that we do a fund-raiser for the Oceanfront Community Center. You know that in my free time I volunteer there."

"I know. That's why you haven't dated in forever and a day." Queen wagged her finger at Eboni.

Eboni sighed and ignored Elizabeth's comment about her sad personal life. "Anyway, besides volunteering, I've donated all of my tips to the center too. But it's not enough. You know business at the salon has dropped lately."

Elizabeth's expression changed to a forlorn one. "I know. I've tried drumming up more customers."

Eboni held up her hand. "We all appreciate your efforts. That's probably what landed you here." She patted Elizabeth's shoulder. "If the center doesn't get more money just for operating costs, they're going to have to close, and at-risk kids will take a wrong turn."

Queen Elizabeth regarded her for a moment before a broad smile lit up her face. "That's what I love about you." She sat up higher in her hospital bed. "Other people would have asked me for money. Hell, my own family has asked me for money just to go to Vegas. Not you. Not my girl. You want to *raise* the money."

Eboni's heart beat stronger. "I learned from the best. Working with you, I know that only hard work will get me what I want."

"You're right. You know I'm in for anything to help out that center. I know that after your mother passed, that place--"

"And your shop," Eboni interjected.

"Helped you growing up." She patted the mattress beside her. "Right now, I'm a little stuck. This is something that needs to happen soon, right?"

Eboni nodded. When a distressed expression crossed Elizabeth's face, Eboni had a change of heart. "Look, don't worry about it. I'll figure something out. I shouldn't have said anything." She waved her hands and backed up.

"If I wasn't out of action, I would love to help you." Elizabeth's eyes lit up. "I'm hoping Gunnar comes to town. If he does, he can help. Wouldn't it be great for you to see him again?"

Eboni swallowed hard. Did she want to see the man who'd been her first love? She wanted to hate him. He'd had a goal like she had when they'd severed their relationship. She and Gunnar had stubborn streaks as long as the universe.

Before she could answer, the hospital room door burst open. Encompassing the entire frame stood Gunnar. He had his dirty-blond hair pulled back into a ponytail. His crystal-blue eyes drew her attention to his strong face. His jaw looked like it had been chiseled from stone. He looked beautiful and scary all at once, especially with the addition of a black eye.

Eboni couldn't look in his face. She refused to watch any of his matches, but she imagined that his current hard expression matched what he would look like before each of his fights.

Her gaze volleyed between his full, very kissable lips and his barrel-sized chest. The more she stared at him, the more her heart accelerated. This man had given her the deepest heartache she'd ever had. Within a millisecond, she found herself still wanting him. She could kick herself for being so stupid now.

Eboni didn't remember Gunnar being that immense. Seeing him again made her want to stand up to him like one of his opponents. He'd caused her to cry more than she cared to admit. The hell she would allow him to make her feel less than her best. If confronted, she would let him know that.

"Ma, what's going on with you, and who's this daughter you said you have now?" Gunnar's voice boomed throughout the room, and probably all down the hall as well.

Guess the man came for a fight. She wouldn't back down.

Meet the Author

Crystal Bright graduated with a B.A. from Old Dominion University with a major in Creative Writing, a minor in Communications, and an emphasis on Public Relations. She earned her M.A. from Seton Hill University in Writing Popular Fiction. She is a member of Romance Writers of America. For more information about Crystal and her writing, please visit her website at www.CrystalBrightWriter.com. You can also find her on Facebook at https://www.facebook.com/crystal.bright.397, or follow her on twitter:https://twitter.com/CrystalBBright.